PRAISE FOR

"Infused with . . . fresh detail. Betw_____ ___ __ ____ness of the relationship and the summery beach setting, romance fans will find this a warming winter read."

—*Publishers Weekly*

"Fans will love the frank honesty of her characters. [Beck's] scenery is richly detailed and the story engaging."

—*RT Book Reviews*

"[A] realistic and heartwarming story of redemption and love . . . Beck's understanding of interpersonal relationships and her flawless prose make for a believable romance and an entertaining read."

—*Booklist*

PRAISE FOR *WORTH THE WAIT*

"[A] poignant and heartwarming story of young love and redemption and will literally make your heart ache . . . Jamie Beck has a real talent for making the reader feel the sorrow, regret, and yearning of this young character."

—*Fresh Fiction*

PRAISE FOR *WORTH THE TROUBLE*

"Beck takes readers on a journey of self-reinvention and risky investments, in love and in life . . . With strong family ties, loyalty, playful banter, and sexual tension, Beck has crafted a beautiful second-chances story."

—*Publishers Weekly* (starred review)

PRAISE FOR *SECRETLY HERS*

"[I]n Beck's ambitious, uplifting second Sterling Canyon contemporary . . . [c]onflicting views and family drama lay the foundation for emotional development in this strong Colorado-set contemporary."

—*Publishers Weekly*

"Witty banter and the deepening of the characters and their relationship, along with some unexpected plot twists and a lovable supporting cast . . . will keep the reader hooked . . . A smart, fun, sexy, and very contemporary romance."

—*Kirkus Reviews*

PRAISE FOR *WORTH THE RISK*

"An emotional read that will leave you reeling at times and hopeful at others."

—*Books and Boys Book Blog*

PRAISE FOR *UNEXPECTEDLY HERS*

"Character-driven, sweet, and chock-full of interesting secondary characters."

—*Kirkus Reviews*

PRAISE FOR *BEFORE I KNEW*

"A tender romance rises from the tragedy of two families—a must read!"

—Robyn Carr, #1 *New York Times* bestselling author

"Jamie Beck's deeply felt novel hits all the right notes, celebrating the power of forgiveness, the sweetness of second chances, and the heady joy of reaching for a dream. Don't miss this one!"

—Susan Wiggs, #1 *New York Times* bestselling author

"*Before I Knew* kept me totally enthralled as two compassionate, relatable characters, each in search of forgiveness and fulfillment, turn a recipe for heartache into a story of love, hope, and some really good menus!"

—Shelley Noble, *New York Times* bestselling author of *Whisper Beach*

PRAISE FOR *ALL WE KNEW*

"A moving story about the flux of life and the steadfastness of family."

—*Publishers Weekly*

"An impressively crafted and deftly entertaining read from first page to last."

—*Midwest Book Review*

"*All We Knew* is compelling, heartbreaking, and emotional."

—*Harlequin Junkie*

PRAISE FOR *JOYFULLY HIS*

"A quick and sweet read that is perfect for the holidays."

—*Harlequin Junkie*

PRAISE FOR *WHEN YOU KNEW*

"[A]n opposites-attract romance with heart."

—*Harlequin Junkie*

if You Must Know

ALSO BY JAMIE BECK

In the Cards

The St. James Novels

Worth the Wait

Worth the Trouble

Worth the Risk

The Sterling Canyon Novels

Accidentally Hers

Secretly Hers

Unexpectedly Hers

Joyfully His

The Cabot Novels

Before I Knew

All We Knew

When You Knew

The Sanctuary Sound Novels

The Memory of You

The Promise of Us

The Wonder of Now

if You Must Know

A Potomac Point Novel

JAMIE BECK

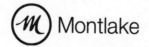 Montlake

Published by Montlake, Seattle

www.apub.com

Amazon, the Amazon logo, and Montlake are trademarks of Amazon.com, Inc., or its affiliates.

ISBN-13: 9781542008716
ISBN-10: 1542008719

Cover design by David Drummond

Printed in the United States of America

This one is for Ria and Bobby, whose wild new life gave me the idea for this story. Thankfully, they are merely thrill seekers, not criminals.

CHAPTER ONE

AMANDA

There ought to be a warning anytime you wake up on a day that will forever change your life. Some harbinger—like a robin, lightning bolt, or black cat—so you don't find yourself blindsided. This morning's brilliant sunshine hadn't exactly screamed, "Beware, today you'll discover that the most destructive lies are the ones you tell yourself."

If anything, the clear blue sky promised a perfect spring day. And so, blissfully ignorant, I stopped at Sugar Momma's on my way home from my routine three-mile walk along Chesapeake Bay. Normally I'd never order a peanut butter–chocolate chunk cookie the size of a dessert plate and a decaffeinated salted-caramel latte with extra whipped cream before nine o'clock in the morning. I'd promised Lyle I'd be good, for the baby's sake. But my husband had been away on business all week. While I wouldn't recommend that anyone lie to a spouse, in this case, I figured what Lyle didn't know wouldn't hurt him.

Honestly, I deserved this little—or not so little—cheat. The pressure of putting together his new company's first real estate development deal was turning my mostly charming husband into a male version of Martha Stewart on steroids. So much so that I almost wished he'd return to his former job: at Chesapeake Properties he'd been a successful commercial broker with less stress.

Lately most of my attempts to alleviate his anxiety had backfired. Thank God I had my mom as a sounding board when his moods blew cold. The day after our last argument three weeks ago, Lyle had come home with a small gift—his standard means of making amends—a silver pinkie ring. Not to complain about his generosity, but I couldn't recall a single "I'm sorry" since we'd met. I'd prefer an apology to a makeup present, but we ended up in the same place either way.

I broke off a section of the still-warm cookie and took a nibble, and my eyelids drooped from cocoa-infused ecstasy. "Oh my goodness, Hannah. This is delicious."

Everything about her and her bakeshop intrigued me, making it my favorite discovery since moving into our new house back in December. The turquoise, gold, and red decor mimicked the bold colors she draped across her generous figure. Crimson lips framed her larger-than-life smile, which made her look younger than the fifty or so years I guessed she was. And she gathered all her blonde-and-pink braids into a single ponytail that was as thick as a fire hose.

I didn't know Hannah as well as I would've liked. We spoke only here, where her animated personality filled the shop with upbeat energy. When I'd sensed her keeping me in the "patron" box, I gave up my attempts at friendship. Yet I often wondered about her life. Pictured her in a busy home kitchen, testing recipes. Imagined her knitting her handmade shawls and vests. Most of all, I questioned what kind of partner could handle all her vivacity.

Not someone like Lyle. He preferred white tablecloths and efficient waiters to an eclectic shop like this—with its mismatched tables and chairs, folk art, and hipster music—but I found the vibe here warm and inviting. A friendly sort of place where you could exhale.

Hannah layered whipped cream on my coffee while winking at me. "Amanda, get yourself another cookie. You're eating for two."

I shook my head, begging off. "I need to watch myself."

"Where's the fun in that?" She tsk-tsked, then proceeded to squirt a liberal amount of liquid caramel atop the whipped cream.

"I know, but it's important to Lyle." When I rubbed my six-month bump, our daughter kicked my hand. My heart swelled. Two years ago I couldn't have imagined anything would eclipse the joy of my wedding day, yet our growing family made each day brighter and everything seem possible. "This morning's little detour has to stay our secret."

Hannah handed me the coffee, grinning. "That's exactly what he always says."

Wait, what?

"He does, does he?" Then why has he acted like he hates this place? I chomped on the cookie, wondering why he'd kept his visits here a secret.

I couldn't exactly ask him when I was planning to keep *my* visit a secret. On the other hand, it wouldn't need to be a secret if I weren't appeasing my overanxious husband. In fairness his concern for our welfare made me feel cherished. Still . . .

"Haven't seen Lyle all week. Where's he been hiding?" Hannah raised her brows while she waited.

I choked on the cookie. Did he really stop in that often? "Away on business."

Hannah had to be exaggerating. Given Lyle's current obsession with diet and exercise, Sugar Momma's heavy aroma of vanilla and butter alone should make him run in the opposite direction.

"Mm, that man works hard. He always looks sharp in his jacket and tie. A man with goals, am I right?" Hannah chuckled, a rich, resonant sound that warmed the soul, like her latte. "He keeps offering to find me a cheaper space in town, but I like this location."

"Don't you dare move, Hannah. This shop is perfect for you." I hoped she couldn't see how baffled I was to be learning these things about my own husband.

"That's what I tell him."

"I'm sorry he's pestering you. He's hyperfocused on his new business." I'd lost count of the skipped dinners and early-morning meetings. Financial freedom might be nice, but I didn't need a big bank account to be happy. I *did* need him.

"Well, you know men. They want to provide."

I'd always suspected his relentless drive to prove himself sprang from his mom's abandonment. No one would call Lyle easy to live with, but my heart ached whenever I thought of the cruelty he suffered in childhood. If healing that wound required me to tiptoe around his feelings or defer to his whims now and then, I would do so happily. He'd taken the leap of trust that I would not leave him like his mother had, so he deserved my devotion.

"He's excited about getting an inside line on some condo development in South Florida. Apparently it's a 'booming' market. I hope we don't have to move there, though. I grew up here in Potomac Point, and my mom's recently widowed and . . . Oh, I don't know. I have torn loyalties, I suppose." I suspected Hannah had lost interest in my rambling, so I stopped.

"Well, good luck to you." She wiped up the whipped cream spatter on the counter.

"Thank you." A bell jingled behind me, and I turned to greet two other women who'd entered the shop. "Hello, Barb. How are you?"

Barb lived on my block. Divorced after five years of marriage, she and her ex-husband, Lenny, shared one preschooler, Collin. She'd kept the house, while Lenny had moved closer to Baltimore and saw his son only every other weekend.

"Hey, Amanda." Barb smiled. "This is my friend Sandy Bello. Sandy, this is Amanda Foster, my neighbor and Collin's nursery school teacher."

"Nice to meet you." I shook Sandy's hand, but my thoughts ran to little Collin and the extra attention I'd been giving him while he adjusted to his new family dynamic. He was not my first or only student facing that confusing upheaval. Some kids handled it better than others.

While Collin still struggled, Barb's mood had improved since her divorce. In fact, at the moment, she and Sandy shone with the contentment that comes from true friendship. I recognized that look from the faces of a lot of the young moms who made playdates for their kids and spa dates for themselves.

In my experience, the young moms tended to view us teachers as "other." Granted, I did know embarrassing truths about many of them. Kids overshare in the cutest ways. But soon I'd be invited into that circle of women, or at least I hoped so. I could use the support as I waded into motherhood, because my two best friends from high school both relocated to other states after college and we'd fallen out of touch. As something of an introvert, I enjoyed cordial relationships with my coworkers, but we never shared intimacies. My sister was still single and childless—unless you counted her cute little dog, Mo—so she couldn't commiserate with the ups and downs of marriage and pregnancy. Besides, Erin had never had much patience for the things that worried me.

Barb placed a palm to her cheek. "I don't know how you handle all those toddlers at once. I'd go crazy."

"Well, it's only three mornings each week, so I get plenty of time to recharge." I smiled, accustomed to these types of comments, though they always surprised me. Kids' brutal honesty beat any comic's jokes, and who could ever get enough sticky-fingered hugs?

When Barb didn't invite me to join them, I said, "Don't let me keep you. Order up. I can vouch for the cookies." I waved the remains of mine and then took a seat at the smallest café table—my favorite despite its wobbly leg. Shellacked postcards from exotic destinations like Tanzania, Brazil, and Alaska decorated its buttercup-yellow tabletop. I'd yet to ask Hannah if she'd been to these places or if she'd merely bought the table from someone else—I didn't believe in prying into people's personal lives without invitation. In today's social media–driven society, privacy was a treasured currency.

I scrolled through my phone. Nothing from Lyle since his late-night text. He'd asked me not to interrupt him during business hours, but we'd never gone a whole day without speaking. As soon as I got home, I'd call to make sure everything was okay.

The overhead speakers pumped out the twangy sound of Iron & Wine's "What Hurts Worse," a song I recognized only because my dad and Erin were music aficionados. One of many interests they'd shared. For my first four years of life, I'd been my dad's "little star." But then Erin was born, and by the time she turned three, she'd become his sun.

I traced the lumpy edge of the postcard from Brazil, one of many countries I hoped to visit. I'd almost spent a semester in London during my junior year of college, but then Erin had wrapped our dad around her finger, like always. After she'd graduated from high school—with *no* plans to attend college—she convinced him to underwrite her backpacking adventure through Europe to get a "real world" education.

Poof . . . another of my plans upended by her.

She hadn't meant to screw up my dream. She wasn't mean-spirited, just high-spirited. And it had been only fair of Dad to give her that money when he'd been helping with my and our brother Kevin's tuition. But if Erin had shared her intentions sooner, I would've worked a second summer job to save enough money to afford the semester abroad.

Then again, expecting Erin to plan anything in advance was pointless. She woke up every day and made random decisions, then strung those days together one by one and called it a life. I spent more time worrying for her future than she did, but the only person from whom she'd ever tolerated any advice is our father. Was . . . was our father.

Laughter caught my attention. Hannah was being folksy with Barb and Sandy, completely comfortable in her own skin. I could envy her for that, but for some reason it didn't niggle me as much with her as it did with my sister.

On her way out of the store, Barb called to me, "See you at drop-off tomorrow!"

I smiled and waved, while Hannah busied herself with the coffee maker.

After savoring my final swig of coffee, I took the empty plate and cup to the counter. "Have a great day, Hannah."

"You too." She waved before shuffling to the far end of her display case to straighten a tray of popovers.

And then, because Lyle's hypocrisy irked me, I added, "See you soon."

Outside, the brisk air fended off a food coma. I inhaled deeply and turned right to finish my walk home. Unlike the east end of town—where I'd grown up—the west side boasted herringbone brickwork sidewalks and iron lampposts with ivy-stuffed hanging baskets. The recent upgrades were part of an expansion due to increased tourism. Lyle and I loved the trendy shops and restaurants, but traffic on Saturdays wasn't ideal.

As I left the commercial district and meandered onto Nukquit Lane, the uniformity of the new residential development relaxed me. We lived on Naeez Court. Each of the five streets that made up our little neighborhood came from the Nanticoke words for one through five. Better yet, the homes, while not identical, were all roughly the same size and style, each set in the center of a well-manicured half-acre lot.

Logic and structure made life easier to navigate.

The older areas where my mom and Erin still lived were populated with 1940s ranch-, cape-, and cottage-style homes, and weak zoning restrictions. Not that I'd noticed when I was young. When I hadn't been at one of Kevin's Little League games or helping my mom bake cookies, I'd been reading books in the hammock or running through the neighborhood on warm summer evenings. But as I grew up, my preference for order over chaos solidified. I'd worked hard and made smart choices to help afford a home on this side of town.

In contrast to my place, Erin's antiquated brick apartment building resembled a crumbling fort, but even that looked more impressive than her cramped apartment. Some nights I'd sit straight up in bed, concerned about how she'd escape that mousetrap in a fire. But anytime I offered to reorganize the clutter or suggested she brighten it up with fresh paint, she'd smile and dismiss me. The pretty Pottery Barn drapes I'd picked up for her this past Christmas remained in a box buried somewhere in that mess.

Despite my best intentions, I never quite did the right thing where she was concerned.

I entered my home through the garage. We'd bought it almost five months ago, yet hadn't nearly finished decorating. Lyle had suggested we get rid of the mishmash of his old-condo furnishings and the things I'd kept from my apartment once we'd married. But our fiscally responsible nature restricted us to purchasing only the essentials to date—a kitchen table and chairs, a Restoration Hardware sofa set from the Maddox Collection and the flat-screen TV that hung above the fireplace, bedroom furniture from Lillian August, and two area rugs to help muffle the echo of the hardwood, tile, and glass throughout the home. We'd selected crisp, clean lines and colors—white, gray, navy. Soothing.

Usually. Today it seemed a little cold and empty.

I twisted my neck from side to side, then sat at the kitchen table and dialed Lyle's number. Straight to voice mail, like it had earlier this morning. I glanced through the french doors that led to the deck and firepit. The night before he'd left, we'd sat by the blaze, discussing baby names.

I'd lobbied for "Willa" in honor of my late father, William Turner. It broke my heart that, thanks to an unexpected heart attack last summer, he wouldn't be part of my growing family. And aside from Willa also being an adorable name, it'd be unique. As a teacher, I'd met more than my fair share of Caitlins, Katies, and Ellies.

Lyle had simply raised his brow at me and pushed for "Penelope," which he thought better suited the blonde curls and blue eyes he expected our daughter to inherit from me.

Penelope Foster . . . Penny. No matter how often I turned that over in my head, it didn't sound right.

Still no word from Lyle, so I called his friend Tom, with whom he was staying while in Miami.

A woman answered, "Hello."

"I'm sorry." I paused. "I might've misdialed. I'm trying to reach Tom Cantor."

"This is Tom's phone, but he just ran out. Can I take a message?" The woman sounded younger—maybe twenty-three or twenty-five.

Not once all week had Lyle mentioned any women at the house. "Um, well, I'm actually trying to track down Lyle Foster. He's staying with Tom."

"Yeah, I know Lyle, but you missed him. He and Ebba left yesterday afternoon."

I blinked. Ebba? I'd heard that name only once before in my life.

"Hello?" came the younger woman's voice.

"I'm sorry." I shook my head in a futile effort to settle my spinning thoughts. "May I ask with whom I am speaking?"

"Gigi . . . Tom's girlfriend." She sounded bored and slightly annoyed, like I'd interrupted her while she was painting her nails.

"Oh." All morning I'd been worried about my husband, but now my thoughts veered in a different, more disturbing direction. "Is Ebba working on the deal with Lyle?"

"No idea. You'll have to ask him."

"I would, but I can't reach him." My voice shot upward, so I cleared my throat. "When will he be back?"

"You know what, I probably shouldn't be giving out all this information about Tom's friend without permission. I don't even know who you are."

"I'm Lyle's wife!" I clapped my palm over my mouth, mortified. Only the sound of my heartbeat broke the ensuing silence.

"Sorry."

Then the line went dead.

Gigi's discomfited tone resounded in my thoughts. If I weren't sitting at my kitchen table, I'd swear someone had shoved my head underwater and was holding it there.

After a minute I dialed Lyle's cell phone once more, straining to speak through my tightening throat. "Lyle, it's Amanda. I haven't heard from you since yesterday morning. I tried Tom's and was told you left the house with someone named Ebba. Is she also working on the deal? Please call me." *One heartbeat. Two.* "I miss you . . ."

I set the phone down and stared into space, mentally walking myself back from the accusations forming in my mind. It could be a coincidence. Sure, Ebba wasn't a common name, but there had to be a reasonable explanation.

I hugged myself. Days ago, we were picking baby names and planning a trip to see the Phillips Collection in DC. Suddenly he's dodging calls and running around with women he failed to mention. What was happening?

Craning my neck to get as close to my belly as possible, I murmured, "Don't worry, Muffin. Mommy will figure everything out and make it right."

I picked up my phone and scrolled through the contacts to find the main number for Lyle's former employer. I stared at it, recalling the one and only time I'd met an Ebba.

Ebba Nilsson. Tall and lithe, blonde and buxom, with a tinkling feminine giggle. She'd laughed often, mostly at anything Lyle had said at the company's most recent holiday party. I'd teased him about his new fan that night but then never mentioned her again. Why would I? I hadn't felt genuinely threatened. We were in love and pregnant. Only good things were happening for us.

A couple of weeks later, on Christmas morning, Lyle had given me my favorite gift: a Foster family memory jar, like the tradition my mom had started years ago in my childhood home. We'd fill it annually with special memories and then, on each New Year's Eve, reread them. Afterward, we would choose our favorite from that year, which would then be kept in a special box for the future.

My eyes closed on that thought, praying that my qualms about Ebba were wrong. Then I dialed the number.

"Chesapeake Properties. How can I direct your call?"

I coughed once so my voice wouldn't squeak. "Ebba Nilsson, please."

"Ebba is no longer with our firm. May I direct you to someone else?"

Without thinking, I hung up and slid the phone away.

Biting the inside of my cheek, I pushed myself out of the chair and paced.

All around me lay evidence of our happy marriage. The striking wedding photo on the sofa table, the embellished throw pillows we'd chosen together, the ultrasound photo pinned to the corkboard above my built-in desk in the kitchen. Sure, career demands and familiarity had rubbed the brand-new shine off our romance and made some days harder than others. But Lyle loved me as I loved him. I knew that with every bit of my being.

He would not destroy the life we'd built together these past three and a half years for a Swedish bimbo.

A sharp knock at the door startled me. I wouldn't have answered, but my mother's voice called, "Amanda, honey! It's me."

I lumbered to the door and flung it open. "Mom . . ."

She looked surprised when I fell into her arms.

"Oh my!" She held me tight, patting my back and stroking my hair. For a second I felt like a kid again, seeking the security of her love, confident that she could fix my problems. "What's happened?"

Uncertainty strangled my vocal cords.

"Come, dear. Let's sit down." My mother led me back to the kitchen table and made sure I was seated. Her kind golden-brown eyes shone with concern, but I was having a hard time looking into them. "Why aren't you ready?"

My mother wanted us to go complete a gift registry for the guests she'd invited to the baby shower she was hosting next month. She'd worn her favorite Lane Bryant dress and kitten heels for the occasion.

"It's Lyle." I swallowed to loosen the knot in my throat. "I think maybe he's having an affair."

"What?" My mother's face pinched while she shook her head. "No way. He dotes on you."

"I thought so, too." I folded my arms on the table and rested my forehead on my wrists, while Mom stroked my hair and squeezed my shoulder. Familiar, gentle reminders that I was not alone, although they did little to settle my stomach.

"Let me fix you a cup of tea, and then you can tell me what's put this nonsense in your head." She set her purse on the table and then absently opened and closed several cupboards and drawers.

"Cups are above the dishwasher." I frowned—my mother had helped me set up my kitchen and visited me at least twice each week. If anything, she knew this kitchen better than I did.

"Oh, that's right." She fuddled around with the cup and tea bag, and eventually turned on the microwave, while I dissected the facts, which, admittedly, weren't clear. Was my mom right? Lyle had never before given me any reason to doubt him. He'd never lied about anything . . .

Well, other than Sugar Momma's.

My mother brought the tea to the table and sat beside me. "Now drink this and tell me what's happened."

I recognized the look on her face. The one she'd worn to convince us that there were no monsters under the bed. Nothing dark and scary had ever reached up to grab us, but that didn't mean there weren't monsters out there.

I couldn't help but wish I had another cookie. "I haven't heard from him since yesterday afternoon—"

She waved that off, wearing a relieved smile. "He's busy working, honey."

Mom had always respected the boundaries of work. As our town's high school librarian, she'd made it clear we couldn't run to her with personal problems during school hours. My father had been in sales, having worked his way up to a regional manager position within a small medical supply company. When we were kids he'd traveled on business one or two days each week. He hadn't been in constant touch with her, and she'd been fine with that. He was always where he said he'd be, and he'd often come home with big hugs and little trinkets for us all.

"I know. But I called Tom, and a woman answered—Tom's girlfriend. When I asked for Lyle, she told me he'd left yesterday—with Ebba."

My mother frowned. "Who's Ebba?"

"I'm not sure, but he used to work with a woman named Ebba at Chesapeake Properties. I called right before you showed up and learned that she no longer works there." I held the teacup in both hands to warm them. It didn't help.

"Well, there you go. Lyle told us he planned to bring partners into this deal so he could quickly repay my loan, right? *Of course* he'd choose partners he already knew he could work well with. He's smart that way."

"Maybe . . ." I mulled it over, recalling all his excitement about our future. But if he'd invited Ebba into the deal, why hadn't that come up in conversation?

"Yes, honey. Trust me. Please don't let your hormones play tricks on you." My mother's certainty reassured me. I *had* been a hormonal mess lately. "Lyle isn't having an affair. He's a good man and devoted husband. Be patient. He'll call any minute now."

The phone buzzed on the table, and I grabbed it.

Erin.

I set it down, unable to deal with her at the moment. It was hard enough to stay optimistic now without her wordless "told you sos" sowing doubts. Not that she'd say it. In fact, she'd brush her hands together, mutter "good riddance," then suggest we get pizza or take a road trip.

"Come on." My mom stood. "Go put on something pretty and let's have our shopping day picking out a crib and bedding and all the sweet things. You'll feel better, and after Lyle calls tonight, we'll laugh about this. You'll see."

I went up to my room to change into a spring dress and flats. My mother's faith had given me hope, and browsing baby clothes would certainly lift my mood. I brushed my hair, thinking about the way Lyle had kissed me goodbye. *"Wish me luck!"* he'd said.

My mother was right. He'd never shown any interest in other women, including Ebba. He could be moody, but he'd never lied.

And then Hannah's laughing face resurfaced from when she'd innocently revealed, *"That's exactly what he always says."*

I stared into the mirror, expecting it to crack as the reckoning that I may not know my husband as well as I'd thought returned.

What if cookies weren't the only secret Lyle was keeping?

CHAPTER TWO

ERIN

Until my dad died, I'd given less than zero thought to my future. Those of us hovering around an average IQ were less burdened by big aspirations and expectations—and that freedom had kept my life spontaneous and interesting. My siblings, Kevin and Amanda, proved my theory that the smarter a person is, the more trapped they get in the whole "big thing," like finding the right school, the right job, the right partner, the right house.

The family gene pool *did* funnel my dad's zest for adventure and winning smile my way. As long as there was a roof over my head, most days I had all I needed to be happy. Lately, though, that roof thing was looking a bit precarious.

If I'd been smarter, maybe I could've become a veterinarian—the perfect job for someone who loves animals more than I do most people. That income would've exceeded what I cleared from the combo of teaching yoga and my budding Etsy business. Still, odd jobs gave me flexibility and autonomy, as well as immediate satisfaction.

But if I'm being completely honest, the specter of my thirtieth birthday had me thinking it might be time to do some adulting and take a few steps away from the poverty line. Lately I'd felt stuck somewhere between where I was headed and where I wanted to be. Without my dad to talk to, I was putting my faith in tomorrow's meditation and yoga retreat as my best hope for answers.

"Let's leave for the institute at six tomorrow." Lexi, my BFF and fellow instructor, rolled up her mat and strapped it onto her yoga bag. She had the face and body of a young Angela Bassett, and rocked short hair just as well.

All around us, women in various states of undress banged around their lockers, blow-dried their hair, and chattered like chickens in a henhouse. The recent influx of young families to town had brought to the studio more women who all looked alike, with their shoulder-length, straight hair, Alala yoga wear, and Céline handbags. Even their freshly plucked eyebrows and real gold jewelry set them apart from me.

My multicolored cocktail-pattern yoga pants had raised more than one eyebrow at Give Me Strength, but I wouldn't have it any other way. They're hilarious, though not as funny as my pair covered with Nicolas Cage's face.

"We don't need to be up in Rhinebeck until noon." I shut my locker. "Seven's the perfect time to go."

"Unless we hit traffic, need a bathroom break, or anything else crops up. We've spent a lot for this weekend, so let's not miss anything. Tony's already busting on me for going on this retreat when I'm a yoga *teacher*."

He had a point, but her boyfriend didn't get restless when life got humdrum. I did, hence my justifying the trip I couldn't afford as a necessity for my future. It *could* give me an edge if I ever found a way to open my own studio, one of many business ideas—along with expanding my Shakti Suds soap products and dog grooming (once I learned how)—that required money I didn't have to spare.

"Max won't be thrilled if I wake Mo up that early." My boyfriend had never been a morning person. Or much of a dog person, frankly.

And once freed from his crate for the day, Mo stuck by someone's heels at all times.

"When is Max ever thrilled about anything?" Lexi quipped.

I could only shrug. Max hadn't been excited about writing, art, music, or even interesting food since his regular Sunday brunch solo gig at the East Beach Café got canceled five months ago, and I'd rather not think about the effect his apathy had on me. "Fine, fine. I'll pick you up at six fifteen."

"Good." Lexi shouldered the gym's heavy glass door open. Like everything else around here, this trendy fitness center looked like something straight out of a magazine. Glass, brick, metal. A.k.a. sterile, unoriginal, and unimaginative.

Silly, really. No one needed upscale finishes to enjoy a rewarding yoga session. Give me a cozy space with soft lighting and some hand-rolled natural incense sticks any day. Better yet, small groups of students who weren't competing with each other to see who could hold a pose longest or best. Hello, people! Kinda missing the point of yoga!

But a paycheck is a paycheck, so I dragged my butt here several days each week to tone women who didn't have to work so they could fit into their designer clothes and sip wine at lunch without guilt. Making the emotional-spiritual connection would be up to them.

"See you tomorrow, Lex!" I waved goodbye before trotting across the street to Sugar Momma's, the only truly awesome new shop on this side of town. I shouldn't splurge, but Hannah's chai was the best, and her love for color exceeded my own. If I ever got fired from the gym, maybe I could work here part-time.

"Good morning, Hannah." I planted my hands on the counter and smiled.

"Woo-hoo, those pants say happy hour to me!" Hannah joked.

"Maybe we should wait until after lunch," I teased. More people should be like us, laughing at the absurdity of life instead of freaking out like my mom and sister had when I'd recently shorn the left side of my head and cropped the hair on the other side in short, uneven chunks.

"I guess it is still early." Hannah raised her index finger. "Hey, you just missed your sister. She left about ten minutes ago."

"Really? That's too bad." I forced my facial expression to match those words. Amanda and my mom were already pissed at me for bailing on this afternoon's baby shower shopping spree. If I'd run into my sister here, I'd be leaving with the chai and a major guilt trip.

Who needed that? I *already* felt bad about choosing Max's dad's birthday lunch instead. But the truth is, Amanda and my mom have similar tastes, and they don't particularly like mine. At least Charlie laughs at my jokes and likes to play cards. Given the choice between hangin' with people who want to change me versus those who don't, why wouldn't I choose the latter?

I didn't even need to be with them to know everything they'd pick today would be white and pink, with lots of lace, ribbon, and ruffles. Sure, that stuff's sweet, but not at all as unique as the little onesie I found on Etsy right after learning about the baby. It had a picture of a gaming remote and read "Player 3 has entered the game." I'd been all grins until Amanda offered up the same awkward smile she'd worn after she'd unwrapped any birthday or Christmas gift I'd ever given her. There was no doubt in my mind that my niece would never wear that onesie except in case of a dire emergency.

Lyle was even pickier than my sister, and twice as certain. Mr. and Mrs. Do the Right This and Be the Right That, as if anything in life was ever actually wrong. Scratch that. Some things were definitely wrong, like murder and disloyalty. But not hairstyles, career choices, and a little experimentation with whatever the world had to offer. Lyle and I hadn't liked each other from the start, so for the past three years I'd seen even less of my sister than before.

"Her belly's getting big now," Hannah said.

That made me smile. Amanda had always been a pretty woman, but now she glowed. I'd marked my niece's due date on my calendar with a red heart. Not that Lyle would let me spend much time with her on my own, if any. That guy's only positive trait was that he gave Amanda a lot of nice things. But if those two ever did let me babysit, I'd be given a list of instructions as long as my arm. Rules, rules, rules. I should've bought a sign like that as a housewarming gift. Then again, it'd be at the bottom of some drawer with that onesie, and I'd be that much closer to being homeless. "Only a few more months to go."

Hannah nodded. "So you want your usual?"

"You know it." I tossed three bucks on the counter and waited for the to-go cup of deliciousness. Totally worth it.

I raised the tea in salutation. "Have an awesome day, my friend."

After running back across the street, I crouched to unlock my bike and then poured the chai into my insulated water bottle to take with me.

Nothing beats biking on spring mornings like this, when the cool breeze whips along the bay and rustles the budding leaves of the oak trees, although they also make me miss my dad even more. I remembered the day we'd transferred the American sycamore seedling from the nursery pot to our backyard. Early April . . . typical overcast skies threatening rain. A chilly breeze whipped across the yard, but I hadn't minded because my dad was smiling at me and we were listening to Coldplay. I'd been ten years old, and it was the first time *I'd* introduced *him* to new music. We'd spent a lot of time outdoors, from snelling hooks on the water to tending to the vegetable garden in the yard, talking about life and laughing at most of it.

A massive heart attack that no one saw coming took him from us almost a year ago. His one vice—those damn cigarettes—had literally killed him. I'm the last person to criticize anyone for a vice, 'cause I've got plenty. But moderation, people. Moderation.

I'd spent the last year grasping at anything—including Max—to fill the void my dad left behind, but the fact that nothing was working was another sign that I needed to change the direction of my life.

As the gentrified part of town faded behind me, the familiar streets of my youth prompted a grin. I'd been biking these old roads since getting Kevin's hand-me-down red trike twenty-odd years ago. My first kiss—Todd Brewer—had lived there on Orchard Drive. Haley Scott, a friend who'd moved to California in tenth grade, had lived there on Aspen Lane. And after I left home, my dad and I had met regularly at Lou's Diner, our favorite spot for coffee and pie despite its broken tableside jukeboxes and desperate need of a new coat of paint. This side of town held its history and its generations-old families. Not the Audi-driving dandies.

I turned the bend onto Oak Court to reach my apartment building, locking my bike in the beat-up rack out front. I've toured interesting cities all over Europe, but nothing quite beats home.

Home sweet home.

Or not, as I was reminded when I passed by Mrs. Wagner's apartment door on my way up to the third floor. I'd lost count of how many cats she kept in there, but the odor that leaked through the gap beneath her door gagged me worse than anything Max let rip after a big meal at Olé Mole.

When I reached into my backpack for my keys, my yoga bag fell off my shoulder. It'd been that kind of morning. Mo barked at the door from inside. My sister's fancy security system had nothing on my fifteen-pound Zuchon.

When I opened the door, I knelt so he could lick me.

"Fluffy McFlufferson. So many kisses!" I squealed, rolling onto my back to play with him for a few seconds. He might be overdue for a grooming appointment, but the retreat registration fee meant I'd need to teach a few more classes to pay for a grooming *and* my phone bill.

On the upside, when Mo's hair got this long, he looked like a puffball, thus the nickname.

"Hey," Max called from his spot on the sofa.

He was still sprawled there in his boxer briefs, remote in hand, exactly like when I'd left two hours earlier. Coming home to the sight of those carved abs and thighs and then dive-bombing the couch with him in a tangle of arms and legs used to excite me. Now I wanted to throw my yoga mat at his head and bellow, *"Get a job!"*

I gave Mo one last hug before I stood. "I thought you'd be showered by now. We should hit the road if you want to get to Philly in time to take your dad to lunch and not have to dine and dash."

"We're not going." Max didn't even look at me.

I glanced at the TV to see what was so captivating that he couldn't tear himself away to have a conversation about the sudden change in plans. *Old School* again. One Will Ferrell movie was more than enough for me, but Max could spend hours on end rewatching them.

"Why not?" I leaned the mat against the wall between the entertainment unit and the corner cluttered with Max's old notebooks, charcoals and art pads, and other abandoned hobby supplies. The same corner I'd been meaning to get around to cleaning because none of my attempts to help him get his mojo back had succeeded. I mean, if a little rejection defeated him, he needed to find a nonartistic career. "Is your dad sick?"

Charlie could be a bit loud, but he'd always been kind to me in a way I'd particularly missed this past year without my dad.

"In the head, maybe." Max snickered at his unfunny joke.

God, he could use a haircut, too. Who doesn't appreciate a small man bun? But his had become a knotted mess.

He still hadn't done more than toss me a glance at that point, so my temper started tapping on my chest the way Principal Kentworth used to tap on his desk whenever I'd gotten in trouble at school.

I crossed my arms. "Hey, Max. Get your hand out of your pants long enough to tell me what's going on. I'd like to know why you've unilaterally changed our plans."

Max heaved a sigh the likes of which should be performed only in truly trying circumstances. "We had an argument, and now I don't feel like celebrating his stupid birthday."

"But I made a cake, and earned another black mark in my mom's scorebook for bailing on her and Amanda today so we could celebrate with him."

Max shrugged. "Sorry, babe."

That endearment used to make my heart sing and my panties wet. Now the only thing my heart wanted to sing when it came to Max was the blues. As for the panties? Dry as Nevada.

"At least tell me why you argued. What was so bad that we can't go wish him a happy birthday?"

He closed his eyes like he needed the patience required to deal with one of my sister's students who'd peed his pants. "Can't we chill and watch the movie, Erin? For chrissakes, it's my dad, not yours. If *I* don't want to go, why do you?"

I blinked, wise to the deflection. Whatever Charlie had said had probably echoed my sentiments. "I'm not leaving this room until you fess up."

"You're being a pill. And don't act like you weren't happy for an excuse to skip out on Amanda's shopping spree." He glowered.

I couldn't deny that last part. I didn't enjoy shopping much even when I *had* money, and most time spent with the dynamic duo otherwise known as Mom and Sis usually makes me feel a little worse about myself—which fact perplexes me because I fundamentally disagree with most of their philosophies. Still, all that well-intentioned advice can make me feel less-than.

"Turn down that movie. You could recite it by heart, so you won't miss anything." I marched across the room and sat on the coffee table.

"He got on my case about getting a 'real' job, okay?" Max blushed.

A touchy subject. Max had dabbled in poetry and short stories but never made much money. To supplement that dream, he'd taken odd jobs at the local hardware store or coffee shops, but eventually he'd argue with his boss and get fired. Resilience wasn't exactly his strong suit, but he'd had such cool goals—or had pretended to until he had a roof over his head at little to no cost to him. Two years ago his good looks, affection, and romantic dreams had drawn me in. I was still grateful for all his tenderness in the wake of my dad's death. But, Jesus, his laziness had been on my nerves for at least two months.

"Well, you know I'm not the corporate type, but there is something to be said for going out every day and doing something to get paid."

"Teaching yoga classes isn't exactly backbreaking work, Erin."

Said the man who'd never taken one of my classes. "I also have my Etsy business."

He rolled his eyes before his gaze landed on the milk crates filled with glass jars, various bottles of coconut and grapeseed oils, scented essential oils, bags of sugar, and soap molds. "Selling soaps and scrubs isn't making you millions, either."

"It makes more than you bring in." I could take a lot of shit from him, but not a slam to Shakti Suds. I loved working with essential oils, packaging the little jars and ribbons, writing notes to customers, which I wouldn't have discovered if I hadn't been sinking into an abyss of grief.

It'd been Max, actually, who'd suggested aromatherapy to help me climb out of that hole. I'd then googled essential oil mixtures that could help with the various stages of grief. Instead of using the diffuser Max had borrowed from a friend, I had taught myself to make soaps and other products to help soothe me while I cried alone in the bathtub.

Whenever I'd given extra product to friends, they'd raved. I figured that since my dad was good at sales and I'm so much like him, maybe I could start a business selling my stuff. In less than a year, I'd built a small but loyal repeat clientele. Pretty good considering I'd been in mourning nearly that whole time.

Mo ran to the door right before someone knocked, barking his head off as if Jason from *Friday the 13th* were on the other side.

"Mo!" I yelled, looking over my shoulder at Max. "Who's this?"

"Uber Eats."

"What the hell?" I hissed. Now it was my turn to heave a big sigh. With a fake smile on my face, I picked Mo up to keep him from jumping all over the delivery person, and answered the door. A young guy handed me a brown bag from Markham's Deli. "Thank you."

I closed the door, set Mo back on the floor, and then peered into the bag. If I had to bet, it contained two bacon, egg, and cheese bagels. With delivery and tip, it probably cost twenty bucks or more. "Who's paying for this, Max?"

"You're the only one with an account." He winked and made grabby hands for the bag.

"Because *I'm* the only one with a credit card." I flung the bag right at his chest.

"Hey!" He scowled, then ripped open the bag on the coffee table to turn it into a makeshift plate.

"You know what?" I put my hands on my hips. "It's a good thing I'm leaving tomorrow for the retreat."

With a full mouth, he asked, "What's that mean?"

In the beginning I'd actually thought that beard was cute, but now it bothered me as much as everything else about him, especially when food got caught in it.

"You're on thin ice, that's what it means. When I asked you to move in last year, I didn't sign up to be your mom."

He got that twinkle in his eye that usually weakened me. In a sultry voice, he said, "Come on, babe. I hardly treat you like my mom."

The fact that his sexy voice didn't melt me proved how bad our chi was out of whack. "We were supposed to split the cost of living to protect the time we needed to pursue our other goals. Yet I've been footing all the bills, and now I'm in credit card debt while you're doing nothing to help. I've got *less* time for my business, and you're *wasting* all yours."

"If money's so tight, why'd you sign up for the retreat?" His entitled tone—his gall to suggest I shouldn't spend my hard-earned money on myself—snapped something deep inside.

"Max, this isn't working for me."

"What isn't?"

"This!" I gestured between us. "You and me. It's probably best if you move out this weekend while I'm away."

At least he put down the sandwich for a second. "You're not serious, are you?"

"I am." I was done. Done, done, done.

"Babe! Don't overreact. I'll pay you back for the sandwich." He rested his elbows on his knees and looked up at me with those big blue eyes, his expression all soft and sad. For a second I almost caved. That adorable man I'd met two years, two months, and fifteen days ago shone through all the ick, and my heart hesitated.

"It's not about the sandwich. It's about having to pay for nearly everything we do because I have two jobs and you have none. It's the way you lie around in your underwear and watch reruns instead of working on a story or poem, or at least doing some housework so I don't have to. It's that beard and the hair that's so overgrown you look like Mo."

His brows rose. "But we have fun, and the sex is still great."

He had me there. The man knew his way around my body like nobody ever had before, and he was still a thing of beauty. If he'd cut his hair and shave, he could probably get work as a local model or something. "I'm turning thirty soon and I need a real partner, not a boy toy."

I didn't know a lot, but I did know that a relationship should make you grow. My dad had once mused that he'd had one old love who'd lit him up like a firecracker yet also left him burned out. Then my mom had come along—steady and assured—to dust him off and help him become his best self. Max and I hadn't done that for each other in quite some time.

"Ouch. You can be harsh, you know." He picked up his sandwich and took another bite, brow creased. "You really want me out? That's it? You're done and I get no say?"

I rose above a petty quip about it being a lot like how I'd had no say in the plans he'd changed today. It wouldn't have been a fair comparison. We'd enjoyed a lengthy, intimate relationship and shared some memorable times together. Yet when I searched my heart for even the smallest ache, I couldn't find it. The past few months had proven that together we would never evolve. "I'm sorry for being harsh. I think maybe this has been coming for a while, and my going away for the weekend gives us the perfect time for a clean break."

He slouched against the cushions and locked his hands behind his head. "You're gonna miss me when I'm gone."

I wouldn't deny there might be some nights when I'd miss him, but I wouldn't miss all the little things that bugged me, and I literally couldn't afford to stay in this relationship. I didn't need a man to define me, and everything about this conversation reinforced that giving Max the boot was step one in changing my life. "Maybe."

"Who gets Mo?"

The air left my lungs. "Mo is mine."

"Why's he yours? We got him together." He crossed his arms now, like he might actually fight me about this, of all things.

His sudden love for Mo only made me angrier. "I bought him. I've paid all his vet bills, walk him every day, and feed him. All you do is lie around with him on that couch. Mo is *my* dog."

"He'll miss me, though." Max cast a soulful gaze Mo's way.

That stopped me. In a way it would be like a divorce, except unlike with a kid, we couldn't explain to Mo why Max wouldn't be around anymore.

Mo was curled up on his little dog bed, watching us both. "Well, I guess you can visit him and take him for walks now and then if you want."

That didn't thrill me, but maybe it would be best for Mo. Truthfully, Max's taking me up on the offer was about as likely as him getting a job anytime soon.

Max narrowed his eyes, but just as he had no resilience when it came to a career, he also had none for our relationship. Quitting was simply his thing. "Fine. I'll be gone by Sunday afternoon."

Without another glance, he stretched back out on the sofa, grabbed his second sandwich, and turned up the volume right as Frank "The Tank" tells Blue he's his boy.

Well, that was that. I pushed off the table and went to the bedroom without another word.

I flopped backward onto my mattress and stared at the ceiling, waiting for tears or doubts or something to take over.

Nothing.

Was this a good sign, or had I simply used up all my tears on my dad? I wasn't sure, but it seemed like evidence that I'd done the right thing. I could pack my bag for my trip. Or maybe I should try to catch up with my mom and sister now that I had the time.

I rolled onto my side with a groan, coming face-to-face with one of my favorite family photos. We'd taken our annual family summer trip to Hilton Head—the one real splurge my dad had made sure we enjoyed every year. We had a tradition of having lunch at a little open-air cabana bar and restaurant called Coco's on the Beach.

Between the deck and the volleyball court in the sand stood a tall pole with colorful arrow-shaped signs pointing in different directions. Each one was painted with the name of a different city somewhere on the globe, along with the mileage to get there. We'd dream about all the places we might go, and after high school I'd had the chance to see many. In this picture, our whole family is standing around that sign, smiling at the camera. My dad has his hand on my shoulder, and if you look closely, you can see Amanda holding my hand. I must've been only five or six—young enough that she hadn't given up trying to be my second mother. At the time, I'd felt smothered by her attention, but looking back, I'd also felt loved.

I grabbed my phone and called my sister, but it went to voice mail. A heaviness pressed on me, but I couldn't tell if it was from looking at that picture of our family that would never again be whole or from the fact that I'd disappointed my mom and sister today.

They loved me in their way even if they couldn't love and accept me *as I was*. My dad had, though, and to honor his memory and wishes for our family, I couldn't continue to drift out of their lives as I'd been doing.

After the beep, I said, "Hey, it's *moi*. Surprise! My plans have changed and I've got a little time. If you get this message, let me know where you are and I'll try to catch up."

I hit "End," my feet restlessly kicking the end of my bed. The small bedroom seemed claustrophobic, but I didn't want to talk to Max. Not that I could avoid him in here, either, where his dirty laundry, sandals, and other items lay about. Rather than take a match to it all, I decided to organize some of his things to help with his packing. Hauling myself off the bed, I then went to the armoire to get to the vintage albums my dad had left me in his will.

Some were fairly valuable, like the Beatles collection box set from 1982, valued at roughly a thousand bucks. Or the *Led Zeppelin* first pressing with the turquoise label, which should net around eight hundred or so dollars. U2's *Joshua Tree* collection box set from 1987—maybe worth six or seven hundred. Then there were others worth less than one hundred dollars. But each one had infinite sentimental value.

Every song resurrected a specific memory of time spent with my father playing cards, washing cars, grilling hot dogs . . . anything. Whatever he'd wanted to do, I'd done with him, and he'd always chosen the perfect background soundtrack for every activity. Those stolen moments had also been a great way to escape my mom's endless lectures and demands. She'd never yelled at me for skipping out on chores or being messy when I'd been spending that time with him. Probably because he wouldn't let her.

At present, my restlessness matched the mood of a typical Bob Seger song, so I grabbed *Beautiful Loser* and slipped the record from its sleeve, resisting the urge to hug it as if it were my dad. I set it on the old turntable he'd also left me. As the few first drumbeats clangored, my heart kicked an extra beat or two—partly happy, partly sad. I glanced toward the bedroom door, picturing Max on the sofa, and then got to work.

It didn't matter where life led me next. I had faith because my own personal angel was looking out for me now.

Que será, será.

CHAPTER THREE

AMANDA

My mother's optimism had gotten me through the day, despite my being jumpy anytime my phone rang. I now sat in front of the computer, double-checking the online registry to make sure the items we'd selected were properly linked. The sweet-looking swaddling blankets and dresses made me smile, but I secretly most coveted one of the practical items—a handsome three-in-one portable crib, diaper bag, and changing station. What a marvelous invention!

I couldn't wait to see my daughter's face. To smell her skin and feel the downy baby hair. To listen to the baby gurgles and press strawberry kisses on her bare tummy. To nurture and teach and drown in all the love for her that was building.

After I'd double-checked everything, I closed out of the computer and made a pit stop at the restroom before collecting the mail.

Making my way back to the kitchen, I sifted through the envelopes, stopping midstride when I saw Lyle's handwriting. He hadn't sent me a love note since our first year of marriage. The envelope was postmarked from Miami two days earlier.

I set the rest of the mail aside and sat at the table while tearing into the letter.

Amanda,

I am writing because a phone call would be more difficult on us both. There is no easy way to tell you that I think I have fallen in love with someone else.

It felt as if my rib cage collapsed. Oh God, I'm an idiot. All day I'd thought the worst-case scenario was some stupid fling, but not *this*. *This* couldn't be happening. I blinked back hot tears to keep reading.

I know the timing is bad with the baby on the way, but I didn't plan it. It just happened. Now I owe it to myself—and to you—to be honest and explore my feelings.

With so much at stake, I need time to figure out what is best for all of us, so it makes sense to do that here while I nail down this deal. I trust your family will give you the emotional support you need while I work through my feelings. I know I'm asking a lot, but if you could give me a couple of weeks of space, I will be in touch as soon as I feel certain of my decision.

Lyle

Not even "Love, Lyle."

As a teacher and lifelong reader, I'd known words could be more lethal than a bullet. Now my body was as cold as any corpse.

I think I've fallen in love with someone else.

Think? A universe of difference existed between "I think" and "I have," didn't it? And he hadn't said he *didn't* love me. Was I grasping? Everything Lyle did, he did with purpose, so he'd chosen that word carefully. Chosen this method of delivery for a reason, although I couldn't figure out why except to guess that it left me no easy way to reply.

I slammed the letter down, then stood in my kitchen, dumbfounded. At once everything felt foreign, including my body. I couldn't move—not even a twitch—his note having severed the connection between my brain and my muscles.

While I'd been loving my husband and nurturing our unborn child, he'd fallen in love with another woman. Absurdly, the musing lyrics of that ridiculous Talking Heads song Erin used to playact, "Once in a Lifetime," became the soundtrack to this horrible moment.

Lyle hadn't even respected me enough to end things before moving on, let alone been willing to work on our marriage. A memory of the first time we met raced forward. November 26, 2016. Two days after Thanksgiving, when I'd gone to the gym to work off all the gravy and pumpkin pie I'd consumed. The electricity in that exercise studio when our gazes locked—his captivating blue eyes luring me like a moth to light. The way he'd waited for me to exit the women's locker room and then walked me to my car, his quick smile drawing me in.

The weekly pink roses he'd sent to my classroom those first few months.

The interesting phone conversations about our pasts and our dreams.

The surprise sailing trip on the bay.

The empathy . . .

"Amanda, if you marry me, I swear I'll make sure you never feel second-best again."

The look on his face when he'd made that vow flickered, causing another sharp inhale. My life with him—his reassurances—had helped me move on from my rivalry with Erin and her place as our dad's favorite.

But apparently I was still easily replaceable.

I'd been fighting that truth my whole life.

The silence in our home sounded different now. More permanent. Yet somehow alive, as if Lyle's ghost were brushing against me, raising the hairs on my skin.

I think I have fallen in love with someone else.

Suddenly, like a movie playing at high speed, I began revisiting the moments of our marriage, dissecting each one, looking for clues, asking myself, "Why, why, why?" Only one conclusion mattered, though: I'd failed at the most important relationship of my life.

Again, those stupid song lyrics taunted me.

I raced upstairs to our closet and grabbed a suitcase, planning to pack a bag and fly to Florida. Then I realized I had no idea where Lyle was staying now that he'd left Tom's.

Enraged, I yanked my clothes off hangers and tossed them in a pile beside the suitcase. Instead of desperately hunting him down, I'd move out and "show him" everything he was about to lose. Ebba might be beautiful, but she wasn't the love of his life. *I* was. He'd told me so a million times, and I was carrying his child, for God's sake!

On that thought, I crumpled to the floor in a heap with my clothes, wailing a raw, otherworldly kind of sound, releasing all the self-pity in the world through gulping sobs. I have no idea how long I remained there.

Later, exhausted, I pushed off the floor and hung my clothes back on their rods and folded others to return to their shelves.

It was then that I noticed the box Lyle kept on the top shelf of the closet. I'd never before been tempted to snoop, but now I wondered if it might contain clues. Balancing on the top of the step stool, I pulled it down and began rummaging. A high school yearbook, old VHS tapes of movies like *The Usual Suspects*, a framed photograph of himself at eight or nine with a woman I presumed was his mother, and a small address book. I held the image of him and his mother closer, studying the woman I'd grown to hate despite having never met her. Where had her new life taken her, and did she ever miss Lyle?

I should burn it, but instead I tossed it back into the box and flipped through the address book, stopping on his father's contact information.

Early on in our relationship I'd promised not to contact the man Lyle had called emotionally abusive. As I stood in my closet now, my hands shook with the temptation to break that promise. I didn't, though. Loyalty matters, even when the chips are down, so I put the box back on the shelf exactly as Lyle had placed it.

Angrily I flirted with the idea of having my own affair, maybe with Doug Silver, the hot dentist. The confident way he often smiled at me and touched my shoulder suggested he found me attractive. But rashness was Erin's style, not mine, so I focused on my daughter. Her needs ranked above all else.

And the embarrassing truth was that I loved my husband. He hadn't said he no longer loved me. He hadn't asked for a divorce. He'd admitted to the affair and asked for time. Given those facts, I could stomach the punch to the gut and forgive him—for our daughter and for myself. I was Lyle's home. It wouldn't take him long to realize what he risked losing for an infatuation.

Until I was certain of next steps, the less anyone in town knew, the better. And family? Well, even if I wanted to, I couldn't turn to Erin. She'd never liked Lyle—the nicest thing she could ever say about him was that he was attractive. I'd rather swallow sour milk than accept the idea that she might've been right about him.

I dreaded Mom's reaction to the affair. I wouldn't tell her yet. I needed time to process all this and talk to Lyle.

I waddled to the bathroom to splash cool water on my face, my stomach cramping, my arms dangling lifelessly at my sides. It'd be pointless to crawl into bed, though, because closing my eyes would lead straight to images of Ebba laughing in her tight, short dress. Did Lyle's former coworkers know about them? If so, they must consider me an idiot—and maybe they weren't wrong. An irritating inner voice accused me of willful ignorance.

Lyle's snappishness these past few months now took on new meaning. My skin crawled when thinking about our recent sex life. I'd attributed the drop-off to my growing belly. But the suspicion that, when we had made love, he'd been picturing *her* ripped through me like my best Shun knife.

On top of everything was the tone of the note—*his* decisions, *his* options—so certain that I'd be patient and obedient, awaiting his decision while hoping he'd choose our family over her . . .

I hated that he knew me so well when I obviously didn't know him at all. I hated that deep down I wanted him to return, beg for mercy, and tell me he could never love someone else more than he loved me. God, I hated Lyle right now, but I still loved him.

How could all these feelings coexist?

Muffin restlessly kicked, distending my abdomen. I dabbed a tear. This man I'd thought would be a model father might actually be a terrible parent.

Like his own.

Another reason not to call Mr. Foster. Grilling Lyle's father wouldn't change my current situation, and Muffin didn't need an emotionally crippled grandfather complicating her life.

To think I'd been excited about the potential of what Lyle's trip to Florida could mean for our future, clueless that he'd been there "nailing down" more than a deal.

I pounded my fists on the marble vanity top with a pained yelp that echoed off the cold surfaces of my bathroom.

Thank God Erin was away this weekend—I'd have more time before facing her. My inability to confide in my sister was a constant source of frustration and regret. Kevin had been nearly three years older than me, so by the time I could keep up with him, he'd preferred his bike, baseball bat, and buddy Tim Hartman to my company. When Erin was born, it was as if my parents had handed me a live baby doll. My mother let me help dress her and rock her and read to her. She was adorable, with her round eyes and wild brown hair. But as soon as she'd graduated from pull-ups, she resisted playing the domestic kinds of make-believe games I enjoyed and, like Kevin, blazed her own crazy path, leaving me to my Barbies and books. To this day, I couldn't count on her to listen to or understand me.

I went back to the kitchen to force myself to eat something. Through the kitchen window, I could see the spot in the yard where I'd suggested we install a swing set mock me. I'd been planning for our growing family while Lyle had been planning an escape. I drank straight from the faucet to soothe my raw throat.

When I tossed the used paper towel, I noticed our Foster family memory jar tucked in the corner, with several little scrolls of paper gathered at the bottom. Things like the memory of making love by the fireplace on our first night in this house. The first dinner party we'd hosted here for my family. The day we'd learned Muffin's gender.

Forever kinds of memories.

Traditions were foundational glue for families—or so I'd believed before Lyle had me questioning absolutely everything.

———

Friday I'd called off work sick and stayed in bed all day. Today my stomach still burned as I drove to my mother's to meet with her and Kevin. I'd been vague when requesting this get-together because I'd hoped to reach Lyle and make this meeting unnecessary. Those prayers went unanswered.

I killed the car's engine in my mother's driveway. Like clockwork, Kevin pulled in before I exited my car. We shared a penchant for punctuality and planners and order. We'd also inherited Mom's blonde hair and blue eyes. Kevin got our dad's larger build and no-nonsense manner, whereas I was petite and always more accommodating than my siblings.

Life as a young partner at the Ballard Spade law firm—not to mention the demands at home from Marcy and their eighteen-month-old,

Billy—consumed much of his time. But while we no longer gathered regularly for Sunday dinners, Kevin had been in touch more since Dad died, taking up the mantle of the man in our family.

He gave me a quick kiss hello. Exhaustion had carved deep lines in his face. "Sis."

"Thanks for coming, Kev. I know you're super busy."

"You sounded kind of desperate. What's going on? Is it Mom?" He started toward the front door.

I kept up with him despite my waddling. "Yes and no. It's complicated." My cheeks burned. "Let's go inside first."

Kevin smiled at my abdomen and squeezed my shoulder. "You look great. I feel bad for Lyle, though. In another two months you'll be miserable. He'll be scrambling to keep you comfortable until the baby pops out."

Tears swam to my eyes without warning.

Kevin was already rapping on the front door before opening it without waiting for Mom to answer, but his face fell at my expression. "Uh-oh. Is this the hormones, or something else?"

"Probably both." I pinched the bridge of my nose, calling out, "Mom, we're here."

A noise in the kitchen caught our attention, so we walked through the living and dining rooms, stepping around a laundry basket on the way. Dirty coffee cups lay abandoned on various tables; a days-old *National Enquirer* draped a chair—a highly unusual state of affairs.

We found Mom in the kitchen, feverishly working to cover something up. A faint whiff of burned plastic hung in the air.

"Hey, Mom." Kevin opened his arms for a hug.

She looked up dazedly. "Oh, Kevin! What are you doing here?"

His large frame dwarfed hers when she went in for the hug. Kevin looked at me over her shoulder, his brows gathered low. "You two asked me to come out to talk." He eased away to look her in the eye, but she avoided his gaze.

"Oh yes. That."

When she frowned, my heart ached anew. Losing my dad so soon after she'd retired had been enough of a blow. They'd been planning a series of trips—an Alaskan cruise, a vacation in Florence—and looking into renting a condo in Sarasota each winter. Like me, Mom didn't adapt quickly to change, so it had taken her weeks to leave the house after his funeral, and months to come to grips with the fact that her husband was gone. My pregnancy had been a catalyst for her turning the corner, by giving her something to look forward to. She hadn't needed me to complicate her life with my mess now.

"Mom, take Kevin to the living room and catch up on Billy's latest antics. I'll fix some tea and meet you in two minutes."

Kevin nodded before guiding her to the other room while chatting. His proud tone as he spoke about his family contrasted mightily with Lyle's. Given how devastated my husband had been by his own mother's abandonment, I couldn't comprehend the way lust was affecting Lyle's thinking—until I recalled the zeal with which he'd once pursued me. Imagining that gleam in his eye aimed at another woman hardened my stomach.

I snatched the turquoise-colored teakettle that had sat on Mom's stove since the '80s and filled it with water. A frying pan with the remnants of a melted spatula stuck to its center lay in the sink. Was my mom losing it? I couldn't handle *that* right now. Please, God, let it be nothing more than stress.

While the water heated, I scraped at the melted bits of plastic, but it was useless. Another thing I couldn't fix. Setting the ruined pan aside, I gazed at the Turner family memory jar. Same aging label. Fewer scrolls for this time of year because, with us kids all gone, only the biggest celebrations made it in there now.

My dad had once suggested we put bad memories in there, too, because at the end of the year you could look back and see how far you'd come. Mom had rejected that outright, preferring to gloss over hardships and unpleasantries. Since the memory jar had been Mom's idea, no one but Erin ever put negative memories in there. Today would be no exception.

When I brought a tray with the teacups into the living room, my brother and mom had seated themselves on the sofa. I moved the stray newspaper and took the chair. No one reached for a teacup.

Having not rehearsed how to begin, I ripped off the proverbial Band-Aid. "Kevin, Lyle is having an affair—"

"We don't know that," my mom interjected, although her vehemence had lessened in the past forty-eight hours.

"It's a fact." I averted my eyes to avoid the flash of disappointment that would flicker through hers. "He confirmed it, but I needed time to process everything before sharing it with you."

Her shoulders collapsed, and she covered her face with her hands. When pity lit Kevin's eyes, I dropped my chin.

"I'm sorry, sis. Did you want help finding a good divorce lawyer? We've got some excellent ones in my firm."

My head snapped up. "No! We're not *there* yet."

"Why the hell not?" Kevin barked like our dad occasionally had when we'd done something stupid—or, rather, like he had when Kevin or I had messed up. Dad had gotten a kick out of Erin's rambunctious attitude and impulsiveness, so he'd met her mistakes with tempered disappointment mixed with a twinkle in his eye. I'd spent my youth working hard for that twinkle—routinely instigating surprise cleanups and doing the laundry for Mom, or making high honors at school—but Erin had earned them simply by breathing.

"Divorce is so final . . . It's too soon for that." I rubbed my stomach. "Lyle's asked for a little time to sort through his feelings and figure things out. I'm not making excuses, but people have affairs—they get bewitched and make mistakes. Sometimes they learn that they had what they needed all along. We have a baby coming. I think he'll come home."

"A little time?" Kevin cursed Lyle's name, earning himself a slap on the arm from our mom.

"Language!" Mom frowned.

"Sorry." He squeezed her hand, then looked at me. "Let's say he deigns to return. Can you be happy with him—or trust him—ever again?"

Before I replied, Mom jumped in. "If Amanda wants to save her marriage, she needs support, not ridicule."

Her attitude didn't surprise me, even if Kevin seemed taken aback. I'd been her golden girl, and golden girls didn't get dumped for bimbos and end up as single moms, especially not if Madeline Turner could help it.

Kevin blew out a breath.

"It bothers me to think of Amanda staying married to a disloyal liar." When he glanced at me, I had to look away. "He's lucky he's not here. I honestly think I'd rip his head off."

He might, too. He'd always been protective of Erin and me.

Now Kevin was already furious, and he didn't even know the full scope of the situation. My stomach cramped again. I must've winced, because my mother's expression pinched.

"What's wrong, Amanda?" she asked.

"I'm stressed out." My voice faltered as I massaged my belly with both hands.

Kevin dialed back his anger. "That's not good for the baby."

"I know!" Another round of tears clogged my throat, but I fought them.

Kevin rubbed his thighs while taking a deep breath. "If you don't need a divorce lawyer, why am I here?"

"Well . . . ," I began. My mom pressed her palms to her cheeks, and the position Lyle had put us in crushed me. "Partly I wanted advice about what I should do *in case* Lyle asks for a divorce—I mean, mostly I'm concerned about custody, but I also wanted to get an idea about child support and alimony, although . . ." I hesitated, bracing myself. "That might be complicated by the fact that Lyle borrowed money from Mom for this deal in Florida."

"What?" Kevin sat up, spine erect, eyes wide. "When?"

"Soon after Lyle started his own business two months ago, he got an inside line on the condo development deal in Florida, but he didn't want to touch his 401(k) because of penalties, and we'd used a bunch of our savings to buy the house. He was scrambling to raise funds in time to scoop the deal. Mom overheard us talking and offered to lend him Dad's death benefit money."

Kev whipped his head in her direction, making her start in her seat. "How much?"

She flinched, and I shuddered along with her. "Most of it."

"You gave Lyle half a million dollars?" Kevin pretty much sprang off the sofa, arms raised before they slapped his sides.

"Not *all* . . ." Mom's voice rose, unaccustomed to having to answer to her children.

I pressed my body into my chair as if it could hide me. Bile filled my throat when I thought about the four hundred thousand dollars she'd lent my husband. We'd both put our faith in him without a second thought, but Mom never would've bankrolled him if she'd suspected he'd been sleeping with another woman.

Kevin ran a hand through his hair, then glared at me. "Was it *his* idea to keep this from me . . . and I assume from Erin as well?"

"We weren't hiding it," Mom insisted. "It was my money. I didn't need anyone's *permission*."

I looked away because, while neither of us had ever spoken of it, we'd tacitly agreed to keep the loan quiet to avoid the appearance of playing favorites. Truthfully, while Erin had been Dad's pet, I'd been Mom's. Maybe that was because I was her first daughter, or because I'd been willing to meet her high expectations. I don't know. I never wanted to question it.

Kevin shook his head. "I'm a lawyer, Mom. You didn't think it might be a good idea to let me structure the loan?"

"I didn't want a lot of guff." Despite her firm voice, my mom's shoulders curled over her chest.

"Stop it, Kevin," I said. "If you've got to yell at someone, yell at me."

His glower's sharp edge slipped beneath my skin like a splinter. He opened his mouth but then, after a quick glimpse of my stomach, clamped it shut. The living room pulsed with tension. With his eyes now closed, he drew another long breath. "Tell me there are loan documents and a bank account we can access."

Now I really and truly wished to disappear.

"Lyle printed a form off the internet—a promissory note. It seemed good enough to cover a family loan. He's meeting with potential investors in Florida now. As soon as they kick in, he'll pay her back . . . probably by the end of this year even."

That's what he'd promised, and despite everything, I believed that much.

"*If* he gets investors. Real estate deals are risky as hell." Kevin pounded the heels of his palms against his forehead. "How could you two be so reckless?"

"I'm sorry!" I croaked. "At the time I had no reason *not* to trust my husband. He's always been hardworking and successful, kept his promises, been good to our parents. Mom offered. I saw no harm. We thought this deal would be a game changer for our future."

"And now?" Kevin spoke through gritted teeth.

"In hindsight, we could've been smarter. But he signed the loan papers. Lyle always pays his debts, but until those investors come through, it might be hard to make both the loan payments and pay child support. That's why I need your advice."

"Amanda, if he only signed a note, then it's an unsecured loan. What happens if he isn't married to you anymore and his big deal flops? He won't be very motivated to figure out how to repay Mom then, will he?" Kevin scrubbed his face with one hand, while my stomach turned at the wrinkle I'd never considered. "Given what he's putting you through, he should return whatever he hasn't already spent on this deal." Kev turned to Mom. "Where's that promissory note?"

"It's in the office, I think." Visibly shaken, she stared at the ground. The thousands of kids she'd intimidated as the school librarian would be shocked to see her humbled.

My skin was now cold and damp. "Mom, look at me. This is not your fault. You were only being supportive and trusting. I should've insisted we involve Kevin."

"Call Lyle and tell him if he doesn't call you back today to discuss the money, we're calling the cops." Kev stared at me, arms crossed.

"The cops?" My brows rose. "What are you talking about?"

Kev raised his hands above his head. "What if he makes off with the money?"

My mouth fell open. "Mom *lent* him the money. He didn't steal it. The whole reason he's in Florida is to tie up that deal. He said he'd repay it, and he will."

"He also said till death do you part." Kevin speared me with that look that made me feel idiotic.

Lyle had broken promises. I couldn't deny that, nor could I fully shake the concern that my mom would be left holding the bag if the deal crumbled. But the leap from bad business judgment to criminal behavior spanned the Chesapeake Bay Bridge.

"Just because he's having an affair doesn't mean he's also a thief. Lyle is my baby's father, Kevin, not a felon." The idea of it! "If he planned to steal the money, why would he suggest and sign that note? There's no need to panic unless he doesn't pay Mom back under *its* terms, not *yours*."

Kevin glared at me, nostrils flaring. His pacing the floor suggested he'd moved on to playing out scenarios in his head. "I don't have a good feeling. Did you check your bank balances?"

"Yes . . . nothing abnormal." I glared, although the fact that I'd checked hardly proved my confidence in Lyle.

"I'll get the note." Ashen-faced, Mom wandered off toward Kevin's old bedroom, which my parents had turned into a home office years ago.

"Amanda, you know the optics are pretty bad, right?" Kevin cracked his knuckles, a habit I'd always found disgusting.

"Jumping to the worst conclusions isn't helping anyone's stress levels. If you're so worried, surely you know private investigators who can track down more details about the deal." I ran my hands through my hair, hoping to somehow stimulate my brain. "He betrayed me, but he's also come clean about it. I'm not happy, but that's not illegal. Please give me a little time to get my arms around what's happening in my marriage before you sound every alarm. This is a private family matter, and we should handle it that way."

He cocked his head, a single brow raised. "You're serious?"

"For God's sake, Kevin. He's my husband. We created a home and have a baby on the way. He's messed up, but he hasn't said he doesn't still love me. And I love him. I know you think that makes me stupid, but there it is. I love my husband even though he's hurt me. That's what I know right now. Maybe that will change, but this is my life—" I shut up as soon as our mom returned with the signed document.

"Here, honey. See?" She waved the pages at Kevin. "We weren't foolish. I made a loan, and I can enforce it."

Kevin took the document from her without reading it. "Amanda, what's the name of Lyle's company? And what bank is he using?"

"I assume he's using Wells Bank, like we do." To be honest, I'd been puking, sleeping, nesting, and working these past couple of months. And like Erin, Lyle often mistook my suggestions as criticism or doubts in his ability to manage his own affairs, so he'd rarely shared the details of his plans with me anyway. Why would he? I was a teacher, not a real estate magnate. "The company is Somniator Syndicate, or maybe

Partners . . . He was going back and forth, so I'm actually not sure what he decided on."

"Latin?" Kevin shook his head again, and I could practically hear Erin's voice in my head saying, *"He's kind of pretentious, isn't he?"* Kev speared me with an incredulous look. "What a pompous piece of—"

"Kevin!" Mom said.

I'd always thought Kev respected Lyle, but his intense disdain today made me question whether he'd hidden his feelings from the beginning.

I buckled from a wave of self-recriminating exhaustion. "Should I lie at your feet and apologize for trusting my husband? Do you feel better saying hateful things about him and shaming me for even *considering* saving my marriage? It might seem weak to you, but it takes strength to forgive and live by the 'for better or worse' part of the vow. Granted, this is definitely a worse part. I'm plenty devastated, angry, and humiliated without reminders from you. But we were happy until this, so maybe counseling can fix whatever broke. I don't know, but my daughter deserves a chance at a whole family. And I deserve the chance to decide whether my marriage is salvageable."

Stubborn as ever, Kev groused, "If Marcy cheated or stole my mom's money, I doubt I'd still love her much."

"Stop saying Lyle stole money. He borrowed it." I shook my head. "And you have no idea what you might be able to forgive until you're faced with it, so don't judge me."

Normally I wouldn't be so defensive, but each attack on Lyle also felt like an attack on me. I wasn't accustomed to Kevin questioning my judgment.

He waved the note in the air. "Without collateral, this isn't worth much more than toilet paper, but I'll look at it at home. Meanwhile, I'll hire an investigator to track down Lyle. Erin should know about all of this, too. We'll all need to band together if the worst comes to pass. In fact, why isn't she here?"

"She's at a yoga camp or something," Mom muttered, mouth pinched, eyes cool. I never wanted her to look at me that way.

"When she gets back, you'll tell her?" Kevin crossed his arms for the umpteenth time since this conversation had started.

"Obviously." Although I'd prefer more time to adjust to my new reality before sharing the embarrassing details with her. If I hadn't needed Kevin's legal expertise, I probably wouldn't have told him yet, either.

Mom went to the bookshelf that displayed decades of family photos and traced a frame with one finger. "I wish your father were here. He'd know what to do."

There wouldn't have been funds to lend if Dad were still alive, but I kept quiet. He'd been so careful planning for retirement and protecting Mom with those policy proceeds. He'd be heartsick that we had handed them over for a deal we knew so little about. All my life I'd followed rules and weighed my decisions precisely to avoid this kind of situation. The one time I acted like my sister, this was the result?

I wouldn't let this be the way our story ended. And I wouldn't let Lyle ruin my mother's future, either. I had no idea how I'd fix this, but I wouldn't rest until I did.

Kevin sighed, studying our mom. "I'm sorry I lost my temper. You're right, it shouldn't be a mistake to trust family. I'm cynical because of the stories I hear at work. Try to relax while we sort it out, okay? I promise I'll do everything I can to get answers quickly."

"Okay." I probably should've felt better about his apology than I did.

Kevin strode over to hug me, speaking softly right in my ear. "Sorry my reaction made this harder. I didn't mean to do that. I love you, sis. I only want what's best for you."

"Thanks." I eased away, having nothing more to say. Kevin hadn't been all wrong. If Marcy hurt him, I'd be equally mistrustful of her.

"I'll call later with a name and number, and we'll get answers as soon as possible."

I nodded with my eyes closed.

Kevin hugged our mom and then saw himself out of her house. Once he left, I slung my arm around her shoulders. "Mom, I'm so sorry. I don't want you to worry. Lyle has loved you from the start because you made him so welcome. You know how much that meant, given his family history. No matter what happens between him and me, he'll pay you back. Hang in there until we get some answers. I swear I'll put things right. You still trust me, don't you?"

"Everything will work out. Your dad is watching over us." She fell silent for a second, having not answered my question.

Last year his unexpected heart attack had rocked our family. I'll never unhear the hollow anguish in my mother's keening when she called me with the news. That anniversary was coming up quickly and weighing on us all, especially Mom, who wanted us to gather together that day. My new circumstances made me dread the occasion all the more.

Anyway, I'd never believed much in guardian angels, but who was I to question that when I still clung to faith in my faithless husband? My mother obviously needed something to believe in while vulnerable. "Mom, what happened with the spatula?"

She looked at me, brows knitted in confusion. "What?"

"The pan in the sink. It looks like the spatula melted."

"Oh, that." Her cheeks flushed. "It's nothing."

"Did you forget to turn off the stove?" Was that kind of thing happening regularly?

"I got distracted by Dodo. She called and we started talking, so I forgot about the pan."

Mom's sister, Dorothy—the one person who had even higher expectations of people than my mother had—enjoyed lording her superiority over the rest of us whenever possible. "Please don't tell Aunt Dodo what's going on."

Mom's eyes nearly bulged out of her skull. "Of course not. It's nobody's business but ours."

The part of me that heaved a sigh of relief also cringed for being happy that my mother would suffer in silence rather than seek comfort from her sister—a dynamic I understood too well. If only Erin and I had learned to lean on each other instead of circling each other like defensive porcupines. Unlike Erin and me, Dodo and my mother spoke daily, but my mother did share my reticence to *confide* in her sister.

Regardless, I shouldn't be selfish. "But, actually, if you want to talk to her about it, I'd understand."

"Good grief, Amanda. If she thinks I can't manage my affairs, she'll swoop in and take over like she did with George."

Dodo had had their elder brother declared incompetent before assuming control over all aspects of his life. My mother had never believed that George's Parkinson's had diminished his mental abilities to a degree that required that humiliation. He died a few years ago, so it was moot now except for the lingering unease it instilled in my mom.

I should be grateful that Erin had no interest in controlling anything. Instead I felt sad that my mother's dysfunctional sibling family history seemed to be repeating itself.

Mom pointed a finger at me. "Not one word of this to anyone but Erin." The childhood scars from her father's highly publicized addiction and professional meltdown had left our mother paranoid about scandal. When working as a federal prosecutor, he'd mangled some high-profile white-collar criminal case while drunk and quickly become the talk of Pottstown, Pennsylvania. The media circus around that had dogged the family. After my mom and her siblings were subjected to playground ridicule, Grandma finally divorced him and moved to Baltimore with the kids, where she eventually remarried.

"Okay. But if things like that—with the pan—keep happening, you'll tell me, right? In fact, would you like to stay with me for a few days?"

"No. I like my house. My things." She wrung her hands, her voice tightening.

"Okay." Truthfully, I would've enjoyed company in that cold, empty house, but I didn't press. "Would you like me to stay for lunch?"

"No, dear. You go home and keep trying to reach Lyle. You're not the only one who's had to fight for love, so don't give up."

I'd always disliked those not-quite-veiled remarks about her being Dad's second choice. So what if her sorority sister, Patty Pollack, had broken his heart first? I'd witnessed the little kisses he'd planted on Mom's temple and the soft smiles shared across the dinner table. He might've been intrigued by the devil-may-care Patty in the beginning, but maturity made him value my mother's steadiness in the end. "I won't."

She patted my cheek. "I need a nap."

"Okay." Fresh out of excuses to linger, I gave her another hug. "Get some rest."

God bless her if she could sleep.

When I got home, I went straight to the computer to look up our credit card account to figure out exactly where Lyle was today, but there hadn't been any new charges in days. I went back several months, looking for evidence of the affair. No hotel room charges. No jewelry store purchases. Nothing obvious or attention-grabbing. I groaned. What did it matter? He wasn't denying the affair, so proof was pointless.

I shut it down and walked through my soundless house, room by room, while dialing Lyle again. Invisibility wasn't unfamiliar. When you don't toot your own horn, your good deeds can go unnoticed—or at least underappreciated. Swallowing my pride and fighting for love had been my life's norms—even with my mom, I'd worked to be her pet.

Lyle had been the only exception. He'd pursued me. Loved me. Admired me. Appreciated me.

Now he wouldn't answer my calls.

Given his note, I hadn't actually expected him to. But this limbo would make navigating the coming days at work and in town difficult.

His voice mail beeped.

"Lyle, it's me. I've given you a couple of days since getting your note." I closed my eyes and leaned against the kitchen island, telling myself not to sound desperate. "I'm shocked. Angry. Mostly I'm hurt. Between the baby and the money you borrowed, we need to talk now. Under the circumstances, it'd be best if you paid my mom back sooner than later." My resolve folded beneath the burden of my unraveling world, and I hated myself a little right then. "I need to talk to you. Even for a few minutes. Please. This feels like being locked in a dark closet . . ." I hung up before I begged even more.

My lungs burned. Saturday afternoon stretched in front of me—a long, lonely day.

I caught my reflection in the microwave glass. Pretty enough, but not exotic like Ebba. Not even edgy like my sister. Maybe a new look would make me feel better. At the very least, it would kill time.

With my purse and keys in hand, I headed to Divaz Salon. Lyle preferred my classic style. Right now I wasn't in the mood to do anything that pleased him, which made it the perfect time to try something new.

CHAPTER FOUR

Erin

When Mo didn't scratch the door at the sound of the key, I expected the worst. If Max had taken my dog, he'd better expect to be hunted down by a wild mama bear fresh off a grueling five-hour drive.

Once inside, I flicked on the light and spied Mo locked in his crate. I dropped my things on the floor before rushing over to set him free. "Oh, Mosley-Mo, how long have you been stuck in there?"

Mo crawled out from his little cave, stretching in a better downward-dog position than many of my students managed. His tail wagged enthusiastically, making me grateful that dogs were easier to read than humans. Mo was always happy to see me, too . . . another key difference between him and some people.

I tickled his belly, then had him follow me back outside to do his business. At the end of long, tiring days like this one, an elevator would be nice. Then again, three flights of stairs kept my butt pert. While Mo did his frantic back-and-forth dance in search of the perfect spot to poo, I checked my phone messages.

Hey, Erin, it's Amanda. I hope you enjoyed the yoga retreat. You're probably tired from the drive, so come to dinner at my house. Mom will be there. I'd actually like to talk about something, too. Six thirty? I'll throw in a pumpkin pie. Thanks.

I checked the time. Five o'clock. Early enough that I didn't have a good excuse to say no. Pumpkin pie was a draw, admittedly, but I could hardly get excited about spending the evening with my nervous-Nellie mom and my "perfect" sister at her "perfect house," where her "told you so" expressions would surely surface as soon as she found out about Max.

Spending the evening writing down all the ideas that had percolated during the retreat would be far more productive. If only I could find a cheap—or free—place to teach yoga, my income could increase enough to create some financial breathing room. Maybe even enough to hang on to my apartment, although this place might not be worth it.

Amanda hadn't mentioned Lyle, so he still had to be in Florida. Thank God. His presence had a way of sucking up all the oxygen.

Mo bounded toward me after relieving himself, so we headed back inside.

"Who's the best puppy?" I chased him up the stairs, speaking in my silly doggy voice. "You are, Fluffy. Yes, you are."

Mrs. Wagner opened her door a crack when we hit the second floor. After giving me the standard disapproving once-over, she said, "Oh, it's you. I heard a commotion."

The stench that wafted into the hallway nearly knocked me back down the stairs. Mo's nose twitched, and then he beelined for her door to get to those cats, but she closed it in our faces before he could slip inside.

"Have a good evening," I sang out while giving her the mental finger. I'd never been anything but polite, yet she judged my appearance despite how she lived in that stench?

I tromped up the last flight of stairs and reentered the apartment. *My* apartment now that Max had gone, or mine until the end of the month, anyway. I'd have to seriously reevaluate my finances before signing a new lease.

In fairness, Max had left things neater than I'd expected. Granted, most of the stuff was mine from before he moved in, so he'd had to pack only his clothes and a few other things. Good riddance to the mustache-shaped napkin holder he'd gotten from his cousin Ned as a groomsmen gift, and to the Jack Daniel's bottle collection. But the living area looked a little pathetic without the colorful jute kilim rug that had been in front of the TV stand. The bookshelf stood nearly naked now that he'd cleared out the great books he'd owned. And the corner of the room was downright gloomy without the glow from his funky industrial table lamp.

Mo lapped some water while I strolled through the space. A hint of the patchouli and sage oils Max had used to combat his eczema pervaded the air. That might linger until I washed all the blankets and pillows. Somehow it felt wrong to erase every trace of him so quickly, so I'd let the scent dissipate on its own.

A teeny part of me suddenly missed his silly grin. The silence struck me, too. Ah, Max had also taken his beloved TV. Well, that was no loss. And in any case, being on my own had never bothered me before. I simply needed to reclaim this space.

Maybe after dinner I'd return, pour myself a glass of wine, and allow myself a moment of melancholy about my fizzled, once-promising love affair. Then I'd fire up a great album and experiment with a new batch of sugar scrubs. At least now I could work without being distracted by Daniel Tosh's crude jokes.

Independence was good. A chance to plan for all my ideas. The prospect of rockin' my thirties had me bouncing on my toes.

First I'd have to survive dinner.

I glanced at my attire—Converse high-tops, yoga pants, a sports bra, and a loose-fitted T-shirt. If I hadn't missed the baby shower shopping extravaganza, I'd show up dressed like this. But "workout clothes at the table" would bug Amanda and my mom, so I pulled on jean shorts, a cute pink-camo top, and my bronze metallic Birkenstocks. After finger-combing the right side of my head, I was ready to face the firing squad.

My thumbs flew across the phone's keyboard.

Be there soon. What can I bring?

Within minutes, she replied.

Nothing. I've got it covered.

She *always* had everything covered. Sometimes I suspected she said that because it came off as considerate while simultaneously squeezing my ideas right out of the picture.

The few times I'd tried to introduce my family to new foods—like an awesome sweet potato–turmeric miso soup from the Herb Box—she and my mom had flashed that polite smile before shooting each other "the look." Then, instead of giving it a fair chance, they took minuscule samples before quietly setting it aside.

I grabbed a half-empty can of whipped cream from my fridge, knowing Amanda probably wouldn't have any. Lyle didn't allow sugar in that house, whereas whipped cream qualified as a major food group in mine. Good for coffee, cocoa, ice cream, and even an occasional squirt in the mouth as a pick-me-up.

Mo had climbed up to his favorite spot on the back of the sofa cushions, where he could stare out the window. I'd take him with me, but the possibility of him scratching her floors or furniture made Amanda a little nervous.

Bending at the waist, I gave him some lovin'. "Sorry to leave you so soon, MoMo, but you hang here and keep an eye on the place till I get back."

After snatching my keys off the dining table, I locked the door behind me. Ten minutes later, my bike was parked in front of my sister's garage. Not a leaf or speck of dirt lay anywhere on her driveway. All the flower beds were neatly fashioned. Cheerful tulips blew in the breeze, heralding spring. Postcard perfect, the way she liked it.

I trotted up the two steps to the front porch and knocked on the door. Lexi and her sister, Aisha, walked into each other's homes without any announcement. Amanda might pass out if I tried that. Then again, I hadn't exactly made her free to waltz into my apartment, either.

It seemed weird that we weren't closer, considering we'd shared a room as kids. While Amanda hated that I was messy, she had also read aloud to me at night and otherwise generally treated me like her personal baby doll. The little cocoon had been kind of comforting at times. But somewhere along the way, things had changed.

Simply put, we were oil and water. Amanda had preferred to pull what I called "bored" games off the shelf on rainy days, never once joining me outside to jump in the mud.

A million of those kinds of differences played out on a weekly basis. Over time, walls had gone up, like that invisible line she'd drawn through our drawers and closet to separate her neat space from mine. It'd gotten only worse since Lyle came into our lives.

Amanda answered the door, her attempt at a smile falling a bit flat. "Hey, thanks for coming."

For once, she didn't pay much attention to my outfit or stare at my hair. Then again, maybe I was too busy staring at hers to notice. She'd chopped at least four inches off the back, and the front was layered to prettily frame her face.

"Wow! What a flattering haircut." I stood on the porch, mesmerized. Amanda didn't often do change. Never, really. She liked routines. Her hair had been straight and blunt for as long as I could remember. This new do made me all bubbly inside—hopeful, though for what I couldn't say.

"Oh." She touched it self-consciously, not quite meeting my gaze. "I forgot. Thanks."

Forgot? My spidey-sense tingled, but I had to tread lightly when asking Amanda a direct question. She often took things I said wrong. If I waited long enough, there'd be an opening. For now, I held up the whipped cream, aiming for a laugh. "Hope you were serious about the pie."

Her eyes widened, but only a half-hearted smile appeared. "Sure. Come on in."

She heaved a sigh when she closed the door behind me. It seemed impossible that I'd already done anything to upset her, other than bring a half-empty can of whipped cream. Or maybe she missed Lyle. She'd never liked being alone.

My mom was busy tossing the salad. She looked so much smaller to me since Dad died, like each day the weight of grief pulled her shoulders a bit lower. No one would call her frail, mind you. She was average height and still a bit paunchy despite having shed at least ten pounds this past year. But everything about her seemed less. She'd always been a serious person. Only my dad had been able to loosen her up—like when he'd pull her away from the stove to dance with him when one of his favorite songs would come on. Without his spontaneity to shake her free, she was shriveling up. I was counting on Amanda's baby to break her out of this funk.

It unnerved me to see her off her game. Although our family had never been wealthy, she always dressed up when leaving the house— even since quitting her job. No one shopped for clothes on a budget better than she did. Her wardrobe staples consisted of conservative dresses and flats or small heels, fake pearl earrings and necklaces, and pink lipstick. Today, however, her navy dress didn't have that starchy fresh press she'd given everything from Dad's shirts to my jeans (despite my protests), and she'd forgone earrings altogether.

"Hi, Mom." I kissed her cheek—pretending not to notice the way she tensed at my affection—then set the whipped cream on the counter. After a weekend of a vegetarian diet and kombucha, I'd happily eat the pie for dinner. "Can I help?"

She frowned. "Don't be silly. I'm not so old that I can't dress a salad."

I swallowed my own sigh, replaying my words to see how she could take them as some kind of statement about her age.

A savory aroma from whatever was roasting in the oven sprang the carnivore in me to life.

"How was the retreat?" Amanda asked while placing water glasses filled with iced tea at the table. She looked ashen except for the dark circles beneath her eyes. I supposed a lack of sleep wasn't uncommon among pregnant women.

"Pretty much what I expected. I'll tell you what I *did* learn—I could make nice bank if I had an inexpensive place to hold a retreat. It's amazing how many people throw down big money for them." Even broke folks, like me.

I risked a glimpse of my mom, who kept fussing about the kitchen. Last month, Max had suggested I ask her for a small loan to help "get us through" until he could make some money. My dad had left her a huge insurance payout, but I wouldn't ask for a penny. Partly because I couldn't tolerate the "You wouldn't need to borrow money if only you'd been a more serious student like my other kids" lecture, and partly because that money wouldn't exist if my dad were alive, so the idea of benefiting from it made me sick.

"Well, you're almost thirty. Maybe it's time to find a more serious job." Mom set the salad bowl in the center of the kitchen table.

Looked like I'd get the lecture regardless. Her dismissive attitude about my interests got old fast. My work might not provide the kind of pension and other benefits working for the schools had, but the only job I could get there would be as a custodian. A bad fit. I'm not even neat.

Amanda cleared her throat and shot Mom a weird look. "Weird" because usually the most I could expect from her was false neutrality. Today, however, she almost looked upset with Mom for nagging me.

"I'm serious about yoga, Mom. I have friends who can't afford Give Me Strength's monthly fee but would love to take yoga with me if I had a place to teach. Besides, a so-called 'serious' job would make it harder for me to work on Shakti Suds, and I think that has potential. This is my year to push myself entrepreneurially."

Amanda nodded after a mega yawn. "I love the Citrus Delight sugar scrub you gave me. It smells terrific."

"Thanks." I blinked in surprise, but my responding smile prompted the first real grin from my sister since I'd arrived. Still, she moved around the kitchen subdued. Her voice mail had mentioned wanting to talk about something, but I wouldn't force that conversation.

"You know what?" she continued, possibly encouraged by my reaction. "You should approach local shop owners and ask them to carry the products."

Naturally she butted in to tell me how much better she could run things. After all, she *was* the "smart" sister.

I shrugged noncommittally, having no interest in her taking over—and taking credit for—my business. Now was a good time to change the subject. "Hey, sorry I missed the baby shower thingy on Thursday. Did you have fun?"

"Oh, it's fine." Amanda waved it off. "I know you hate shopping anyway."

"But I'm excited about the baby. Can I see the registration list?" I asked, curious about why she and Mom remained circumspect about their big day. "I want first choice of gifts."

If I had more money, my niece would want for nothing. Most of Amanda's colleagues and neighbors would be able to afford the better items on the list, though. A month from now the family room would be filled with prettily wrapped boxes and prettier women, plus Mom and Aunt Dodo.

While I couldn't fill my niece's playroom with toys, no one else could craft a line of organic baby soap products—chamomile-infused oatmeal bars—special for her. Once Amanda shared the baby's name, I'd order a monogrammed stamp for the little bars, too.

"I'll send you the links later." Amanda touched my hand. "I'm rethinking the whole party idea, anyway."

"What? Why?" Okay, now I was beginning to worry. Was something wrong with the baby?

"I'm just . . . overwhelmed right now." She and my mom exchanged another peculiar look, but if she didn't want to tell me the truth, I didn't want to know. It's not like she ever took my advice about anything anyway, so why work myself up? "Either way, I don't expect you to get me anything."

Because I was broke. She didn't have to say it for me to know that's what she meant. At least she didn't look smug. And, truthfully, at this point I couldn't even argue. "Of course I'm going to get something for my niece. I'm her aunt Erin, though maybe the first thing I should get is a better name for myself. A nickname . . . something cool, like Zizi." Zizi. Zizi-E—like a rapper.

The oven timer dinged, and Mom muttered something under her breath. She seemed a bit absent tonight, which was also unusual. Even at sixty-two, she had loads of energy and a quick mind. Lots of opinions, too. In that way, she and I did share something in common, except our opinions rarely matched and I didn't impose mine on others as often.

"Let me grab the pork so we can sit down." Amanda crossed to the oven.

I couldn't take the strain anymore, despite my resolve to butt out. "Is everything okay with you and the baby?"

Mom made a sign of the cross. "The baby is perfectly fine, Erin. Don't say such things."

"Sorry." I bit my tongue, having known better than to try.

Amanda pulled a roast out of the oven and set the pan on the stove. Caramel-brown pork and potatoes and a hint of rosemary, apricot, and maple wafted through the kitchen. Her cooking made my temporary discomfort worthwhile.

My mouth watered as if I hadn't eaten in days. "That roast looks perfect."

Man, Lyle ought to bow down and kiss her feet every single day. She kept the house spotless, cooked like a master, and bent into a pretzel to please everyone, especially him. All that could get on *my* nerves, because her striving for perfection made me feel like I never knew my sister. Who was *she*, and what made *her* happy—because pleasing everyone else could not, in and of itself, be a life goal, could it?

Amanda shrugged. "Thanks."

She'd spent years trying to interest me in preparing something that didn't come in a box with plastic wrap, so I expected detailed instructions about how to make this dish. When she didn't elaborate, that sinking feeling returned. "You two are awful quiet. Did you invite me over because of Max? 'Cause I'm fine. I swear."

Amanda's brows pinched. "What happened with Max?"

"I broke up with him." I drummed my hands on the counter. "He moved out while I was at the retreat."

Instead of jumping for joy, my mom started touching her cheek the way she always did when she got nervous. She'd never much cared for Max, though. When I'd invited him to live with me the month after my dad died, she'd accused me of using him to fill a void and said I'd regret it. If anything, I'd expect her to start celebrating the fact that she'd possibly been a little bit right.

Maybe she preferred me to be with someone rather than no one. She probably couldn't imagine my life as a young, single woman. Heck, aside from running the public library's genre-based book groups on Thursday nights, she still struggled with what to do with herself as a widow. No kids to boss around at home or at school, either—except for Amanda. Last fall when I'd suggested she should write a book, she'd glared at me like I'd said she was ugly or something. Meanwhile, I thought I'd given her a compliment. She was a good writer and knew more about books than anyone I'd ever met.

"What made you do that?" Amanda carved the roast with extra zeal.

"Whoa, take it easy. It's already dead." I laughed.

She glanced up, cheeks pink from embarrassment.

"Kidding!" My gaze bounced between her and Mom, who didn't appear to be listening much to anything we were saying. I almost made a crack about bad sex to test my theory. "Max and I weren't having fun or inspiring each other anymore, so we parted ways."

"Was he upset?" Amanda's jaw tightened while she plated juicy slices of pork, potatoes, and squash.

"Not really." It didn't reflect well on me to admit it, but I wouldn't lie. "At least he didn't seem to be."

"And you're okay?" Amanda looked at me incredulously.

"Why wouldn't I be?"

"You dated for two years. You've been living together for a while. I thought he was 'the one' for you. That's what you said." She looked so sad about it, like I'd broken up with her or something.

I shrugged. "Guess I was wrong."

"So you *didn't* love him," Mom interrupted. "Even when you insisted that you did?"

Finally, she was paying attention. Nice job with the not-quite "I told you so," too.

"I loved him enough to support him these past several months while he floundered around without any job. But it's not like you fall in love and then, wham, it lasts forever. Feelings change. People grow. Relationships evolve. The things that made us work well were no longer working—he'd stopped all of his artistic stuff, didn't lift a finger to help me, and, honestly, he got a little boring—"

My sister's unexpected sob shut me up.

She never cried in front of me. At least not since the time she'd come home excited about being admitted to the National Honor Society only to have her achievement overlooked because I'd gotten hurt after falling off our roof. I'd gone up there to hide from Mom because I knew she'd gotten a call from the middle school principal about a food fight I'd started in the cafeteria. To be fair, I'd dumped the pasta on Emmerson's head because she'd been picking on poor Wendy Jones that day. Anyway, looking back, I did have a habit of inadvertently ruining my sister's celebrations. "Amanda, I'm sorry you're so upset. Shocked, though. You never much liked Max. You thought he smelled funny."

"Don't pick on your sister," my mom admonished as she reached over to soothe Amanda.

I stood there, blinking, confused about why Amanda needed comforting over my breakup with a man neither of them liked. "I've had a weird vibe pretty much since I arrived. What's going on?"

Amanda wiped her eyes and sniffled. "Let's all take our plates to the table, then I'll explain."

Suddenly my appetite waned. Unlike when Mom and Amanda typically made a mountain out of a molehill, tonight their somber moods rattled me. We all took our plates and sat while I searched my memory for any hint of trouble in the Turner family that I'd missed last week.

The chances of my getting out of this conversation without inadvertently causing more conflict were pretty slim without my dad around. He'd been a much-needed buffer, and never misunderstood my meaning or intentions in these kinds of family discussions. Given my sister's tears, anything I did or said could be the wrong thing now, like that stupid Thanksgiving four years ago, when Amanda had made a pumpkin cheesecake instead of pie and then gotten upset with me for voicing my surprise. That conversation had been about to tip into yet another argument when Dad cut it short. *"Amanda, your sister was only looking forward to your pumpkin pie, but I bet we'll love this, too, once we try it.*

Now pass me a slice." He wasn't here tonight to stop us from going down a rabbit hole, so my best bet was to eat in silence and let it all unfold. Amanda pretty much pushed her food around with her fork before putting it down and sipping her iced tea.

My mom reached across the table and patted her hand. "It's all going to be okay."

I sat back, antsy and growing warmer by the minute. "It's obvious you're upset, and I want to give you space, but the suspense is killing me." Maybe a joke would break the tension. "Did someone rob a bank?"

Amanda's bleak gaze snapped to mine, stunning me into silence. "Lyle is having an affair . . ."

She kept talking, but my mind shut down at those words. That rat bastard!

When I'd caught him with that hot blonde on Valentine's Day, I'd felt even more suspicious of him than usual. Lyle had been startled when I'd run into them at the Kentwood Inn, where I'd stopped in on Max's behalf to ask about auditions for its new live-music nights. They'd looked almost conspiratorial to me, the way they were looking into each other's eyes.

"Happy Valentine's Day, Lyle," I'd said sardonically while staring at him, my gaze flicking briefly to the bimbo's face.

He stiffened so slightly I questioned whether I'd imagined it. "Erin."

I raised my brows expectantly, then extended my hand to the woman. "Hi, I'm Erin Turner, Lyle's sister-in-law."

The blonde gave nothing away but a hint of steel in her spine. "I'm Ebba Nilsson." Then she'd tied her scarf tighter around her neck and pulled her blonde curls out of it to cascade over her shoulders.

"Ebba and I work together at Chesapeake Properties," Lyle added smoothly. But he'd also shifted his demeanor, stepping slightly away from her. "We were having lunch with a potential tenant."

The fact that he'd offered a detailed explanation before I'd even questioned him had struck me, too.

"Oh, and here I assumed you stopped by to make reservations for a romantic dinner with Amanda." I'd waited for his reaction, which didn't come. But Ebba's mouth curled upward a touch. I looked over Lyle's shoulder. "Where's your client?"

He and I locked gazes. There in the depths of those striking blue eyes lay all the coldness he hid from my sister. "He left five minutes ago for another meeting. I had to stay and pay the bill. Now we're on our way back to the office, so if you'll excuse us." He grinned insincerely. "You have a pleasant day."

I'd waited on the porch, watching them wander down the walkway, scrutinizing their body language for any overt sign of something nefarious. They'd done nothing I could latch on to, yet I couldn't shake my misgivings.

I'd never trusted Lyle—not from the first. But there hadn't been any evidence that day to take to Amanda. And after the way she'd shut down on me the first time I'd criticized him, I couldn't have simply shared my suspicion. Not with her basking in her first trimester and their recent move to this house. Plus we'd all still been reeling from Dad's death, so I hadn't wanted to stir up more drama without smoking-gun proof.

She'd fallen so hard for Lyle from the start, blind to all his faults. His boasting annoyed me, but worse was how he'd systematically made Amanda more reliant on him—sowing doubts about her friends, like making derogatory remarks about Cindy Dunlap's influence simply because she planned girls' nights out, or persuading Amanda to put off working toward her master's degree because he could support her while she raised their children. He used my sister's eagerness to please him against her, and got away with it by lavishing her with praise and affection. God, he made my skin crawl.

Meanwhile, I'd only ever been completely open with her, and yet she trusted him more than she trusted me—that much was as clear as her crystal chandelier. In a "he said, she said" situation, he would've won and she and I could've ended up seriously estranged.

But damn it. Damn, damn, damn. No way would I confess that sighting now. That'd be worse than useless, and the blame for everything would land back on me despite *Lyle* being the liar.

"Wait, wait . . ." I waved my hands after hearing something about Mom and her money. "I'm sorry. I missed everything you said after the very first sentence. What's this about Mom's money?"

Amanda set her elbows on the table and hung her head, hands covering her face, hair dangling all around. Now that drastic haircut made sense. What we women did to feel better I'd never quite understand, but I had a tattoo and an extra piercing as the result of various disappointments, so no judgment here.

My mom interjected with the clipped voice she always used to stop a discussion before it started. "I lent Lyle money to get this deal in Florida under his belt. We're waiting to hear back from him about all that."

My stomach dropped as if the floor had fallen away. *I* hadn't asked for Mom's money—Dad's money—but *Lyle* took it? "Waiting to hear back?"

Amanda reexplained about the promissory note and the coworker.

I stole a look at her belly and completely lost my appetite. God, I wished I'd risked the argument back in February. I'd mentioned it to Max at the time, but he'd raised an eyebrow and warned me that if Lyle was as bad as I thought, then I'd better not alienate my sister, because one day she'd need me. Looked like that day was now. Still, if speaking up would've planted the slightest seed of doubt about him and prevented this loan situation, estrangement would've been worth it.

Crap. Biggest effing mistake in my life—and that's saying something. "I'm so sorry, Amanda. What can I do . . . besides track down this other woman and make her life a living hell?"

My sister had never shared my bloodlust, but today a fleeting glimmer of vengeance lit her eyes. "Please don't do anything. I'll solve this on my own. It's just been difficult because Lyle hasn't been easy to reach these past few days."

She twined her fingers together on top of the table, probably regretting the mini breakdown.

I narrowed my gaze, trying to read her better. She loved that man, no matter how foolish that seemed to me. This had to *gut* her. If only she'd be open with her feelings, maybe I would know how to help. "You seem strangely calm for someone whose husband is off with another woman."

She lowered her hands from the table. "I've had a few days to get used to the idea."

I crossed my arms, recalling how people in high school had taken advantage of her generous nature to get what they needed—study outlines, rides, extra cash because she was flush from babysitting money—but rarely had reciprocated. I would've dumped pasta on all their heads, too, if I could've.

How dare Lyle! My love for movies like *Goodfellas* prompted all kinds of evil ideas to the point where energy pulsed through my arms and shot to the fists that I'd formed. "We need to take Ebba down. I mean, she's a class-A bitch to sleep with a married man whose wife is *pregnant*."

"Language," Mom admonished.

Amanda shook her head, looking sadder than I'd seen her since we buried Dad. Man, I was almost glad he wasn't around to see this. He'd be devastated, and would probably be upset with me for not saying anything, too. Then again, if he'd been around in February, I would've asked for his advice. "I'd prefer it if this could stay between us for now. I'm not ready for the whole town to pick sides."

"Okay." It chapped my butt that Lyle was getting away with so much. Even worse—*he'd* known he would, too, because he knew Amanda's history of smoothing things over. Boy, I wanted to punch him. My thoughts circled back to the sheer hypocrisy of his taking a loan from my mom. "Not to belabor this, but if Lyle's business plan's so great, why couldn't he borrow money from the bank?"

Amanda's eyes flared to life in his defense . . . and probably in hers for complicity. "He didn't ask Mom for the money. She overheard us talking about how a bank loan wouldn't come through in time to jump on the deal."

On the surface that sounded plausible, but I'd never trusted Lyle. He'd been too polished. Too solicitous to my parents. Too sweet to my sister.

I didn't go to college, but I knew plenty of pop psychology, and his behavior smacked of everything phony and manipulative. Amanda's pathological need to please had been the perfect fit for a guy like him. He'd hooked her harder than an Eagle Claw snell did a striped bass. "I guess now Mom wants to be paid back pronto."

"He probably already invested some of the money, but I've asked him to send back whatever is left until he and I work out our situation." She and Mom exchanged a meaningful look.

"Did he agree?"

"We haven't actually spoken." Amanda barely met my gaze. "I've left messages."

This kept getting stranger, and the lack of alarm in her voice had *my* bells clanging.

"How do you know nothing bad has happened? I mean, even under the circumstances, isn't he at least keeping tabs on the baby? Maybe you should call Rodri." Rodrigo, my high school buddy turned cop, might be able to get to Lyle faster than we could.

"We're not involving the cops in our family's private business. The affair, the loan. Good God, Erin. Think for once," Mom snapped.

That was rich coming from the woman who'd handed her savings over to Lyle, but I let it pass. If I had to be the punching bag for her stress, so be it. "I can't believe that bast—sorry—*guy* took Dad's blood money."

"It isn't blood money." Mom bugged her eyes. "If your father were alive, he would've helped your sister, too. Lyle's business success would secure Amanda's and my granddaughter's future, so I helped."

Despite the certain tone, she fiddled with her sleeve and pursed her lips.

Maybe I'd crossed a line, but frustration shook me. And contrary to our mom's opinion, my poor dad would be furious about this situation. He'd never much trusted Lyle, either. Maybe he hadn't said it in so many words, but he hadn't disagreed when I'd told him I thought Amanda marrying Lyle was a mistake. In any case, that money had been for Mom's comfortable retirement, period. "How much?"

"None of your business." After a lifetime of my hearing the fierce tone she'd used to control every kid in town, the hollowness in this attempt echoed.

My hackles rose. "That nonanswer tells me I don't even want to know what you might lose on this investment."

"It's not an investment. It's a *loan*. We have a loan document." Mom's stab at looking smug also failed.

"Oh, I see." I rubbed an eyelid. "We're going with the fail-proof 'wait and hope that everything turns out okay' plan."

"Not exactly. Kevin's sending a private investigator tomorrow." Amanda's cheeks glowed like embers.

I raised my brows. "I'm surprised *he* didn't insist on the cops."

"Affairs and loans aren't crimes, no matter what you two think. It hurts that neither of my siblings support my marriage." Amanda's voice cracked as she rubbed her belly.

Support her marriage? I'd kicked Max out for way less than this. Then again, my silence this winter had helped create this whole mess, so I could hardly be indignant.

As if no one else were in the room, Amanda yammered while staring into space. "One day I had a life that made sense. The next, it vanished. I'm still in shock . . . like I'm falling into a bottomless pit with nothing to grab on to. Rage collects in my chest and then bursts like big sorrow bombs. I'm humiliated . . ." She paused, then snapped her gaze to me. "But if Lyle wants to come home, I'll consider it. He didn't grow up like us, with a good example of family and commitment, so maybe he's freaking out about becoming a dad, or he doubts my love and this is his way of testing my commitment. I mean, I have been a little obsessed about the baby lately, so he might've felt ignored. I don't know what comes next, but unlike you, my love doesn't just die. And I can't believe his has, either." Her voice broke on that last sentence as she pushed out of her chair, then tore up the stairs as fast as her big belly allowed.

My mom hung her head, but her shakiness appeared to be about more than Amanda's little breakdown. "Why can't you ever be supportive of your sister? This is a terrible time for her. She's pregnant and scared, yet you have to make everything harder."

"Mom, that's not fair." I would scream about how she put the worst interpretation on everything I did, but no one needed something more to worry about.

Mom's eyes got misty, making me the total heel. "Everything's always so easy for you. A big game. You have *all* the answers."

Anyone paying attention would raise an eyebrow. A woman in my shoes—very tattered ones at that—hardly had all the answers. But I did know a few things about life and people. "You've had a few days to process this. Did you expect me to simply smile and ask for seconds?"

My mom closed her eyes with a dramatic sigh. "We promised Kevin we'd fill you in. What's done is done. I don't have to answer to you or him, but if your father were here, he'd expect you both to support your sister. I know my opinion never mattered much to you, but his did, so I hope you'll think about that."

She marched off to check on Amanda. I scratched my head, literally, unsure how I'd become the bad guy when clearly Lyle deserved that title. If anything, this conversation—this blame when I'd done nothing wrong tonight—confirmed my decision not to breathe a word about what I'd witnessed this past winter. Better I find some way to make Lyle pay for what he'd done than to stick my own neck in the noose.

And yet knowing that they'd never forgive me for my silence irked me because Amanda was already angling to forgive *Lyle*. Quite ironic—or hypocritical. If I wanted to cast up her mistakes, I could go all the way back to third grade, when then-sixth-grade mean girl Missy Pendleton teased me for dressing in the orphan look from *Anastasia*. Instead of sticking up for me, Amanda kept quiet. She never, ever made waves. In that particular case, it could've been because she'd agreed with them or because she'd wanted to be part of that cool crowd more than she'd cared about my feelings.

Not sure. Never asked.

My appetite had long fled, so I wrapped my food in foil for later, loaded my dish into the dishwasher, and walked out the door.

Tonight sure had screwed up any zen I'd found at the retreat. Getting away from this side of town and home to Mo and my Etsy stuff couldn't happen fast enough. The ride flew with my legs pumping hard enough to burn off the energy I might've turned on Lyle and Ebba had they been around.

Mo greeted me with his good cheer despite having no idea how badly I needed those sloppy kisses. Once he settled, I went to the crate where I stored the coconut oil, then hefted a five-pound bag of sugar, some food coloring, and a variety of essential oils onto the table. Before locating the measuring cups and spoons, I went to my room to pick some music—maybe Bowie.

I flung open the armoire—and then my heart stopped.

Empty!

All my albums were gone, along with all Max's clothes.

No. No, no, no, no!

I sprinted back to the kitchen to find my phone and then dialed Max. Not shocking that he didn't answer. My fist hurt from beating out a steady rhythm on the counter while waiting for the flippin' beep.

"Max, if this is some idea of a joke, I'm not laughing. You'd better bring my albums back over here right now or I *will* call the cops." I was not my sister, in case that wasn't already clear.

I hung up. The pulse point at the base of my neck throbbed like the opening of Van Halen's "Hot for Teacher."

I began tearing the apartment apart, looking under tables and the bed, inside other drawers, behind the curtains. Anyplace I could think where he might've hidden the records to mess with me.

It took only about ten minutes—one benefit of a shoebox-size apartment—to confirm that Max hadn't merely pulled a prank. He still hadn't returned my call, either. Tears backed up on me, making my throat ache. My albums. My one lasting comfort and connection to my dad and what he loved. I pictured him up in heaven, shaking his head at all of us.

I flopped onto the couch. Mo jumped up beside me, seeking another belly rub. Mindlessly, I indulged him. It'd be awesome if a belly rub could fix all *my* problems.

If Max didn't call me by morning, I'd ask Rodri to have him arrested. Truthfully, though, if Max scratched any of those records, *I* might be the one who ended up in jail.

CHAPTER FIVE

AMANDA

Little Laticia Nelson pressed so close to me she was practically sitting in my lap. She flipped back to the first page of *Olivia*. "Mrs. Foster, read it again."

Mrs. Foster. The name I'd proudly taken two years ago might be usurped by Ebba. Bitterness bloomed.

"How do we ask nicely?" I nudged gently, redirecting my thoughts. All around us, boys and girls played on the checkerboard carpet or colored at the art table beside the reading nook.

"Please!" She clapped her hands together and quivered as if forced to trap all her energy in her body.

Someday not long from now, my own daughter might also love to be read to over and over. The anxiety of becoming a single parent tainted that joyful thought. So did sorrow that my daughter might not ever live under the same roof with her father. And shame for not seeing any of it coming.

I looked at page one and began. "This is Olivia . . ."

"Okay, kids, let's clean up," Darlene Silvestri, my coteacher, called out. "It's time to go."

A quick glance through the classroom door's window revealed parents waiting to collect their kids. Now and then a dad showed up instead of a mom or other caregiver. With Lyle's being his own boss, I'd been anticipating picking up our daughter together and having lunch before he returned to work. Would that be another dream lost? "Sorry, sweet pea. We'll read it again on Wednesday. Please go put this back on the shelf so we know where to find it, okay?"

"Okay." Laticia slid off the bench with the book in both hands and marched directly to the shelf, where she neatly slipped it into place.

I smiled. I'd been like her—a lover of books, a good listener, a neatnik. Those habits had mostly served me well, but Lyle's recent about-face had me questioning everything. None of my ways had secured his affection or my future. Meanwhile selfish people like him, and reckless ones like Erin, had all the fun.

"Are you okay?" Darlene asked when she came over to reorganize the puzzles.

"What?" I blinked before standing and straightening my shirt.

"You've been a little absent today. Are you tired? I remember how hard it gets to sleep as you get bigger." She laughed. "And once the baby comes, it's harder for different reasons."

"I'm sorry I've been out of it. A lot on my mind, I guess. I'll pull my weight on Wednesday." I couldn't bear Darlene thinking less of me as a teaching partner. But lying had never come easy, so pretending my life wasn't falling apart posed a tremendous challenge. The hives on my neck should have been a giveaway, but she hadn't noticed.

"No worries at all. I'm only checking in to see if you need anything." She looked at the door. "We'd better let the parents grab their kids."

Before I answered, Darlene had crossed the carpeted area and reached the door. Even if I'd wanted to confide in her, I couldn't stand it if my colleagues ridiculed me the way Kevin and Erin had.

As usual, the kids lined up, bouncing on toes or outright jumping up to catch their parents' attention. I waved at my neighbor Barb, while Darlene released the children one at a time. If my marriage ended, perhaps Barb would share single-parenting advice. The reality of it hurt so much I pushed it aside. For now, I breathed a sigh of relief that my job had ended for the day. I'd done my best for my students, even if I hadn't been at the top of my game.

"Want to grab a quick lunch and a little gossip?" Darlene asked as we did one final sweep of the room. "I guess you've already heard that Susan Miller's new baby isn't her husband's. Now he's threatening to sue for custody of Sadie. I mean, I do feel bad for him, but how can he not have known sooner?" She grimaced while tossing two broken crayons.

Sadie was an adorable four-year-old in another classroom here at the Tot Spot. It ripped me up to think of her as a pawn in her parents' battle. Worse to know that if my marriage ended, I'd be the subject of such "friendly" gossip.

"That's tragic for all of them. Sorry, I can't join you for lunch, though. I've got errands and an appointment." My dismissiveness should stanch further questions. I had no intention of discussing my upcoming appointment with the private investigator, Stan Whittaker. Lord only knew what *he* must think of me. But with Lyle's disappearing act, the need to locate my husband had intensified. Still, I didn't want Darlene's radar going up, so I said, "Rain check?"

"Sure." She smiled. "Have a good afternoon."

I waved goodbye and then went straight to my car, closed my eyes, and let my head fall back while inhaling slowly. When my phone rang, I jerked before grabbing for my purse to dig it out. An unfamiliar number. "Hello?"

"Amanda, it's me."

"Lyle?" I choked on his name, but the surge of relief from the sound of his voice made everything else fall away. "Why haven't you called sooner? I've been so upset. Everyone's so upset."

"I'm sorry. I'd hoped my letter would buy some time to sort through things before we spoke. I went to Abaco for a few days to sniff out redevelopment opportunities. Service there is spotty, then my phone dropped out of my shirt pocket into the sea when I was tying up to the dock."

I couldn't focus on his words with all the things I wanted to say competing for my attention. Mostly I considered the nights I'd spent crying while he'd apparently been cruising the Bahamas. Fury climbed up my throat. "When did you become a man who'd treat a whore to a vacation on my mother's dime while your daughter and I were heartsick at home?"

He heaved the kind of sigh one breathed in the face of a petulant child. "This is exactly why I didn't want to talk yet. If we can't be civil, there's no point."

"No point?" I stared at the arborvitae that edged the parking lot, processing a remark that reduced the past few years of my life to nothingness.

"You know what I mean. Amanda, it kills me to have hurt you like this, but, please, let's not say things we can't take back." The soothing tone that usually worked on me sounded patronizing.

"I think I'm entitled to some anger, Lyle. You've made me question everything I believed in. Meanwhile, my mother is a nervous wreck about her money. I've been agonizing all weekend while you've been dallying in the Caribbean. To top it off, Kevin and Erin are breathing down my back, ready to call the cops."

"Of course they are. Kevin's paranoid, and Erin never liked me no matter how much I did for you and your parents over the years."

Kevin was shrewd, not paranoid, although Lyle was right about Erin. When he'd mowed the lawn for Dad that summer after his knee replacement, Erin had practically choked on her thank-you. And anytime Lyle gave me a piece of jewelry or pretty new outfit, she'd made it seem like it had more to do with his ego than with his love for me. Then again, unlike my sister, I'd totally missed Lyle's potential to do harm.

"Erin thought you were a phony, and your affair proves her right. You're a liar and a coward." Hurling insults didn't feel as good as I'd hoped, nor would they change the facts or remind Lyle of the happy life we'd had together.

"If that's how you feel, you must want a divorce."

The chilling lack of remorse in his voice made me feel like I'd been thrown into the bay on a cold March day. "Don't twist my words around to put this on me. *You're* the one who broke our vows." A sob broke apart before I could stifle it. "Why? Why did you do that?"

"I didn't plan it, Amanda." He now sounded sorry, but I didn't quite trust anything he said or did. And his feelings were beside the point. "I don't know what else to say that won't hurt you more."

My hopes of reconciliation dimmed. "Please. I need to understand what happened, Lyle. Where did I go wrong?"

I closed my eyes, pressing my skull against the headrest as if its support would somehow cushion the blow.

"It's a lot of pressure to live up to—your standards of perfection and thoughtfulness. Plus the work of keeping you on the pedestal your sister kicked you off of with your dad. And you're content to live the rest of your life in your hometown. At first it was charming—so different from my childhood—but after working with Ebba on some commercial deals, something changed. She's adventuresome and shares my sense of humor. She's not set on living the rest of her life in Potomac Point. With her I can imagine a different kind of future. One with infinite possibilities and no moral high ground."

Each of his words exploded in my chest like copper-tipped bullets. I looked down, expecting to see blood. With shallow breaths, I wondered if this was what my dad's heart attack had felt like and if heartbreak could cause cardiac arrest. "But when we met, you craved a home and a family where you felt loved and secure *because* of your childhood. My parents welcomed you in and tried to fill that void. I've been giving you exactly what you said you wanted . . ."

"You did and I'm grateful. You healed me, and I'm sorry I've hurt you, Amanda. I never wanted that. If you believe nothing else, believe that."

If I'd healed him, why was he leaving me? "Don't you love me anymore?"

The silent pause said more than any words could. A sour taste flooded my mouth. My body broke into a cold sweat.

"It's complicated. Part of me will always love you, but now I'm in love with her, too. No matter who I choose, I'll have some regrets and hurt someone. As for you and me, it's hard to imagine that you could really forgive me for Ebba."

On one hand, I wanted to shout at him to stop saying her name. On the other, it was no wonder Lyle couldn't conceive of the forgiveness and love I offered. His mother had walked away from him rather than fight for her family. His dad had then blamed him, making him feel more unwanted.

"It won't be easy, but when I think of everything we have . . . or had . . . If you come home, I'm willing to try—for us and for our daughter. Doesn't she deserve the stability you didn't have growing up?"

"Yes." His tone scraped with a raw edge it held whenever he thought of *his* family. "But we don't always get what we deserve."

We sure didn't. "Would you really choose a woman who'd interfere in a marriage over trying to fix us and be a father?"

"What if I'm not what's best for the baby? Maybe I'm not capable of that commitment full-time."

What was he saying? "You were the one who suggested we start a family. Why would you do that if you weren't happy?"

"I wasn't unhappy, and it's what people our age do—they start families. I got caught up in the fantasy. But Ebba's flawed like me. We fit better. Maybe I'm simply not a good enough man to deserve someone like you, Amanda."

"Stop blowing smoke, Lyle. We aren't teenagers breaking up. We're husband and wife with a baby on the way. So much will be affected by our decision. You're letting your trust issues destroy us. Please slow down and look at what you're doing before you ruin everything over a fling."

For a second, I thought he might've hung up on me he was so quiet.

"You're right. This is a huge decision." He paused. "While I'm stuck here locking down investors, give me a little more time, okay?"

The mention of the deal felt like manipulation. "If this deal is so awesome, why aren't investors jumping all over it?" I stopped myself from saying more, unaccustomed to questioning my husband's motives, then blurted my growing fear. "Is there even a deal at all, Lyle, or is that a big lie, too?"

"Yes, there's a deal." Indignance—always his first reaction to being questioned about anything—replaced the syrupy tone he'd been using. "Do you need proof?"

I didn't like the places my thoughts were sailing.

"*I* believe you." My impending meeting with a PI said otherwise, but Lyle didn't need to know that. "But proof will help my mother rest easier, and keep Kevin and Erin calm."

"Remind everyone the first loan payment isn't even due until the beginning of next month." The steel in his voice gave me pause, but we were both tense. "I used the money to buy the land, so I'll send you the deed. Will that satisfy everyone?"

"It certainly won't hurt." I almost apologized, but I stopped myself.

During the ensuing silence, I wondered if he'd ever known how much I'd loved him. How I would've done anything for him. If he'd wanted a life of adventure, I would've gone with him, even if I'd had reservations. All he'd ever had to do was ask. Instead, he'd turned to someone else and left me alone and devastated.

Now I faced single motherhood while he played fast and loose with fatherhood. Should I have suspected this could happen? We are, after all, a product of our genetics.

After I pressed my thumbs against my eyes, I checked the rearview mirror to see if my mascara had run, and noticed Barb coming off the school playground with Collin. Shoot.

"I guess there's nothing more to say today." No doubt he heard the quaver in my voice.

"I'm sorry I can't tell you what you want to hear today, but I'm trying to be honest with everyone."

Too little, too late.

When I said nothing, he added, "I'll call you next week."

"Goodbye." I hung up, more confused and heartsick, wondering if he'd really thought himself unworthy of me—and if that were true, whether I'd done something to make him feel that way. Had I been too needy, like he'd intimated? My headache intensified. Frantic to flee the parking lot before Barb spotted my splotchy face and made me the next subject of pitiful whispers, I started the engine.

With only thirty minutes until my meeting, there was hardly time to grab something from Oak & Almond on my way home.

Heading in that direction took me past the police station—a handsome colonial-style three-story brick building. My thoughts began to stray, then Erin—whom no one could miss in that skimpy red shirt and decade-old biker boots—burst through its doors.

Erin's head jerked up at the screech of my tires. She stared at me while I circled into the parking lot and leaped from my car, my heart pounding against my ribs. "You promised you wouldn't say anything, yet here you are asking Rodri to dig around in Lyle's and my business."

She scowled. "Since when have I ever broken a promise to you?"

Strictly speaking, never that I was aware of. However, she had let me take the blame for denting Dad's car even though *she* was the one who'd banged into it with the Kohl's shopping cart. I'd covered for her because I knew our mother would've grounded her and made her miss out on the Fourth of July party she'd been talking about for weeks. "Then why are you here?"

Erin crossed her arms beneath her ample chest, her speckled cheeks and neck announcing her emotions. "Max stole Dad's albums."

"What?" I reached for her arm, imagining the unholy string of cursing that must have spewed from her lips when she discovered them missing.

It made sense that Dad had left those to Erin given their shared love of those classic tunes, but they were his most personal possessions, and he'd not given a single one to Kevin or me. He'd left me a little money, which I'd used to buy my living room furniture, so in that way I had a piece of him here with me. But it wasn't the same thing.

"I found out last night when I went to play one. I left him a message warning to call me back *or else*. Well, twelve hours later, still no call, so I asked Rodri to issue an arrest warrant. Those albums are worth thousands, which makes Max a felon. If he gets caught, he could be fined big-time and go to jail." She shook her head, the tiny diamond chip in the crease of one nostril glinting in the sun.

She acted tough, but this couldn't be easy for her. It wasn't the monetary value that mattered. Those records were her biggest connection to our dad, whom she'd loved more than anyone or anything in her entire life. Bad enough I'd felt replaced in my dad's eyes, but watching those two share the kind of relationship that I'd once hoped she and I might build had rubbed salt in that wound. Based on my mom's occasional comparisons of Erin's attitudes to those of the infamous Patty—Dad's first love—I think even she envied Erin's bond with Dad.

"I'm so sorry, Erin." Neither of us was having a good week.

"For accusing me of breaking your trust?" Erin cocked her head.

I glanced at my feet before peeking up at her. "Well, that too."

After a brief pause, her shoulders relaxed and her eyes filled with sympathy. "Have you heard from Lyle?"

The recent call had depleted me, so I deflected rather than fill her in on the less-than-satisfying conversation I'd yet to process. "I'm meeting the investigator now."

"Oh, that should be interesting. Want some company?"

"No, thanks." Meeting Stan and discussing Lyle would be hard enough without my sister hovering and adding her two cents.

She wrinkled her nose. "I know you don't want my advice, but if you want Lyle's attention, send him a clear message. Go straight to Rodri. I guarantee that'd make him jump."

For a split second a heady rush of revenge tore through me. I could screw Lyle over the way he was screwing with me. But he'd said things that made me question my role in all this. What if I'd unintentionally pushed my husband away exactly like I seemed to do with my sister?

The stakes required me to remain calm and protect my daughter's best interests. Besides, Mom didn't want *anyone* learning about the money.

"Lyle hasn't stolen anything"—when that deed hit my inbox, I would prove that—"and going public before I know the fate of my marriage is *not* an option."

"I don't get protecting Lyle just because you're afraid of gossip." She shook her head. "Then again, maybe gossip would bother me more if I had your perfect track record."

Perfect? I'd had plenty of disappointments, including the way the baby sister I'd adored couldn't run far enough away from me our whole lives. Or how I always remained an outsider—with my dad and sister, my sorority, even with acquaintances like Hannah . . . and now with my own husband.

She scratched her head. "But, man, I'd be stoked if you'd give Lyle his due and move on to find something or someone better."

I wouldn't let Erin—whose choices rarely made sense to me—bully me into publicly shaming my husband or embarrassing my mother by prematurely involving the police.

"Like your provocateur way of life is working for you?" I raised one brow and glanced at the police station.

"'Provocateur,'" she mimicked with a smile. "I like that."

Naturally.

Then she shrugged, kicking the toe of her boot against the pavement. "Maybe I don't live a life you'd be proud of, but at least I face my mistakes head-on."

I stroked my stomach, thinking of the precious life born of my marriage. Her existence alone meant my marriage could never be considered a mistake.

From what I could tell, my sister had no idea what it meant to love someone more than she loved herself. No idea what real commitment—real strength—required. No concept of self-sacrifice. She'd dumped Max when that got boring or hard or whatever it was that had made her choose to walk away—quite easily, I might add. And as recently as my baby shower registry day, she'd picked the fun of Max's dad's birthday over the chore of doing something she didn't enjoy (shopping). "I've got enough to deal with without your judgment."

"Well, then don't nearly kill yourself while hunting me down, assuming the worst of me . . ." She crouched to unlock her bike without sparing me another glance.

She wasn't wrong about that part. I'd started this argument before learning about the albums, but I couldn't quite bring myself to apologize again. "I hope they find Dad's records. I mean it."

She hitched one leg over the bike. "Oh, trust me. Max had better hope they find him before I do. But either way, I *will* get those records back."

She winked and then pedaled away, strong and sure like she attempted most things in life, despite being single and broke, with no firm or immediate prospects of improvement in either category. Amazing. A demoralizing flicker of envy struck. For all my accomplishments, that confidence eluded me. It was the one trait I hoped my daughter would inherit from my sister.

I slipped back into the driver's seat and slammed the door, praying Stan was a kind man.

Five minutes later, I pulled into my driveway. A man who looked remarkably similar to Uncle Bob—my dad's brother, who lived in North Carolina—got out of the silver Ford Focus parked along the curb. Barrel-chested, a shock of salt-and-pepper hair, caramel-colored eyes. Slightly bowlegged, too, with a neatly trimmed beard. The sight of him—and the inescapable reality of my life—made me want to cry all over again.

As the investigator made his way toward me, Michelle Callow eyed him from across the street while she retrieved her mail. The social-butterfly mother of superstar twin middle schoolers, she had a habit of being the unofficial "authority" on everything to do with motherhood, education, and sports training. She also didn't shy away from gossip. Wearing a bright smile, I waved at her as if there were nothing at all remarkable about this burly older man visiting me in the middle of the day.

"Mrs. Foster?" The man extended his hand. "I'm Stan Whittaker."

"Hello." The formality seemed silly given the intimacy of his mission. I shook his hand, trying not to stare too closely at him. "Please, call me Amanda."

His kindly eyes sparkled. I restrained myself from seeking a hug. After all, he was *not* my uncle, and now wasn't the time to indulge a longing for my father. Blinking to clear my misty eyes, I gestured for him to follow me inside while clearing my throat. "Can I get you some water or iced tea?"

"No thank you."

"Okay." I set my purse on the kitchen counter. "Shall we sit at the table, or do you prefer the living room?"

He scanned the house as if he were memorizing everything, keeping hold of his soft-sided briefcase. "Actually, if you have an office, let's begin there."

"That's fine." I led him through the house to Lyle's office, checking my emails for the deed Lyle had promised to send.

We'd been so proud of this small, walnut-paneled room, with its french doors and built-in bookshelves that currently displayed Lyle's real estate broker awards. How different it all looked to me now—the liar's den. Those late nights "working" in here had probably been a cover for private messaging and phone or FaceTime sex.

Bile rose up my esophagus—a bitter punishment for my oblivion.

"Do you mind if I sit at the desk?" Stan asked.

I cleared my throat. "Not at all. But I should mention that this might be unnecessary. I spoke with Lyle less than an hour ago. He's still in Florida meeting with potential investors, but he promised to send me the deed to the land he bought."

"And you believe him." That statement held no judgment. In fact, it was almost a question, like he was nudging me to continue with the inquiry just in case.

I glanced at my feet, wanting to defend Lyle yet unable to give Stan an unequivocal answer. After all, I'd been so aggrieved by the state of our marriage I hadn't thought to ask specific questions about the project—like an address. "Let's proceed with the understanding that if the deed comes in and checks out, we'll call this off and I'll work out my marriage—or divorce—with lawyers."

"Understood."

"Should I log you on to the computer?"

"In a moment. First, I'd like to ask you some questions about your husband's affairs—business affairs, that is." He grimaced. "Sorry."

"It's fine." Inside I died another tiny death. That humiliation would continue times one hundred once others in town learned the truth.

Questions. Whispers. Plenty of phony comfort. That I'd been so openly proud to be his wife made it all worse.

Rumors chum the waters, like with the Millers, or when Laura Blair's husband slept with their nanny. People always questioned how the spouses couldn't tell what was happening. Even I'd wondered that about Laura, but now I knew. When you love and trust someone, you don't think to be suspicious. You don't look for clues or betrayals. You simply live and love with no more thought than it takes to breathe.

Stan took a seat and removed a legal-size yellow notepad from his case. Something about that old-school manner inexplicably calmed me. I trusted him, and not only because my brother had referred the ex-cop to me. "Kevin sketched out some basic details to make it easier on you. But I'd like to quickly review the facts to confirm that I've got accurate information."

"Certainly." I stroked my stomach absently.

Stan proceeded to recite Lyle's full name, birth date, birthplace, and other such information, including his work history—or at least that from the past few years. I added Lyle's social security number, Tom's contact information, and what little I could recall about the condominium-development deal. When we finished with that, Stan asked me to log on to the computer.

"You're welcome to stay here while I search through the files." He glanced up at me.

I stared at the screen, trying to anticipate what embarrassing things he might uncover. "What are you looking for?"

"I'll start with the search history. You'd be surprised how many folks don't think to clear it regularly. It could offer important clues about what he's been planning. And if he automatically saved passwords, that'll make it easier to get into other sites."

"Oh." I nodded dumbly, although my head was already swimming. "I'm sorry. I should've thought to do those searches."

He patted my hand. "It's hard to think clearly when your emotions are running high."

"Thank you." His kindness meant everything because I'd beaten myself up every waking moment since Tom's girlfriend, Gigi, had hung up on me. "I'd rather not stand over your shoulder unless you need me here. If you have questions, give me a holler, but I'll be better off doing something else. Otherwise, my stomach will churn."

He looked at my belly. "Let's not add to your stress. I'll dig around and call you if I have questions."

"Perfect." I stood and uttered, "Good luck," although it seemed a weird thing to say under the circumstances.

He winked. "No luck needed. I promise, I'll find the truth."

I offered a weak smile, picturing Lyle's face. Those spellbinding blue eyes. The little cleft in his chin, and his long, lean frame. The way he'd share the morning's most interesting news stories over coffee and then kiss me on his way off to work. If he walked through the door, I'd be as likely to fling myself into his arms as I would to throw a vase at his head. I'd never known I was the kind of woman who might forgive this kind of betrayal, but I'd also never been put to the test.

As hurt as I was, a part of me still wanted to forgive him.

The part of me that Lyle had made feel fully understood and appreciated from our first moment in the gym, that had quit my elementary school job to take the nursery school position so I'd have more time for him and our baby, that had happily worked hard to make our home and relationship a refuge from the stress and disappointments of the world.

The part that had trusted in my happily ever after.

On my way upstairs, the house phone rang. When I got to my room, I saw Aunt Dodo's number. She shared Michelle Callow's tendency to lecture, but deep down I believed she meant well. She probably would've been less involved in "fixing" the rest of our lives if she'd been able to have children of her own.

Closing my eyes, I sat on the bed, hoping to manage this conversation without disclosing anything my mother wished to hide. "Hi, Aunt Dodo."

"Oh good. You're home."

"Yes. Is everything all right?"

"You tell me. I can't reach your mom, and she never sent me the baby shower list. It's only a few weeks away. I'd like to order my gifts and wrap them."

"Oh, thank you. But I'm canceling the shower . . . or at least putting it off. That's probably why she hasn't sent out the list."

"Heavens on earth, why would you cancel? This is a celebration! My first grandniece."

I smiled, grateful for her enthusiasm yet aware my own happiness was no longer as complete. "Thank you for being so excited, but I'm feeling overwhelmed. It's coming to the end of the school year, and with the anniversary of my dad's death . . . it feels like the wrong time."

The disgrace of using my father's death as part of a cover story made me want to throw up. My father had loved children and been particularly tickled when Kevin made him a grandfather. When Lyle and I first discussed having a baby, I'd secretly anticipated sharing something with my dad that wouldn't involve Erin.

"Amanda, listen to me, dear. You can't wait for the perfect time to do things, because there is no perfect time. Once this baby comes, you must be ready to go, go, go. Now, come on, let's have a party."

"I appreciate the pep talk, but Lyle's out of town on business and I'm . . . I've got a lot to handle. Maybe after the baby comes."

"But then you won't have all the things you need. Oh dear. I have to speak with Madeline. If it's too much for you to host at your house, she should host it. I'll come a day early to help set up."

"Oh no, Aunt Dodo, please don't." Her tendency to boss everyone around would not only be unhelpful but also would send my mother into a tizzy.

"Don't you worry. I know how to handle my baby sister. See you soon. Kisses." And then she hung up on me.

I should warn my mother, but this day had sapped all my energy. Experience also had taught me that sisters had to manage their own relationship. After all, neither Mom's, Dad's, nor Kevin's attempts to wrangle Erin's and mine had ever made a difference.

Grabbing all the pillows, I then stuffed some around my awkward figure for support. Little by little, my body felt as if it were sinking into the mattress. My eyelids drifted south . . .

"So you think I can do it?" Lyle stood in the kitchen, orange juice in hand, looking at me with hope in his eyes.

"I know you can. You're driven, persuasive, savvy . . . and irresistible. If anyone can sell that old factory, it's you." I buttered my toast.

Lyle set down his glass and came over to wrap his arms around me, giving me a kiss that made me weak in the knees. "Thank you. You've no idea what your support means. Marrying you will always be the best decision I ever made."

I hugged him, resting my cheek on his shoulder. "I feel exactly the same way."

"Amanda!" A man's voice called my name from downstairs. For a second after waking from my nap, my heart was at peace. I thought Lyle was downstairs and it had all been a horrible dream. Then I replayed the voice that belonged to Stan, and the nightmare continued.

"Just a minute!" I rolled off the bed and risked a quick look in the mirror. Gah—nice deep wrinkle across my cheek. From the top of the steps, I gazed at Stan. "Sorry. I dozed off."

"No worries. When my wife was pregnant, she slept whenever she could. Your body needs the rest." He nodded with a warm smile.

I made my way downstairs, thinking he must be a gentle husband and father. "Do you have questions?"

"Yes. Let's sit in the kitchen."

"Sure. I could use some herbal tea. How about you?"

"That'd be nice, thanks." He followed me and took a seat while I quickly made two peppermint teas—from the gift basket Erin had given me when she learned I was pregnant—and then handed him one. "Ooh, smells great."

I took my seat before sipping from my cup. "So what can I help you with now?"

"Well, first off, were you and your husband in the market for a boat, or talking about a Caribbean cruise—like a private charter yacht?" He looked hopeful, which made my stomach drop.

Lyle had grown up near Lake Michigan and become an accomplished sailor by his teens. He'd always wanted his own boat, but I'd suggested we save that money, arguing we could always rent a sailboat, like he had for one of our first dates. He'd splurged to charter a gorgeous sailboat that day. He'd looked so happy and free at the helm my heart ached to remember it.

I'd never been to his family home in Michigan, though. That third time I'd suggested meeting his dad had drawn a severe argument that ended with my promise to never bring it up again, so I'd finally stopped. In any case, now I couldn't help but wonder if that freedom he experienced on a sailboat had always been his heart's true desire.

I shook my head. "No. Why?"

He clucked. "Well, I found a lot of searches for long-range miniyachts. Charters and used ones for sale."

Only then did I recall the Abaco part of my earlier conversation with Lyle. Oh God, he'd taken Ebba for a sail, like he'd done with me. The image of him at the helm revisited me. Handsome and proud, the wind in his hair. Another of my special memories now sullied. "Lyle mentioned something about a weekend in the Bahamas. While tying a boat to a dock in Abaco, he lost his phone. It's why he called from a strange number. Could that be what he'd researched?"

Stan's bushy brows tightened. "Could be. Do you have that phone number? I'm not legally allowed to track that, but the police could . . . if you get them involved."

"It's in my recent-calls list." I let the remark about the cops pass as if I hadn't heard it. "Anyway, Lyle loves boats. He could've been fantasizing about what he'd buy when his deal paid off."

Even I heard the pathetic hope in my voice.

"Maybe." Stan flipped through his notes some more. "I also found searches for foreign incorporations and banks—the Caymans, BVI, Isle of Man, and such."

Isle of Man?

I didn't know anything about the law, but movies had taught me enough to know that people hid money in the Caymans. Did he plan to hide his business income in order to reduce alimony and child support payments?

My heart rate skyrocketed, which was bad for the baby. I must've been blanching, because Stan touched my hand.

"Amanda, relax. Breathe and drink more tea, or maybe get some water. I know things don't sound promising, but I swear to you, if he's hiding money, we'll find him and get justice."

How sweet of him to pretend that Lyle was not up to tricks, but I knew he didn't believe it. Even *I* now experienced doubts, but I nodded nonetheless. "What if he's plotting something . . ."

"Here's the good news. The vast majority of these guys aren't nearly as smart as they think they are. Like in this case, with him failing to scrub his browser and such, they leave clues. And this woman—Ebba— she'll have left clues, too."

"Will you be talking to people about *her*?" I bit my lip. Half of me desperately wanted to learn every detail; the other half would rather know nothing.

"She's a big piece of the puzzle."

"But then people in town will talk." I practically slumped onto the table. It would be harder to patch my life back together—with or without Lyle—with everyone whispering and judging me. "Could there be another explanation . . . maybe the Cayman Islands have something to do with this Florida deal?"

A stretch, but hope was seductive.

I covered my face with my hands and drew a deep breath.

"Amanda, I'm very sorry. And trust me, you're not alone. Many wives have been where you are, looking for ways to protect their families and their children's future from men who've let them down."

"You must think my holding out hope is foolish."

"No. Don't let anyone make you ashamed to have invested your heart in your marriage. And it's not uncommon for wives to refuse to involve the cops for a bunch of reasons, so don't feel guilty about turning to me first. Or for holding out hope. There's still a lot we don't know, and maybe he'll snap out of this midlife crisis before things go much further. I'll certainly exercise discretion while looking into Miss Nilsson's life."

"Thank you for your kindness." I pushed my hair back. "I wish I didn't feel so powerless. Weak. *Idiotic.*"

"From what I can see, your husband is the idiot not to appreciate the life he had here." He smiled, and I again subdued the urge to seek a hug.

"Worst-case scenario—what happens if there is no deed and he runs before we find him?"

"Let's not jump ahead. He's promised to send the deed, and he might make a timely payment to your mom. Like you've said, being an adulterer doesn't make him a thief, too. I hope, for your sake, that's the case."

He hadn't answered my worst-case question, which told me that my options were limited. "Thank you for your discretion. I'll forward the deed when it comes and let you know if I learn anything more."

We both stood, and Stan followed me through the entry to the front door.

"I'll be in touch. In the meantime, take care of yourself and that baby. Whatever happens, don't panic. Your family will help you through." He patted my shoulder before walking to his car.

I closed the door, grateful to Kevin for sending me the perfect PI. Having a family to lean on made me lucky.

I dragged myself back upstairs to our closet, where the majority of Lyle's clothes and shoes remained neatly organized. No wonder I'd had no clue that he'd planned an extended getaway.

As I fingered his jackets, his cologne wafted through the closet, stirring a vision of him in the midst of his morning routine. He'd shower, shave, then do twenty quick push-ups—just enough to open his pores—before spritzing himself with Terre d'Hermès. Sometimes, when he had an especially important client meeting, he'd ask me to assist with his tie and cuff links. I'd enjoyed helping him put himself together—like teammates—and then sending him off with a kiss.

The toxic brew of fond memories and sorrow gave me a headache. What made me so dispensable? With my father for Erin. Tommy Cantor for Jasmine Berry. Now Lyle for Ebba. I'd given my all to make those men happy. To make them proud of me. To earn their love and respect. Still, when push came to shove, they each preferred the company of someone else. Someone more carefree . . .

I eyed that box with Lyle's father's last-known contact information. If I crossed that line, Ebba would win, because Lyle would never forgive me.

The phone rang. *Mom.* "Hi, Mom."

"What did you say to Dodo?" Her terseness made me start.

"That I was thinking of canceling the shower."

"Now she thinks I'm a terrible mother for not taking better care of you, and she's pressing me to host this shower here. Oh, I could just strangle Lyle."

I literally bit down on my tongue to keep from lashing out. I'd only tried to help her by canceling the shower. Couldn't she see that everything wasn't about her? She had a lot at stake—I got that—but *I* could use some comfort, too. "I'm sorry. I'll call her later and take the bullet, okay?"

"No, I'll handle Dodo. I'm fed up with how she bosses me around as if I'm a child."

Dodo's dictatorial tone could be draining, but she cared about us. "She's been worried about you since Dad died, Mom. It's sweet."

"You always give everyone the benefit of the doubt." Her tone proved that wasn't a compliment.

If I didn't believe that most people meant well, there'd be no point in investing in *any* relationship. "Speaking of that, Lyle finally called me this morning. He's sending me the deed to the land he bought. The PI promised to double-check it along with all the other information he gathered today."

For several seconds, nothing—not a grunt, gasp, or peep of any kind—came through the line.

"That must've been a hard conversation. Are you okay? What did Lyle say about Ebba?" My mother mispronounced the name, giving it a long-*e* sound.

"He's torn . . ." A lump strangled my throat. "I can't talk about this now, Mom. I'm exhausted."

"Oh, honey. I remember how hard it was, being in love with your dad while he was still getting over Patty." She sighed. I appreciated her empathy, although our situations were hardly similar. "Persistence paid off, though. Drink lots of water and get plenty of rest."

"I will." I wandered to my sofa and sank against the pillows. "Have you spoken with Erin about Dad's records?"

"No, why? Did she ruin them?" Mom clucked at the other end of the line. "How like her . . . so disorganized."

"No, Mom. Max stole them. Erin filed a police report today."

"Oh! William's records gone, too?" The emphasis on "too" broke my heart. Despite her empathy, she wasn't about to accept anything Lyle told me at face value. That my husband could be worse than Max made me cringe. While I'd always hoped to find some common ground with my sister, our poor taste in men was not what I'd had in mind.

Projecting more confidence than I felt, I said, "It's been a terrible week, but let's hold on to hope. You know Rodri will hunt Max down for Erin, so the albums will be recovered. And Lyle has a proven track record in real estate. This project will come together, and you'll get your money back."

"That still leaves Dodo. She cannot learn any of this, or I'll never hear the end of it. Truly, she'll blab to the whole family." Mom paused, probably projecting to cousin Sue's inevitable snark without concern for how she was adding to my burden. "I wish your father were here . . ."

So did I.

These past few days, a little gap had opened between my mom and me. A fall from grace on my part. Collateral damage from Lyle's behavior. All my life, she'd been the one person whose approval I could count on. I couldn't stand to lose it, too, yet could hardly blame her, given the situation. "I could use some company today. Would you like to bake a pie or something?"

"A pie?" She sounded confused, then sighed. "I guess that would be nice."

"I'll swing by the market and come to your house." It might help to be together in her kitchen, where we'd baked more treats than I could remember. My mom made the flakiest crust in the county—even had a blue ribbon to prove it. I couldn't do squat about my marriage today, but I could protect the other relationship that I needed to be happy. "Blueberry sound good?"

"You know I love blueberry."

The smile in her voice lifted a weight off my chest. "See you soon."

While I changed into casual clothes, the doorbell rang. I made my way downstairs, stunned to see the Bon Fleur truck in my driveway.

The delivery woman handed me a lovely bouquet of pink roses exactly like the ones Lyle used to send to my classroom. My heart swelled with hope. "Oh, these are gorgeous. Thank you."

"Have a nice day." She waved before wandering back to her truck.

I closed the doors and took the flowers to the kitchen, adding more cold water and a couple of drops of bleach to preserve their freshness. With my nose buried in the petals, I wanted so badly to accept this gift as a good sign. Plucking the card from its plastic holder, I then took it from the envelope and read:

Amanda,

No matter what happens, I'll always love you.

Deed will come from the lawyer soon.

Lyle

I crushed the card in my palm, heartbroken. The flowers hadn't marked a decision. They were to keep me on ice or in limbo or whatever other words described this uncomfortable space of uncertainty.

Did he not understand how hurtful his gesture was? Perhaps I'd been wrong to think someone with his background capable of giving and accepting healthy love. He would probably argue that these flowers were a show of affection. That he could've left me dangling after that phone call with no further word.

Maybe he meant the gesture as a kind remembrance of better times. But no matter how beautiful the bouquet, right now I'd rather Lyle had simply sent that deed.

CHAPTER SIX

ERIN

"What do you mean you can't find him? This town's not that big, Rodri. He's broke, too, so there aren't many places he can hide." With the phone tucked between my ear and shoulder, I stooped to unlock my bike while half the women in town strolled past. I didn't care who overheard me, though. Enough was enough. It'd been almost forty-eight hours, for God's sake.

"We'll keep looking, but he might've split town. In fact, if I were him, I would've taken off after stealing your albums." Rodri chuckled. I did not.

Max wouldn't have fled to his dad's. Old Charlie wouldn't put up with him lying around the living room all day. With no siblings to turn to, that left his mom. Now *that* had possibility. She babied the crap out of him, resulting in his massive case of Peter Pan Syndrome. Not that either of them saw it. Joan—that was her name—lived in Atlantic City. Twenty-five dollars in bus fare would put him across state lines. That sneaky weasel. "He could be with his mom in Atlantic City. Try there."

"That's not my jurisdiction."

As usual, rules stood in the way of easy solutions. What was it with society and rules? People were always looking for excuses to bend or break them. Wouldn't it be simpler to get rid of them altogether?

"Get a local cop to pick him up. Or drive me there so we can haul him back ourselves." I imagined Max's stunned expression when he opened the door to find us standing there. "I'd love to get my hands on him."

"That'd be entertaining, but, no, I can't do that." He paused. "I'll be honest. Extradition is expensive and time-consuming. Paperwork galore. You'd be surprised how many people get away with pretty big crimes by crossing state lines. This theft isn't likely to be something that the department will pursue with much vigor if Max is in Jersey."

"Well, that sucks!" I stood, holding the phone again now that I'd freed my bike. I needed those albums. Like, *needed* them to function. That music kept my dad alive for me. I thought better when pairing the right album with a particular problem. I couldn't move forward without those records. And the whole reason I'd kicked Max out was to get my life together, so I needed this major distraction to end yesterday.

"Sorry. I'll look into it, but we've got bigger crimes to solve. You'll have to be patient."

We'll see about that.

"Fine." I had to be careful not to give anything away. "Please call me if you learn *anything*."

"Erin, trust me. I know what those records mean to you. I'll do everything I can, okay?"

He meant that, but I couldn't sit around waiting, especially when *I* wasn't bound by his rules.

"Thanks." I closed my eyes. Rodri had been a good friend for half my life. Tons of people assumed we'd slept together, but we never had. Ours was not *that* kind of love. Too bad, really. My parents would've been happy if I had ended up with a nice, stable cop from a decent family. Instead, I'd chosen Max, who'd turned out to be worse than a simple loser. A heartless, cruel thief. As bad as Lyle, if I were being honest. Boy, that didn't make me happy. I'd never before considered myself a dupe.

"Wanna grab a beer or something this week?" Rodri sounded distracted, like someone else was waiting for him to finish the call.

"I won't be good company until I find Max. But call me later. Bye!" I hung up and hopped on my bike, heading for Nuts & Bolts to find Max's BFF, Joe, a mechanic and fellow stoner. The low-lying body shop had been in his family for two generations. Dingy white paint flaked off the brick exterior like old bark. Not that I cared about its state of disrepair. Joe was Max's friend, so his family business meant less than nothing to me. Heck, I hadn't even owned a car since the rusted-out Volkswagen I'd bought at twenty-one finally gave up the ghost two years ago.

In my haste to get to Joe, I didn't bother locking my bike. Instead I leaned it against the wall and strode right into the garage, coughing from the stench of oil and engines. "Joe Marinelli, get your butt over here!"

Joe popped his head out from under the hood of a nice-looking Cadillac. "Erin?"

He'd pulled his dark hair into a short ponytail, but one section had fallen forward. The baggy work attire didn't hide an otherwise smokin' body. Six feet three. Clooney eyes and a sweet smile. Yeah, Joe was a hottie, but not any more motivated than Max. If it weren't for his dad keeping him employed, he'd probably be sponging off folks like Max did.

I marched over to him, my hands on my hips. "Where's your lying thief of a friend?"

Joe sucked at poker, as proven by the numerous times I'd beaten him. He had many tells, like, right now, the way he scratched his ear and avoided my gaze. "Dunno."

"Bull." I extended my arm, palm up. "Hand me your phone, please."

"What?" He half laughed, waving me off like I was a powerless little flea. "Why?"

"The phone, Joe." When he continued to play dumb—or be dumb, I couldn't be sure—I barked, "I've already gone to the cops. Make no mistake, I'll do anything to get my dad's albums back, and I don't care who gets hurt in the process. If you don't cooperate, Rodri will be here in five minutes to write you up for obstruction."

Thank God for my gift of projecting toughness. It came in handy more often than I could say. Actually, maybe I owed my mom for that, because she'd honed it with her chronic stream of criticism.

"Aw shit, Erin." He scowled with a sigh and then put his phone in my hand.

"Unlock it."

He took it back, pressed his thumb to the button, and then handed it to me like a petulant child.

"Thank you *so* much." I turned my back on him and dialed Max. Unlike with *my* recent calls, he answered Joe's on the second ring.

"Hey, Joe, 'sup?" Max's happy, dippy voice hit my eardrums like a knife scraping china. Not for the first time, I ached for how someone I'd loved had done the worst possible thing he could think of to hurt me. No wonder my sister was so flabbergasted by Lyle. I should be more patient with her.

"It's not Joe, but don't you dare hang up unless you want the cops on your tail." In my mind, I resembled a fire-breathing dragon.

"Erin?"

"Yeah, it's me." I closed my eyes, gathering strength. "You know why I'm calling. I want my albums back yesterday, Max."

A pause. "I don't know what you're talking about."

I stomped my foot, yelling, "Do *not* get cute with me. We both know you took them, and if you don't bring them back today, prepare for an unholy war."

He huffed, acting blasé. "You'd have to find me first."

Time to roll the dice on my hunch. "You're at your mom's, dumb-ass."

"How'd you . . ." He stopped himself, but now I had confirmation. "I didn't steal anything. You owed me something after the way you kicked me out."

I owed *him*?

"Don't be a dick. I never even asked you to repay the charges you ran up on my card last month, though I probably should. You know what those albums mean to me. Just bring them back and I'll tell Rodri to call off the extradition paperwork." Max needn't know that paperwork hadn't gone into effect.

"You went to Rodri?" he yelped. Good. While it would've been nice to have heard a bit of guilt with that fear, I wasn't holding my breath.

"Yes, and he'll be at your mom's door tonight unless you return my property. Thousands of dollars of stolen property, Max. *Felony*-level crime. You want that on your record?"

I smiled when he cursed, but then a long pause made me wary.

He heaved a sigh. "I don't have them."

Desperation—not at all my choice emotion—pushed past all bravado. Tears were clogging my throat. "Please. Let's not end our whole relationship on this crappy note. I don't want that, do you? All I want are my records."

"Sorry, Erin. I sold them and then used the money to come here. Lost some at the casino . . ."

My heart stopped. I hadn't considered this complication. Jesus, I had no time to waste. "Sold them to whom?"

"Some dude Clyde knew who collects classic records."

Clyde—Max's buddy who played jazz guitar at local clubs like the Lamplight. "What 'dude'?"

"I don't remember. Eli something. He's there in town."

If I could've reached through the phone to strangle Max, I would've. "Eli who? Where in town? Apartment, house, condo? East side or west?"

"Hang on, let me see if I can find the email," he said, pausing. "But you swear you'll call off Rodri?"

If Max needed to think he had some bargaining power, I'd oblige long enough to get what I needed. "I don't care if I never see you again. I told you, all I want is my property."

A few seconds later, he said, "Eli Woodruff, 152 Willow Lane. Okay? We square?"

"Square?" I shook my head, although only Joe could see me. "You're unbelievable. You'd better take my next call. If I can't find this Eli person, this isn't the last you'll be hearing from me."

"Yeah, yeah. Put Joe on the phone, okay?"

The fact that I'd been hoodwinked by a guy who'd been using me for only a roof and a warm bed *really* chapped my butt. "First let me thank you for ensuring that I never have a single moment of regret for dumping you."

I handed Joe the phone before Max could say something else to enrage me. On my way out of the garage, I overheard Joe apologizing to his friend, which made me want to run back and toss a wrench at *his* stupid head.

I hopped on my bike, planning to make an unexpected house call on this Eli person, then thought better of that. Who knew what kind of creep he'd be? If memory served, Clyde had some strange friends. I pedaled back to the station, where Rodri was getting off for a late lunch break. "I know where my records are. Max sold them to a guy here in town. I was going to go get them on my own but thought it'd be better to get you involved. Can we go now?"

He scowled. "You can't come."

"Please, Rodri! I need to see them and make sure they're all there. I swear, I'll come but keep quiet." When I remembered I hadn't yet shared Eli's name and address yet, I added, "If you don't let me come, then I'll go on my own without involving you."

"Erin, the guy could be dangerous." The concern coloring his expression made my stomach hurt. But I never gave up any advantage that came my way—not when they were as elusive as shooting stars.

"I know, so don't make me go alone. I promise I'll stay in the car until you make sure it's safe. Please bend the rules this one time."

"Aw, shit." Rodri glanced around as if checking to make sure no one overheard us. "You know I can't ever say no to those big brown eyes. Get in the squad car and swear you won't do anything without my say-so."

"I swear." I hoped I'd keep that promise, too, and truly I did. I locked my bike up at the rack before climbing into his front seat.

"I know I'll regret this." He slid behind the wheel. "Address?"

After giving him the information, I breathed a huge sigh of relief. "Thank you. I owe you huge. Now let's hope this guy is at home. He has to give my stuff back, right? Stolen goods and all."

Rodri nodded. "Yeah, we'll get your stuff back. How'd you get this info so fast?"

"Gimme a little credit. It's not too hard to trick Max." I rolled down the window, feeling like I could breathe for the first time since discovering the albums were gone. Losing them was like losing my dad all over again.

"Songs are miniature stories," he'd told me once, when he'd sweetened an afternoon of garden chores by propping a speaker in an open window so he and I could listen to U2.

I'd always hated to read, habitually losing focus partway through any story, so I'd chewed that over while cutting back and digging out the old shrubs before planting new ones. Finally I'd proclaimed that songs changed the world more than books did because people remembered all the words to songs but not to books.

I still remember the way he smiled at me, shaking his head without argument. I miss how he accepted my way of seeing things without forcing me to see them his way. I also remembered him saying U2 would probably outlast many other bands, and he was right. Sadly, they also outlasted my dad.

Rodri pulled down Willow Lane to a sweet little Craftsman-style house, dark green with maroon accents and a covered front porch. The surrounding thatch of trees gave it an enchanted look. Not the kind of home a thief or dangerous person—or friend of Clyde's—would live in. In fact, it looked more like something Amanda might like, with its neat yard and shrubs.

When I went to open the door, Rodri grabbed my arm. "You stay put."

"Fine." I slumped back, sulking.

After Rodri got out of the car, I rested both arms out my window, straining to watch the action. Shouldn't be too hard when the driveway was barely a stone's throw from the front door. Within a minute, a man answered and stepped onto the porch.

A striking man who looked like he could be Jared Leto's brother. He had a hint of facial hair, but more like he'd forgotten to shave for two days than any real attempt at a beard or 'stache. An oval face—hollowed cheeks, fine nose. His hair begged to have fingers running through it . . . thick and glossy and a touch wavy.

Even from a distance, I liked his vibe. Loose-fitted jeans and a well-worn T-shirt covered his lean, fit frame. His bare feet appealed to my casual nature. He wore a thick leather bracelet on one arm and a silver one on the other. From what I could tell, he had no tats.

He stood there peering at me over Rodri's shoulder. When our eyes met, the air all around me heated. From where I sat, his eyes looked pale, but I couldn't tell if they were green or blue. Either way, the round shape fit the keen yet somber expression. He oozed an old-soul quality that would never be complicit in the purchase of stolen goods.

A serious hottie, but given Max's and Lyle's recent behavior, lust was trouble I didn't need to borrow.

Rodri waved me up to the porch, reminding me why we had come. The albums. God, nothing would be right in my world until those were back in my possession.

Eli's eyes dipped ever so briefly to my bare midriff before he jerked them back up. If he thought my knee-length Easter egg–print yoga pants, jog bra, and Birkenstocks odd or ugly, he didn't show it. The stiff soles of my old sandals clomped on the wood steps.

"Erin, this is Eli. He wants to confirm which albums are yours, in case some of the ones he bought weren't stolen. I don't have the report with me . . ."

"Oh," I said, then risked an up-close look at Eli. He didn't look pissed or defiant, which was a good sign. "Hi, Eli. Nice to meet you. I'm sorry to barge in like this, but I have to get my dad's records back."

"So I've heard." His voice was even prettier than that face. Clear and rich, masculine without being too deep or raspy. "Hope you understand why I'd like a little proof that they're all yours."

"What if I rattle them off right now?"

Both men stared at me with some surprise. Eli crossed his arms, distracting me by calling my attention to the muscle movement beneath his T-shirt. "Go ahead, then."

"Sure." I looked down, giving my head a tiny shake to concentrate, then wondered if Eli could pick up a pencil with his long, thin toes. Focus! "There were three crates. How about I do them in order of value, starting with the most valuable? David Bowie's 1974 *Diamond Dogs*—the original cover that got pulled. Then there's Nirvana's rerelease of *Bleach* from 1992. The Beatles' *The Collection* from 1982. Probably next is U2's *Joshua Tree Collection*, the '87 box set. Led Zeppelin's *BBC Sessions* from 1997. Pink Floyd's *Dark Side of the Moon*, with the gatefold sleeve. Springsteen's first pressing of *The Rising*—"

Eli held up his hand. "Okay, okay. It's your collection." He looked almost like he was stifling a smile, although he had nothing to smile about. The poor guy was out several grand. I shouldn't feel guilty about that, but I did.

He turned to Rodri. "I had no idea the guy didn't own the albums, Officer. He seemed more desperate than devious."

A fair observation of Max.

"I believe you." Rodri waved away Eli's concern about being arrested. "Unfortunately, you do have to give them back. But you can file charges against the guy who sold them to you, and you can file a lawsuit to get your money back."

"That'd probably cost me as much in lawyers' fees as I'm out." Eli shrugged.

I narrowed my eyes. He seemed way too relaxed about letting thousands of dollars disappear. "What did Max charge you, if you don't mind telling me?"

"Fifteen hundred dollars." Eli stared at me as if waiting for a reaction, and he got one, no doubt.

I raised my arms with a glare intended for Max, who wasn't even there. "That idiot. Seriously . . ."

Rodri looked at me. "Are they worth *that* much more?"

Eli and I simultaneously said yes and then stopped and looked at each other.

"I could probably get close to five grand for the collection of those ones I named," I said, suddenly aware that Eli's gaze was traveling from my boots up my legs. "The rest aren't expensive, but they're old favorites . . . reminders—"

"You might get seven for the whole collection," Eli interrupted.

"So then, one could say—in a way—you knew you'd gotten a steal, huh?" That came out flirtier than intended or appropriate, and Eli's slow smile stirred a slight flutter.

With a half shrug, he said, "Let me grab them for you."

"Need a hand?" Rodri asked.

"Sure." Eli held open the screen door.

"I'll help, too." I stepped inside without an invitation, eager to see my babies. Eli didn't object.

His place smelled homey—like coffee and fresh bread—maybe with a hint of pine. Hardwood floors and oak wainscot added an extra cozy warmth. Mo would love to curl up on that comfy-looking garnet-colored sofa and stare out the window, though the rest of the furnishings were unremarkable. Eli kept his home neat, but not in the sterile way I could feel in my sister's clean house. But what struck me most were the guitars. At least six that I could see: four acoustic, two electric.

Lots of people thought they had stuff to say, but artists—creative people—actually dug into the big questions about life and love. Maybe I hoped hanging out with them would reveal answers I still hadn't found. I wondered what Eli could teach me, then reminded myself of my quest to figure out my own life.

Eli couldn't teach me squat about myself, so I'd simply be grateful that the decent man with a beautiful face was handing me back my property without a fight.

"Over here." Eli motioned for us to follow him to the dining room, where the albums remained neatly placed on the floor as if awaiting a permanent home. I teared up with relief.

We each hefted a crate and marched them out to the squad car and carefully set them in the trunk.

Rodri shook Eli's hand first. "Thanks for cooperating. You should file some kind of report or claim, even if only in small-claims court."

I didn't disagree, but I also didn't want Eli to waste his time or more money. "I hate to say it, but Max is broke, so even if Eli got a judgment, I doubt he'd see any money. Max gambled and lost the money he got from the sale." I grimaced. "Sorry."

Eli nodded, looking at me with that half smile, like nothing about this was worth getting too upset about. "It's fine. It's half my fault. Like you said, I should've asked more questions when he charged me so little."

I stuck my hand out, admiring him for being a stand-up guy during a week when it'd be easy to give up on men. "Thank you for making this easy on me. I'm beyond relieved to get them back but feel terrible leaving you with nothing. I don't have money, but I make bath products—all organic—and I teach yoga. If you want free soaps or yoga instruction, I'm your girl. Call me anytime. My name is Erin Turner."

When I caught Rodri's eyes rolling upward, heat rose in my cheeks. I hadn't meant to be so eager.

Eli grabbed my outstretched hand with both of his. "Thanks. I'll keep that in mind."

Everything about his manner put me at ease. In a way, his calm acceptance reminded me of my father.

"I need to get back to the station." Rodri tugged at my arm.

My stubborn legs resisted, but Rodri had been a good friend today, so I forced myself to comply.

"Bye!" My voice sounded like a seventh grader with a terrible crush. Good God, how humiliating.

As Rodri drove away, I found myself humming "Here Comes the Sun" for no particular reason. No doubt this day would make its way into Mom's memory jar. An unexpected good memory in the middle of a lousy week.

This had to be a sign—a good sign.

Things would get better for my sister and me.

I just knew it.

CHAPTER SEVEN

AMANDA

For every high, there was now a low.

An hour ago, a recent deed for property in Broward County, Florida, arrived in my inbox. It had taken Lyle a couple of days to make good on his promise, but it had come. Thank God. I'd sent it to Stan, breathing easier for the first time in days. My marriage remained an open question, but at least my husband wasn't a thief. Once he got investors, my mom would be okay again, even if I never was.

Then, thirty minutes ago, my mother's next-door neighbor, Mrs. Morton, had called me after she'd found my mother passed out near the mailbox. She'd also called the EMTs, who'd arrived before I did. Mom's pulse and blood pressure were fine, and they'd found no serious injuries but suggested we monitor her for signs of a mild concussion. Meanwhile, my heart had yet to resume its normal rhythm.

My mother signed the Refusal of Medical Aid form and handed it back to the female EMT while the male finished packing the blood pressure cuff. I thanked them for their thorough exam before they closed the ambulance doors.

"Oh my goodness, Amanda. I'm so embarrassed." My mother covered her face as the vehicle pulled away from the curb. My brain could scarcely keep pace with the gauntlet of little disasters life had thrown at us Turner women lately. But words rarely helped someone as much as a hug did, and since no words came to mind anyway, I wrapped my arms around her.

Neither of us liked being a public spectacle, so we broke apart quickly. The vacant look in Mom's eyes had become more frequent this past week. Although I now felt confident she'd be repaid, the guilt over putting her through all this remained.

I picked out a stray bit of leaf stuck in her hair before looping my arm through hers and leading her inside. We'd not fully recovered from losing my dad, making my mother's downward spiral that much more painful to watch.

With my hand pressed gently on her back, I said, "Sit and rest while I straighten up."

"I can help." She bent to pick up a throw pillow that had fallen off the sofa.

"You just fainted, Mom. Please let me do this small thing for you."

While she fussed with the pillow, all I could think about was that this pattern couldn't continue.

With a heavy sigh, she pulled at the hem of her favorite day dress— navy with white flowers, bought last spring. "I got a grass stain."

That much I *could* fix. "Go change and I'll spray it for you."

"I think I want to lie down." She rubbed her temple, reminding me uneasily of the possibility of a concussion.

"I'm not sure it's a good idea to sleep right now."

"I'm exhausted, Amanda. I'm not sleeping at night." She turned and walked toward her room, waving over her shoulder while I shoveled another pile of blame onto mine. "Let me take a catnap . . . Wake me in fifteen minutes."

I supposed that couldn't hurt, and no one could withstand the silent pleading of the bags beneath her eyes. I followed her to her bedroom, where she kicked off her shoes, changed into a cozy tracksuit, and lay on the bed.

"Fifteen minutes." I grabbed the stained dress from the end of her mattress, then closed her door and went to the laundry area to apply a stain remover. On my way to the kitchen, I collected two discarded mugs and a plate. A cold, burned potpie sat on the counter near the sink. Had it been out all night? I sniffed it, wrinkled my nose, and scraped most of the contents of the pan into the trash.

Through the window above the sink, the swaying of the sycamore branches at the edge of the backyard drew me into a trance. Twice in one week my mom had burned food, and now a random collapse? I swayed, dizzy because the person who'd been my rock was crumbling like she had in the weeks following Dad's funeral.

Oh, how she'd shrieked when Erin had suggested we cremate Dad and toss his ashes in the bay. For days after, she'd barked at us for the smallest reason.

But much worse were the weeks that followed. Quiet, long days when she'd refused to dress or shower. When I'd stopped by at random times to find her napping or crying. Kevin had temporarily taken over handling her bills for her, but she rebuffed my offer to pack up Dad's things for three months.

Yet even with that erratic behavior I'd never sensed her being a danger to herself. Not like now. This mental fog seemed rapid, but then again, perhaps I'd missed it unfolding under my nose exactly like I'd missed Lyle's affair.

I might cry if I had any tears left. Tears hadn't helped me anyway, and they sure wouldn't help my mother.

The last bits of gravy and peas fell into the sink as I rinsed the pie pan before putting it in the dishwasher. Like pieces of my life, the mess circled the drain and disappeared while I watched it happen.

I shook out my hands, which had balled into fists, and got to work. Within ten minutes I'd finished loading the dishwasher, wiped the counters, refolded the throw blanket, fluffed the sofa cushions, and vacuumed the living room. The instant gratification restored some sense of control, and perhaps offered a bit of penance, too.

Mom clearly needed some TLC, so I fixed her favorite turkey and Dijon sandwich. After pouring a glass of diet soda and rinsing a cluster of grapes, I took the plate to the dining table, where the place setting for one pinched my heart.

If I closed my eyes and concentrated, my dad's deep voice and pleasant chuckle still echoed off the walls. Mom used to complain about the nonstop music and the tinkering noises coming from the basement or garage, but now she probably missed those things the same way I'd been missing the otherwise annoying sneeze from Lyle's seasonal allergies.

Out of the blue, I recalled the morning of my wedding. I'd slept in my old room and gotten dressed here, too. My mother had gone from pressing Erin's bridesmaid gown—which had gotten wrinkled lying at the bottom of Erin's closet for weeks—to helping fasten the myriad tiny buttons up the spine of my dress.

"How do I look?" I'd asked my mother and Erin once my veil was in place. "Too much?"

Lyle and I had decided on a church service, with my siblings serving as the best man and maid of honor because he would have no family in attendance.

Mom clutched her chest. "Perfectly gorgeous."

I looked at Erin, which wasn't easy given her rather open distaste for Lyle. She winked. "You look like a picture-perfect cake topper."

Mom tossed her an annoyed look and then opened the bedroom door so I could go out to the living room, where Kevin, Marcy, and Dad were waiting. It was one of the few times in my life where I'd had my dad's undivided attention. He teared up upon seeing me in a fluff of white silk and organza, then gently hugged me so as not to muss my gown and makeup. "My beautiful little star, you could not be any prettier. I hope Lyle treasures you as we do."

He winked then, much like my sister had.

Now, not even two years later, I stood in that very spot in the living room—my mother a widow, myself on the verge of divorce. While I'd give anything for my father to be alive, I was glad he never saw what had become of my marriage.

When I went to wake my mother, she looked puny in a bed that seemed too large without my dad there to fill the other side.

I touched her shoulder. "Mom."

Her eyes opened. "Amanda?" While she reoriented, I noticed the sleep-aid pill bottle on the nightstand and frowned.

"I forgot you were here." She pushed herself upright.

I shook the bottle of pills. "Have you been taking a lot of these lately?"

She nodded. "I told you I'm having trouble sleeping."

"I didn't realize it was *this* bad." I returned the bottle to the nightstand.

"It started after your father died, but it's gotten worse lately." She slipped her feet into her slippers.

She didn't need to say the words for me to assume the blame. Lately, lugging guilt around was my full-time job.

"When was the last time you took one?" I crossed my arms.

"This morning around seven, but only because I didn't get a wink of sleep last night. I finally dozed off for a bit this morning, but maybe the pill hadn't fully worn off by the time I went to the mailbox." She must've sensed my concern, because she got defensive. "I'm not overmedicating, Amanda. I'm fine. Everything is fine."

"This time," I almost said, but didn't want to further agitate her.

"Understood." Food should help absorb whatever drugs remained floating around her system, so I grabbed her hand. "I made you a sandwich. Come eat."

She looked at me as if I were walking her into some kind of trap, but she relented. "Thank you, honey. That was thoughtful."

Well, almost everyone would say I was nothing if not thoughtful. What they didn't know was how I sometimes wondered if loneliness drove my compulsive need to please others as much as kindness did.

The starkness of that solitary place setting struck again. "I'll sit with you."

Meals for one sucked—to borrow my sister's vernacular. It occurred to me, sitting with my mother now, that I should've invited her over for dinner more often this past year. Without Dad's company or her old job, each hour had to feel like a month. She took daily morning walks with her buddy Lorraine Dahill and volunteered for a few hours each week at the town library, but that left many hours to fill.

I'd been too consumed with my own grief and then my pregnancy to have considered how she might've enjoyed company in the evening. I didn't like to admit that . . . not when I'd always thought of myself as considerate.

"Aren't you hungry?" She took her seat with a cared-for smile that softened the knot in my stomach.

"I ate already," I lied. Since finding out about Lyle's affair, my appetite had pulled a disappearing act. Amazing how well one could subsist on prenatal vitamins and the minimum amount of protein needed to support Muffin's healthy growth.

My mind wandered in the ensuing silence. My mother needed a new hobby or a roommate, or both. Under other circumstances, I might've asked Aunt Dodo to come for an extended visit. Now, that would only intensify my mother's stress.

The preschool term ended soon, and then I'd have time for daily visits, when I could also help with housework. But an hour or two per day wouldn't protect her from burning pots and fainting spells, and I had much to do to prepare for the baby. Mom would be offended by the suggestion of in-home health care.

I needed Erin's help.

Not an easy solution, given the way those two bickered. In truth, I'd never understood why they couldn't at least bond over their mutual love for Dad. *All* our lives would be easier if their relationship improved.

I couldn't do anything about Lyle's affair, but I could help my mom and my sister to get closer—literally and figuratively. The fact that it would help me out didn't hurt, either. "You know, Erin must be pretty lonely without Max."

My mother continued chewing—a reluctant nod her only acknowledgment. Success would depend on me tiptoeing through a minefield.

"Isn't her lease up soon?" I asked.

Mom shrugged. "I have no idea. Why?"

"I guess I've been thinking about how she and I were both betrayed, but at least I have a close relationship with you. Without Dad around, Erin's sort of on her own."

Mom snorted. "It's not like we ban her from our lives. She keeps us at arm's length."

"I only meant that she's alone, and we both know that's not easy."

"You're sweet to worry about her, honey. She can surely use all the help she can get." She took another bite of the sandwich.

I'd spent my childhood doing everything to avoid being the target of that kind of dig. At least this time Erin hadn't been here to hear it. It must've been exhausting brushing off those comments day after day.

On a positive note, Mom's wisecrack had given me an opening. While I didn't know the details of my sister's finances, she could probably use a financial break. "Actually, *you* could do her a big favor if you let her move in with you for a while to save some money while she figured out her next steps . . ."

I didn't make eye contact, feigning nonchalance.

"You're kidding, right?" She frowned. "If I offer help, she'll accuse me of thinking she can't hack it on her own."

True enough, but I had a solution for that, too. One I wouldn't share with Mom, though. I only had to convince her to let Erin move in. "For the sake of argument, if she said yes, would you be okay with that?"

My mom took another bite while thinking. Her serious contemplation suggested she might be even lonelier than I presumed. "I do like her little dog."

Oof. The dog, not her daughter? What if my plan backfired and drove them further apart? Maybe this was a mistake.

Mom continued, "I suppose it wouldn't hurt if she moved in for a while. William would offer if he were here . . ."

With no time to waffle, I nodded, knowing my dad's wishes would cinch this side of the equation. "Daddy would love that."

My mom balled up her napkin. "This will sound silly, but sometimes I get so mad at him for dying on me. How often did I beg him to quit smoking? But those cigarettes were more important to him than we were. If he were here, I'd kill him for leaving me too soon. Nothing is the same without him."

I couldn't begrudge her the reflexive need to blame someone or something for her pain. Some losses are simply too infinite to accept. I'd been sewing a quilt for our guest room when my mother had called with the news. Lyle had been in his office but came to check on me when he heard me sobbing. He'd gathered me in his arms despite my fists slamming against his chest. When I finally collapsed against him in a puddle of tears, I'd had two thoughts. One was wondering whether my dad had ever realized how much I'd wanted to be closer to him. The second was that at least I'd had Lyle, who loved me as I was, unlike my less fortunate sister, who'd been dating Max, a man I knew could never come close to being a substitute for our father. How ludicrous I'd been to not know that *no* man would ever fill that void.

Patting my mother's wrist, I said, "I miss him, too, Mom."

She squeezed my hand. "Let's change the subject."

Okay, then.

Since Lyle went rogue, our conversations had been strained like this one, with each of us walking a wide circle around frightening questions that didn't have clear answers. This must be how Erin felt with Mom—always careful and at a loss for safe topics. "I noticed your tulips."

"Let's hope the deer don't eat them all." She wiped her mouth with the crumpled napkin. "Thank you for tidying up and making my sandwich, but I'm fine now. You should rest while you can. You'll need strength when the baby comes."

Color had returned to her face and she seemed alert, so I took her up on her suggestion. "Promise you'll call if you start to feel woozy."

"I'm fine. But, yes, I'll call if anything changes."

"Okay. And what did you decide about Erin? If I float the idea by her, would you let her move in?"

"Sure. We should be able to manage a few months without killing each other, and it'll deter Dodo from visiting." Her joking was a sign she might even secretly be looking forward to it.

"Great." I had to get to Erin before Mom changed her mind. "I have a ham at home if you want to stop over for dinner."

"Maybe."

Equivocation on a dinner invitation—rare indeed. "I'll call you later."

If I warned Erin of my arrival, she might put me off, so I drove the few blocks to her place. Before entering the decrepit building, I drew in a deep breath, which I held all the way past that second floor. There weren't words for that crazy cat lady's apartment stench.

When I knocked on Erin's door, Mo went berserk. Erin's laughter drifted into the hallway while she called him her crazy MoMo. She must've peered through the peephole, because there was a pronounced pause before she opened the door. "What's wrong?"

I bent down to scratch Mo's ears. "Do you have a few minutes? Something happened today, and I could use some help."

She made a face and stared at the stairwell window behind me. "Are pigs flying?"

"What?" I turned to look, confused.

"You want *my* help?" she asked, then smiled. It surprised me that it could make her this happy when she never seemed to care much for my opinion. "Come on in."

"Thanks." I scanned the room for a clean place to set my bag before giving up and leaving it on the floor by the door. Only then did I recognize an old Bruce Springsteen song playing in the background, laced with the distinct sound of vinyl. "Did you get the records back?"

"Yes!" She nodded. "I tracked Max down in New Jersey and threatened him, so he gave me the name of the guy he'd sold them to."

Only Erin would take risks and make threats to resolve her problems. "How could you confront that guy by yourself? That's dangerous."

She rolled her eyes. "I'm not *that* stupid. Rodri came with me, but that hadn't been necessary. Eli was awesome."

Her sudden smile hinted at something more than mere gratitude. "Eli?"

"Eli Woodruff. He lives here in town." She wrapped her arms around her waist, swaying. "Very chill and understanding. He was hot, too. I know it's not the time to start up with someone new, but there is something about him that presses my buttons."

Her moving on from a long-term relationship faster than Speedy Gonzales reminded me of Lyle, prompting a burst of anger. "Did he ask you out?"

"No. We barely talked. Like I said, Rodri was there, so it was all about the albums. I did get a peek inside his place. It's super cozy. You'd like it—very tidy." She gesticulated like she was re-creating the space in her head.

"Does he have a girlfriend?"

"No idea, but it sounds like you hope so." She frowned. "I really didn't get a chance to learn much, but I think he's sad about something. He looked a little sad, anyway, but I could be wrong."

At times, my sister's severe hair, piercings, and such made her appear intimidating, even threatening. But her animated musing made her very attractive, even if I envied the sweet rush of a new crush. "What's he look like?"

"A '90s-era Jared Leto. And there were guitars everywhere. I saw at least six."

"Another musician." I hoped my eyes hadn't rolled again, but, truly, hadn't she learned her lesson with Max?

"I have no idea, but I know what you're thinking. A—you're wrong, this guy's not like Max. He has his own house and he lives like a grown-up. He looks a little older, too . . . maybe Kevin's age. And B—I'm not seriously looking."

"So you don't plan on calling him?" My sister was bold that way, unlike me. I always waited to be asked.

"Wow. I see you've taken a crash course in interrogation from Mom."

"I'm not interrogating," I said, although maybe I was. "I'm curious, that's all."

"Well, I offered to make him free soaps or give him free private yoga lessons, since he lost his money on the albums. If he tracks me down, I'll see what happens." With that, Mo came over and jumped on her. She scooped him into her arms. "Oh, don't worry, Fluff. You'll always be the real love of my life."

Lyle was allergic to cats and said dogs were babies that never grew up. But I liked both. If I had a pet now, maybe I wouldn't be so lonely. I glanced around Erin's apartment, which hadn't much clear floor space. "Maybe I should help you straighten up in case he wants to come do yoga?"

Erin glowered. "No. This is me in all my glorious mess. Either he likes me or he doesn't. I won't pretend to be you to impress him."

"I doubt he'd be impressed by me. Especially lately." Nobody would.

"Well, he hasn't called, so clearly he isn't impressed by me, either. Guess we're both having a losing streak lately." She laughed at her off-hand remark, which told me she didn't mean it as an insult. It hurt anyway. "Besides, my main focus is on myself and my business, so love will have to wait. But what's this help you need from me?"

"Oh, that." I'd almost forgotten the reason I came. It had been nice to think about something other than Lyle and Mom for a few minutes. "Can we sit?"

"Want some iced tea?" She set Mo back on the floor and trotted over to the refrigerator. Mo followed and stopped at his water bowl.

"Sure." I sat at the little dining table. One end had enough clean space for a couple of glasses. The rest was covered with all kinds of products, some of which smelled like pine and citrus. Both were better than the patchouli odor that had clung to Max like a second skin. "You know, with school ending soon, I'd be happy to help you organize Shakti Suds. Maybe I could help you with a newsletter, too? I've done a lot of them for the nursery school."

Erin handed me a glass before taking a seat beside me. "Maybe, but let's talk about why you came over."

Once again she ignored my offer of help. Our long-standing dynamic.

"Well." I sipped my tea, working out the best opening. "The EMTs were at Mom's today."

Erin lurched forward. "Why?"

"She's fine now . . . sorry. I should've led with that." Her panic threw me. Erin put up such a good front of not caring that I sometimes forgot it couldn't be true. "Mrs. Morton found her passed out beside her mailbox. She'd fainted. No major injuries."

"Why did she call you when I live closer?" Erin scowled.

I suspected because I ran into Mrs. Morton regularly when stopping by our mom's, but I didn't want to escalate hurt feelings. "I'd given her my number after Dad died . . . for emergencies."

"Oh." Erin sat back. "Does Mom faint a lot?"

"Not that I've ever known."

"Well, lately she's been more stressed than usual." Erin didn't say more, but I guessed we were both thinking about Lyle and the loan.

"I'm getting concerned." I risked another glimpse of my sister. "I know she's only sixty-two, but she's still grieving Dad's death—"

"Of course she is," Erin interrupted. "I still am and probably always will."

"As will I." My chin tipped up, resenting the implication that her being Dad's favorite meant she grieved him more than I did. "All I'm saying is that with this extra financial stress . . . I think she's alone too much."

"What's being alone have to do with her fainting?"

"I think loneliness is affecting her—she's not sleeping and eating well."

She nodded, tapping her fingernails on the table. "You don't like being alone, either. How are you holding up?"

Dissecting myself had not been the purpose of my visit, yet I needed to talk to *someone*. Mom wasn't an option, and I refused to go outside the family in case Lyle decided to come home. That left me with no choice but to take a leap of faith. "So-so."

Erin listened to my update about Lyle's phone call, his indecision, the flowers, and the deed. If I'd expected her to see anything positive or hopeful, I'd be disappointed.

"What a dick—keeping you on the hook like that. Making out like he's the poor 'torn' victim, then sending you *flowers*? Total BS." She grabbed my hand. "You know, this is his loss. Tell me you know that and then walk away."

I shrugged, unable to lie. The end of my marriage seemed very much my loss.

Erin released my hand and stroked my arm. "Amanda, look at me. None of this is your fault."

"Isn't it?" I blinked my watery eyes. "I missed all the signs."

My sister's face drained of color, which didn't make sense. I braced for her to say something else that would inadvertently hurt me.

"You're not the only one who ignored signs. We both did." Her gaze wandered as she got lost in her thoughts, but her contrite expression didn't make sense. She had nothing to do with my marriage. I was about to ask her about it when she continued, "Look at me with Max. I left him alone in my apartment after we broke up. Trusted him to be a good guy, pack his own things, and go. Yet he stole from me. Is that my fault?"

"Of course not."

"*Exactly.* Don't take the blame for Lyle's behavior." She wrinkled her nose before asking, "Even if he sent flowers and a deed, he's still down there with another woman. Why are you still interested in saving your marriage?"

The leaden feeling returned, sinking me in a murky lake of emotion. Erin said the word "marriage" as if it were some abstract concept, which to her it was. But to me it was my life. My place. My everything. How could I *not* want to save it?

I laid my hands on my stomach. "I've read about couples surviving infidelity. And my baby . . ." My voice croaked as the biggest fear surfaced. Lyle might be distracted by lust now, but someday he would want a presence in our child's life. "I don't want to split her holidays and birthdays and summers. I don't want to miss a single moment of her life."

Erin stared at me for what seemed like a long time. Her resigned expression proved she neither understood nor condemned me. "I know it's hard for you to let go of the perfect picture in your head, but you don't need him, Amanda. You're so much better than he ever was."

The compliment—while surprisingly lovely—didn't make it easier to hear criticism about someone I'd cared about. "I loved him. Loved my life with him. Waking up snuggled close. Sharing meals and walks and dreams. And he did things you never saw, like handing a homeless man his coat on a cold night, or the money he gave Jed Symons to help with bills when he was out of work last year." At that point I stopped. Bombarding her with words wouldn't convince my sister of how happy I'd been, or of the sense of peace his love had given me, because she'd never liked Lyle. Yet I wouldn't pretend I didn't yearn to recapture those feelings.

"There are other guys out there who can snuggle, talk, walk, and help you raise your daughter. Heck, maybe even one who will make you laugh. I don't recall ever hearing you and Lyle laugh, and that makes me sad. Don't you want to laugh?"

We'd laughed. Maybe not the kind of belly laughs that made soda spit from your mouth, but Lyle and I shared lots of little inside jokes, like when he'd mimic that BatDad guy from YouTube he weirdly idolized. It was so out of character it always made me laugh. Or the way he'd sing-talk in the mornings, as if we were actors in a musical. He woke up playful, which was a nice way to start each day. In any case, if I had to choose between belly laughs and security, I'd choose the latter. Then again, Lyle had hardly left me with a sense of security. "I think it's safe to say we're not looking for the same things in a man."

"Really? I bet we both want someone who likes us as we are. Who gets us, supports our dreams, and, most important, is great in bed . . ." She wiggled her eyebrows.

I chuckled from surprise. "So you don't miss Max? You're not even a little lonely here by yourself?"

"Not really." She paused, wrecking my grand plan. "If anything, I wish I'd dumped him before he dwindled my bank account. I'm not sure I can afford to sign a new lease this month, which puts me in a bind. I mean, there aren't many cheaper places in town that lack hypodermic needles lying about, you know?" She laughed and gulped some tea.

I didn't find her predicament funny. It did, however, confirm that my plan would benefit both her and my mom. "Maybe there's a solution that could help you and Mom, although you could never tell her that we cooked it up together."

"Cooked what up?" Her gaze narrowed.

"Well, what if you moved back home for a couple of months? You'd save money, and you could help me make sure Mom doesn't hurt herself or get too depressed. I mean, with Dad gone, she's lonely."

"Mom and me under one roof without a buffer won't work. She barely likes me." That belief—the sole crack in Erin's confident armor—made a brief appearance before she shrugged it off. Years ago I might've considered her attitude babyish. After all, I dealt with her being Dad's favorite forever without complaining. But now I understood the difference. Dad might not have adored me as he did Erin, but he never picked on me as Mom did my sister.

"That's not true. She just doesn't understand why you don't care about her opinions. And you aren't exactly patient with her, either. Maybe it'd be good for you two to spend this time together."

Erin stared into space. "I mean, it is pretty bad if she's passing out in the yard."

"And burning pots on the stove."

"Really?" Erin grimaced. "That's dangerous."

"I know. But she can never know we think she needs a babysitter. Can you let her believe she's doing *you* the favor—financially?" I flashed my most pleading eyes. "We already lost Dad. I don't want something to happen to Mom, too."

Erin stretched her arms across the table and pressed her forehead to its surface before pulling back. "I could use an extra six hundred bucks in my pocket each month, but, my God, I can't imagine living in that house without Dad."

We stared at each other for a beat or two, tethered by silent, shared heartache.

I cleared my throat before patting her hand. "That'll be hard. But you both loved him so much. Start with that common ground."

Erin was close to capitulating. I could feel it, and I wasn't prone to that sort of thing.

She shook her head. "I couldn't take the humiliation or her rejection."

"Let me broach it like it's my idea. I think she'll actually enjoy feeling useful . . . and it'd just be until she gets back to normal."

"If she and I don't kill each other first." Erin rolled her eyes.

"I'll be the ref."

"Refs are supposed to remain neutral . . ." She cocked a brow at me, calling me out for often taking Mom's side. "Gosh, I don't know. My stomach's already queasy from the thought."

"Dad would want us to watch out for her." I'd never been this manipulative, but Erin couldn't resist that plea. She'd thank me later.

She glanced at Mo, who'd climbed up onto the back of the sofa to stare out the window. "Mo would love the fenced-in backyard and the shade of the sycamore."

I felt a pang because when she and Dad had planted it eons ago, he'd envisioned lazy summer days in its shade.

"Let me talk to Mom." I'd wait an hour and then call Erin with the green light. "If it works out, I'll help you pack."

"You shouldn't lift heavy stuff." She turned to scan her small apartment. "I might leave most things behind anyway. I mean, the prior tenant left that couch when I rented the place. I could sell my bed and other stuff, pocket the cash, and move into our old room for a while."

I nodded enthusiastically because I hated almost everything in this apartment. After she saved money, I'd help her shop for new—or gently used—stuff. "Okay. Let me go work some magic on Mom. I'll call you later."

She stopped me when I stood to leave. "Hold up. Have you heard back from the PI?"

"Not yet." I unbuttoned the top button of my shirt and tugged at the collar. "He's checking on the deed, among other things."

"I'm sure you'll hear something soon."

I shrugged, wishing I could feel a fraction of her eagerness, which told me something I didn't want to acknowledge about my husband and our relationship.

"I'm sorry. I wish I . . ." She hesitated, appearing to weigh her words. "I wish this wasn't happening to you. You don't deserve it."

This was the second time she'd been almost desperately gentle with me, yet I felt more embarrassed than pleased.

"Fairness never factors much into my life." That wasn't sour grapes but a simple acknowledgment that I'd worked harder for things most other people took for granted. "Meanwhile, Lyle should've been home days ago. People are asking questions, making it hard to keep the truth quiet."

"Why hide it?"

"Initially, I didn't want to complicate a reconciliation. I'm losing faith in that hope, but it hurts to admit that to myself, let alone talk about it with others."

"Won't your friends support you?"

Friends? As I said, things others take for granted don't come easily to introverts like me. "Not without judgment . . . and pity." I averted my gaze.

"Screw them, then. They aren't real friends."

I tilted my head, certain she missed the irony. "Even you have judgment and pity."

She laughed while holding up her thumb and forefinger. "Only a little. But you shouldn't have to hide. Call Lyle out for *his* behavior. Make *him* the object of disgust."

"Except I'll bear the brunt of all the censure and gossip while he's off in Florida, despite the fact that I didn't do anything wrong."

"That's Mom's fear talking. Break through that noise."

I stiffened. "I'm not ready."

Erin grunted something. "Am I allowed to full-out hate Lyle yet, or is it too soon? 'Cause I really want to hurt him."

"Sometimes I do, too." I let the shock of that fan through me. "One second I'm fantasizing about cutting up his sports coats and burning his pictures, then the next breath I'm hugging his clothes and crying."

Erin set a hand on my shoulder. "When you're ready for the bonfire, call me."

I dabbed my eye and chuckled. "Thanks."

"Anytime. Now, before you go, I have one favor to ask."

Uh-oh. "Shoot."

"Would that PI do some digging on Eli?"

"No!"

"I'm kidding." She batted my arm. "I mean, I'd love the scoop on the guy, but I'd never spy on him. Once I've got a plan for Shakti Suds, maybe I'll find another way to learn his secrets."

I remembered the time she took a job with Molly Maids to get inside a guy's house. Her plan had backfired when she used Clorox Clean-Up with bleach on his marble countertops. "Don't do anything rash."

The diamond chip in her nose glinted. "But that's the best way to do most things."

CHAPTER EIGHT

ERIN

Shipping products continued to be my least favorite part of building my Etsy empire. Without a car, I'd resorted to transporting boxes to the post office in a rusty red wagon purchased last autumn at a garage sale. Not so great in the rain or snow, which required me to beg friends or family to borrow their cars. On a positive note, I lived only three-quarters of a mile from the post office. The trip to and from there did double duty as one of Mo's daily walks, and sunny days like today translated to some quality vitamin D production.

"Come on, Mo. Stop sniffing other animals' poo." I jerked the leash a tad to redirect him. Crossing the street safely with a dog in one hand and a wagon filled with boxes in the other required focus and a bit of luck.

I didn't like coming on Wednesdays because Mary worked on Wednesdays and she didn't like Mo—or any dog—inside the building. As I was of the "better to ask for forgiveness" persuasion, that didn't stop me from trying. I couldn't leave Mo tied up outside by himself.

After rolling the wagon up the handicap ramp, I shortened Mo's leash and bent to lift my three packages from the wagon. *It* wouldn't be stolen because no one would want the rickety thing.

"Erin?"

I immediately recognized the voice behind me. *Eli!* When I turned around, my heart launched into an imitation of a Neil Peart solo. "Wow, this is a surprise!"

I supposed we could've passed each other in town before without noticing. I mean, I didn't pay attention to most men, especially not while dating Max. Then again, it'd be hard to miss Eli, who looked fine this morning in belted caramel-brown khakis and a midnight-blue shirt.

He smiled. "Had to overnight something to Nashville."

"Well, it's nice to see you again." I wondered briefly if he had family there.

His gaze moved from my wagon to Mo, who sniffed him like he kept bacon in his pockets. Eli crouched to scratch my dog behind the ears and, man, was I jealous. Mo's tail wagged nonstop. Even I wanted to thump my foot with pleasure at the sight.

"Aren't you cute." Eli glanced up at me. "What's his name?"

"This is Mo. The greatest dog ever, despite being overdue for a grooming." I couldn't help my grin. Mo filled my heart with light.

"Lucky me, meeting the greatest dog ever." Eli's slow smile rose to warm me like a sunrise.

"He likes you." A fact that confirmed Mo's superior intellect. "Or you have treats in your pocket. Hard to be sure."

"No treats." Eli chuckled as he stood. "You've got your hands full. Would it help if I sat here with Mo while you take care of those packages?"

Gallant too. Like my dad.

"Would you mind? I wouldn't impose, but Mary works on Wednesdays, and she and Mo do not belong to a mutual fan club."

"Obviously Mary has her head up her . . ." Eli winked and then held out his hand for the leash.

I set my chin on top of one box in order to keep them from toppling while I transferred the leash, so I couldn't savor the electrifying brush of our fingers for near long enough. "Thanks so much. I'll be right back."

"Take your time." Eli waved me off.

Boy, postage killed my margins. A large order of sugar scrubs was heavy, and I tended to underestimate the shipping costs. If I didn't investigate better options for small businesses soon—another of the to-do items that always fell to the end of my list—Shakti Suds might die before it got off the ground.

Mary and I did our business with little joy. People like her confused the crap out of me. If you've got a job dealing with the public, why not smile? Make some small talk. Tell a joke. Anything to break the monotony for yourself, if not to enhance the customer experience. Good grief.

One by one, I pushed pennies across the counter to pay the bill. Admittedly, Mary's annoyed stare only made me go slower.

The dire state of my finances should make me rejoice about moving in with my mom in two days. *Ha!* Lots of feelings about that swarmed my thoughts, but joy had yet to appear in the lineup. A lack of privacy ranked high on my list of concerns, but not as high as the inevitable bickering.

She always corrected every single thing I did. Like when I emptied the dishwasher to be nice, but she complained about how I put away the silverware. First of all, why buy two different sets? Second, it wasn't like I put forks in the same tray as spoons, so who cared if the plain set got mixed together with the patterned set? Plain forks and fancy forks were still forks, for crying out loud. My dad had agreed with me, but then had given my mom a kiss before he redistributed the silverware to make her happy.

I pocketed my receipt, eager to set aside my moving-day concerns and return to Eli and Mo. When I got outside, I found them seated on the bench. Two pretty, young twentysomethings were flirting with him and Mo, but he wasn't encouraging them. When I came up, he smiled at me. "You're back."

The young women shuffled off.

I sat beside Eli instead of immediately taking the leash. "Thanks so much for your help. It's much easier to do that without Mo at my feet."

"You're welcome." He squinted in the sunlight. "What were all those boxes?"

"Soaps and sugar scrubs. Remember, I offered to make you some? My products are all organic. Any scent you want."

"Men buy that stuff?" His expression showed doubt.

"Sure!" Truth be told, most of my customers were women, but I could expand to new markets. "There are masculine scents made with sandalwood or bergamot or lemongrass—or a combination of those."

"That sounds nice, actually." His melancholic, kind eyes crinkled at the outer edges when he smiled. It'd be easy to get lost in those expressive teal pools.

Any other time, I'd surprise him by quickly delivering some experimental batches. But I'd promised myself that with Max gone and this move to Mom's, I'd focus on myself more, which meant I should sit on my flirtatious impulses. "I enjoy coming up with creative ideas and playing around with different molds. I'm planning a line of chamomile soaps for my soon-to-be niece. The only holdup is waiting for my sister to tell me her name so I can order a monogrammed mold."

A shadow passed over his eyes, hinting at that sadness I felt when we'd first met. I wondered what triggered it.

He continued stroking Mo, who looked content to remain nestled beside Eli's thigh. Like I said, smart dog. "Is this your first niece?"

"Yes, but I have a nephew up near Baltimore." I loved little Billy, but he didn't live here in town. "I'm superstoked to become Aunt Erin to another kid—although that name's so boring. My sister isn't a fan of my chosen nickname, though."

He smiled again—shadow erased. "What's that?"

I made a Z with my arms as if I were doing an Egyptian dance. "Zizi-E. Much more hip, don't you think?"

His eyes, which stared directly into mine for the first time today, lit with humor and, dare I say, attraction. Oh, man, I might be in trouble, because if he liked me, it would be hard to put on the brakes. "Definitely."

"How about you? Are you an uncle?"

"No." He shook his head. "I'm an only child."

I frowned on reflex. My siblings and I weren't best buds, but I also couldn't imagine childhood—or adulthood—without them. Not that there hadn't been some days when being an only child had sounded pretty good. "Does that get lonely?"

"At times. It's not all bad, though. My parents fawned on me. I never had to share their attention or resources, so I got to do things they might not have afforded if they'd had more kids."

Might I have made that trade—all my parents' attention and resources but no siblings? Riding lessons had been an unattainable childhood dream. I'd loved the look of those velvet helmets and riding pants. Horses too. But even through all the arguments and tattling, no horse would've been as good as a sister who braided my hair and a brother who drove me everywhere once he got his license.

I sometimes wished our birth orders had been different. I liked being the baby, but if Amanda had been the oldest and Kevin the middle child, he and I would've played well together. He didn't scream when I brought frogs into the house, or care if I wore my favorite pajama pants to the park. But without a doubt, the worst part of being an only child in the Turner home would've been being the sole object of my mother's scrutiny. Thank *God* Amanda gave her one daughter she could be proud of.

I looked at Eli, curious about childhood days without siblings to bicker and play with. "What kinds of things?"

He raised one shoulder in a half shrug. "Great summer camps in faraway places. Music lessons."

That did sound nice. None of us Turners ever got to take private lessons at anything, although we'd played sports for town and school teams, and we'd had all the basics—fishing rods and bikes and skateboards. Best of all, we'd had our dad, who made the best homemade kettle corn, gave the biggest hugs, and laughed as easily as I did. "I noticed all the guitars in your house. Are you a professional musician or a hobbyist?"

As soon as the crease appeared between his eyebrows, I wanted to rub it away. "I was a songwriter."

He'd mentioned sending a package to Nashville. "'Was'?"

A truck shifted gears on its way up the hill behind us, its low rumble like a thunderous warning.

"Been taking some time away from it all." He didn't need to say more for his tone to tell me that whatever drove him to step back wasn't something he would discuss. "Spent more than a year traveling around Asia before moving here recently."

"Why Asia?"

"I needed to immerse myself in something completely different—a whole new culture, new foods, new topography."

Sounded like he'd gone on a sort of spiritual journey. If I had the money, maybe I'd take off for parts unknown to speed up my own evolution. "So what brought you here?"

"An old friend. He's taken over his parents' business—a music bar and restaurant called the Lamplight."

"You know Phil?" The bar owner, Phil, was Kevin's age, but they weren't close. Kev had been an athlete, not a quiet kid like Phil, who'd been into deejaying in high school. If I recalled correctly, Phil had gone to school at Belmont to learn the music business—which would have sounded like an awesome plan to me if only I had liked school—so I'd thought it a little sad when he ended up coming home last year. But then I'd learned that his dad was sick—MS or something—and his mom had needed help. Now Eli's connection to Clyde—who played there and helped Max book some gigs on open-mic nights—made more sense, too.

"*You* know Phil?"

"Everyone knows that family and the Lamplight, especially those of us who love music, which I do. Mad kind of love—as you probably guessed from my albums. I think songwriters are the most talented storytellers on the planet." The statement brought my dad to mind so sharply I felt a twinge. "Did you perform your own stuff, or write for others?"

"Both, but mostly I sold my songs."

"Anything I'd know? And bear in mind I know a lot of songs, not only the pop stuff most people hear on the radio."

He graced me with another of his wide, appreciative smiles. "'Come 'Round Home' and 'Only You' got a lot of play." He looked at the ground like he'd been caught bragging, but I almost shot off the bench.

"Brad Peyton's hits?" I loved good country music, especially when sung by a bass with a rich vibrato. "Wow! I'm super impressed now. Where do you get your inspiration?"

That shadow came racing back to his eyes. He was bent over, elbows on his knees, fingertips tapping together. "Let's just say it's lost now."

The air around us got heavy, like the thickness that settles in before a storm, except the sky remained blue and sunlight poured over us. I hadn't been wrong about that sorrow I'd sensed, although the scope of it seemed bigger than I'd originally guessed. A divorce maybe? Or like me, a beloved parent snatched away. God knows I'd slept more during the first six months after my dad died than I had in the six prior years combined.

I probably should've kept my big trap shut, but I couldn't stop myself. "You know, I'm not the smartest person. In fact, my family would tell you my life is a hot mess. But the one thing I do know is that nothing lasts forever—not the good or the bad. Whatever's got you blocked, I hope you find new inspiration soon. I know you will, actually. Probably when you least expect it."

I looked away then, choosing to focus on Mo and his kisses. Kisses I might rather get from Eli—let's be honest.

Eli didn't say much except to mumble a quiet thanks before he stretched his legs and rose from our bench. "Well, I'd better let you get back to your day. Nice bumping into you, Erin."

My heart sank to my toes when he effectively ended our conversation. Apparently, he didn't want a pep talk.

"Thanks again for your help. First you get ripped off by my ex, next you dog-sit free of charge. My IOUs are piling up." I subdued the instinct to grab his shoulders for a quick hug, settling for a wave. "See you around!"

He offered a casual salute as his final goodbye. I told myself it was for the best. I had a move to deal with anyway.

All in all, still the best post-office run ever.

Take that, Mary!

———

"You guys rock." I high-fived Lexi's boyfriend, Tony. Not only had he let me borrow his pickup to move my stuff, but he'd also helped carry the few pieces of furniture I kept.

Mom had been anxious, telling me where I could and couldn't put my things. I couldn't really get mad. It was her house. At least she didn't mind watching after Mo while my friends helped me unload the truck.

To avoid winding through the house and down the narrow basement stairs, we'd brought my boxes and furniture through the basement slider in the back. For the time being, most of my nonessentials would remain stored in the unfinished part of the basement so they'd be easy to move again when I found a new apartment.

"No problem, E." Tony mopped his brow with his forearm, then patted Lexi's butt. "Meet you in the truck?"

"Be there in a sec," she said. Once he'd gone, my best friend spun around. "You know, this finished part of the basement could be a great little yoga studio."

Intrigued, I surveyed the level rectangular room. My dad and I had upgraded the flooring about seven years ago with laminate, so it would be durable, easy to clean, and soft beneath the feet. Natural light from the sliders flooded the space, and if I hung some crystals near the doors, they'd cast little rainbows everywhere. "You're right, Lex."

"If you move some of those pieces against the walls, you'll clear enough floor space for five or six students." She rested her hands on her hips, nose wrinkled. "Man, I'd kill for a free place to do private lessons."

"Don't envy me. I'd have to convince my mom to let me invite 'strangers' to the house, which isn't a slam dunk." If Amanda asked, it would be, but our mom trusted her judgment more than mine. Come to think of it, considering the Lyle situation, Mom probably wouldn't trust Amanda now, either. Being downgraded had to sting.

On the other hand, Dad would've been an easy sell. He'd loved when I tried new things.

No matter where my gaze fell, I saw him. Every picture. Every old fishing rod. The pea-green lounge chair he'd fought hard to keep that my mother now couldn't part with. The only thing missing—aside from him—was the scent of cigarette smoke. I didn't miss that. Anytime I smelled it, my heart hurt.

"Hm. Well, good luck. I'd better catch up with Tony. See you tomorrow!" Lexi waved and then closed the slider behind her on her way out. It sealed with a thunk, perfect for my somewhat trapped circumstance. Seeing Lex run off with Tony also reminded me of my very single status. What if I got horny? Mom wouldn't tolerate me bringing men here for sex. Could I take care of myself in the room next to my mother's without her knowing? The shower? At least I wouldn't be sharing the bathroom with my siblings this time around.

Before I got too depressed about the drawbacks, I told myself to embrace the positive. Cheap living. Doing the "right" thing by watching out for Mom. Making Dad proud. And maybe celibacy would be the key to my success.

Enough of that. I desperately needed a snack, which meant no more hiding out down here. Time to face my new roomie.

My backpack remained near the stairs. I grabbed it and took the steps two at a time to reach the kitchen quickly. Mo gave me one of his drive-by ankle licks, as if testing to make sure I was still me.

"Oh good. You finished quickly." Mom crossed to the refrigerator and pulled out a pitcher of lemonade. "Are you thirsty?"

"No thanks." I plopped onto a chair, hoping to look more relaxed than I felt, and grabbed an apple. I supposed I would have to spend time with her to monitor her wellness. "What should we do on this lovely Friday?"

She stared at the backpack I'd set on the kitchen table. "You could start by removing your backpack. That thing belongs in a closet, not as the centerpiece on my table."

And so it began.

I unzipped it. "I brought a little thank-you gift for letting me crash here for a bit." I handed her a tissue-wrapped package of three gardenia-scented soap bars and a bath oil. A bit sweet-smelling for me, but she should like it. I'd read that older people's sense of smell diminishes over time.

"Oh." She set down her lemonade, temporarily disarmed. "That's thoughtful. Thank you."

She held the gift awkwardly, like she didn't quite trust it not to explode in her hands.

"You're welcome." While I chomped on my fruit, I watched her fiddle nervously with the package while neither of us said more. Against my better judgment, I asked, "Actually, want to help me make a batch of sugar scrubs now? It's fun to experiment with different aromas. And if you like it, I can teach you to make soaps."

"Not now."

"Why not?" I wiped the apple's juice from my chin.

"Because that sounds messy and I have company coming. Why don't you go shower and then run out and do whatever it is you normally do when you're not working." She turned, setting the soaps on the counter and placing the pitcher of lemonade and glasses on a tray. Clearly she didn't want me to meet her mysterious company. So, naturally, I had to dig into that.

"Who's coming? Aunt Dodo?"

Her hands went up like a traffic cop. "No one you know."

"You're being kinda squirrelly." Was a *man* coming to visit? I didn't know how I felt about that.

"Fine." She tipped up her chin. "I've been on a wait list with a renowned medium, and an appointment opened up. I confirmed it before you set your move-in date and didn't want to reschedule. Given everything happening with your sister, I really need to speak with William."

My jaw came unhinged. Amanda hadn't exaggerated her concerns. Before I could question my mother, she hustled me out of the chair. "Now go on and shower. Please, Erin. Don't embarrass me."

I slung my backpack over my shoulder, tossed the core in the trash, and picked Mo up with my free hand. "Fine. But I want to meet this psycho."

"Psych*ic*, not psycho." She scowled.

We'd see. This would be more interesting than sitting around watching those afternoon talk shows she loved.

By the time I'd showered and dressed, the special guest had arrived. I hung back in the hallway, straining to listen, expecting that Mom might be talking about me.

An older-sounding woman said, "Madeline, remember, I'm only a vessel. I can't promise to summon anyone in particular but will pass along messages from those who want to be heard. Whoever comes through does so in love, so don't be afraid. I'm going to close my eyes, and together we can pray . . . may this session be for the higher good."

What kind of nonsense was *that*? I crept closer.

My mom said, "I'm picturing William on our wedding day—so handsome in his tux, before he got that potbelly that helped kill him."

Yeah, he could've lost fifteen pounds, but the cigarettes had nailed his coffin shut. That and maybe a little stress caused by the expense of Amanda's "fairy-tale" wedding reception. All those flowers and champagne . . . for what? Whenever I finally got married—if I did—it'd be barefoot in the backyard with only my closest peeps and Mo, and a really funky dress. And hopefully I wouldn't be facing divorce less than two years later. Not that *that* was her fault.

"Please don't say more. The less I know, the better. If I ask a question, yes/no answers are best. I'm not getting anything yet . . . or maybe . . . something about the number three?" the woman said.

"Yes! We have three children." My mom—who'd already broken the yes/no rule—sounded flabbergasted, but, seriously, anyone could look at the family photos to make that guess.

No longer worried about making a "bad" impression, I barged around the corner and set Mo on the floor. He crouched while making unusual groaning noises. Completely different behavior from how he'd greeted Eli the other day.

"Hello, ladies." I wandered over to stand behind one of the dining chairs. Before my mom said anything, I stuck out my hand to the stranger with bottle-dyed red hair. Judging from her wrinkles, I put her in her late sixties. She wore casual, loose-fitting clothes. Multiple rings bedazzled her fingers. "Hello, I'm Erin, the youngest of those three kids."

"Hello, Erin. I'm Nancy Thompson." She looked at me expectantly, as if I should be awed or at least recognize her name.

"Nice to meet you, Nancy. Can I be part of this little séance?" I held a phony smile in place while she pulled a sour face at my choice of words.

"I'm a psychic medium." She stared at me, but I wasn't about to genuflect. "We're hoping to communicate with your father."

"Sit, Erin." Mom must've decided that it'd be less embarrassing to let me participate than to argue. "Maybe William will show up if you're here."

Whenever she acknowledged my special bond with my dad, I preened even though I suspected it had made her jealous at times. Not that my dad hadn't loved her, too. He had. But he and I had laughed at nonsense jokes, hated brussels sprouts, preferred picnic tables to fancy restaurants—we simply clicked in ways that no one else in the family shared. "Great."

The look in Mom's eyes warned me to behave, so I sat with my hands folded on my lap, wondering what other surprises I'd encounter in the coming weeks. Normally, I'd applaud her broadening her horizons, but this bizarre change in behavior made me a little nervous.

"Fine. What do I do?" I turned to Nancy.

She gestured widely with her hands. "First, get comfortable and think about your father. Picture him someplace meaningful."

Hocus-pocus in my book, but this would be one of those rare times I wouldn't mind being proven wrong. I often felt my dad's presence, or at least I'd found more stray pennies this past year than normal, which Lexi told me were signs from my dad that I'm valued. It's amazing what we'll believe when desperate.

I closed my eyes; otherwise, my ability to concentrate would last about two seconds before Nancy's bling distracted me.

For some reason, the time I failed a middle school science test came to mind. Mrs. Smith had seated students by how well they scored on each test, with the first seat of the first row being the best score, and so on to the last seat of the final row. Needless to say, I'd spent most of that school year in the last two rows, but the time I landed in that dead-last seat had sucked big-time.

My mom's nonexistent sympathy hadn't surprised me, nor had her suggestion that I beg Amanda to tutor me. As if my perfect sister lording her smartness over me would've actually helped or improved my confidence.

When my dad had come home from work, my mom had lamented my failure. Instead of issuing a lecture, he'd grabbed me from my room and gotten our fishing rods. We'd walked to the closest dock—the one at the end of Autumn Lane—baited our hooks, and cast the lines, sitting with our legs dangling over the edge, toes dipped in the water.

Neither of us had been fishing seriously at that point, and we'd both known it. He had only brought me there for comfort. His sitting beside me saying nothing had been exactly the presence of love and acceptance I'd needed to help me face however many days it would be until the next test (and hopefully better results).

With Dad it had rarely been what he said—but more what he didn't say—that counted. In his quiet way, he'd let me know that that science test was only a drop of water in a giant ocean, and I shouldn't give it any more significance than I did any other thing that happened.

He'd been wearing his Ravens cap that afternoon. Why I recalled that detail, I couldn't say.

I popped one eye open to find Nancy's closed. The chestnut hairs on her arms stood on end. Mo had curled into a ball, nose tipped up, alert and sniffing the air. Nancy's rings must have mesmerized him. My mother's eyes were closed tight. Her urgent desire to "reach" my father practically bled from her pores and intensified my discomfort with participating in this farce.

"I'm getting something . . . the word 'cast' . . . ," Nancy said.

"William sold medical supplies!" my mother exclaimed, as if this were proof of anything.

"Yes or no, please." Nancy nodded, eyes now open. "Maybe William's trying to tell us something . . . or warn us of an accident."

Oh no. That would not do. My mother already worried enough without paying for false red flags. "Nancy, can I ask a question?"

She peered at me, her expression wary. "Go ahead."

I cleared my throat. "What do you charge for these readings?"

"Erin!" my mom exclaimed.

"I'm curious." I shrugged and returned my attention to Nancy.

"One hundred dollars per session."

My brows rose. "How long is a session?"

"An hour."

"And you charge that even if you don't say anything that can be directly attributed to the dead—something that can't be discovered with a quick Google search?" That had been a little rude, but I needed to wake my mom up before she burned through hundreds of dollars to learn nothing we didn't already know.

Dad was dead. None of us liked it, but a dead man couldn't help us solve our problems even if he could talk or leave us pennies. Plus he'd be plain pissed about the loan. If Nancy *could* talk to him, I hoped she wouldn't deliver that message.

"I'm a Lily Dale–accredited medium and only practice evidential mediumship." Nancy glared—a lame stab at intimidation.

That gobbledygook meant less than nothing to me, so I shrugged.

Nancy brusquely turned to my mom. "Perhaps we should stop. Negative energy is not optimal."

Well versed in the "blame it on Erin" game, I waved both hands before I further aggravated my mother.

"I'll go." I stood before being told to leave. "I've lots to do anyway, especially if I want to teach private yoga classes in the basement." My mom's head swiveled toward me, but I kept talking before she could say no. "Carry on. Say hi to Dad if you hear from him."

I took Mom's silence as tacit approval of my yoga plans. As for her pursuing this thing with Nancy, we'd discuss it later. A onetime roll of the dice seemed harmless enough, but if my mom was turning cuckoo, I'd have to tell Amanda and Kevin.

As I passed behind Nancy, I caught a whiff of her perfume, which made me stop and lean close. "Ooh, you smell good. What are you wearing?"

She looked skeptical, her brows knitted. "Tocca."

"Thanks!" I bounced away, calling for Mo to follow me to my new—old—room while looking Tocca up on my phone. Not a cheap fragrance, but I could research its notes to concoct something similar for my soaps. Maybe I'd call that line "Oracle."

I snickered at myself, 'cause, come on, that would be funny.

CHAPTER NINE

AMANDA

"You're early." I glanced over Erin's shoulder in search of my mother, whom I didn't see.

"Hello to you, too." Erin handed me my mail, wearing what I'd first thought were neon paisley microshorts until closer inspection revealed a mishmash of brightly colored skulls. "I came early to gossip a little before Mom shows up."

I suspected this newfound desire was more about escaping our mom after fifty-odd hours of living together than about talking to me. Especially as I'd grown increasingly unhinged with no word from Lyle or Stan. On TV, PI work happens in a snap. In real life, not so much.

There'd been lows—in the quiet of the evening—when I'd considered driving over to Mom's. Even the awkward tension there might be preferable to sitting alone, staring at photos, and kicking myself for having been so trusting. Each day Lyle remained in Florida with Ebba was changing me. I felt a shift, deep down, like the turn of a screw. A permanent hardening that I couldn't be sure was better for me or worse.

"Okay, but I'm in the middle of getting dinner ready." I backed up to wave her in.

Erin kicked off her shoes by the door. "I thought you were making spaghetti."

"I am."

"Don't you just boil water and open a jar?" Her quizzical tone proved she wasn't joking.

Her disinterest in cooking puzzled me, yet she existed fine on granola cereal, canned soups, sandwiches, and eggs. Lucky for her Max hadn't been particular about his diet.

"I'm making a homemade ragù." Meatballs slow cooked in the sauce, along with some pork ribs, hot sausage links, onion, and plenty of garlic. A go-to comfort food.

As she made her way down the hallway, Erin grabbed her chest. "It smells so good. I love you!"

That made me smile. With everything else going downhill, I soaked up any affirmation. "Hopefully, its taste will live up to your expectations."

Erin scrubbed one hand along the shorn side of her head. "Want me to clean lettuce?"

I hesitated. There is a proper way to clean lettuce: first you chop it into small pieces, then rinse and dry it with the spinner and crisp it in a metal bowl with paper towels to absorb any remaining water. Keeping the lettuce crisp also requires making sure that diced cucumber, tomatoes, and onions are placed at the bottom of the bowl, beneath the cleaned lettuce, so the liquid in those veggies doesn't make the lettuce soggy. Unfortunately, I'd seen Erin make a salad. She rips the lettuce in a haphazard fashion and leaves too much water on the leaves, then dumps everything on top with a dash of salt! But between questioning my perfectionism and the more crucial issues on our figurative plates, I didn't want to be a jerk about the salad.

"Sure." I tossed the mail on the counter. "There's romaine in the refrigerator."

Based on her expression, one might think I had sprouted a third eye. I supposed I didn't often accept her help.

I could admit to being particular, but I took care of my own needs and never asked others to meet them for me. A week ago, the idea that my habits might've driven Lyle away had crushed me. Now a silent rage slithered up my spine.

Erin located a knife and the salad spinner. She tossed the lettuce onto the cutting board while blurting, "Did you know Mom's paying a medium to talk to Dad?"

"What?" I dropped the wooden spoon into the pot of sauce I'd been stirring.

"Yup." Erin nodded while chopping. "I'm not sure what she expects Dad's ghost to do, but she's flushing what little money she has left down the toilet."

I closed my eyes, absorbing that blow. Erin hadn't meant to take a jab at me, but we both knew why Mom's finances were strained. "Did you tell her to stop?"

"I told her the 'medium' didn't impress me, but that just made her more determined to enjoy it. Anyway, I'm not pissing off my new landlord by telling her what to do a second time." Erin cringed, shaking her head. "But *you* could probably get away with it."

The downside of being Mom's favorite: both Kevin and Erin relied on me to approach her with anything controversial. "Level with me. How bad is it?"

"Not horrible." Erin rinsed the basket of torn leaves before giving the spinning device a half-hearted pump. I suppressed the urge to take it from her and wring the lettuce dry. "I mean, she's a little forgetful. Repeats herself more than usual. She misplaced the car keys once—left them in the fridge beside the milk. It took us an hour to find them. I found a fork in the garbage can yesterday. But she hasn't burned the house down or fainted again."

Keys in the fridge? Forks in the garbage? Plenty of mothers suffered "mommy brain" hiccups, but ours wasn't chasing toddlers. "Should we call a doctor?"

"Not yet. I mean, she *is* sixty-two. Maybe forgetfulness is normal at that age."

Maybe. I hardly trusted my judgment lately, nor would I want to insult Mom by suggesting that she was losing it.

"Are you two getting along?" I hadn't meant that to sound patronizing. Although a minuscule part of me felt threatened by the idea of Erin winning Mom over like she had Dad, I wanted only to make sure Mom wasn't beating her down.

"Well, she's letting me offer yoga lessons in the basement." She screwed up her face. "Actually, that alone proves she's not herself."

Wow. Even when we were teens, Mom didn't want our house to be the hangout house. She'd had enough of other people's kids at her job. If Erin and I had been more compatible, that probably wouldn't have bothered me. But being discouraged from inviting people over had made socializing harder for me—a shy person who didn't get invited everywhere.

"You're teaching at the house?" I'd never been able to keep up with my sister's plans, mostly because she didn't plan ahead. "Did you get fired from Give Me Strength?"

"No, I didn't get fired." She shot me a peeved look. "I can manage both. The more money I make, the sooner I can find my own housing." She then barked a surprised laugh. "I just figured out why Mom isn't stopping me from teaching in the basement."

Normally, that kind of realization elicited a snarky aside, but Erin had a decided lightness about her. Single at her age and basically homeless, yet nothing troubled her for long. I could use a dose of whatever ran through her blood.

"You seem pretty cheerful, all things considered."

"I'm saving money. I'm helping with Mom. I've made plans to make more money." She planted her hands on the counter, lettuce abandoned and wilting beside her. "Things are moving in a good direction, as long as I don't get sidetracked."

"Sidetracked by what?"

"More like by whom." She drummed her fingers against her lips. "I keep thinking about Eli."

"The guy who bought Dad's records?" I still thought of them as Dad's, not hers.

She nodded. "I saw him this week. He was coming out of the post office when I was heading in. He offered to watch Mo while I shipped my packages, then we talked for a while."

"Did he ask you out?" Her ability to move on from Max without skipping a beat mirrored Lyle with Ebba, making me hot.

"No. I must be losing my touch," she joked before making an exaggerated pout. "Did I tell you he's a songwriter? Or he was . . . he's taking a break."

That sounded awfully familiar.

She wagged a finger. "I told you already, he isn't like Max. He's a *real* songwriter. He's written songs for Brad Peyton."

"Seriously?"

"Yes." She nodded proudly despite having had nothing to do with it. "I think something bad happened to him, though. When I asked him about where he got his inspiration, he made a vague reference to having lost it. Then he mentioned having spent a year wandering around Asia. What do you think that all means? Addiction? A bad breakup?"

"Well, if he's nursing a broken heart, you could end up with one of your own. Be careful." It struck me then that I'd never seen her heartbroken—except over Dad's death. That had slowed her to a crawl, leaving her listless and puffy-eyed for months. She'd clung to Max like a life raft when, for most of her life, boyfriends had come and gone without much drama.

To me, that was only possible if she'd never let them all the way into her heart. If that were true, then despite what we'd both been told all our lives, perhaps *she* was the smarter one. I'd give anything to numb the violent pain of my torn heart. To not despise the fool in the mirror.

"You're probably right, although what-ifs don't usually worry me." She sighed and dumped the lettuce out of the strainer and into the bowl. "I did decide to leave a batch of soaps—a mix of lemon, sage, and bergamot—on his porch today. I also left my upcoming yoga class schedule and Mom's address. I mean, I owe him something for how Max robbed him blind."

I slapped my palms to my cheeks, which were as hot as the pot of ragù and probably twice as red. "You did not."

"I did." She grimaced. "What can I say? Change is hard. I can only repress so many impulses before I blow."

"Won't you be embarrassed if he doesn't call or show up?"

"A little, but then again, if he doesn't respond, c'est la vie. I'm curious about him and what's got him so blue. If he's on a journey of self-improvement, maybe we can help each other along—as friends."

Seemed to me that if Eli wanted to know her, he'd reach out without the prompting, the way Lyle had when we'd met. Not that *that* had worked out well. "It was a nice gesture, and I'm sure he'll like the soaps. How's the business going?"

"Still fun."

Not the answer I'd hoped for. She put so much effort into those products it'd be nice to see it pay off. "Is it growing?"

"A little." She averted her gaze.

That gnawing frustration that used to build when I'd helped her with Spanish or prealgebra homework festered. "Are you tracking your customers and getting feedback? What about providing incentives— you know, buy ten and get the next one free, or something?"

Erin crossed her arms and spoke through a phony smile. "I've got it under control."

I'm not creative like her, but I knew my organization skills could help her take her business to a new level. I could really use a distraction this summer, too. This could be an opportunity to combine our strengths if she stopped viewing it as a contest. Before I made another suggestion, Erin said, "Enough about me. How are you?"

I shrugged, still unaccustomed to trading intimacies with her. "Okay."

We both knew it to be a lie, but she didn't call me out. Like two blind people feeling their way through new surroundings, we fumbled around our fledgling friendship.

"Any new info?" She peered at me, trying to peek beneath the surface.

"Not yet." I straightened the copper canisters of flour and sugar that didn't need to be realigned, then spotted the discarded mail—a handy excuse to escape this conversation. "May I go handle this mail for a few minutes?"

"Sure. Mind if I grab a drink?" Erin turned toward the refrigerator with the salad bowl in hand. Refrigerating wet lettuce made it slimy, but I let it go. Priorities.

"Not at all. And could you fill a large pot with water and put it on the stove, please? I'll be right back." I wandered to the office. Lyle had always managed our finances, but it was looking like I'd be handling them from now on. While I mindlessly sifted through the bills, the red "Second Notice" stamp on one from our bank intensified the sick feeling that had begun during my conversation with Tom's girlfriend, Gigi.

Apparently, Lyle hadn't made any mortgage payment for two months, which made no sense. He'd been militant about his stellar credit rating of 800. Even if he no longer cared about hurting me, he wouldn't harm himself.

It had to be a banking error. I searched the desk drawers for our checkbook yet found no receipts or pay stubs. Then again, Lyle paid most bills electronically.

Rubbing my chest didn't stanch the acid pumping up my esophagus. I shook my hands out before logging in to our account, then blew out a breath and clicked on the loan account. No recent payments there or in the bill-pay section.

My right leg bounced beneath the desk as I switched over to our checking account to make the payment. *Ohmygod!* A sharp inhale burned my lungs while I switched to look at the savings balance next. Less than eight thousand dollars remained there—down from almost forty thousand from when I'd last checked. That plus only two grand in checking didn't leave me enough to cover the two outstanding loan payments and the next one due, let alone the other costs of homeownership or those associated with childbirth. I logged on to our investment account to find it similarly depleted with the exception of my pathetic 401(k).

Tears blurred my vision as the screw in my gut tightened further.

A noise from the kitchen reminded me that I wasn't alone. I quietly closed the office door before dialing Lyle. Voice mail. In a terse whisper, I said, "Lyle, I got the late notice on our mortgage, and money is missing from our savings. You had no right to take all that. Call me back!"

Immediately afterward I dialed Stan, only to be met by another voice mail. My throat inflamed. "Hi, Stan, it's Amanda Foster. Please call me back as soon as you get this message. Lyle's now depleted most of our joint accounts and didn't pay our mortgage. I need an update on the deed and everything else."

That deed had to be a fake . . . a ruse to put me off a little longer.

With long, slow breaths, I forced air in and out of my lungs. I should've protected myself as soon as Lyle said he'd fallen in love with Ebba instead of worrying that taking action would push him further away. Idiot! Now I'd have to channel Meryl Streep to pull off hosting my mom and sister for dinner tonight without letting on about this crisis. My money, my home, my entire future—vanished like my husband.

I pressed the heels of my palms to my eyes. This evening *had* been about the three of us enjoying an hour of peace together. Now, Lyle had stolen that from me, too.

I'd handed him my entire heart. How could he use me, lie, and walk away without a single regret? He'd polluted our love—and all my happy memories. My chest tightened before a worthless surge of hatred drowned me in self-pity. I couldn't catch my breath. More evidence that I wasn't ready to hack it as a single mom.

I wouldn't have believed Lyle could be this selfish—this cruel—or that he could hurt his own child this way. What had Ebba offered to make him willing to transfer everything—his affection, our money, our future—from me to her?

I snatched some tissues and blew my nose.

My sister would come looking for me soon, and my mom would arrive any minute. I decided to wait for Stan's update before sharing this new information with her. My poor mother deserved one nice meal in blissful ignorance before the world came crashing down around her. Her episodes were sure to get worse with that stress. After pinching my cheeks, I pasted a pleasant smile on my face before leaving the privacy of the office.

Erin's butt greeted me when I rounded the corner to the family room.

"Shouldn't Mom be here by now?" she asked from her downward-dog position.

As if she had ESP, the doorbell rang. Thank God, because another Mom misadventure would've sent me over the edge. "I'll get it."

"Great, I'm starving." Erin jumped up and headed to the kitchen while I went to the door, dabbing my sweaty face with my shirt on the way.

"Hi, Mom." My voice might've trembled. I kissed her hello, but she brushed past quickly. It occurred to me that the last time she'd been here was the day our lives had started to fall apart. Our new normal consisted of stiff upper lips and foolish hope that everything would eventually be made right.

"It smells delicious." Mom walked ahead of me, and we both arrived in the kitchen to find Erin setting the table. Without saying a word, Mom went behind her, fixing the placement of the silverware to move the spoons and knives from the napkins on the left over to the right side of the plate.

Erin shot me her "I'm annoyed" look but thankfully kept her mouth shut.

Only then did the psychic medium cross my mind. I believed in spirits and the afterlife but was less certain that some people could talk to the dead. Something about taking money from the most vulnerable, grieving hopefuls didn't sit well with me, either. Then again, talking to Dad would be an amazing gift.

"You look a little tired, Mom. Still not sleeping well?" After salting the boiling water, I dumped a pound of bucatini into the pot, keeping myself in motion so that they didn't notice my own puffy face.

"I'm getting only four hours a night."

"Stop eating cookies late at night. Sugar before bed messes with sleep big-time." Erin drummed her hands on the counter. For all her bravery, our mom intimidated her.

"More likely it's the nonstop music into the wee hours." Mom flashed a mocking smile, and even I heard a little bite in her tone. That had to hurt my sister. But given all that I was losing, I wasn't unhappy to remain Mom's favorite. Not a proud admission, and in my heart, I did want them to be closer.

Erin appeared to swallow whatever retort she might've spat if they weren't living together. In a complete switch, she smiled at me. "Let's talk about something fun, like what you're naming my niece. I'm dying to know so I can get started on my gift."

Willa. The name danced on the tip of my tongue. Not Penelope or Penny or any other nickname. She fluttered in my belly as if hearing my thoughts. My precious child, whom I loved with every breath in my body. How could her own father rip away her security, her home, her future? During the years I'd blamed his parents for hurting him, I never once suspected he could become them.

"Sis? You okay?" Erin tapped my shoulder.

I blinked, embarrassed by the stray tear I wiped away. "Willa."

Lyle didn't deserve a say in her name. Not after all he'd done.

"What?"

"Willa. That's what I want to name Muffin . . . after Dad." My gaze turned to my mother, seeking her opinion. Her misty eyes confirmed my choice.

"I love that name." She squeezed my hand.

I then risked a glance at Erin, oddly self-conscious because she might've wanted to reserve Dad's name for her future child.

Gazing into space, Erin pushed an errant hank of maroon-tinted bangs back from her forehead. "I hope she has Dad's smile and dimples." She didn't remark upon the name itself. Instead, she tested a strand of pasta. "Zizi-E will teach her how to fish, like Dad taught me. And I'll make sure she knows all the best music."

Zizi-E. My sister would undoubtedly continue to call herself that in a crusade to win me over or wear me down, or both. It did fit her better than Auntie Erin.

Lyle would hate it—its key selling point at the moment. "Is the pasta done?"

"Al dente." Erin nodded.

My mother poured everyone some seltzer. While I removed the pot from the stove, the landline required for the home security system rang. Its answering machine kicked on before I finished draining the pasta.

"Hello, Amanda, it's Stan. I got your message about more anomalies. Sorry I missed you—"

"Hi, Stan. It's me." I reached the phone before he hung up.

The air in the kitchen crackled with anticipation. Erin set about ladling the pasta with sauce and fixing plates while my mother stared at me.

"Oh hey, Amanda. Well, I wish I had better news, but while the deed itself is real, I can't tie Lyle to the entity that bought that land or to that scribbled signature. The general partner of that entity is named Greg Toscano. Does that ring any bells for you?"

I shook my head, then choked out a no when I remembered he couldn't see me.

"Well, there's no mention of Lyle or Ebba in any of the real estate documents involved in that transaction, either." When I didn't reply, he asked, "You still there?"

Was I? Not really. At the moment, I felt as if I were floating outside my own body, looking down on the disaster that had become my life. I cleared my throat. "Mm-hmm."

"I hate to pile on, but I've also discovered a recently formed Cayman partnership, Somniator Partners. Its general partner is another foreign entity, so I haven't yet pinned it to Lyle, but this entity bought a used sixty-foot 1988 DeFever in Miami for close to four hundred thousand dollars right before your husband went to Abaco."

"What's a 'DeFever'?"

"It's a long-range yacht. Like I mentioned, Somniator is owned by another foreign entity—like a shell game—but the names and dates and such all fit together with the info I pulled from your home computer and other searches. My guess is that your husband washed your mom's money through these shell companies to make it difficult to track and tie to him."

My knees buckled, so I leaned against the counter for support. "That can't be right. Maybe there's another Somniator . . ." Even as the words came out, I knew they didn't make sense. My brain couldn't—or wouldn't—catch up to the painful truth.

"Like I said, I'm still digging, but if I were a betting man, I'd go all in on my theory. I haven't uncovered a single real estate transaction in Florida in Lyle's or Ebba's name or the names of entities tied to either of them. I also haven't found any Maryland, Florida, or Delaware entities registered to Lyle. I just spoke with Kevin about all of this and then told him to let me talk to you while he cools down. As you know, he's hot to involve the authorities, but that's complicated by the fact that the promissory note to your mom doesn't specify the use of funds."

"Why does that matter?"

"Well, the loan itself didn't require the funds go toward or be secured by a particular asset—the real estate. Ostensibly, he could have borrowed that money for anything according to the documents, so now you'll have to prove fraud, which is tough. The conversations about the actual Florida deal are mostly he said, she said at this point. Absent more hard evidence and the fact Lyle hasn't missed the first payment yet puts us in a weird sort of limbo—although the fake deed is a good start. Similarly, he can use joint assets for any reason, so that's not a crime in and of itself, but tracing those wires—with your permission—might help us tie Lyle to these entities or their bank accounts. If I can do that, it'll help us with fraud claims. My goal is to put together a colorable claim for wire fraud—a federal crime."

"That letter he wrote referenced the Florida deal . . . ," I said absently. Proof of mail fraud. In hindsight, Lyle's deceit and manipulations seemed so obvious. I'd never been the dumb girl before. It figured my first time would be a whopper. "I'm still confused, because he might be a liar and thief, but he's never been stupid. If all my mother's money paid for the boat, the savings he took can only last so long. How does he plan to keep this going?"

"I suspect that's where Ms. Nilsson comes in. Turns out she's got family money. If he can woo her into marrying him, he'd get access to her funds, too." He cleared his throat. "Sorry. I know this is hard to hear, but it's possible she's unaware of all the facts at this point."

My hand gripped the base of my throat. "So now what?"

"You'd mentioned that your husband was in Abaco recently. My guess is that they're probably cruising around the Caribbean. Boats don't have to file travel plans like planes do, so it makes our job a little harder. Most yachts have GPS and other navigation safety equipment, though, so with the MMSI number—the maritime mobile service identity—we can track him via public apps like Boat Finder as long as he's got his AIS turned on, which he should for safety purposes. If he docks somewhere, we will hope the authorities can pick him up."

I let the "authorities" remark go because that conversation would send my mother over the edge. "In other words, we keep waiting?"

"You keep waiting, and I keep digging. I want to build a solid case so we can go to the FBI instead of local cops. Lyle doesn't know you've hired me. The way he's been calling, sending the deed, and such tells me he thinks he's still a few steps ahead of you. My bet is that he's trying to woo this woman, so he'll be sailing around those islands as long as he thinks you aren't chasing him."

I closed my eyes, unable to reconcile this reckless, selfish version of my husband—the fugitive with a bosomy mistress—with the man I'd known and loved. My temple throbbed as my brain tried to keep up with Stan's summary.

Meanwhile, he kept talking. "Boats break down all the time. He might need to wait a few days in one spot for repairs. And weather can ground him, too, so a storm at sea might keep him in one place long enough for us to grab him. We'll catch up to him. Be patient, and if he calls, don't let on."

My entire body had overheated to the point where I shook feverishly. The intrigue and fodder of an international search for a felon meant we'd leapfrog ahead of the Millers and Blairs in terms of gossip-worthy conversation. It could also affect my ability to keep my preschool job, let alone any attempt to get my old job at the elementary school. Mom could lose her mind under that scrutiny.

Maybe the deal Erin had struck with Max would work for me.

"What if we don't want to involve the authorities?" I couldn't look at my family. "Can I offer not to press charges in exchange for him paying back the money and signing over custody and the sale of the house?"

"Well, I can't advise you to offer that deal because, technically, that's extortion and illegal."

"Why is it illegal?"

"The short answer is because when the state prosecutes a crime, it does so on behalf of the people of the state—or country in federal cases—so the victim doesn't have the right to get a bunch of benefits in exchange for the criminal not being prosecuted. That's not to say some people don't do this and get away with it, but it isn't legal, especially if you're grabbing for things like custody that go beyond simple restitution." Yet something in his voice suggested that he wouldn't turn me in for doing so, either.

Erin had broken the law with impunity. But I'd never been a risk-taker or a criminal, and I wasn't sure I wanted to let Lyle turn me into one.

"Once we involve the authorities, it could drag on for years, right? Won't the government seize all his assets?" Then my mom might see only a fraction of her money down the road. "Custody and my house and everything else would be an open question, too."

"Unfortunately, that's all likely, yes."

"In other words, we're basically victimized twice." A gross injustice given how faithfully I'd always followed every rule.

"Let's focus on what we can control. With your permission as joint account holder, I'll track recent electronic transfers and maybe tie them to these offshore entities."

Nothing he'd said made me feel better, but that wasn't his fault. "Okay. Thank you."

I'd just hung up when Erin asked, "Lyle bought a boat?"

Any remnants of hope for my future dissolved in my chest, wrenching a hiccuped sob. I grabbed the now-wilting pink roses I'd kept—my last contact with Lyle—and threw them in the trash with a groan, then shuffled to my seat, robotically summarizing Stan's update.

My mother folded and unfolded her paper napkin like an accordion, her mouth twisted in an unpleasant moue. Erin handed me some tissues.

"There's basically no question now that Lyle's stolen Mom's money. Let me call Rodri."

Being a felon's daughter would cast a long shadow over Willa. That reality turned my stomach. "Stan said to wait. The loan document didn't specify how Lyle had to spend the money, and he only has circumstantial evidence linking Lyle with this company and boat. Besides, Rodri is local. We need to get the feds interested if we want to arrest him in another country."

"So you *will* involve the authorities once you get all the evidence?" Erin looked at Mom and me.

"The legalities might drag out for years . . . Mom might not recover much, if anything." There *had* to be a solution that made her whole. I grabbed my head, needing time to think.

"I can't believe *you'd* risk breaking the law." Erin bugged her eyes.

I scowled at her hypocrisy. "You did."

"First of all, Max's crime was peanuts compared with Lyle's, so the stakes were way lower. Second, I've got nothing to lose, Amanda. But you're going to be a mother. You shouldn't even consider something reckless."

"I didn't say I would! I'm simply looking at options," I yelled. "You might be comfortable making snap decisions, but I like to think them through, so give me more than two seconds to process what Stan told me."

"Well, hooray for finally having a temper." Erin flung her arms outward. "Let the fury come and don't let Lyle off easy."

"You think I haven't been furious since this began? Willa won't have anything like the life I wanted for her, but maybe the *least* I can do for her is use Lyle's crime against him to secure full custody." My voice had hit birdlike screech levels, but it couldn't be helped. "If that means he gets to stay out of jail, maybe it's for the best. And don't look at me like I'm weak or crazy. Stan says plenty of women pursue solutions that don't involve cops. I've got to think about Willa's future, first and foremost."

Erin sighed, conflict screwing up her face. "What if you fail, Amanda, or *you* get arrested? Is that best for Willa?"

She had me there, but I was too busy trying to punch my way out of this coffin Lyle had buried me in to concede any ground.

Mom had remained silent throughout our argument, but one look at her reminded me that I wasn't the only one with everything at stake. "What are you thinking, Mom?"

Mom's gaze darted from my sister to me. "I don't know. I don't know . . ."

I covered my face like one of my students who wished to disappear.

Erin chimed in. "At least start divorce proceedings."

"Stop! Please stop." My palms slapped the table. "Just because something is right or true doesn't make it simple. I'm so overwhelmed I don't even know where to begin, let alone know what to do with this devastating pain." I pounded on my chest. "*You* probably can't imagine feeling lost and hopeless and stupid and worthless, but there it is. He's left me with next to nothing. I can't even pay the mortgage. I could lose this house—and I can't sell it without his consent since we're both on the deed. I'm basically now a broke single mom. God help me if that woman becomes my daughter's stepmom. And where will I live? Can I get my old job back and afford to pay for help raising my daughter? I've got all this running through my mind every second, so I don't need you pushing me to blow up every last semblance of the life I'm still mourning on *your* timetable, Erin."

She and my mother exchanged worried looks, unaccustomed to my temper. At least it gave me a second to catch my breath.

"You can't still love him, can you?" Erin asked in the softest voice I'd ever heard her use.

"Right now I've never hated anyone more. But two weeks ago I thought my marriage was near perfect. Several days ago, it still had a small chance." I closed my eyes. "My head knows it's over, but my heart still aches for the life and love I thought I had."

Mom tapped her glass with her fork. "Girls, we've got to pull together."

"I'm sorry, Mom. I know you're worried, too." I glanced at Erin, who gazed into space, clearly biting her tongue. "Once we've got the evidence, if you want to go to the police, we will."

My mom raised her chin—defiantly so. "I'm not interested in becoming the laughingstock of town if we can find a way to handle this ourselves instead."

"Mom!" Erin slapped her forehead.

"Stop, Erin." Mom held up a palm. "Trust me. Life here will be unbearable if all of this comes out. It'll be worse than what happened with my dad, because I worked in these schools for three decades. Everyone knows me. There'll be no hiding from everyone's pity, scorn, or schadenfreude. For Pete's sake, I'd have to move to escape the shame. And Dodo would insert herself in my affairs like she did with George. What good does it do me if Lyle sits in jail but I never get my money back? He still wins. Even if a bargain with Lyle is illegal, he can't turn us in for extortion without exposing his own crimes." She nodded to herself. "He's pragmatic. He'll cooperate if we catch him, and Amanda can keep custody without dishonor bringing us all down—"

"I can't believe how far you'll go to avoid a little gossip," Erin interrupted.

"It's not 'a little gossip.' It's *forever*, thanks to Google. And it isn't only me that would suffer. My granddaughter will suffer forever, too, anytime anyone searched her name or her dad's." Mom sighed. "Your sister is smart. She'll find another way."

I closed my eyes to avoid seeing my mother's self-recriminations and my sister's scorn. But our predicament proved I wasn't very smart at all.

Erin clucked. "Let's not make decisions based on some fantasy that Willa will get through life without knowing the truth. That won't happen unless you plan to lie to her forever. That's not the best role-modeling, is it?" She stared me down, challenging me with the very advice I used to give her during her less-than-honest teen years. She'd rarely listened to me, like the time she cheated on an earth science test with an answer key she'd gotten from Briggs McCrady despite my pleas and then got caught. There was probably a lesson in that for me, but the temptation to control my own destiny for a change was too strong.

"I don't know what I'll tell her or when, but that's my choice, not yours." Granted, I didn't have many options, and all of them were terrible. I grabbed my stomach, which had cramped. "I can't imagine taking Willa to visit Lyle in jail."

"Why would you let that liar near her?" Erin shook her head.

"I might not have a choice!" I barked. Did a felony conviction terminate parental rights?

"Erin, don't stress your sister in her condition." Mom jumped out of her seat and rubbed my back. "Relax and drink some water. Take a breath, honey."

Erin stood with her arms crossed, her face pinched in frustration.

I gulped water from the glass my mom had handed me, then met my sister's gaze. "It's black-and-white to you because you don't have to think about anyone but yourself. I'm looking for a solution that doesn't destroy more lives. That's not so simple."

Erin's face got red, and I saw a flicker of hurt in her eyes. But she didn't lash back in anger. "You're wrong, sis. The answers *are* simple. You're making them complicated. But I'll stop pushing if you tell me one thing—what do you want? Don't think about the baby or Mom or anyone else. For once, ignore all that and tell me what *you* want."

"I want my life back! I want my husband to look at me like I'm a beautiful sunrise again. I want my daughter to know a father's love the way we did. I want to know I can keep this house and not have to get a full-time job and pay a nanny to raise my daughter. I want my marriage to be what I thought it was . . . ," I cried.

The disappointment in Erin's eyes couldn't be missed. "Oh, Amanda."

"Don't pity me."

"It's not pity." She grabbed the back of the dining chair. "You've spent your whole life chasing perfection—with school, food, this house—but it's time to wake up to reality. There is no perfect. There're only messy truths. Willa will be better off with a mom who can face them than one who is trying to raise her in a Norman Rockwell cocoon."

"Stop talking, Erin. Please." Mom speared her with the look that used to precede some kind of punishment. Her only leverage these days would be kicking Erin out, which I didn't want to see happen.

"I've lost my appetite." Erin took her plate to the sink. Her gaze flickered from Mom to me. "Believe it or not, I'm not your enemy. I'm trying to help. You're smarter than me, and maybe most people would look at our paths and judge yours better—this Lyle stuff excepted—but you could learn a thing or two about how to make the best of bad situations, and how to believe in yourself despite flaws and failings."

She squeezed my shoulder before looking at Mom. "See you at home. I'm going to experiment with soaps for Willa."

I wanted her to stay but wouldn't ask. Maybe the idea of her making something pretty for my daughter appealed to me. Or maybe I was too proud to admit that I could learn from her.

One thing was certain, though. Lyle shouldn't get to make all the rules anymore. The only way to grasp what he was capable of—and to protect my daughter—would be to better understand how he'd become this man I didn't know. To learn about his past meant talking with his dad, but taking that step meant opening a door I might not be able to close.

For weeks I'd been doing everything I could think of to avoid this moment, but now I let the pain of the end of my marriage hit me fully, my body slowly folding in on itself as I cradled my belly, with my mother rubbing my back.

With deep breaths, I told myself we would be fine. Willed myself to rebuild stronger and smarter for the future.

Surely I'd survived the worst already.

It could only get easier from here.

CHAPTER TEN

ERIN

Last night I'd been in the kitchen, working on a cold-process soap recipe when my mother returned from Amanda's. She'd taken one look at me in my goggles and gloves, shaken her head, and waved good night. Earlier that evening, I'd been glad for the distraction of making a sample batch of chamomile and oat soap for little Willa. Ironic when everything about our family situation made me feel dirty.

I loved my niece's name, though. Had I even told my sister that?

The soap molds would set on my racks for another few days, awaiting the custom-made stamp I'd ordered online—a butterfly with the letter *W*—for embossing the hardened soaps. Someday I'd teach Willa to make soaps. We'd dye them bright colors and cast them in funky molds. Of course, we'd start with a melt-and-pour process so she couldn't get hurt from the lye. Amanda would insist on that precaution—probably forever.

I should call my sister to apologize for coming down on her so hard. She wasn't completely wrong about my hypocrisy. I've never had to make decisions that affected an unborn life—unless you counted the baby-soap ingredients, which were hardly significant.

For weeks after my dad's passing, I'd struggled to choose which pants to wear, much less manage life-altering decisions. While Lyle's departure made *me* want to celebrate, my sister was grieving a huge loss. Just as I had not appreciated Max's attempts to expedite my mourning, my sister didn't need me to tell her how to feel. More important, she deserved my faith that she'd eventually come around to do right, like she always did.

And yet, as wrong as I might be about many things in life, I was right about one: she had to start believing in herself.

Amanda worked today, so I'd wait to hash things out when we wouldn't be rushed. This morning I'd make peace with my mom by preparing breakfast. My sister would've whipped up protein pancakes with quinoa and fresh mango or something, but I went with the sweet Dunkin' Donuts salted-caramel coffee Mom loved and a stack of toaster waffles. Seemed like a lot considering that I usually made do with a cup of yogurt.

Mom shuffled into the kitchen—her blue robe's sash tied snugly beneath her breasts, her hair brushed away from her face—wearing an apprehensive expression that reflected my mood.

"Have a seat." I pulled out a kitchen chair, flashing a smile meant to put us both at ease.

She sniffed the sweetened air. "What did you do?"

"I thought we might enjoy a little breakfast before I start my first yoga class downstairs." I set a cup of coffee in front of her, then buttered the waffles and smothered them in syrup.

Her brows rose as she scooted her chair up to the table and immediately cut into the short stack. "This is nice."

If she remembered that she'd served us toaster waffles as a reward when we were young, she didn't mention it.

"I feel bad about last night." A not-quite apology of the variety I usually gave her. It neither disappointed nor surprised me when she didn't reciprocate. "At the risk of reopening a can of worms, you have to know I didn't mean to hurt anyone's feelings. In my heart of hearts, I know Amanda will be fine. She's smart, and once she gets over her shock, she'll land a full-time teaching job and we'll help her raise Willa."

When my mother concentrated on cutting her waffles rather than reply, I continued, "But, Mom, I'm worried about *you*. Dad's social security income and your pension cover your daily needs, but not emergencies or serious health issues. That insurance money was your safety net. Recovering it has to outweigh protecting your reputation. Sooner or later the truth about Lyle will leak. Delaying the inevitable only gives him more time to flee. If I actually believed you and Amanda could trap him yourselves, maybe I'd get on board. But Lyle isn't as dumb as Max, so it won't be as easy. Please reconsider. Involving the cops is the only way to get justice."

She closed her eyes on a sigh before lifting her chin to meet my gaze.

"It doesn't help when you point out the obvious, Erin. I'm plenty worried on my own, but I can't go back and do things differently. *I* lent those funds for reasons that made sense to me at the time, and *I'll* live with my mistake, even if it costs me all that money." She pounded the table twice with her palm. "Justice that entails my humiliation doesn't interest me, especially when it doesn't guarantee I'll be repaid. You don't understand because you've never lived through interviews and a trial, the media circus . . . It's extremely stressful, and stress is dangerous for pregnant women, you know. I couldn't live with myself if escalating this situation sent your sister into premature labor. I would hope you couldn't, either."

"Of course not." Another pop of guilt singed my subconscious like lye. My silence in February had given Lyle ample time to plot his devious plan. A confession might underscore my sense of urgency to my mother, but I couldn't make myself do it when the truth would only divide us at a time when we needed to pull together.

"How many strangers will be in my basement today?" Her abrupt change of subject yanked me from my dilemma.

"They aren't strangers. In fact, you probably remember Lucy Cahill from high school." I hadn't been friends with Lucy, who was a few years older than me, but every kid had spent time at the school library. "In any case, only three have reserved space for my first official class."

Not too bad, considering the only advertising I'd done was posting flyers at Sugar Momma's, the post office, Stewart's Grocery Mart, and the laundromat. Fewer students meant individualized attention. And I felt good about giving beginners an affordable option.

After washing down a bite of waffles with a swig of coffee, Mom asked, "What do you charge?"

"Fifteen bucks." Less than half my hourly wage at Give Me Strength, which could add up to a decent supplemental income.

Mom nodded. "Forty-five dollars for an hour of stretching is pretty good."

Not half as much as Nancy Thompson made, but I kept that crack to myself. "Ideally, I'd like a class size of about five students four times per week. I could add one or two evening classes if the interest is there . . ." Annualized, that could add around twenty grand to my income. If I could also grow Shakti Suds from making two grand per year to ten or fifteen, I could move out of here to someplace half-decent.

"Those people won't be coming upstairs, though, right?"

"No. I hung a sign on the front door directing them around back, so you can run around in your underwear and curlers and no one will be the wiser." I wiggled my brows.

My mom almost smiled, but she fought it like always. I swear she spent her whole life refusing to joke around with me, as if her not laughing at my silliness might somehow make me more mature. Yet again my dad's absence snuck up on me from behind. If he were here, we'd be snickering. I missed that deep chuckle, which had often ended with his arm around my shoulders and a kiss on the temple or a tweak of my nose. *Oh, Daddy.*

I blinked back quick tears and took my mug to the sink, dumping the majority of the sickeningly sweet coffee down the drain. My mother continued to savor hers. Six months of this quiet tension might well end up feeling like twelve. It'd be nice if we could have some fun together while I kept her safe. An idea struck. With as much enthusiasm as I could muster, I asked, "Why don't you come take my class? It's important to remain limber as you age—for injury prevention. Plus it's meditative. Reduces stress . . ."

"I haven't taken an exercise class in years. Are you trying to make a fool of me in front of a former student?" She frowned before ingesting another large bite of waffle.

As if I'd ever set out to embarrass anyone. It got tiring to count to three and brush off these slights. In the past I'd done so because I'd had my dad, so I'd given up on pleasing my mom. Now that he was gone and we had huge problems to deal with, I wouldn't waste energy on petty shit. "There's no judgment in yoga—you do what you can. But if you're uncomfortable in front of others, we can do private sessions at night. It'll be fun. You know, Dad sometimes took my classes."

She set down her silverware, staring at me like all my hair had grown back. "He did not."

"He did." Even now I could picture him showing up in his Loyola gym shorts and T-shirt, determined to master crow pose despite his potbelly. "Then we'd go get ice cream afterward. Pistachio, at Dream Cream."

Dream Cream had been one of his favorite haunts. He'd slipped into another world when he ate a cone—lick by lick—savoring each bite. *"Delayed gratification,"* he'd say.

"Why would he keep that from me?" she asked of no one in particular, scowling.

Who knew why people kept little secrets? I suspect Dad had kept to himself lots of trivial things he and I did. He'd worked in sales, which had enabled him to sneak in breaks during the day. Mom had never minded being alone in the late afternoons when she believed he was working. But if she'd known he'd left her there to come play with me, she might've curtailed his freedom by handing him a miles-long honey-do list.

"I'm sure he told you. You probably forgot. It's not like it was important stuff." A glance at the clock reminded me to get downstairs. Rather than play telephone by asking what Amanda had said last night after I'd left, I'd get those details straight from my sister later. "See you in an hour."

"Erin"—Mom turned the cup in her hand—"thank you for breakfast, and for your concern. How about if I go pick up more of those mini mason jars and help you with another batch of lotion tonight?"

I had no words. Two days ago I suspected she'd helped me only to make sure everything got cleaned up properly. Now, out of the blue, she wanted to spend more time with me? Those waffles were miracle workers!

"That'd be awesome. And you're welcome for breakfast." A bit of the heaviness that had settled in my bones last night lifted as I descended the stairs.

Before anyone arrived, I lit a Japanese-style incense stick to infuse the room with the calming blend of ginger, lavender, and clove. The colossal box of summer clothes I'd meant to take upstairs remained in the middle of the floor, so I lugged it to the bottom of the stairwell. Next, I hit "Play" on "The Light" by Sol Rising and dimmed the lights. The spicy incense's faint aroma quickly permeated the room, so I snuffed the stick out in water.

While I stacked foam blocks in one corner, a tap on the slider behind me made me glance over my shoulder.

"Eli?" I jumped, unprepared to see him. Lightweight gray Nike joggers hugged his slim hips. A navy short-sleeve shirt fitted snugly around his biceps. I rolled the door open, aware that my grin gave so much away. "This is a surprise."

"Your invitation was hard to resist." He stepped inside, a cautious smile playing on his lips. "Is it okay that I didn't make a reservation?"

"Sure! Only three women are coming today, so it'll be intimate." The word lingered between us.

Eli cleared his throat and scanned the basement. "Cute house."

"Oh, it's not mine. I grew up here. Moved back in this week—temporarily—thus the moving boxes." I gestured toward the box by the stairs. "My mom's been under a lot of stress and acting a bit off, so I'm keeping an eye on her." To avoid creating bad karma, total honesty was required. "Plus I'm a little low on cash and couldn't pass up free rent."

"Hopefully, things will improve for your mom and you." He sucked his lower lip beneath his teeth, but his eyes remained fixed on mine.

My body temperature rose like mercury in a thermometer. I didn't particularly welcome this feeling, and yet it was a nice break from all the tension in my life. "Thanks."

Eli's lips twitched when he glanced at my Nicolas Cage yoga pants. He seemed amused, in a good way.

A man's attention didn't normally faze me, but our awkward pause made me blurt, "Can I get you some water?"

"Sure."

As soon as he answered, Jessica London came through the door. "Hey, Erin. I'm so excited you're doing this." She took in the surroundings and smiled at Eli. "I could never afford Give Me Strength, and this vibe's much better."

"Thanks, Jess. This is Eli." The way her eyes lit up when she extended her hand toward him made me edgy. "Eli, Jess."

I handed him a paper cup to break up their handshake.

While he drank and Jess found a spot, I took a Sitali—or cooling—Pranayama breath before Lucy and a woman named Christie Bell wandered in. After everyone unfurled their mats, I started class, reminding myself to make eye contact with everyone, not only Eli.

"Thank you all for sharing your morning with me. For this flow class, you might need some yoga blocks, which you'll find in the corner. As always, if at any time something doesn't feel right, adjust or take child's pose to rest. There's no contest. It's your practice. And remember, where the mind goes, energy flows, so focus on your breathing and position. Now we'll start in mountain pose while we set our intention for the practice. Stand with your feet hip-width apart. Close your eyes and face your palms forward, fingers extended. Draw your first ujjayi breath—the ocean-sounding breath—in through the nose, out through the mouth, full and expansive." I drew three as examples. "Send that breath to the spaces inside that are depleted as we come to the mat . . ."

Teaching class was never as meditative as practicing on my own, but the focus on breath and body did take me out of my head. Oxygenation and stretching shook loose the tension carried in my shoulders and back. Deep focus on deepening a position cleared stray thoughts.

Tons of people could get themselves off Xanax if they'd give themselves the gift of yoga. Maybe I could create a tagline around that idea.

Class continued for the next fifty minutes with me leading a series of poses, occasionally walking among the students and tweaking their bodies to prevent injury. Touching Eli and having him watch me move around the room made me unusually self-conscious.

The end of class brought a sigh of relief. "Namaste."

Jess, Christie, and Lucy rolled their mats and handed me cash on their way out. Eli lagged behind, having stayed in Savasana longer than the women and then taken his time preparing to leave.

"You're a great instructor." He lowered his chin, flashing another shy smile, which in turn made me the richest woman in Potomac Point despite my empty pocketbook.

The subtle flirtation prompted me to tease him. "Been to many yoga classes?"

"Define 'many.'"

"More than one?"

His eyes twinkled. "More than one, less than twenty."

"Can I entice you to make it a regular practice?" He had the right body for it—long and lean and flexible. He also possessed the patient and calm temperament required. Mostly I thought it could help him work through whatever weighed on him.

"Done."

My heart squeezed. Were we flirting? I thought so, but his subtlety made me less certain.

He reached into his pocket and pulled out a twenty-dollar bill.

"No way." I clamped my hands beneath my armpits. "If you read my note, you know you're getting free classes to alleviate my guilt about taking my albums back."

"But they were *your* albums . . ." He hesitated, then tucked the bill back into his pocket. "By the way, thank you for the soaps."

"You're welcome. Did you like the scent?" A person's body oils and odors altered a fragrance, so my products would never smell the same on someone else as they did on me.

"It's great." He raised his forearm under my nose.

One quick sniff proved it was a winner on Eli. Our gazes locked again. "I'm so glad."

We stood there frozen in another awkward pause. Normally, I'd bulldoze right through this stage, but Eli's hesitant manner and my personal goals made me cautious.

I bent to roll my mat. "Will I see you again in my class?"

"Chances are good." He watched me until I stood again. "So where's my buddy, Mo?"

"Likely upstairs lounging on the back of the sofa like the king that he is, staring out the front window to track all the neighbors." Mo loved lazing around in the sun's warmth while keeping guard.

"Ah." His wandering gaze landed on the abandoned moving box. "May I carry that up for you?"

"Hard up to see my dog?" I teased, recognizing his excuse to hang out longer. My mom wouldn't be happy for Eli to traipse through the house, though—especially if she actually *did* walk around in her under-wear. But I couldn't think up a nice way to turn him down, so like always, I'd beg for forgiveness later. "I'll take you up on that offer."

Eli set his mat on top of the box before hefting it and following me up the rather dimly lit, narrow staircase. Mo must've heard us coming, because he and his wagging tail were eagerly waiting in the kitchen, where he jumped on my legs.

"Little Fluff, did you miss me?" I lifted him to my hip to get some kisses. "Do you remember Eli?"

I petted his head and faced him toward Eli, whose arms were still occupied by my large box of clothes.

"Oh, sorry." I set Mo on the floor. "My room is this way."

The dynamic duo of distraction otherwise known as Mo and Eli had prevented me from hearing Nancy Thompson in the dining room with my mother. Mom must've called her for an emergency session after last night, and then hoped they'd finish before I got out of my class.

"Oh, hello." I'm pretty sure my attempt at not frowning failed. "Sorry to interrupt."

Could everyone hear my sarcasm, or did it sound that way only in my head? Fortunately, my mother was too preoccupied with the hand-some stranger in her living room to care.

"Mom, this is my friend Eli. Eli, that's my mom, Madeline Turner, and her . . . friend Nancy." Like my mom, Nancy had also become engrossed in Eli. Who could blame them? He was by far the best-looking thing in the entire house.

Eli nodded. "Good morning, ladies."

"Sorry to interrupt. Just passing through." My goal now? Keeping Nancy from explaining her presence, it being far too early in our acquaintance for Eli to discover exactly how crazy Turner women could be and that my mom paid to talk to dead people. Yet suddenly sadness hit me, because for Mom to bring Nancy back so soon reeked of desperation, which suggested she was still deeper in grief over Dad than I'd believed.

"We'll leave you alone," I said, brows pinched thanks to the unhappy revelation.

We'd taken one step toward my room when Nancy blurted, "Karen says it's time to be happy."

Eli tripped, dropping the box, his face now as pale as Mo's white fur. He stared at Nancy, lost and aghast. "What did you say?" Pain sharpened his words.

Nancy's gaze ping-ponged between my mother and Eli. "I'm getting a message from a woman named Karen. I don't know who is the intended recipient."

Eli's expression hardened as color rushed back to his face. Avoiding my gaze, he mumbled something that sounded like "Outta here" before bolting through the front door, leaving his yoga mat behind.

My ears funneled sound like the inside of a conch shell. Could Nancy actually talk to the dead? And if so, who was Karen?

I retrieved Eli's mat and chased him outside, leaving Mo behind.

"Eli, wait!" Dewy grass clung to my bare feet, but I caught up to him before he got into his car. "You forgot your mat."

His haunted eyes flashed with discomfort when he took it from me and tossed it in his back seat. "Thanks. See you round."

"Wait." I reached for his arm, but he flinched, so I pulled back, raising my hands. "My mom's paying that kook to communicate with my dad, who died last year. I've told her she's flushing her money down the toilet, but your reaction makes me wonder if maybe there's more to Nancy than sneaky Google searches. Please, can you tell me what spooked you?"

His chest rose and fell on a heavy exhale.

"That 'kook' might've delivered a message from my dead wife." He'd been staring at the house when he said that, so he didn't see my face fall.

His dead wife.

"I'm so sorry." It felt like a medicine ball had landed on my stomach. "Something about you seemed sad, but given your age, I never thought widower."

As soon as those words emerged, I wished I could spit my foot out of my mouth. Eli didn't show any sign of having heard me, though. He remained fixated on the house as if Karen might appear in the window. He stood like a sentinel, his hands on his hips, sorrow etched across his face.

My gaze followed his, but my thoughts wandered. "That's why you stopped writing songs . . ."

He faced me then. My breath stayed locked in my lungs; he swallowed hard. Concentric circles of tension vibrated around us, holding us in place.

Death and grief loomed everywhere. My sister, my mother, Eli . . . Even I still clung to my dad's memory every single day. "Eli, I'm not the most tactful person, and maybe you don't want to talk about this . . . but I know that emptiness . . . that excruciating absence of someone. Knowing you'd cut off your arm to hear another 'I love you,' or spend every penny you had to make them laugh. Last summer I barely made it out of bed most days. By fall, I still struggled to go to work and get through a day without tears. To make sense of why the person who most loved me was taken from me without warning." I dabbed my eyes before massaging my throat to untie the knot that had formed. I recalled unloading my sorrow on Hannah one day when I'd first discovered her shop. "Sometimes it's easier to talk about hard things with strangers than with friends. So if you ever feel like unburdening yourself, I'll do my best to help you get through another day."

He turned back toward the house, his hands now flattened against the roof of his Subaru. I didn't dare move or make another peep, knowing I'd already probably said too much. Although his gaze didn't waver from the living room window, he seemed a million miles away. "Karen loved the mountains and stars, campfires and guitars."

A couple of heartbeats ticked by while I waited for wherever that statement might lead.

"She was a diabetic. We knew we'd taken a risk with her getting pregnant. But it'd been proceeding so well we'd let our guard down. At around twenty-eight weeks, she suggested a weekend camping trip to the Great Smokies, a few hours outside our house in Nashville. She had her meds, we'd had no signs of any trouble. Great forecast. Air mattress. Two nights . . . 'What could happen?' she'd said. 'It'll be our last chance to enjoy camping for a while.'"

He paused, eyes misty. I almost stopped him from continuing rather than watch him relive the pain or fall apart in front of me. The grisly details of whatever went wrong weren't any of my business, but I couldn't walk away after inviting him to share. "She woke in the middle of that first night, bleeding pretty heavily, crying from thinking she was miscarrying. That was her only concern—the baby. But by the time we got to the nearest hospital—an hour away—she'd stopped crying because she'd gone into shock. Placental abruption, then complications from massive blood loss. Both she and our baby died . . . my son . . ." Tears welled in his red-rimmed eyes, which he dabbed with the heel of his hand.

"I'm so sorry, Eli." I stroked his arm, wanting nothing more than to offer a comforting hug, yet sensing from his tightened muscles that one would not be welcomed. It'd take a lifetime of yoga to work through that pain.

He squeezed his eyes closed, pinching the bridge of his nose. "If I could go back, I'd insist we adopt, but she was so damn sure . . . so optimistic. That's how she approached everything. Embracing life and challenges. Refusing to be limited by her illness. We should never have gone someplace remote like that, but she'd had me believing in her fairy tale, like always." The corner of his mouth quirked up in a fond smile before his voice broke apart. "If I'd been smarter, she might still be here."

I knew that feeling, too. If I had begged my dad harder to stop smoking. If I had paid more attention to his huffy breath instead of teasing "the old guy." If I hadn't gone to Dream Cream and helped him clog his arteries. Jesus, the way we tortured ourselves over fates we didn't control boggled the mind.

If Amanda were standing behind Eli, she'd be giving me all kinds of hand signals to keep my trap shut. She'd be rightly worried, too, because despite my desire to be helpful, I had a bad habit of saying the exact wrong thing. This would likely be another of those times. "For what it's worth, your wife sounds like my kind of person. She lived life on *her* terms, so she wouldn't fault *you* for what happened. I bet she loved almost every second of her pregnancy, too. It's tragic—what happened—but try to remember that she made all those decisions with you. You've got to stop blaming yourself."

He dragged his gaze away from the house. "Easier said than done."

"Most things are." Those words echoed through my thoughts, considering the decisions my family had to make and all the blame we passed around. My dad had excelled at taking the sting out of distress and putting life in perspective. But even if he saw us foundering without him, it didn't mean he could send a helpful message through Nancy. "Think it's a coincidence that Nancy mentioned a name that meant something to you?"

"Dunno."

Against all reason, I allowed for the *possibility* that Eli's dead wife had actually made contact with Nancy, because it might help Eli feel better. "If it's true, it sounds like Karen can't rest until you're happier. Maybe you should start writing songs again. Keep living . . ."

His breathing turned labored, so I shut up. But if her death also killed his passion for songwriting, then he needed a new muse so he didn't shrivel up and die, too—metaphorically speaking. Maybe I—

"I've got to go, Erin." He slipped into the driver's seat without making eye contact with me. "Sorry. I'll see you . . ."

I hoped so.

"Take care, Eli." He probably hadn't noticed me waving goodbye. Once his car turned the bend and disappeared, I stood on the road, replaying his awful tale—imagining his beautiful face screwed with alarm, picturing him slumped over his dead wife and child, lost and angry and benumbed—and my lungs filled with sand.

He'd come for yoga and been sideswiped by Nancy. How dare that woman think it okay to blurt out messages without any idea of the consequence? What damage might she do to my mother? I jogged back inside to confront her. "What made you say that to Eli?"

Nancy laid her hands on the table. "Someone named Karen gave me a message. I can't interpret it beyond that."

A convenient nonreply. "Gave you how?"

Nancy peered at me, looking mistrustful of my motives, but ultimately her ego made her prove herself. "Think of me like a tube. When a spirit wants to pass a message, it lowers its energy frequency. Before coming to a reading, I meditate in order to raise my energy frequency to meet spirits in the middle. When a presence comes, energy warms down my legs—sometimes I get goose bumps—so I back away and let that energy come through. Some mediums get visual cues, others can get scents. I mostly receive verbal ones."

That she could turn herself into a telephone from heaven sounded like bullshit.

"Swear to me on your kids—you got kids, right?—that that was real. That you didn't somehow look up Eli's license plate before coming inside and then learning something to mess with him." I didn't know what to believe, or even what I wanted to believe. But my question was stupid because Nancy wouldn't admit to scamming us.

Her eyes flickered. "I never do anything to mess with people."

"Erin, apologize." My mother nervously twisted her earring while Mo looked on from his perch on the sofa. "Nancy came to help me reach your father. What would she gain by hurting your friend?"

Nancy never did swear on her kids.

"I don't know, but it's careless to share messages when you have no idea how they'll affect—how they'll hurt—the recipient." I picked up the discarded box of clothes and looked at my mother, concern and anger pulsing through me. "I can't stop you, Mom, but you've been warned that this can end badly."

Mo jumped off the sofa and followed me to my room, where I deposited him on my bed and then paced, shaking out my hands. I'd need another round of yoga to calm down because pacing this tight space wasn't helping.

Not much had changed in here since Amanda and I had slept in the two twin beds laid out in an L shape, each with a pink comforter embellished with purple and white owls. The old posters and small dresser didn't bug me, but the sense of still being that same odd kid whose opinions were disregarded sure did.

I grabbed piles of clothes from the box and stuffed them into the drawers to distract myself. The dividers Amanda had eventually inserted to keep her side of each drawer organized made me snort. Her side had always held neatly folded items, while mine had mingled socks and pajamas and shorts without care. If she could've divided our entire room, she would've. Admittedly, I'd taken full advantage of her willingness to clean up, make my bed, and put away my laundry. These days I'd be on my own.

Fifteen minutes later, my mother knocked on the door.

"Come in." I leaned against the headboard, sitting cross-legged. Mo climbed into my lap, his little face perched on one knee, staring out the window.

Mom wandered over to sit at the foot of my bed. I braced for a lecture, so I was stunned when she quietly said, "I came to check in. You seemed rattled."

"I'm fine." A white lie, but seeing as how I didn't understand my own thoughts, I could hardly explain them to her. *She* wasn't the parent I'd ever poured my heart out to, and now wasn't the time to begin. "What about you?"

Mom pressed her hand to her chest, a childlike smile appearing. "I know you're concerned, but I'm heartened. Nancy got a message to your friend, which makes me confident that we'll hear from your father, especially if you and your sister help." Given the breakdown Amanda had last night, asking her to participate in this farce seemed unwise. Yet how could I snuff out the little bit of joy and hope now reflected in Mom's eyes? For the first time, I felt selfish for processing only my own grief this past year when I might've helped her with hers, too. "If we're all together with Nancy, William will have to show up."

Her whole face softened after mentioning my dad's name.

For all our differences, we'd both adored him. Yet as much as I'd loved my father, it wasn't the same as losing a spouse.

Parents and children don't share the same intimacies that couples do. They don't wake up together. They don't make major life decisions as one. They don't create new life together. They don't even live in the same house after a period of time.

Yes, I loved my father, but I'd had my own life, too—jobs, hobbies, boyfriends, and friends. On the other hand, my mother had built her whole life around my father. Truly, she started forty-two years ago, when she'd first comforted him in the wake of a bad breakup with some other woman at college. No wonder she was frantic to turn to him now—to get his advice about how to help Amanda and what to do about Lyle.

And Amanda had been right about the fact that I couldn't relate to her pain. I'd yet to love a man other than my father with my whole heart and soul. Losing a spouse had broken something different in Mom and my sister than losing Dad had in me. They might never be whole again. Nor would Eli.

"That's a beautiful wish, Mom, but I don't share your faith in Nancy."

Her forlorn expression made me feel like an ogre. "Not even after what happened today?"

"I can't explain today . . ." Reiterating my license plate theory would earn me only an eye roll and a dismissive wave of the hands, and also make me feel like a shit. "But even if it was one hundred percent authentic, would you actually want to hear from Dad through that woman? It's freaky, and we'd have no way to verify the truth of anything she'd tell us." As gently as I could muster, I added, "Given our other priorities, ghost hunting doesn't seem like the best use of time or money."

She stiffened. "Well, I've got plenty of time, and it is my money, so I'll use it however I please."

I raised my hands in surrender, now defeated and drained. Not good, because I had even less of a filter under these conditions. "Okay, but if you go broke, we'll both be living in my crummy old apartment."

"Psh." She fell silent, her lips twisted. I petted Mo, wishing Mom would leave me alone to think, but the way she picked at the quilt warned me the conversation was about to take a turn. "So is this Eli someone special?"

"He's the guy who bought Dad's albums from Max."

Her stricken expression implied that she'd misinterpreted me.

"He didn't know Max had stolen them," I hastened to add. "He handed them over immediately upon finding out. He's a good guy. A songwriter."

"You like him." She raised a brow.

"What little I know, I like." I snuggled Mo closer, as if he could protect me from her probing.

"It's a little soon after breaking things off with Max to throw yourself into something new, isn't it?"

As if anyone's heart could be bound by so-called rules of propriety. "I'm not throwing myself at him. I merely offered him some free classes because Max cost him so much money."

Not entirely the truth, but close enough. She didn't need to know the effort it took to repress the urge to jump his bones.

"Good, because whoever Karen is, he still loves her. That much is plain as the nose on your face."

That ice water took a minute to shake off. My mom had this way of saying things—honest, true things—that hurt even when she didn't mean them to. This was one of those times, and as usual, she wasn't wrong.

Everything about Eli's earlier expression and voice had dripped with longing for his wife. He hadn't said how long ago she'd died, but he'd previously mentioned not writing for a couple of years. A long time to remain withdrawn from the world. "If you believe Nancy actually spoke with her, then she told him to move on."

Mom slowly shook her head, chin tucked. "You can't compete with a memory, Erin. A ghost of one's beloved is a perfect incarnation of what used to be, untarnished by bad memories or faults. You will always suffer by comparison. I don't want that for you."

I knew my mother was speaking from experience. No matter how many times my dad had told anyone who would listen how he'd hit the jackpot with my mother, she never, ever fully forgot that someone else had been his first love.

Meanwhile, my entire life had been a series of suffering by comparison—to my siblings, other students—so this wouldn't be any different, but I kept that to myself. "Well, I can't help how I feel."

Mom sighed. "You're stubborn."

"Maybe." Mo licked my face and gave me sloppy doggy kisses, which were better than no kisses. "Mom, do you get lonely? I mean, you're alone a lot. Maybe you need to join a club or find a new friend . . ."

She batted my knee. "I've no interest in dating."

"I said 'friend,' not 'boyfriend.'" Interesting that her mind went there, though. Sort of cringey, but interesting. "Then again, you are only sixty-two. Dad wouldn't want you to live the next twenty or thirty years without any romance." The mere thought made me a little sad for her.

Mom practically sprang off the mattress. "If you don't want to talk about Eli, fine, but don't nose into my personal life. For goodness' sake, I'm too old for hot pants. I'll see you later."

She scurried away, leaving me scratching my head. Hot pants? I snorted.

My class at Give Me Strength wasn't for another hour, so I lugged myself from the bed and put on an old Doors LP to chill out. "People Are Strange" had begun to play when a crashing sound made me leap off my bed. "Mom?"

Silence.

I trotted through the house, calling for her. By the time I reached the empty kitchen, my heart was racing. I flung the door to the garage open.

"Oh shoot!" Mo and I ran to the driver's side of the car, which she'd backed into the garage door before opening it.

Mom sat behind the steering wheel, her white-knuckled hands wrapped around it, tears in her eyes. My heart thundered from panic and guilt. Why had I worked her into a tizzy when the whole reason I was living here was to make sure this kind of thing didn't happen?

I flung open the car door. "Are you hurt?" After scanning her from head to toe, I breathed a sigh of relief. No blood.

"I'm fine. Completely fine." She glanced up at me, pleading, "Erin, don't tell Dodo about this."

Dodo was the last thing on my mind, for God's sake. Crossing my heart, I peered back at the rear bumper and the dented garage door. Two additional expenses we couldn't afford. "Not a peep."

Between Nancy Thompson and accidents like this, my mom would be as broke as I was within months. I dreaded calling Amanda, who didn't need more bad news. Mom's continual oopsy-daisies were becoming more troubling and dangerous at a time when the Turner family did not need more stress.

"Let's go inside. I'll get you some water and call the garage door company." She leaned on my shoulder as she pushed out of the car, and I kept hold of her elbow until she was seated at the kitchen table.

She'd always seemed so together and invincible. Watching her falling apart made me aware that I relied on her toughness more than I'd realized.

While filling a water glass, I saw the clouds blocking the sun, dimming the light in the kitchen. Hopelessness had never been my thing, but with Amanda, my mother, and Eli all in distress, the blue mood enveloped me. A sluggishness I'd not felt since the early months of missing my dad's quiet presence returned.

I handed my mother the glass and took a seat. "I won't call Dodo, but we have to tell Amanda. This is the third or fourth dangerous incident in a couple weeks. It's time to make a doctor's appointment to rule out anything worse."

"No!" She slammed the glass on the table.

"Mom, please. We lost Dad too soon. Don't ignore your health, too." Warm tears swam in my eyes. Despite our peevish relationship, I did love my mother. Her behavior of late had me getting concerned about dementia, like *her* dad had suffered.

"Okay." The hardened look in her eyes resembled blue ice. "But only to prove that I'm fine."

"Thank you."

In one of the rarest moments of my life, I hoped my mom *would* prove me wrong.

CHAPTER ELEVEN

AMANDA

To break the silence, I cranked the soundtrack to the most recent *Pride & Prejudice* movie upon returning home from work. That music still moved me despite my own fraudulent Mr. Darcy. Channeling Lizzy for the courage needed to handle the task ahead, I sat at the kitchen table and smoothed out the handwritten page of questions for Lyle's father that I'd compiled this morning. To protect my daughter, my mother, and myself, I had to be better able to predict Lyle's behavior, which meant I needed the facts about his entire life instead of relying on his version.

It was past time for this step, but somehow my heart hadn't gotten the message. It fluttered violently despite my having practiced my introduction at least four times during the short drive home. With the phone held to my ear and my eyes closed, I held my breath while it rang.

"Hello?" came a gruff, bored voice.

My body stiffened. It took two heartbeats before I could answer. "Mr. Foster?"

"Take me off your list—"

"Wait, I'm not a telemarketer. I'm . . . I'm Lyle's wife." So much for practiced eloquence. My gaze settled on the empty space of the kitchen desk that used to house my engagement photo. After my family had left last night, I'd taken every photograph of Lyle out of their frames and cut them into pieces. It struck me then that I'd never seen a picture of Lyle's father. My husband had never even described the man's appearance, so I imagined a paunchier, graying version of Lyle, which didn't calm me down. When he didn't respond, I asked, "Mr. Foster?"

A long sigh came through the line. "Is he dead?"

Goodness, what a question. No wonder Lyle had left home.

"No!" Despite the many recent moments when I'd wanted to kill him. Maybe not literally, but pretty darn close.

"Yeah, I suppose people like him have nine lives."

I blinked. People like him? An unkind remark, but given what little I knew of this man, I'd expected a derisive tone, not this melancholy one. Having prepared for combat, I had to shift gears and ease my way in.

"Sorry to call out of the blue. I would've reached out sooner, but Lyle never let me. Now I have no choice, because I need to better understand the scars his mom caused. Will you answer a few questions?"

"'Scars his mom caused,' eh?" He scoffed. "Sounds like he sold you the same cock-and-bull story he told his first wife."

I slumped back on my chair as if struck by an arrow. Each breath hurt. "His *first* wife?"

Lyle hadn't mentioned that on our marriage license. Not that another lie should startle me at this point. He'd had another wife. A wife! Of all his lies, the one in which he'd said he'd spent a lifetime searching for me somehow suddenly hurt the most. I'd been his *second* choice—my destiny, it seemed.

"Dana, or no—Deanna . . . Yeah, Deanna. Only met her once. Sweet girl. Real giving, just like his mother, who spoiled him rotten, God rest her soul."

God rest her soul?

A chill trickled down my spine. First wives and dead mothers were not part of my script. "I'm sorry . . . I . . . Lyle told me his mom left when he was young."

"Like I said, cock-and-bull."

"So she didn't leave?"

"Not on purpose. She died when he was twelve."

Had Lyle used the word "abandoned," or had I filled in the gap when he'd said his mother had left him? Lyle had watched me mourn my father and never once commiserated about having lost a parent. Who *was* the man I'd married, and how had I been so easily manipulated?

"I'm so sorry . . ." My brain chased each new surprise like a rat seeking cheese. "I'm sorry. I feel foolish. So many lies . . . I don't know what to ask next, or what I expected . . ."

"Listen . . . er, what's your name?" He gentled his voice.

"Amanda."

"Okay, Amanda. I'm guessing my son's finally turned on you, and now you're looking for a reason why it all went wrong?"

Heat flushed through me. "Close enough."

He clucked on the other end of the line. "He never mentioned Deanna?"

The part about his mother "leaving" might be hazy, but I'd remember a prior marriage.

"No." I shook my head although he couldn't see me.

"He probably told you I wasn't a good father."

"Well . . ." This call had been a mistake. Instead of answers there were only more questions. I fidgeted in my seat, uncomfortable and not at all sure *any* Foster man could be trusted. "It was obvious you were estranged, and he made it sound like you were . . . hard on him."

"I was, but only to keep him from running off the rails. He probably kept you away from me because he knew I wouldn't lie for him."

Lie about what? His mother? His first wife? Was there more?

"I'm so confused. It's not like his mother's death or a prior marriage would've changed my feelings. Why would he care if you told me the truth?"

"Because he's a narcissist. He creates his own truth to control others and feel good about himself. At this point, he probably believes his own lies."

"That can't be right. I mean, he's done some awful things lately, but he can also be generous and considerate."

"He mimics empathy and generosity, but it only lasts until he's frustrated or disappointed. Bet in the beginning he treated you like a queen. Made you the center of everything, right?"

"Yes." I sat straighter. An unpleasant tang filled my mouth in anticipation of more facts I might not want to know about Lyle or myself.

"Mm-hmm. He sucks people in with charm, then turns them into puppets. Gives them just enough attention to keep them dancing, and withholds affection if you cross him."

Even when you don't cross him. "So he never loved me." The words fell from my lips without thought.

"Honey, you can't look at it that way." Mr. Foster continued. "He probably cared about you as much as he can care about anyone, but Lyle's all about Lyle. He'll turn on you, beat you down, and make you feel guilty if you do or say anything to challenge him. Everything he does ultimately is about propping up his ego."

Bit by bit the images of my relationship reshuffled through this dark filter as the subtle ways Lyle had let his disapprovals and disappointments be known in order to pull my strings.

"Not sure if he was born that way or his mom created a monster, but he's not right in the head." Lyle's dad coughed.

I remained reluctant to confirm that statement—whether because of what it said about Lyle or about me I couldn't be sure.

"Even so, I never kicked my son out. He left because I saw through him. He's got a gift for lying. Tells you ninety percent of the truth, then twists that last ten percent to change the whole context. Been getting away with that since he was six. I warned Meggie, but she didn't see it, or didn't want to. In her eyes, her little Lyle was perfect. That's what she told him every day, all the while making a million excuses for his bad behavior." He sighed. "You got kids?"

Unsure of his trustworthiness, I told a half truth of the ilk he'd bemoaned, which made me feel worse. "Not yet."

"Well, good. They aren't always a blessing. And like I told that Deanna, Lyle should never be anybody's father. Not unless he gets help."

My ears suddenly felt boxed as I sat there breathless and glad for the chair beneath me. "Do Deanna and Lyle have children?"

Willa deserved to know if she had a half sibling, even if it wasn't clear whether that would be good or bad news.

"No. She annulled the marriage before it got that far. I only know that much because he threatened me after he found out about our conversation. Then he left Michigan. Haven't heard from him in a little more than three years."

So Lyle had moved here immediately after that fight, found his new patsy—me—and started a new life. Bad enough he left me for Ebba, but now it seemed our entire relationship had been a lie, all the way back to those first "I love yous." Fresh tears threatened at yet another loss. Did the fact that I wanted to believe he'd once loved me make *me* a head case? "I'm sorry."

"What are you sorry about, girl? You haven't done anything wrong other than maybe turn a blind eye."

Turned a blind eye. Dragged my family into a web of lies. Given my baby a monster for a father. "I'm sorry I bothered you with my problems, but thanks for your time."

"You sound like a nice girl. My best advice is to leave my son and find a good man." His words sounded remarkably like something my own father might say to a woman in my situation. At least my father would never see how spectacularly I'd been snowed, and how the entire family was suffering for my mistake.

Lyle's dad had been so forthcoming I almost mentioned my pregnancy, then decided to first have Stan verify what I'd been told and learn more about Mr. Foster.

The ball in my throat made swallowing a challenge. "Thank you."

"Take care." He hung up unceremoniously, as if we'd talked about the weather or his favorite book.

Meanwhile, my body was numb. I couldn't connect all the lies to the truth of my life, or maybe it was the other way around—I couldn't connect the truth with the lies of my life. In the jumble only one truth stood out. When you pour everything you have into a belief, letting it go is like killing a part of yourself, even when you know it's the only way to survive. Somehow I had to perform a sort of lobotomy yet remain whole enough to mother my daughter.

My phone vibrated, dancing across the table. *Erin*. I waited for it to drop to voice mail, then, a minute later, learned that my mother had driven her car through the garage door.

I never swore, but—Fuck. This. Day.

———

"Think Mom'll give Dr. Blount the same cold shoulder she's giving us?" Erin bent to tie her bright-red Converse high-tops, unconcerned with whether others in the waiting room were listening.

"She's never rude to strangers." Frayed patience made me huff, but Erin took it in stride. I hadn't yet told her about Lyle's father, because I could manage only one crisis at a time. "Let's be thankful Dr. Blount squeezed her in today."

"How'd you get that kind of pull?" Erin stood and shook out her hands—a longtime restless habit.

"Her special-needs son was in my first-grade class two years ago. We got particularly close when a difficult student took to bullying Robbie on the playground."

"Flippin' bullies. Will there ever be a day when people stop demanding that others conform to their own expectations?" Before I could reply, she said, "Let's go downstairs to that little café and grab something while we wait."

"Sure."

Once we reached the café, I hunted for a table while Erin searched for something satisfying.

She met me a few minutes later, having purchased seltzer and a chocolate chip muffin, and a milk for me. "Should we have told the doctor *all* of the circumstances Mom's facing?"

"Today is only a baseline neurological and memory assessment. We mentioned extreme stress. The source can't be as relevant as the fact that it exists, can it? Plus she was already upset. I didn't want to embarrass her more." Bit by bit, I shredded a paper napkin. "Let's pray that it's only our current situation that's causing Mom's absentmindedness. At least that can be fixed."

Erin made a doubtful face before popping the tab on her can.

"What?"

She shrugged. "Grandpa had dementia . . . but even if Mom's trouble is situational, there's no guarantee *that* will resolve anytime soon, or ever. We both know Lyle could get away with it, especially if you don't involve the authorities. Then she'll be depressed and broke. She needs rainy-day money for another twenty to thirty years—"

"You think I don't know that?" I snapped, suspecting a part of Erin was enjoying my fall from grace.

She set down what remained of her muffin. "Don't bark at me because you don't like the facts. We need to be realistic so we can figure stuff out. I can kick in some rent to help, but my living at home is *not* a long-term solution. And even with me there, accidents still happen."

"Clearly." I twisted the cap off the milk and swallowed a gulp while shifting the guilt from myself back to her.

Erin winced. "You think you can do better? Be my guest."

"I'm sorry." I set the milk down, ashamed and exhausted. I didn't want to be at odds with Erin. I'd never wanted that, yet we'd never learned how to break that cycle. "I'm not myself today."

Erin relaxed into her seat. "I thought you looked pasty. Maybe you should get checked out, too."

"I'm fine."

"But the baby . . ." Erin bit her lower lip, genuine concern in her eyes.

Trusting my sister had never been easy, but in a single year I'd lost my father and my husband, and was now facing the possibility of slowly losing my mother as well. Erin and I needed to become friends. If we'd managed that sooner, I might've trusted her instincts about Lyle from the beginning. Although it felt as if I were flinging myself in front of a bus, I pushed myself to try. "If I tell you something, will it stay between us?"

Erin tugged at her earlobe, grimacing. "The part of me that can't imagine anything worse than what I already know doesn't want to hear another word. But you obviously need someone to talk to, so hit me with it. I promise to keep it in the vault."

"It turns out that Lyle not only lied to me about his childhood, but he was also married before."

Erin's eyes narrowed, but she didn't look shocked. "Did Stan find this out?"

I walked her through my conversation with Lyle's father, stomach tight in anticipation of snarky comments and a series of eye rolls. She remained thoughtfully silent instead. I sat back, hands clasped together and resting on the table. "I expected an 'I told you so.' You always said Lyle was too good to be true."

My sister wouldn't meet my gaze. Seeing her acting uncomfortable in her own skin—something rarer than a pay phone—unnerved me.

"I'm not happy to have been right. I wish I would've . . . spoken up more." Finally she met my gaze. "A narcissist. What does that really mean?"

"Trust me, I'll be doing some homework."

Erin waved a hand. "Don't look back, Amanda. We can't change past mistakes, so let's deal with the facts and move forward."

That MO did *not* surprise me, nor did it persuade me. I never charged ahead without first understanding how I'd arrived at where I was.

"Did you file for divorce?" she asked.

I rubbed my forehead. "I know I should, but I'm paralyzed. He's taken most of our money. I don't have a full-time job or health insurance—and I'm about to give birth. I don't even control my home, because we're both on the deed. How will I raise this baby now? I'm ill-equipped, and for the first time in my life, I've got no options."

"You have options. Your old boss loves you. Start subbing, and sooner or later you'll get rehired. Mom and I will help with the baby. Kev will help you with the legal stuff . . ."

Her matter-of-fact delivery made it all sound easy, but she'd ignored my emotionally crippled state. The code I'd believed in—the golden rule I'd lived by—had failed me. Without that life road map, I couldn't navigate ahead. "Lyle strung me along these past weeks. I'm mortified by the hours I've wasted thinking about how to forgive him. And just when I was feeling a little stronger, the *full* depth of his deception has knocked me down again." I looked at the ceiling, blinking to stave off fresh tears, thinking it a miracle my body could still produce them. "I don't know how you live on the edge of constant uncertainty without getting an ulcer."

Erin snorted. "Gee, thanks. As backhanded compliments go, I suppose that wasn't the worst."

I reached for her hand and then released it. "I didn't mean to insult you. Sorry. My brain is fried today."

"Fix it, because we need to call Kevin. I know you wanted to wait for info from Dr. Blount before we filled him in, but that could take days. At least make him happier by giving him the green light on preparing divorce papers."

I hung my head. Lyle was sailing around with Ebba, sipping wine and laughing at me, while my sister and I sat in a medical-center lobby worrying about our mother, who was falling apart because of that man. "I know my marriage is over, but it's hard to admit to failure."

"Take it from me, it gets easier with practice." Erin smiled, joking to make me feel better. "You didn't fail. *He* did, and somehow we *will* make him pay for it."

A new knot tightened in my chest. Vengeance had never before been part of my vernacular, but loathing born of humiliation was premium fuel for that kind of bloodlust. The hatred in my heart scared me. "I'll tell Kevin to file the papers."

Something in my expression must've cued Erin in to my thoughts. "How about we start by torching all Lyle's stuff?"

"I need to sell it to help pay the bills." I rubbed my stomach because connecting with Willa reminded me of my one remaining spot of joy.

"Ever practical. This is why you're the smart one with options." Erin set her chin on her fists. "You know if I had more money, I'd help you."

I could hardly meet her gaze. We'd probably relied on each other more these past weeks than during the past ten years. Not for the first time, I promised myself it wouldn't take tragedies to push me to do better. "Thank you."

"Kevin could probably lend you some money until you can sell your house."

I shook my head. "Proving 'spousal abandonment' won't be quick. The bank will foreclose before I jump through all the legal hoops to sell the house without Lyle's consent. My best chance to avoid bankruptcy is to negotiate with Lyle to cosign a listing agreement as part of a deal to keep Mom from filing charges."

"Back to illegal deals?" Erin shook her head, all camaraderie fading. "Normally, I'd applaud any decision that went against your lifetime of rule following, but not this."

"Please let's not argue. You know I'd never consider it if any other option would restore Mom's finances and protect Willa's future. Honestly, it's more like a plea bargain than a crime. Once the cops get involved, Lyle could enter into a deal for lesser charges or even somehow escape conviction. Either way, the assets seized will sit and lose value. I'll lose the equity in my house and still have to deal with him on custody issues. The rumors might even make it hard for me to get a job in this school district. Isn't his freedom a small price to pay for closure on those other things? Everyone wins."

"Everyone including the asswipe with the 'Get Out of Jail Free' card." Erin slouched low in her seat, her brows pulled together.

"I can't indulge my ego when I've got to look out for Mom and Willa. The truth is, there aren't any clear-cut answers."

Erin guzzled the rest of her seltzer before crumpling the can in her hands. "I know how much you hate that."

"Who doesn't?"

"The lawyers . . . They live for that shit." Erin chuckled. I shouldn't have laughed with her, but joking did provide a little relief. "So let's talk about this Nancy Thompson business. Are you up for doing that with Mom? Because I'm not."

"Of all of us, I'd expect you to be the most open to it."

Erin shot me a deadpan expression. "Why? Because I like yoga?"

"Sort of?" I wrinkled my nose. But that wasn't the truth. "You were especially close to Dad. I would've thought you'd jump at a chance to hear from him if possible."

"Key words—'*if* possible.'"

She didn't deny their special connection, and I appreciated that honesty even though it still stung. We both knew which of us was each parent's pet. The difference was that she didn't yearn to be equal in Mom's eyes, while I'd always resented the way Erin had taken my place with my dad, even if it hadn't been her intention. After all, she hadn't asked to be born. Had she and I been closer, maybe her relationship with Dad wouldn't have smarted. I don't know, and never will. In any case, I *was* a little curious about Nancy. "You still don't believe, even after what happened with your friend?"

"That made it worse. Nancy knows Mom will believe anything she tells us now." Erin twirled her can round and round, staring at it with a scowl. "I can't explain this morning's 'message,' but it's too convenient, right? We're to accept that Eli's wife's spirit passed a message to Nancy at the precise moment Eli walked by? I mean, magic is awesome, but people aren't actually cut in half in a box and put back together. Unless Dad comes over a speakerphone or whispers in *my* ear, I'm not interested in what Nancy's selling."

Her topsy-turvy thought process revealed a weird logic, but with the anniversary of Dad's death on the horizon, and everything in our lives in limbo, the part of me that respected my father's advice was willing to roll the dice. Then again, Eli hadn't enjoyed receiving his message.

We'd spent enough time talking about me. I wanted to change the subject. "Mom never explained why Eli was there in the first place."

"He showed up for yoga." A wistful sparkle lit her eyes. "After class, he offered to carry the heavy moving box upstairs for me. Then Nancy dropped the K-bomb, and kapow." She emphasized the explosion with her hands.

"That had to be a huge shock. Will you check on him?"

"I can't barge in on him while he's processing potential messages from the grave. Plus"—she pointed her index finger at me—"and don't you ever tell Mom I said this . . . she made a good point about him still being hung up on his wife. With everything else going on now, romance seems ill-fated."

We certainly had bigger crises to contend with, but Erin's tempering her impulses rocked me. "I disagree."

She cocked her head, peering at me. "I expected you to be proud of me for 'cooling my heels,' as Mom might say."

"Normally I might, but maybe we'd all be happier if one of us found some joy. What's more joyful than new romance? Plus the fact that Eli is still devoted to his wife speaks well of his capacity for commitment and love." Unlike my husband, who had no problem changing wives as often as some women changed their shoes.

"He does seem gentle and kind." The little upturn of her mouth gave me a pang. I missed feeling that way about Lyle. Erin said, "If you ever meet him, you'll sense it."

Doubtful. I'd fallen for Lyle, so my "sense" for good men was faulty, which meant I should mind my own business.

"On second thought, you're probably right not to push, especially when you've never been particularly interested in something more permanent. He's been hurt badly, so you couldn't walk away so easily like you did with Max."

Erin rapped her knuckles on the table, frowning. "I put up with Max's crap for months before I finally ended things."

"All I meant was that Eli's vulnerable now. Don't toy with his heart on an impulse."

Her eyes drifted upward as she sighed. "Not everyone throws their whole heart in the ring from the get-go."

"No, but from what you've described, he sounds more like me than you."

Erin slumped back in her chair. "Well, then there's no problem, because he'd get annoyed by me, anyway."

Her tone had been light, but she wouldn't have said it if on some level she didn't believe that she annoyed me sometimes. A sad fact, but if she were being honest, she'd admit that irritation ran in *both* directions. My reluctance to take risks and her disinterest in domestic pastimes left us with little to share. By the time we'd reached adulthood, we'd accepted it and carved out parallel lives that intersected for family events.

When Lyle burst into my life, her dislike of him made it easy to drift even further apart. I'd ignored her opinions because my life had become full of excitement and acceptance—or so I'd thought. Another bad decision to add to my growing list of mistakes. I didn't want to continue making them, and it was past time to close the distance between us. "He might sometimes, but he'd still find you lovable."

A quirk of her lips disrupted her deadpan expression. Playfully, she fluffed her chunky waves of hair. "Well, I *am* sort of unique."

"For sure." The shorn head, nose ring, and odd clothing used to embarrass me—possibly because all I'd wanted was for her to fit in so others wouldn't talk about her. Now I realized how petty they'd all been, and how weak I'd been for not sticking up for her. I almost said something, but my phone rang. *Mom.*

The moment with my sister was over. "Hey, Mom, are you finished?"

"Yes. Where are you two?"

"At the café downstairs." I scanned the medical center's cavernous lobby. "We'll meet you by the elevators."

"Fine." She hung up.

"Uh-oh." I shoved the phone in my bag and stood. "She's not a happy camper."

Erin tossed the muffin wrapper in the trash and crushed her can before putting it in the recycle bin. "Bad news?"

"It's too soon for any news. She's just mad that we forced her to come."

Erin grimaced. "More embarrassed than mad."

Embarrassed to seek medical care. That sounded ridiculous, but our mother was a proud woman who'd spent most of her life overcoming her father's legacy, determined to prove herself to be nothing like him. That shaped her aversion to unwanted attention, as my need for her approval shaped mine. I had to find a way to break the decades-old cycle to spare my daughter this unhealthy anxiety despite her father's crimes.

By the time we made our way to the elevator bank, our mom had arrived. "I hope you two are satisfied now. Let's go."

She marched ahead of us, clasping her clutch to her bosom.

"Did Dr. Blount offer any preliminary opinions?" I asked, holding my belly while trotting to keep up with her.

"That's not your business, like making people think I'm losing my mind isn't your business." She burst through the doors into the bright sunlight.

I squinted. "Mom, we haven't even told Kevin yet, let alone 'people.' But we're concerned given the pan, the keys, the fainting, the garage. You've got to admit you've been off lately."

She whirled around, wearing the stern expression she typically reserved for Erin. "With good reason, Amanda."

I shrank from the rebuke.

Mom rarely yelled at me. I'd always hated when it happened, and I still did. "I'm sorry. You know I am."

I couldn't feel any smaller unless I became invisible, which would have been preferable to being reminded, yet again, of what my husband had done.

"Let's chill." Erin set her hands on both our shoulders. "Mom, so you're a little embarrassed by the oopsies and this appointment. Embarrassment won't kill you. Learn from me and roll with it. We hope this appointment was unnecessary, but as you always tell me, better safe than sorry."

"Hmph." Mom huffed. "You've never listened to me."

"And aren't I the last person you want as your role model?" Erin said it with a smile as she tweaked Mom's nose, catching Mom by surprise. I might've laughed if I didn't envy her carefree attitude about my mother's viewpoints. She opened the front passenger door for our mom and then slid into the back seat.

As the ignition turned over, I said, "Mom, I know it's been a trying day, and I'm sorry to add to it, but I'm filing for divorce."

"Oh, honey. I suppose it's time." Mom made the sign of the cross. "We'd better get our stories straight."

"What *story*?" I asked.

"You certainly won't advertise the affair and theft. Blame everything on irreconcilable differences." She clucked to herself. "Even with that, Becky Morton and Dodo will be all over me with questions."

My mouth opened and closed like a fish out of water.

"It'll be worse if you get busted lying," Erin scoffed.

Mom twisted in her seat to face Erin. "It's called discretion. Besides, Lyle's gone, so Amanda can control the narrative. It's better for all of us that way, especially her. It'll be much easier to move forward with Willa if she doesn't have to deal with snickers and pity."

Maybe. Or maybe keeping secrets would increase my stress. Either way, I hated being talked about as if I weren't present.

"For all we know, Ebba has friends who know the truth. Secrets never stay hidden forever. Just tell the damn truth!" Erin said. "He's an asshole, and people should know it."

"Language!" Mom turned back around. I was surprised that the vicious glare she sent through the windshield didn't crack it.

"Stop talking about me like I'm not here," I said.

My mother faced me. "Ignore your sister. You understand what I'm saying."

"Wouldn't a judge be more inclined to penalize Lyle for the affair with higher alimony and child support?" I mused.

"Judges don't care about that," Mom huffed. "And you can't trust Lyle to abide by a divorce decree, anyway. The *only* hammer you have is the ability to keep him out of jail. Anything you don't get from him when we present our bargain will be lost. Accept that and move forward."

Every time I caught my breath, she knocked the wind out of me again by filling me with doubt. The worst part was that, in addition to ending our marriage, Lyle might actually be destroying the lifelong relationship I'd always considered secure.

"Okay, Mom, let's walk it back a bit. Filing for divorce is a big enough step for now." Erin squeezed my shoulder. "We should celebrate. Let's make something fun for dinner, like mac and cheese with bacon—or french toast."

I put the car in reverse, not feeling the least bit celebratory about my divorce or future. I needed time alone to think through everything I'd learned and to speak with Kevin. "Sorry, I can't. I have to prepare for parent conferences."

"They're three years old. How hard can that be?" Erin asked, then shifted to a prim voice. "Mr. and Mrs. Peterson, little Johnny is the top finger painter in our class. And he counts to twenty without resorting to using his toes. His potty training is by far the best we've seen all year."

"Ha ha." Some people see me as a glorified babysitter. Never mind my early childhood development and education background. Or the creativity and flexibility I demonstrate to keep children that age engaged in learning and reading. Or the communication skills I possess to be able to converse well with kids that young and their parents.

Sometimes I wondered if anything I'd ever worked hard at in this life mattered to anyone but me. Lyle had convinced me that he appreciated my devotion and enthusiasm. It had been the greatest gift I'd ever received—but it had also been a lie.

The effort I put out for others rarely returned in equal measure—except with the children. They loved me. I hoped my daughter would, too.

"Erin, don't tease your sister. When you have kids, you'll want someone like her taking them seriously." My mom reached across the seat and patted my thigh, marginally lifting my spirits.

"I'm only kidding." Erin rolled her eyes, thinking we couldn't see her, but I caught it in the rearview mirror. "So, Mom, when *will* we get the results from your tests?"

In a blink, the giant tangle of questions about my future got swept off the table. Perhaps I should be grateful for the break, but what I most needed was a hug.

"*We* won't get anything. I'll hear something within the week."

"That's fast!" Erin sat forward, chin on the back of the seat like a dog. "What'd they make you do?"

"Please, Erin. I just answered a thousand questions for the doctor, and now your sister's getting divorced. My head hurts." Mom opened her purse and pulled out a bottle of Advil.

My head hurt, too—not that they cared.

Erin raised her hands in surrender, rolling her eyes again as she slid back onto her seat. At this rate, their living arrangement wouldn't last very long. The mountain of problems I had to manage was grinding me down.

Muscle memory had me navigating around the potholes and slow-ing for the speed bumps in the old neighborhood while my mind wan-dered. The Uptons had changed out some old boxwoods for hydrangea. Little ranches and cottages dotted the streets, and most of the houses needed fresh paint or new roofs, or both. But today these homes seemed well loved. Well *lived*. The lack of uniformity gave the neighborhood personality, and I could no longer remember why I'd wanted to leave it all behind.

We rode in silence until we got to Mom's house, which could also use a coat of fresh paint. I put the car in park in the driveway and leaned over to kiss her cheek, wanting to end the day on a better note. "I'll talk to you tomorrow."

"Okay." She got out of the car.

Erin paused on the edge of the back seat. "You okay?"

I didn't want to cry but was grateful she'd thought to ask. I nodded, so she scooted out and closed the door. She then looped her arm through our mom's and pointed at something in the sky as they made their way up the walkway. Neither stooped to pull the weeds growing between the pavers, nor did Mom resist Erin's hold on her. Mo made a brief appearance after they opened the front door, and then they all went inside.

My hand rested on the key as I debated turning off the ignition and following them instead of facing another evening alone. I missed companionship. Warmth. The welcoming smile of someone who loved me. Most days my mom provided those things, but while carbs and cheese and Mo cuddling on my lap sounded like heaven, I knew no one would be handing out hugs tonight. Work would have to be my solace.

Other teachers—lazier ones—phoned in parent conferences, but I'd sworn I'd never become one of them. My personal life might be in pieces, but Lyle couldn't steal my professional reputation without my help.

Yet once I entered my home—a prison I couldn't even sell—the walls closed in.

While a plate of leftover pasta spun in the microwave, my gaze drifted to the memory jar—now a farce. My jaw clenched as I pictured Lyle and Ebba snuggled on the bow of a yacht like Kate and Leo. In one swift movement, the jar crashed to the floor.

The microwave beeped, but I remained frozen amid the glittering shards scattered across the tile. A dozen or so pink scrolls of paper lay among the wreckage.

Squatting, I picked one to read.

Lyle bought me chicken noodle soup from Oak & Almond because I was sick, and he did two loads of laundry so I could rest.

Gestures like that had coaxed me into believing in his love, his lies. What I hadn't recognized until after my conversation with Lyle's dad was how he'd crowed about those actions for weeks afterward, making me work twice as hard to thank him for such thoughtfulness. I grabbed another scrap of paper.

Watched the Jim Gaffigan special on TV with Lyle and laughed so hard my stomach ached.

Date night at home had been my favorite. Our little cocoon—or love nest, as some say. That's what this home used to be.

One by one, I collected the rest of the scrolls, scanning each to discover that Lyle hadn't contributed a single memory in three months. He'd probably been carrying on his affair for the duration, planning his escape while luring me deeper into a life he knew I could never count on.

I released the papers into the trash like unwanted confetti, then got the broom and swept up my spectacular mess. No tears, only anger spreading through my limbs like a fever.

All my life I'd been reliable. A team player. Generous with my time and love. Loyal. Hardworking. Self-sacrificing. What had it all gotten me? No one thought me any more special than anyone else. My own husband didn't even care enough about my feelings not to humiliate me and steal from my family.

What would my habits teach my daughter about love and commitment? About me? If I didn't want Willa to feel unworthy and underappreciated like me, I'd have to change everything . . .

But first I had to prepare for the parent meetings.

CHAPTER TWELVE

Erin

"Are you sure you want to add lime to this geranium scent?" My mother wrinkled her nose while sniffing it.

"Absolutely." I continued stirring the coconut and almond oils together with the beeswax and shea butter in the double boiler. "But first we add the vitamin E, remember?"

She gave me "the look" that said she was sick of me testing her memory every day. Five days since the doctor appointment and still no news. I raised my hands apologetically while she measured a teaspoon of vitamin E oil and put it in the glass bowl.

Her behavior had actually been better lately—except for the day she went to the pharmacy to get her cholesterol medication but came back with only sunscreen and shampoo. When I realized what she'd done, I ran back to get her prescription and left it on her bathroom vanity without calling out her brain fart. Things were tense enough with Lyle on the run. Oh, then there was the chicken that got charred to a crisp, but Aunt Dodo had a habit of calling when my mom was cooking, and I couldn't quite blame her for getting sidetracked. But other than those incidents, she'd been focusing very hard on proving that she was "fine."

"Now let's add the essential oils. The lime is a nice contrast note. Trust me, you'll like it. A perfect summer scent. You won't even need perfume." I stepped back and let her take over so I could pop into the garage to get the mini mason jars.

I stared at the now-empty corner where I normally stashed my supplies. Crap! I ducked back into the kitchen. "Mom, did you throw out my box of mason jars?"

"No." She glanced over her shoulder. "I put them up on the shelf by the lawn mower. If you want to run a business, you need to be organized, Erin. You should be keeping inventory lists and looking for discounts on supplies."

"When I get bigger, I'll worry about that."

She shook her head like she used to when I'd doodle while Amanda tried to help me with homework. "You can't grow a business if you aren't organized and following a plan. We should be testing things and tracking what works and doesn't. Let's not wing this." She went back to stirring the ingredients.

Let's? We?

Shakti Suds was *my* baby—my vision—yet if Dad had been living, I would've welcomed his help and input.

I'd already taken Amanda's idea about contacting local stores, although I didn't tell her I'd done so because I couldn't willingly give her another reason to feel superior to me. However, this situation with Lyle and Mom's forgetfulness had forced us to work together, and that hadn't sucked.

Maybe I should get Amanda more involved—officially. It wouldn't be the worst thing for me to pass off the things I hated to do—math! and organization—so I could concentrate on the creative side of my enterprise. And Lord knew she could use something to think about besides Lyle.

The idea made me a little sick to my stomach, though. I'd have to weigh the pros and cons more . . . maybe talk to Kevin about how to structure it.

"I thought you'd retired from ever working again." I looked at my mom.

"I have, trust me. This is only a good distraction until this Lyle business is settled."

"Well, then, how about we finish this batch without making plans for an empire."

"Fine, but we should go to Home Depot today to get some sturdy shelves for the garage. I'll make labels and create one central place for all these oils and bottles and things."

I had to admit I didn't mind that help. "I can't go today. I've got plans."

She looked up. "What plans?"

I couldn't tell her about my plan to investigate Ebba Nilsson, so I hedged. "I'm taking the soaps we made the other day and some sugar scrubs to Castille's."

Nalini Bhatt, the owner of the upscale local store that specialized in women's lingerie and pajamas, had agreed to let me conduct a little trial in her shop. Granted, her place was a bit chichi for my taste, but women who would pay sixty dollars for a bra shouldn't blink at spending eight bucks for a bar of organic homemade soap.

"You've sold them all already?"

Mom rarely graced me with an impressed expression, so I hated to erase it so quickly.

"Not yet. Castille's will sell them for a cut of the revenue. I made pretty lotus-flower labels with my website info listed on them so if people like the products, they can reorder directly from me."

Mom nodded, tapping her temple. "Good idea, honey."

"Thanks." I nodded, encouraged. "I'll grab the mason jars so we can fill them with lotion, then can I borrow your car?"

Mom hadn't driven much since the little accident. "Sure. Amanda's coming over for help with baking for her school fair tomorrow morning, so I don't need it."

Good. Mom wouldn't be alone for long, which meant I wouldn't have to worry about her microwaving anything covered with tinfoil again. Luckily I'd caught that one before she hit the "Start" button, but, yeah, that actually made it three incidents in five days. Guess she wasn't doing as well as I wanted to believe.

"Notice that the keys are on the hook . . . ," she said, with a haughty raise of her brows.

"Yep." I didn't react—as I hadn't done any of the bazillion times she'd pointed out all the things she'd done right this week. "I'll be right back with the jars."

———

After spending twenty minutes at Castille's arranging small displays at the checkout counter and in the storefront window, I tossed my empty boxes in the trunk of Mom's car and headed over to Chesapeake Properties.

My dislike of Lyle meant I'd never once been to his office or met his coworkers, so no one would know that my real name wasn't Roxy Cummings. While Stan ran down leads through online research and whatnot, I would carry out my own investigation. My years of working in restaurants and gyms had taught me a thing or two about how much women liked to gossip. After scanning the website to look at the agents who still worked there, I'd singled out two—Meghan Armstrong and Jane Bauer—who looked most likely to have been friendly with Ebba. In my experience, attractive women tended to band together.

I got out of the car, slightly self-conscious in the conservative dress I'd purchased years ago for "grown-up" events. Mom had bought my lie about dressing up to make a good impression at Castille's. Concealing my real plan would let me avoid her disappointment if I failed. Truthfully, she might've told me not to come. Sidestepping that conversation meant I wasn't breaking a promise.

Time to get into character.

I opened the realty shop's door and glanced around the open room to find seven polished mahogany desks but only three agents busy at work. Lucky for me, I spotted Jane Bauer from my research. Averting my eyes from the other agents' gazes, I beelined for Jane's desk.

"Good morning." I stuck out my hand. "I'm Roxy and I'm looking to buy my first house. My friend told me about this agency—actually she mentioned a broker, Ebba Nilsson—so here I am. Are you her?"

Jane shook my hand. I could tell she bought my cover story, so I relaxed. "No, Ebba left a few weeks ago, but her specialty was really commercial properties, anyway. I'm Jane Bauer, a residential property specialist, and I'd be happy to assist you."

"Oh, terrific." I took a seat, mentally telling myself not to tip my hand too quickly.

"So, Roxy, are you new to town, or have you been here long?" Jane smiled pleasantly.

"I've been here almost two years," I lied. "To be honest, my boyfriend and I are breaking up, and I need to get out of our apartment and away from the memories, you know?"

She made a sad face. "Oh, yes, I do. I'm sorry about that, but a pretty little place of your own will show him what he's missing, won't it?"

"For sure." I grinned, hoping to keep my lies straight.

She took out a yellow legal pad and wrote my name across the top. My mother would admire her picture-perfect penmanship. "Tell me what you're looking for."

"Something new but small. Two bedrooms, max. I like an open floor plan." Hopefully, a natural opening to bring up Ebba again would happen soon, but while I was there, I might as well learn what the town had to offer.

Her expression turned more serious. "Would you be willing to look at condos?"

"I wasn't thinking about them, but maybe. What's your opinion?"

"Well, a lot of single women like condos because they don't have to deal with yard maintenance, they like the amenities like pools and small gyms, and they like the built-in community."

"Ooh, I didn't think about that. I suppose condos are filled with people my age."

"Including men with good jobs." She smiled conspiratorially.

Ugh. I couldn't think of anything I'd like less than a group of ambitious prepster dudes barking up my tree, but this kind of chatty conversation could pave the way to bringing up Ebba. "Good point. It's hard to find single men around here."

"Tell me about it." She rolled her eyes.

I cackled like we were long-lost friends. "Okay, let's look at condos. Now, I don't have a huge budget. I was thinking two hundred grand tops."

"That will limit our options, but I know of two developments with open units in that price range. One has a nice pool and party room, too." She smiled and punched a bunch of stuff into the computer.

"Sounds perfect! Maybe I could move in in time to break out the bikini."

"It'll be like living in a resort." She waved a hand in a "you go, girl" manner.

"I like your spirit." I high-fived her. "I'm glad Ebba wasn't here."

"Thanks." And then I saw it—a gleam in her eyes as if she was pleased to have been deemed better than the absentee broker.

"It's weird, though," I said, wading in carefully. "My friend gave me the impression that Ebba was a real go-getter. Top broker. Why'd she quit?"

"To be honest, it's a little bizarre. She'd grown secretive all spring. We suspected she'd met someone, but she wouldn't really tell us much other than that he was charming and successful and getting out of a 'bad situation,' which I guessed meant he was still married. We never saw her out with anyone, which also points to an affair."

"Well, that's really awful if it's true. But doesn't she still need a job?" Hopefully my curious-but-dopey act was working.

"No, actually. Apparently, they're sailing off together—literally."

"That sounds crazy."

"Right? I like the Caribbean as much as the next person, but living on a boat full-time would be claustrophobic."

"Exactly. Those islands could get boring fast."

"Well, they won't be there forever." Jane looked around at the other brokers—one of whom was on a call, the other on his computer—then leaned a little closer, holding her hair to one side. "To be honest, Ebba was a good broker, but those awards started to go to her head. She got a little boastful, so when she quit, she did 'casually' mention how excited she was to become an international real estate investor. They're sailing down the chain of islands all the way to some island off the coast of Venezuela. It sounded risky to me, but whatever. I bet she regrets it in about a year."

"It does sound risky, especially if this mystery man actually was married. I mean, once a cheater, always a cheater." And a thief. And an absentee father.

Jane planted her palm on her desk for emphasis as she said, "Ex-actly."

"It sucks to be single again"—then for a second, Eli's face flickered through my thoughts—"but it's better than being with an asshole."

"Amen, sista!" Jane laughed, and suddenly guilt swamped me for leading her on with my fake name and pretend house-hunting. I couldn't ever use her as a Realtor without her exposing the truth about me, but I would send her business whenever I learned of others who were looking to upgrade. "So shall we go check out these two condos?"

"Right now? Oh, gosh, I really only stopped in to get the ball rolling. I assumed we'd need to set up appointments. How about you give me your card, and I'll call you later today to do that? I've got a bunch of errands I need to take care of right now."

"Sure." She smiled and handed me a business card. "It's been nice talking to you. I'm sure we can find you the right place to start over."

I stood and shook her hand again. "Jane, you have no idea how grateful I am for all your help today."

On that note, I turned and darted out the door, eager to share what I'd learned so the cops would have what they needed to trap Lyle. The drive across town seemed to take forever, but I smiled when I saw Amanda's car parked in front of the house. I whipped into the garage and practically jumped out of the front seat.

"Hey!" I yelped after dashing into the kitchen. Not only weren't Mom and Amanda baking, but I didn't detect a whiff of sugar or browned butter. Mo hadn't come running at me, either. My heart sped up, wondering if something else went wrong while I'd been gone. I cupped my hands to my mouth and yelled, "Mom?"

"Back here," came a voice muffled by the closed kitchen window.

Was she hurt? I raced to the deck, where I nearly crashed into Amanda and Mom enjoying a cup of coffee. Mo's tail wagged as he trotted over to greet me, but I was too shaky to pick him up.

Mom frowned at me, setting down her cup. "What's wrong? You look wild."

"I know where Lyle's going!" The chair I'd yanked scraped against the deck before my butt hit its seat. Mo jumped on my shins, so I lifted him onto my lap.

"How?" Amanda's face paled.

When you live in a town of eighteen thousand people, it's big enough that you don't know everyone, and today that had worked in our favor. "I went to Lyle's old office and pretended to be looking for a new house. While getting to know another broker, I got some deets about Ebba, and one thing led to another."

"What broker? What 'deets'?" Instead of jumping for joy, my sister trembled. In fact, she might've stopped breathing, too.

"Jane Bauer."

Amanda slapped her head. "Jane's a huge gossip. Oh God, did she know about Lyle?"

"No. Relax. I went in as if someone had recommended Ebba, so Jane said she'd quit." As I recited the conversation back practically word for word, I'd hoped my sister would calm down, but instead she turned green. "Amanda, this is good news. Let's call Stan and Kevin."

I thrust a phone at her, but she didn't take it.

"What's wrong?" I shot my mom a quizzical look. In return, she offered up that pinched expression that informed me I'd done something she didn't like.

Amanda squeezed her eyes shut, nodding. "I'll call him."

She hoisted herself out of the chair, which wasn't easy with that round belly, then disappeared inside.

When I went to follow her, my mom called, "Stop!"

My hands shot out from my sides. "Why aren't you excited, or at least relieved?"

She pitched her face upward as if begging my dad for some wisdom about how to deal with me. "I realize you're trying to help, but did you stop for one minute to think about how hard it is for your sister to hear about Lyle's grand cruise with his mistress?" She shook her head, letting the rustle of the sycamore leaves fill the temporary silence. "You expect her to move on without paying any respect to what she's losing. Yes, you were right about Lyle all along, but your sister loved him, Erin. He was her husband, not some high school boyfriend. Life as she knew it is over. That's hard for most people, but especially for someone like her, who works so hard to keep things together. You could try being more sensitive."

I scratched behind my ear, having no ready comeback, mostly because there wasn't one. "Sorry."

"Don't apologize to *me*."

I peered through the window but didn't see my sister in the kitchen. "Okay. I'll try harder, but, my gosh, can't we celebrate the fact that this nightmare might be over soon? We should book tickets to Turks and Caicos or something today, 'cause I want a front row seat to his arrest."

"Arrest?" Her demeanor shifted from concern to self-preservation in a blink. "Lyle hasn't missed his interest payment yet. Until he does, that's premature." Mom purposefully tapped her fingernail against the arm of the deck chair four times.

Things never went anywhere when Mom's fingernails got involved. My skin prickled and tightened from frustration.

"Lyle wouldn't be sailing off to South America if he planned to make those payments. When's it due?" I asked.

"Monday."

In two days. I guessed we'd argue about the cops on Tuesday, then.

Amanda returned, still clutching her phone. "Well, that yacht Stan's been tracking is in Turks, so it's more evidence that *The Office*—that's the boat's name—is in fact Lyle's and making its way south. He's still working on linking all the wire transfers from our bank to Lyle and the company and the boat. Until that's tied up, Lyle could claim to be borrowing or leasing the boat from a friend or something, or using Mom's money for something else. Who knows? He's obviously the best liar."

"So we wait?" Mom asked, looking almost relieved that she had a reprieve from notifying the authorities.

Amanda shrugged. "Stan suspects Lyle plans to hang out around Venezuela because, while technically there's an extradition treaty between it and the US, it's considered a fugitive-friendly nation, especially with all the current political upheaval. Lyle could live there a long time without having to worry about being extradited."

When neither of them said more, I let out an exasperated raspberry. "We have enough circumstantial evidence to convince the authorities to investigate. If they issue warrants, they might get access to information Stan can't. It's crazy to sit on our hands and let Lyle get away." So much for being sensitive to my sister's feelings.

"I said no!" My mother fisted both hands and beat them against her chair.

Amanda flinched. "Lyle doesn't know I hired a PI, so he thinks he's fooled me with that deed. He and Ebba aren't rushing anywhere, so we have a little time. But I have to agree with Erin, Mom. Maybe it's time to involve the police."

Mom shook her head. "You said we could offer Lyle a deal first. One that gets me my money and *you* your house and sole custody."

"An illegal deal," I reminded them both.

Amanda's face pinched as her gaze darted from me to Mom. Her fingers were turning white around the phone still in her hand. "Mom, even if I caught up to Lyle, he'd probably laugh in my face and try outrunning the law before he'd hand over anything to me." Her free hand rubbed her forehead. It struck me then that this was—in my memory—the first time she'd ever defied our mom. "If he gets to Venezuela, we'll have lost everything, and I'll be in limbo for years trying to prove he abandoned me."

"But the alternative is becoming the talk of the town. Poor Amanda Foster and her stupid mother, both duped by that con man!" Mom scowled. "Our reputations will be ruined. Even if he's arrested, I'll probably get very little money back, and you'll lose your home and have no guarantee of custody once Lyle gets out of jail."

"It's hard to pretend life is A-okay when people ask me when Lyle's coming home. 'I'm not sure' isn't working so well anymore. Ebba's coworkers suspect she was having an affair. Once people know Lyle and I are done and start putting together the timeline, gossip will spread. Playing dumb will make us both look stupider than the truth does." Amanda tossed the phone aside and rubbed her breastbone.

"You're not stupid. He played us all," I said, harkening back to that cold February afternoon when I should've acted on my instincts when my radar had sensed the sex in the air, despite how Lyle and Ebba had played it off. But Amanda had been happily planning for the baby, never mentioning any problems, so I'd let it go.

"Talk about the divorce like we discussed—irreconcilable differences. But don't mention the money," Mom insisted before she pushed herself out of her chair and took her empty cup inside, mumbling something about Dodo.

Once she'd gone, I whirled on my sister. "Don't listen to her."

"Please don't push me." She gazed blankly at the yard before briefly closing her eyes to catch a breath.

One look at her belly and the stress etched on her face kept me silent. At least she'd started to see reason. Eventually she'd do the right thing. She always did. The funny part was the fact that *I* wanted to follow the rules for a change.

My sister's pained stare broke me.

"Amanda, I'm sorry if I overstepped today. I got impatient, but I didn't mean to upset you more."

"It's not your fault I'm upset." It would be if she knew the whole truth. It'd be a relief to simply confess, but unburdening my conscience now seemed more selfish than helpful. Amanda turned to me, her face flushed. "I just—it kills me that Lyle's sailing around with no remorse whatsoever. He never loved me." Her voice cracked.

She rarely showed her pain to me—at least not this directly—and I desperately wished I could take it away. "He doesn't love Ebba, either. He only loves himself."

I held my breath then. The last time I'd made a remark of that ilk had been their first anniversary—the "paper" one. She'd had their wedding vows transcribed in calligraphy on large sheets of paper, which she'd framed, so I called to see how he'd liked it. When she described what sounded like a tepid reaction and then told me he'd given her a box of stationery—something that hadn't taken much time or effort—I'd popped off a cutting remark, at which point she'd insinuated that I was jealous and then hung up on me.

Today she didn't defend Lyle—a promising change. Instead she shrugged. "I'll survive, but how will it affect Willa to have a dad who couldn't care enough to stick around?"

Given our awesome father, I couldn't imagine that. I wondered, however, if Amanda was also projecting a bit of her own feelings of rejection, too. Our father had never neglected her, but she'd yearned for a relationship with him that never fully formed because they were such different people. Sensing a need for a lighter topic, I said, "Let's take things one day at a time. Want some help baking now that Mom's pissed off at us both?"

She flashed a half-hearted smile. "No offense, but when's the last time you used an oven?"

"Fair enough. Go buy out the counter at Sugar Momma's and save yourself the effort. I think you need to rest, Amanda. You've lost your glow."

"Hard to glow when my life is falling apart." Amanda tucked a section of loose hair behind her ear. "How about we talk about you instead. Have you heard from Eli?"

I shook my head. Each morning I'd stare at the sliding doors, hoping he'd show up to yoga, but he'd steered clear of this house and me since the K-bomb. "I finally googled him, though. He's cowritten a ton of songs, produced a bunch, too. He never let on about all his success, which makes me like him more. I also found pictures of his wife and him at the CMAs. She was pretty in a soft way, like you. Fine features. Fair-haired."

Amanda protectively cradled her stomach. "When I think about what happened to his wife and baby, I feel sick. I don't know what I'd do if I lost Willa. She's all I have."

It saddened me that she believed her child was *all* she had. She needed a new perspective, and a new goal. Revenge worked for me. "The only person anything bad will happen to is Lyle. I'll make sure of that."

But as my words made their way into the universe, I regretted tempting fate. When Amanda shivered, I prayed it was from the cool spring breeze whipping across the yard.

CHAPTER THIRTEEN

AMANDA

The last time I'd been to Sugar Momma's had been the day I'd gotten my first inkling about Lyle's lies. Now, despite its welcoming yellow-and-blue-striped awning snapping cheerfully in the breeze, the little shop resembled a crime scene more than a haven.

Townsfolk milled around the local stores and bistros, enjoying the warm weather, oblivious to the ways my life had fallen apart. When I got out of my car, I kept my gaze down, unwilling to make eye contact with anyone familiar who might question me about Lyle and wish us well with our baby.

That thought shot heat to my cheeks.

My phone rang on my way to the door, so I huddled outside the entrance. "Hello?"

"Amanda, it's Stan again. We got so caught up in our conversation about Lyle's whereabouts that I forgot to tell you that I confirmed his mom died when he was twelve, and he did marry a Deanna Parker, who got an annulment a year later. Mr. Foster Sr. pays his bills on time and has held a job at Chrysler for twenty-plus years. He lives a quiet life, frequents a local social club, and likes to go on fishing trips."

Like my dad. Perhaps Willa could have a grandfather in her life after all.

I settled one hand on my stomach, my head rising with hope. "Are you saying nothing about Mr. Foster gives you pause?"

"From all accounts, he's a stand-up guy living his life in the same community where he grew up."

A man who appreciated truth, roots, and the comfort of home. Exactly the kind of person I could relate to. "Thank you so much. Is that all?"

"Pretty much. I'll be back in touch when we have everything together to take to the FBI."

"Don't contact the authorities just yet. My mother and I . . . well, we're weighing all options."

A heavy sigh came through the line. "Your options are pretty limited. But you know, there may be a legal way to get the title to that boat transferred before Lyle is arrested. I was speaking with a buddy, and he said the FBI sometimes authorizes an OIA—otherwise illegal activity. They might be willing to do that with regard to Lyle in order to get a confession and button up their case."

Me, an operative? No one would believe it, least of all Lyle. "How would it work?"

"Basically they'd 'deputize' you for a limited purpose. You'd probably wear a wire and confront Lyle with the proposed deal—the boat title in exchange for not pressing charges. If you get him talking, he might confess, but even if he doesn't confess, if he takes your deal and signs over the boat, it's a stronger case."

"But won't they seize the boat as soon as they arrest him?"

"Not from what I'm told. It'd be your mom's to sell. They might seize his other assets, which would include your house."

"Couldn't I wrap my house and custody into that deal?"

"'Fraid not."

I should jump at this for my mom's sake, although the greedy part of me remained heartsick that I wouldn't get what I needed. I'd give up ten years of my life span to make sure Lyle never had any say in Willa's life. "It's something to consider."

"In these situations, it's best to set your emotions aside and let the authorities do their jobs. The sooner we alert them, the better."

"I know." But he didn't understand how impossible it would be to force my mother to face public shame a second time—especially when she couldn't easily move to a new community and start over like she had as a child. I'd gone my entire life without crossing her. If she didn't give me her blessing, I wasn't sure I could kick off my first time with something so permanent. "I'm about to enter a store. Can we talk later?"

"Sure thing. Have a good day."

A good day? I hadn't had one in weeks, and probably wouldn't have one for months to come.

Uncertainty gnawed at me, leaving me raw. I probably should've turned around rather than open the shop door.

Inside, lively chatter competed with the background music. A teenage couple stood in front of me in line. The lanky boy's hand sank into the petite girl's back jean pocket. She leaned against his side, laughing at something he said.

A month ago they would've made me grin. I might've even thought sweet things about Lyle as a result of seeing young love in full bloom, blissfully clueless about the truth of my life.

When I reached the counter, I faked a smile as big as the frown I'd been sporting a moment ago. Yet my head buzzed from the fever pitch of my disillusionment. "Hey, Hannah. I'm hoping you might be interested in doing a small community favor."

"A community favor?" She motioned with her hands. "Go ahead. Hit me."

"The preschool where I work is having a little fair and bake sale tomorrow to raise money for new books and things. While I like to cook, I don't make anything as delicious as what you sell. Would you be willing to donate some cookies and muffins to the cause? I'd advertise your shop and hand out business cards at the fair." I flashed my best hard-up-teacher smile.

Hannah nodded, flicking her wrist. "Sure, dear. I've got grandkids. You can never have too many crayons and books in those classrooms. Is three dozen enough?"

"More than enough. Thank you so much. You've really helped me out of a bind today." And then I overcame my insecurities long enough to do something I had never done before: put her on the spot. If I were being honest, this was the real reason I'd come. "You know, it surprised me the other week when you mentioned that Lyle stops in often."

"Really? He'll pick up goodies for the office. Other times he'll stop in with clients to kill time between showings." She tied up the second box she'd filled.

"Hm." For weeks I'd been swallowing my feelings, ashamed and hiding. But something snapped now, making me glad that no one had come in behind me. Lowering my voice didn't prevent it from emerging with a bitter edge. "I'm guessing one of those 'clients' was a young, buxom blonde."

She gave me a look, as if my intimation confirmed something she'd suspected. When she handed me the bagful of free baked goods and some business cards, she pointed at my stomach. "Now you go on and take care of what you're cooking in there. Nothing matters more than that. Kids are where our true happiness lives." She patted the spot over her heart.

My face must've been cherry red, so I appreciated that she neither pitied me nor gossiped about whatever she'd seen Lyle do. "Thank you for the treats. You have no idea how much I appreciate it."

The sting of grateful tears pricked my eyes, so I threw a ten-dollar tip on the counter before turning to dash out of the store. Although

I regretted putting her in that position, numbness spread through me like mildew.

When I arrived at the house I was soon to lose, I stood in the middle of my kitchen, blinking into the emptiness. This home no longer felt like mine. Neither did my life. I couldn't stomach being there, surrounded by reminders of my marriage.

I climbed the stairs, determined to scrub Lyle from the house. One by one, I folded and stacked his winter sweaters and slacks, the various brown and black leather shoes and loafers he'd worn, silk ties, dress and casual shirts, and cuff links, and then loaded them into clear plastic garbage bags. The task revealed what was missing from his wardrobe: bathing suits and sandals, the Tommy Bahama shorts and shirts we'd bought in Naples last year, both pairs of his Maui Jim sunglasses. More clues that, had I been paying attention when he'd packed, might've tipped me off about his "business" trip.

Instead, I'd sweetly kissed him goodbye, wished him luck, and waved as the Uber pulled away for the airport, having had no idea that it would be the last time I'd ever smile at him, kiss his lips, and feel whole and happy.

I growled and then strode to our bathroom to empty his vanity of soaps and colognes and every other personal item that reminded me of him, tossing each one in the trash.

When I'd finished, I sat on the edge of our bed, trying that yoga breathing Erin preached about, but it didn't bring peace—just noisy breath. Getting rid of Lyle's personal things hadn't helped, either. The bed, the linens, the paint on the wall—everything we'd picked and purchased still threw him and all my failed dreams in my face.

I rubbed at my sore throat, choked by loneliness and sorrow. None of the pretty things—the marble counters and high-end fixtures, the reclaimed hardwood, the huge windows—muted the pain. Sharing a roof with my mom and sister might be a little awkward now, but it would beat being alone, surrounded by Lyle's memory. Even my old twin bed, the 1990s decor, and a messy roommate would be heaven compared with this cold palace.

I returned to our closet to pack two bags for myself.

While sorting through my own things, I remembered Mr. Foster—a man who deserved to know that he'd be a grandfather.

Sitting on the tufted bench in our closet, I scrolled through my phone history, my thumb hovering over Mr. Foster's number. Mom would warn me not to involve a stranger, but I had to do the right thing—for Mr. Foster's sake and for Willa's. Little girls needed a father's love, and without hers or mine around to fill that role, I couldn't deny my daughter her only living grandfather. The artery in my neck throbbed, but I pressed "Call."

He picked up on the second ring. "Hell-o."

The cheerful greeting made me picture a man happily watching ESPN with a beer or a burger.

"Mr. Foster, it's Amanda. Lyle's wife."

"Oh, I didn't expect to hear from you again." The matter-of-fact delivery gave no hint of his feelings about me.

"Well, I have more information for you . . ." I stalled, uncertain about where to begin.

"If it's all the same to lyou, maybe you could spare me the details. It doesn't feel good—hearing how my son uses lies about his mom and me to hurt other people. If I'd met you before you got married, maybe I could've helped, but I can't be much use to you now."

His pain put mine in a different perspective. No parent ever imagines him- or herself in those powerless shoes. "I can see where it would be hard on you."

"Ignorance is bliss, you know? I hadn't been ashamed of any new trouble for years until you called."

"I'm sorry, but this is important. I actually have good news, but first I need to ask something. If Lyle would reach out for help to avoid

consequences, could you do the right thing even if it would hurt him?"
I bit my lip.

"Hurt him how?"

My heart thumped. "Fines. Possibly prison."

"Jesus. What'd he do?"

"He's defrauded my mother out of a substantial amount of money and fled with his mistress." How easily my new reality could be reduced to one bitter sentence. "I'll share details another time, but I need an answer. If he contacts you, would you help him hide?"

I waited out a long silence.

He coughed. "Parenting has never been easy, and this kind of decision makes you question everything you think you know about yourself and love and fairness."

"I'm very sorry." He wasn't the only father with a child who'd turned into someone no parent could respect. Still, I couldn't imagine that Willa would grow up to be a monster, even if she had her father's DNA. "Yet I need an answer."

My foot jiggled for what seemed like forever while Mr. Foster seriously contemplated his heart and conscience. "I wouldn't break the law to protect him, if that's what you're asking."

I took that to mean he'd lend emotional support and maybe help with lawyers but wouldn't help him hide or escape. Good news for me, and for him, because now he could learn about Willa.

"I'm glad you said that, because I'm pregnant with your grandchild. Coming up on seven months. It's a girl. I'm planning to name her Willa for my late father."

I'm not sure what reaction I expected, but I got silence.

"Mr. Foster?"

"Maybe you should call me Richard."

I smiled. "Okay, Richard. Did you hear what I said?"

"I'm going to be a grandfather?" I recognized a familiar sound in his voice—awe mingled with a sort of terrified joy, as if letting the excitement in might somehow put it at risk. "Seven months, you say? Things between Lyle and me are bad, but I can't believe he didn't tell me." He fell silent a moment. "He obviously took my warnings to heart after Deanna, but I meant it when I said I'd never lie for him like his mother did."

I vaguely wondered what Lyle had done to Deanna, but that was pointless. "My daughter won't be able to count on her father, but I'm hopeful you'll be a man she can respect and love who will love her back. If you want to be that for her, then you're welcome to come meet us in August, after she's born."

"Wow." His voice broke apart a bit. "I'm sorry. I didn't expect all this. From one extreme to another . . . I'm a bit overwhelmed."

"I understand. I didn't mention Willa the last time we spoke because I was reeling from all Lyle's lies and needed to verify what we'd discussed. The PI checked into your background a bit, too. I'm not proud of that, but I needed to protect Willa. I hope you understand."

"Of course." He clucked. "I've gotten used to being alone—looking ahead and seeing myself getting old here in this living room all by myself. Never gave grandkids a thought. This is welcome news for sure."

For the first time all day, a genuine smile split my face. Willa would have a man who could dote on her because he had no wife or other grandkids to divide his attention. That might help her to be confident like Erin. "I'm glad."

A beat of silence passed. "Does Lyle know you've called me?"

"No. He still thinks I believe that he's in Florida working on the business deal my mother lent him the money for. He'll be unhappy that I contacted you, but I'm well past caring. He's left me unable to afford to keep my house, yet unable to sell it without his signature. I'll probably need to file for bankruptcy on top of finding a better-paying job as a single, working parent."

I covered my mouth with my free hand, stunned by my flippant tone and careless confession. I'd been acting more like Erin than myself lately. Although I'd never admit it aloud, this bold streak made me feel the best I had in weeks.

"I'm sorry my son has caused you and your family so much pain and trouble. I'm not a rich man, but I can help with some of the child-care costs . . ."

My nose tingled. The amount didn't matter; his kindness brought on fresh tears. "That's very sweet, thank you, but that's not why I called. Please don't worry about me. One way or another, I'll solve my own problems."

I had to learn to stand on my own, for Willa's sake.

"You're giving me a chance to be a grandfather after what my son has done, and that's priceless. Truly. I want to help, for both your sakes."

"Let's discuss that later. I've got more pressing things to address before Willa's born."

"Okay. I look forward to meeting you both. If Meggie were still alive, she would've been tickled to have had a baby *girl* to spoil." And then, as if realizing the implications of what he'd said, he fell silent again. "May I ask . . . what kind of time is Lyle looking at?"

"I'm not sure. We haven't gone to the cops yet. It's complicated, especially with Lyle having fled the country. We've considered negotiating to get him to agree to return the money if we don't press charges."

"Sounds risky."

"Yes." My willingness to consider bending the law to suit my needs—or my mother's needs—nagged. I'd never before believed in an "ends justifies the means" philosophy, but neither could I pretend that my innate sense of fairness was overly troubled by the alternative.

"If you need help, call me. Maybe I could finally make Lyle do the right thing."

I tried to picture Lyle's reaction to seeing his father and me, arm in arm, boarding his stupid yacht with the only deal that could keep him out of prison. How utterly magnificent it would be to wipe that smug look off his face, and to witness Ebba's crestfallen expression when she learned she hadn't won anything worth having. Better yet, I'd leave *them* reeling and penniless, the ultimate victory and justice. A delicious, vengeful giddiness bubbled inside.

"Thanks, but, again, I only called to tell you about Willa."

"Will you keep in touch during the pregnancy?"

"Sure." I gave my head a little shake at our surreal situation. "Listen, I'm sorry to cut this short, but I've got to run."

"Okay. You take care."

"You too." I sat there with the phone in my hands, almost disbelieving what I'd done. He'd been thoughtful and kind and generous, which should make it easier on my mother when she found out.

I stood and surveyed Lyle's things, which lay in garbage bags all around me. Time to take out the trash.

After I dropped Lyle's belongings at the consignment store, I mulled the OIA over during the drive to my mother's. The specter of public disgrace terrified me, as did the threat of mandatory visitation for Willa while Lyle remained in prison. But breaking the law wasn't something I would've ever considered before my husband betrayed me, and I did not want him to fundamentally change who I was.

My life would be worse if, once I worked through my sorrow—and someday I would—I couldn't recognize myself anymore. With each mile the answer became obvious. If only doing the right thing wouldn't put me at serious odds with my mother for the first time in my life.

Once I pulled the car into the driveway, I sat in the front seat and stared at the place that, for better or worse, had molded me.

Being the middle child made me invisible for much of my childhood. Even when I'd proudly pedaled my tricycle on the driveway, Kevin would whiz past on his two-wheeler, drawing "attaboys" from my parents. After Erin was born, evenings entailed my mother helping Kev with his second-grade homework while my dad bathed Erin and read to her before putting her down. Each night I'd quietly played with my dolls and waited for someone to notice me, which typically occurred only after I'd gone out of my way to do something thoughtful for my parents.

For years, I'd told myself that doing good meant I *was* good. That doing better made me better. Yet looking back I can't help but wonder if family dynamics, insecurities, and jealousies had warped me to the point where I no longer knew if I did things because I wanted to or because it was what pleased someone I loved. And if the latter, then what did that mean, and who was I, really? Was I someone with the courage to do what needed to be done when it wouldn't please others—specifically my mother?

I wouldn't find the answers sitting here, but talking to my mother shouldn't be this hard.

Whatever happened next, I vowed my daughter wouldn't need to "achieve" to get my attention. And she'd be able to talk to me about anything without punishment.

Those promises made me feel better about facing the firing squad inside. I grabbed my suitcases from the back seat, forced a smile, and went through the garage. My mother was on the phone, but her expression stopped me in my tracks.

Little mason jars covered the kitchen table, along with an open bag of sugar, some oils, and food dye. It stunned me that Erin involved our mother with Shakti Suds when she never let me help.

"Dodo, I'll call you later. Amanda just showed up." She nodded with the receiver in hand. "Yes, I'll be sure to tell her, and I promise we'll reschedule the baby shower when things settle down. Bye." She hung up and sighed. "I told Dodo about the divorce before she heard about it from someone else. At least I won't have to host her for three days now that we've canceled the baby shower. She sends her love."

"Mm. That's all she had to say?" I knew Aunt Dodo had opinions about me, Lyle, and divorce. Her judgmental nature had never annoyed me as much as it did Erin, probably because most of the time Aunt Dodo respected me and my choices.

"She wondered what was so irreconcilable that you couldn't fix it. Don't worry about it. I'll deal with my sister." She set her hands on her hips. "Going somewhere?"

I wished my mom hadn't lied to her sister, but arguing about that right now wouldn't pave the way for me to move in.

I pushed the luggage aside. "I can't stand my house. Everything there reminds me of Lyle, except it's all different now—twisted and ugly. Lonely. I thought I'd feel better here with you and Erin. But if I'll be in the way . . ."

"Don't be silly. Stay . . . although, if memory serves, sharing a room with your sister won't be relaxing."

Now that Kevin's old room was a dedicated office—cluttered with a desk and file cabinets—it wasn't an option for me. But oddly, I didn't mind.

"Don't say that. Besides"—I gestured to the mess—"it looks like you two are getting along. Are you helping her with her business?"

"She's pretending to do me the favor of keeping me busy, but secretly I think she knows she needs the help. It is a little relaxing to work with aromas for the sugar scrubs." She had a slight sparkle in her eye, and I was surprised that Erin had stealthily diverted our mother from grief. Perhaps I never gave my sister enough credit.

"Let's get you settled." Mom went to lift one of my suitcases. "So far Becky hasn't asked questions, but seeing your car here every day could raise some. And before you get upset about the irreconcilable-differences cover, remember it's the truth. After all, you can't reconcile with a thief. Months from now, when the divorce is final and we've settled things with Lyle, you'll be grateful that you didn't blab. Trust me, honey, never give people a reason to whisper about you at the grocery store or neighborhood party. It's nobody's business what goes on in this family."

I understood—empathized, even—with the desire to craft a palatable version of the truth. Her past aside, pride was a strong motivator, and marital affairs did inspire feeding frenzies among my colleagues and others. Yet if we kept telling half truths, we'd never create an environment that encouraged—embraced—the actual truth. But announcing my decision could wait until Erin arrived, because I wanted to have the conversation only once.

"Voilà." Mom grimaced as we entered the small bedroom carpeted with used towels and discarded clothes. "Some things haven't changed."

One only had to visit Erin's old apartment to know that much. "Do you think she'll mind the invasion?"

"It's my house, Amanda. Even if she minds, she won't argue."

That didn't make me feel better.

"Thank you for letting me stay." I held my belly when I bent over with a grunt to pick up some of my sister's things off the ground. "Where is Erin, anyway?"

"Walking Mo." Mom heaved both suitcases onto the small bed. "I'll let you settle in while I clean up the kitchen."

"What's for dinner?"

Mom shrugged, smiling at me in that worried way she did when one of her kids was hurting. "How about grilled cheese and tomato soup?"

We could do better than canned soup.

"Let me cook something. When I finish here, I'll see what you've got on hand and maybe run to the store. Now that I'm home, my appetite should return." When I kissed my mom's cheek, she gave me a hug and pat on the back. My fingers and toes prickled back to life as numbness faded.

"Suit yourself." She smiled and left me alone.

I hadn't slept in this room since graduating from college twelve years ago. It hadn't changed. Same white eyelet curtains. Same creaky dresser. Same scent of dusty old papers and aging vanilla candles.

Before I unpacked, I tossed Erin's discarded socks and dirty clothes in the hamper, then folded the few things that appeared to have been tried on and rejected, setting those items on her bed. We'd had epic throw-downs about this space, like the time she sneaked my new bikini to wear to the beach and then put it back damp and sandy. But having now shown up without invitation, I'd sit on my impulse to complain. Maybe this time around we could be better roommates and make the connection we'd failed to find as children.

While I was stowing my empty suitcases beneath my bed, Erin returned. From the muffled conversation in the other room, I assumed they were discussing my arrival.

Bracing myself, I went into the kitchen to make myself useful. The baking supplies I'd brought this morning sat unused, reminding me of all that had happened today. On the upside, cookies for dinner would be my plan B.

Mo jumped up on my legs, eager for love like me, so I smothered him with friendly petting. "Hey, Mo. Are you happy to see me again?"

I glanced up at my sister, awaiting an answer from the person of whom I'd actually been asking that question.

"I'll say this . . ." She smirked, a half smile in place. "Life's been interesting lately."

That much was clear. Less clear was whether she wanted me there.

"What do you think?" Mom held an open jar up to Erin's nose. "I call it Peppermint Pop."

Erin failed to stifle a grimace. "It's a little strong, like an Altoid."

"I *like* Altoids." Mom took her little box of jars. "These will be for me, then."

"Good initiative, though." Erin rubbed Mom's shoulder.

Oddly, I felt like an intruder. "Before we get all cozy, I've got more news to share. You might want to sit down first."

"That doesn't sound good." My mom pressed one hand to her temple and took a seat. Erin simply crossed her arms and leaned back against the counter. I might've unpacked prematurely, because Mom could freak out once she learned all my plans.

"I told Lyle's father about Willa." I raised my hands to stanch oncoming criticism.

My mother slapped her cheeks and gave some anyway. "Oh, honey. You don't even know the man. Why would you do that?"

"Because it's the right thing to do. Willa needs a man in her life. Kevin's busy in Baltimore with his career and family. Uncle Bob's got his own grandkids. Stan checked up on Richard—that's his name—and he's a decent, lonely man. He was lovely about it. Even offered to help with child support after he learned about what Lyle has done."

"You told him *everything*?" My mother pounded on the table before standing to pace, casting me furious glances. "What if he warns Lyle?"

"Mom, take a breath," Erin began, leading me to believe she supported my decision. Then she asked me, "Do you trust him?"

Her expression suggested she did not.

"They haven't spoken in more than three years. If push came to shove, I trust him to put Willa's needs ahead of Lyle's." Strangely, I smiled at the affirmation that Lyle hadn't completely killed my ability to trust someone—or at least not someone I'd had checked out by a PI.

"All righty, then," Erin said with a nod.

Mom cast her an irritated glance while muttering, "At least he's in Michigan. And he shouldn't want to spread the word about his son's criminal behavior any more than we do." She rubbed her temples so forcefully they might bruise. "But what good can come of inviting a stranger into our lives? That man raised Lyle, and look how *he* turned out. What makes you think he'll be a good influence on Willa?"

As a teacher, I'd seen good parents with troubled kids and troubled parents with wonderful kids. "Don't blame Richard. Lyle was born manipulative and made worse by a mother who enabled his entitled narcissism. I can't see the future, but we have to do what's right."

Erin smiled. "I'm proud of you."

I narrowed my gaze, searching for hints of sarcasm. "You make it sound like I don't usually do the right thing."

"But this time you didn't wait for approval. Maybe that's the silver lining in this whole situation." She opened the refrigerator, grabbed the OJ, and finished it straight from the bottle. Her chipper mood didn't make that compliment less backhanded.

"What's that mean?" I asked.

She shrugged one shoulder. "You don't usually do things without a consensus, but now you're making your own decisions, for better or worse. Backbone is a good thing."

"Meaning I'm normally weak?"

Erin grimaced. "'Weak' is harsh. Let's go with 'indecisive.'"

The fact that my mother failed to jump in or roll her eyes suggested my new "backbone" rattled her.

Was that how everyone saw me—a weak and indecisive person rather than a conscientious and cautious one? "It's hurtful when you paint me that way, you know."

"Oh for God's sake, Amanda. You and Mom are always pointing out things you'd like to change about me. Don't live in a glass house. Can't we learn to say what we feel and be okay with it? Otherwise this new living arrangement will result in one of us ending up in jail before Lyle."

She had a point.

Time to go all in and drop the next bombshell. "Well, if that's how you feel, you'll be thrilled to hear what else I've decided."

"Oh bother," my mother moaned, hanging her head. "What now?"

"Mom, keep an open mind. Stan found a legal way to get the boat. It's called an OIA operation—an otherwise illegal activity. Basically, the FBI can deputize me to help carry out a sting." I then explained the details as I understood them. "Obviously, it won't settle custody or give me control over my house, but if successful, we'd get the boat to sell, so you'd get paid back quickly. Plus Lyle will get a real comeuppance, and if Ebba's an accomplice, she'll land in jail, too. This is our best chance for real justice."

My mother covered her face with her hands, shaking her head. "So you don't care if our family loses all respect, or that your father's name will be remembered this way? You'd have Willa's life begin under a cloud of salacious gossip, and make me face the children I've taught and *their* kids, and my neighbors, as an idiot? I can't bear it, Amanda. Please. Don't make me uproot my life at sixty-two."

"Mom, it's terrifying and difficult, but it's not about only us. I've given this a lot of thought. I told you, if I confront Lyle with no backup, he'll probably laugh in my face and take off. So in the bigger scheme of things, this is our best chance of getting you your money back and of keeping Lyle from hurting *another* woman."

"This is a mistake you can't undo. It will take on a life of its own, and with the internet, it will never die!" Mom looked up, wild-eyed. I stood, arrested by her accusatory gaze, unaccustomed to being the disappointing child. Was this how Erin felt all the time? I guessed I ought to get used to it, because I had to have a "backbone" for Willa. She begged, "Let's try it ourselves, and then, *if we fail*, we go to the cops—"

Erin interrupted. "If you do that, Lyle has time to get away. Worse, if the authorities do catch up to him, he could squeal on Amanda for extortion."

"Damn it! Damn all of it." Mom waved her fists around before grabbing her car keys from the hook.

"Where are you going?" I asked.

"Somewhere to think." She glared at us both, although Erin brushed off Mom's outrage like she'd shoo a mosquito.

"Mom!" I called as she slammed the door to the garage in our faces. I whirled on Erin. "Should we stop her?"

"Nah." She inspected the bananas before choosing one to peel, calm as ever. "I don't want to give her the chance to wear down your resolve. You've made the right call. I can't wait to see Lyle's smug face when the cops raid his boat."

"Mom's not all wrong. This might not work out the way we hope. Kevin and Stan haven't gotten back to me yet about if the FBI will take this case and do the OIA. If not, we end up with all the negative publicity and none of the upside. Mom will never forgive me."

"I bet they'll go for the sting. If you can get a confession, it makes their case a slam dunk." Erin tossed the peel in the trash. "I know it's hard, but it's okay to stand up to Mom. Somewhere Dad is cheering."

That perked me up, having rarely been the one to surprise Dad with an act of courage. "I hope you're right."

"I am." She gave me a brief hug.

"Thanks for being supportive, and for not grousing about my moving in. I know it isn't what you expected when you agreed to keep an eye on Mom."

"You won't hear me complain about a free maid." She winked. "Seriously, it's good for us to hunker down together until things with Lyle get settled."

"Who would've thought we'd both be home again?"

The corners of her mouth drooped with her shoulders. "Fair warning, living here will make you miss Dad more. I 'see' him everywhere. On the other hand, Mom and I are getting along better."

"Well, looks like I might need your help with her."

"A role reversal!" She chuckled.

Wasn't it just. "If only Dad were here, maybe I'd get to be *his* favorite for a day."

Erin's grin faded. "I know you think Dad loved me best, but that's not true. We liked the same music and shared inside jokes, and he enjoyed my traits that made you and Mom uncomfortable, but he *loved* you and Kevin as much as me. Sometimes I think he went easy on me because the rest of you always cringed at my differences."

The impact of her words hit me from all angles, knocking my knees out from under me. "Did you . . . did you think I didn't like you?"

My head spun from the very idea because, for my whole life, I'd thought it the other way around.

"Don't start feeling guilty. I know deep down you and Mom love me even though I embarrass you." She flashed an impish smile, but if she believed what she was saying, it had to hurt.

"I'm sorry I made you feel that way. All I ever wanted was to be close. I tried so hard to get you to want to play with me, but you always ran off."

"I ran from your *dolls* and games like 'house.'" She crossed her arms. "Besides, if I'd brought you along to break all the rules, you'd have tattled."

"Only if you were doing something unsafe." Those words came out defensively—so much so that I had to laugh at myself. "Oh gosh. No wonder you ran."

Erin smiled with that same twinkle in her eye that Dad had. For the first time in weeks, my chest felt warm and fuzzy.

I grabbed my sister into another hug and squeezed tight. "I feel like we're finally coming to understand and count on each other. It means so much to me."

"Same here." She patted my back but eased away, averting her eyes. "Anyway, I'm heading out with Lexi for open-mic night at the Lamplight. Her boyfriend is singing, so she wants to stack the audience with fans."

I would've declined an invitation to join her in favor of making amends with Mom, but on the heels of our breakthrough, it would've been nice to have been asked. Then again, my giant belly didn't scream "bar buddy." "Have fun."

Erin affected a mock bow before exiting the kitchen.

Leaving me alone. Again.

I guessed Mom had gone to Dad's grave. Even a year later, she still turned to him when she got upset. Habits of a nearly forty-year marriage must be hard to break. One benefit of getting out of mine early would be learning to turn inward for answers. It wouldn't be an easy shift, but Willa needed me to be tougher by the time she arrived.

For now, I'd make one of my mom's favorite meals. As I opened the refrigerator door, a loud whoop rang out from the bedroom, followed by a hearty "It's like old times!"

In every way, my sister was coming through for me. Never in all these years had it occurred to me that my behavior had driven some of hers. She'd hidden her self-doubt so well I hadn't thought anything I did or said ever mattered to her. Our little talk had been a good start at being more honest.

With no more secrets and unspoken grievances between us, maybe now my sister and I would finally become friends.

CHAPTER FOURTEEN

ERIN

Apparently Mom's earlier "thinking" had resulted in a decision to answer Amanda's questions with yes/no answers, period.

My sister had to regret moving home at the exact time she finally stood up to Mom. Being surrounded by bad juju in that empty house across town must've been unbearable for her to willingly suffer this wrath. Mom's mood aside, we had to make it work because Amanda and Willa belonged with us.

My sister's inexperience with disapproval left her vulnerable, though. I suggested ignoring Mom until she surrendered. That always did the trick for me, but Amanda didn't have my alligator skin. In the time it took me to pick an outfit, shower, and laze around my newly cleaned room, she'd already cooked dinner and done a load of laundry to win back Mom's good graces.

Lexi honked her horn a second time, so I barreled through the living room to avoid being trapped by the tension, quickly waving goodbye.

I told myself my staying home tonight might cause a setback in Amanda's battle for independence. But I also tore out of there because it was easier to run away than be cast aside once the "star" child made amends. A part of me—a selfish part—wondered whether Amanda's return would affect the little rhythm Mom and I had forged while watching *Jeopardy!* and making sugar scrubs. We three Turner girls—soon to be four—faced weeks or months of breaking old habits and forming new ones.

And, aside from all those reasons to bolt, there *was* the fact that I hoped to bump into Eli tonight.

But running out the door didn't make it easier to ignore my sister's misery. She'd been brave today, calling Lyle's dad and moving forward with the cops. We'd had an awesome sisterly breakthrough, yet I still hadn't told her or Mom about my run-in with Lyle and Ebba. My dad had warned me not to build a relationship on lies, but this truth was more likely to destroy the progress we'd made.

I darted across the lawn—red Converse in hand—and flung open the dented door of Lexi's Corolla.

"You look hawt, E!" Lexi smiled, eyeing my supershort, fitted black dress with white and red stripes running down each side. By pairing the dress with my sneakers, I'd put together a trendy getup, if I did say so myself.

"Thanks." I buckled up before she pulled away from the curb, without mentioning the motivation behind my outfit. "Where's Tony?"

"I dropped him at the club first so he could do a sound check. You know how he gets, taking this so seriously, like he was Garth Brooks or something." She giggled, but when Tony sang onstage, he *was* Garth Brooks in her eyes.

Like every reference to country music lately, this made me think of Eli, who might actually know Garth Brooks.

I wondered if he'd recovered from his surprise ghost-a-gram since he'd scrambled away from Nancy and me on Monday. Each morning my yoga students had grown restless while I'd stared at the sliders, giving him an extra minute to show up. And every single time he didn't, the sky seemed duller. Then I'd remember my mom's advice and decide his disappearing act might be for the best. But tonight the buzz of anticipation swarmed my stomach. If he was at the Lamplight, I would check up on him. "Are we eating at the bar or stopping somewhere cheaper first?"

"Did you forget about the ladies' night special on open-mic nights? How 'bout we drink our dinner? We can get a bucket of Bud and a bowl of peanuts pretty dang cheap."

"Split an order of wings and I'm in." I reached over to hug her shoulders while she was driving. "You're the best date ever. Does Tony know how lucky he is?"

"He does." Her satisfied smile reminded me of how my sister used to grin when discussing Lyle. But in Lexi's case, she'd found the real deal. "You know, you haven't said boo about Max these past few weeks. Do you miss him at all, or are you ready to move on?"

"I don't miss him." That sounded idyllic, but it actually made me a little sad. Watching Amanda agonize over her divorce had me questioning whether I lacked some essential gene needed to form a loving attachment to any man other than my dad. "I could move on with the right guy."

With no trouble whatsoever, I conjured Eli's face. Practice makes perfect, like my mother claimed. If I closed my eyes, I could picture the way his solemn eyes lit up whenever the first hint of his soft smile peeked through, like the sun cutting through fog. Man, that little smile did things to me.

"How about going out with Tony's drummer, Dan? He's pretty chill, and cute. Big brown eyes—all soulful like you like. We could double-date all the time."

I nodded noncommittally but preferred Eli and his teal eyes. Lexi knew nothing about him, though, because bringing him up would invite questions I didn't want to answer. "What time does Tony go on?"

"He's second in the lineup, so probably between eight thirty and nine o'clock. There's another singer after him and then two comics."

"Ooh, comics." I cringed. "They're pretty painful in a joint like this. Maybe we can cut out before they go on."

"Oh, come on, E. You gotta support people with the balls to get up there and try."

"You're right." I practiced a fake laugh with a snort to see if I could pull it off. "Think that'll convince 'em they're funny?"

Lexi shook her head as she threw the car into park. "You are so weird."

"Thank you!" I opened the door and got out.

The Lamplight took its name seriously, with oil lanterns twinkling outside and in. My parents used to come here on dates to listen to live music. Mom would put on one of her fancier dresses, her hair done up, lipstick glossy and perfectly applied. I'd catch my dad patting her butt on their way to the car, and she'd half-heartedly shoo his hand away while flashing a flattered smile.

That sudden memory made me ache for yesteryear. For the chance to have done some things differently, and for another dozen years' worth of hugs from my dad.

The Lamplight seemed like the only thing that hadn't changed in the intervening years. Deep grooves marred its wood floors. High-backed red-vinyl-cushioned booths flanked the walls, creating little hideaways. A dozen or more café tables, all chipped and sticky because the waitresses couldn't keep up with the spilled beer and barbecue sauce, were scattered around the open space. Some nights they pushed those tables aside to make room for a dance floor, but on open-mic night they positioned them here, there, and everywhere to give the illusion of a full house.

Max and I had hung out here from time to time early in our relationship, when he still got amped about music. Those had been exciting days, when we'd happily discussed everything and anything to learn as much about each other as possible. He'd been quick to laugh and high on his own dreams until he butted up against rejection.

Some nights I wondered where it all went wrong, and whether *his* attitude hadn't been the *only* problem in our relationship. Had my disjointed lifestyle caused Max to lose his way? Had I expected to rise with his balloon and, when that didn't happen, popped it so he fell back to earth with me? Those answers eluded me, but one truth was clear: he and I hadn't brought out the best in each other.

In truth, I didn't even know what my best was—an uncomfortable confession to make so close to my thirtieth. Even recently I'd gotten swept up into our family drama instead of focusing on making those big changes I'd vowed to make. But perhaps that was fate's way of showing me that my best required help from people whose skills complemented mine.

"So we down with a bucket of Bud and some wings?" Lexi asked while scanning the room, presumably searching for Tony.

"Yep. Go give your honey a good-luck kiss. I'll grab us a table and place the order." I waved her off, nabbed a small table near the front, and flagged a waitress. My once-over of the room didn't reveal Eli. Bummer.

Lexi returned before the food and beer arrived. Then the lights dimmed, and the first musician—a fiftysomething soloist with a growly voice—strummed his guitar.

He wasn't half-bad, but the three beers I'd sucked down in forty minutes made me an easy audience. His average music gave me an excuse to zone out. My thoughts kept wandering to my mother and Amanda, and whether things would get better or worse for us. For the first time, I understood what it meant to be "in a funk." I wished I could shake it off like Mo did bathwater. This malaise wasn't as crippling as the grief I'd experienced a year ago, but I felt like a bird caught in an oil spill, gummed up and losing buoyancy.

During the dead zone between Growly's set and Tony's, I excused myself to use the restroom. On my return, movement in the back booth caught my eye. Granted, the dark corner made it difficult to see, but something about the man seated there made my body hum to life. When he looked up, my responding smile hurt my cheeks.

I waved before it occurred to me that Eli had chosen that particular booth to avoid people—maybe even to avoid me. Now he looked a bit like a cat burglar in a spotlight. Tapping into newfound maturity and empathy, I offered a friendly nod and began turning toward my own table, but then he waved me over.

A glance at Lexi showed that Tony and his two bandmates setting up had her full attention. She wouldn't miss me for a while.

Eli studied me as I approached, making me self-conscious. I didn't know what I hoped to gain by the "chance" run-in. From the first time we'd met, something about him had tugged at my chest, and my efforts to resist that pull were failing.

I slid onto the bench opposite him, determined to play it cool.

If my dad were here, he'd tell me to be myself so that, whatever happened, I wouldn't have regrets. That advice had never been hard to follow, yet Eli was like a new world that I didn't know how to navigate. A world with one rule: don't discuss Karen. I repeated that in my head a few times to make it stick.

Then I promptly went with the most honest thing I could say. "I kinda hoped to see you here tonight."

"Is that why you came?" He sat back, hiding his hands beneath the table, gaze searching mine.

"Not entirely. My friend Lexi"—I hooked a thumb over my shoulder in her direction—"asked me to come support her boyfriend, the guy setting up now. Did you come alone?"

"I did."

Good. "You don't seem shocked to see me."

"I'm not."

I teased, "Is that why *you* came?"

"Not entirely." He raised one shoulder with a slight tip of his head, grinning. "I like open-mic nights. You never know when you might hear someone with talent and original material."

He straightened his shoulders, fidgeting a bit in his seat. His apparent nerves made me feel less like a freak.

"Are you scouting or something?" That idea prompted several thoughts. First and foremost was the fact that someone like Eli had the power to make a person's dream come true, whereas someone like me did not.

"Not officially." He brought his hands back atop the table to toy with his half-empty beer bottle. I couldn't tell whether his anxiety was because he liked me or now regretted our not-entirely-accidental run-in.

"It's great that you're keeping your toes in the business." Jesus, to hear me you'd think Max also stole my conversation skills.

"I'll never quit music altogether, even if I'm no longer writing. It's too much a part of me to fully walk away." He tucked his chin, looking twice as cute when a little embarrassed, although I didn't know why that admission made him uncomfortable.

Fortunately for him, I could demonstrate how to well and truly make a humiliating confession. "You're lucky you have something that matters that much to you. Most of us don't."

He pulled a sip from his longneck while keeping his gaze locked on mine. "Seems to me you have a lot of things that interest you . . ."

Namely him, at the moment.

"Passing fancies, as my mom calls them." I almost covered my mouth after that unintended confession.

He narrowed his gaze. "So there's nothing you're devoted to?"

His pointed question unmoored our little booth. If my goal was to make him *less* interested, I was killing it! Actual self-improvement would have to wait until a later date. Right now, I had to spin my fatal flaw. "I've got too many dreams and ideas, so I can't devote myself to one thing."

The relief from my mildly clever answer got cut short in a matter of seconds.

"Dreaming's easy. It lets you feel productive while you avoid the work it takes to make a dream reality." He sipped his beer while that observation simmered. "You don't strike me as lazy, though. Maybe you don't try so no one can say you failed?"

Those words triggered a long-forgotten memory, dazing me like a camera's flash.

"Why are you quitting the dance team when you're finally old enough to audition for the Christmas show?" My dad cut into his apple and ate the slice straight from the paring knife.

I shrank in my seat, swinging my feet while drinking chocolate milk. Amanda had been picked to play Clara in *The Nutcracker* when she'd been in fifth grade. I'd probably end up as one of the mice. "I'm bored of it now."

He handed me a slice of his apple. "Bored, or scared?"

"'Scared'?" I laughed a little too hard before biting into the apple.

"Part of trying new things is learning what you like and don't like, so if you're bored, then quit. But, Erin, getting good at things requires commitment and learning how to come back harder if you fail the first time. Promise me you won't quit things because you're scared you're not good enough."

"Erin?" Eli leaned across the table, his hand stretched out almost far enough to touch mine. He didn't, but heat radiated between us, brushing against my skin nonetheless. "I'm sorry. I didn't mean to offend you."

"It's fine." I waved him off, still shaken by the memory of my dad as a younger, healthy man. I wanted to hold that image close, or, better yet, have him back for one more day. More dreaming . . . "But since we're speaking about not trying things, you haven't come to another yoga class."

"Nothing personal." Eli swigged more beer while I tried to read his giant, soulful eyes. "I'm . . . not over the shock from what happened last time."

Tony's voice momentarily snagged my attention. Lexi had her chin on her fists, probably smiling at him while he sang the opening line of "Wild Horses." I turned back to Eli, sidestepping the Nancy topic. "That's my friend's boyfriend. He's a foreman by day. What do you think?"

"He's not half-bad."

"But only half-good?" I teased. Tony could carry a tune, but that was about the limit of his ability.

"He looks happy enough singing for this crowd." He pushed his empty bottle to the edge of the table. "When you love to play, it fills your soul whether there are ten or ten thousand people listening."

Eli had no idea about my Google-stalking him and Karen. That had led me to a bunch of his work—an impressive list of cowritten songs plus a few YouTube videos of him performing. His singing voice sounded a bit like Don Henley's, which I wouldn't have predicted. Regardless, I'd give up a full cup size for a private concert. "Do you miss performing?"

"Sometimes." His nonchalance didn't fool me, though.

I gestured to the stage. "Why don't you get up there?"

His gaze shot into space while his fingers drummed the table. When he finally returned from his mental meandering, he said, "'Cause my old songs make me sad, and I haven't written anything new."

"Oh." I interlaced my own fingers together instead of reaching for his hand. Don't say it. Don't . . . Oh, hell. I was gonna say it. "If your wife actually spoke through Nancy, maybe she wants you to write again."

Crap.

His blue eyes turned the grayish color of a stormy sea.

"Sorry," I mumbled, glancing toward Lexi to escape Eli's glare. She shot me a questioning look. My subtle shake of the head was meant to keep her away.

Eli shifted in his seat again, and I half expected him to ask me to go. "The thing is, I've been creeped out ever since that day. There've been times since Karen died when I would've sworn I felt her—when I'd honestly believed I had—but they'd been more like a dream or a wish. Now I'm walking around wondering if she's here with me all the time—watching me, hearing my thoughts, listening to my conversations—like right now, sitting here with you. I hate that idea, which makes me feel shitty because I loved her and would give anything for her to be alive. I'm truly effed-up."

The layers of emotion he'd unpacked settled around me like discarded diary pages tossed in the air. The moment felt fraught, as if our booth had become a spring-loaded booby trap I could trip with one wrong word.

"It's hard for me to know what to say because I've never lost someone I loved that much. Well, I loved my dad, but that's different. Still, part of me likes the idea that he might be around all the time, and that he actually hears me when I'm talking to him. And that maybe he's enjoying when I play a favorite album and picture something we'd done together while listening to it. Sure, there are some things I wouldn't want him seeing or knowing"—my cheeks grew hot because I was thinking about sex, at which point I started looking at everything but Eli—"but he probably wouldn't want to see them, either, so I bet he'd make himself scarce whenever they cropped up. Heaven is supposed to be better than earth, so there have got to be better things for spirits to do than spy on us twenty-four seven, right? I guess I think spirits only come back now and then to check in and make sure people are getting on okay without them."

When I looked up at Eli, he surprised me with a wide grin. "You're odd. You know that, right?"

His affectionate tone kept me from being offended. Besides, who can fault a guy who admires uniqueness? "So I've been told. My dad found me charming, so I've never felt the need to fit in."

He drummed his thumbs on the table again. "Your dad sounds like a wise man."

"He was wise and kind and warm and wonderful." Traits Eli seemed to share. No wonder I felt some familiarity even though we barely knew each other.

"Can I ask you something?"

"Sure." I leaned forward.

"Why are you here on a Saturday night alone?"

"I'm not alone, remember? I came with my friend." I pointed in Lexi's direction again, in case he hadn't believed me before.

"I meant, why aren't you on a date?"

My brows rose. "You know how well my last relationship turned out. Add to that my brother-in-law's latest stunt, and you'd get why my focus is elsewhere."

He frowned. "What did your brother-in-law do?"

"Oh shoot." I covered my mouth while debating how to dig out of this hole. In truth, Eli hardly seemed like a guy who mingled and gossiped.

"Can you keep a secret—I mean, seriously keep one?" When he nodded, the idea of discussing Lyle with someone other than my mom and sister came as a relief. "The short version is that he ran off with a bimbo, leaving my sister alone and pregnant. There's more to it, but Amanda and I don't have the kind of relationship where I feel I can say more, if you know what I mean."

"Mm, only child here, so I can't claim to get the nuances of sibling relationships."

"I remember." We smiled at each other, perhaps both harkening back to the bench outside the post office. With the music playing in the background, anyone—including me—could've mistaken *us* as being on a date, eagerly learning bits and pieces of information about each other. If Karen *was* floating around, I hoped she liked me enough to whisper in Eli's ear that he could lean on me as he took his first steps forward without her.

"That's all unfortunate," he added, "but you seem too young to be cynical about men."

"Not so young. Just immature." I winked, and he chuckled. "And not entirely cynical. There are plenty of men out there like my dad. But my thirtieth birthday is soon, and I need to get myself together before I involve anyone else."

"That doesn't sound immature."

"An anomaly, I promise." I laughed. "Meanwhile, you talk like you're an old man, yet you can't be more than thirty-four."

"Thirty-six . . . despite the baby face." He circled his face with one hand.

"It's the eyes." I could stare into them forever—so bright—like a sunny sky after days of rain. For a few precious seconds we gazed at each other as if there weren't another thing on earth worth seeing.

The waitress killed the moment when she stopped by to check if we needed refills. We both declined. After she left, Eli folded his arms on the table. "Everyone's a work in progress, so don't put your love life on hold while you evolve."

I'd been around the block enough to recognize the subtle cast of that line, and starving fish that I was, I risked the bite. "If the right man came along—someone honest and interesting—I'd probably throw my heart in the ring again."

Another period of silence passed before he leaned across the table, dropping his voice. "Since you're spilling secrets, maybe I should share one of my own."

Please, God, don't let the purring in my chest be heard over the twang of Tony's guitar. "Do tell."

"The truth is . . ." He swallowed thickly. "You're the first woman I've met since Karen that's made me feel anything at all. That's why I came to yoga, and also why that psychic shook me up so bad. I felt guilty, like my being there had hurt my wife, no matter what she supposedly said in her 'message.'"

Hearing his secret taught me what winning the lottery would feel like, which was equal parts an urge to shriek and an inability to breathe. Amanda would have a smart response—something empathetic and interesting. I wanted to leap over the table and wrap him in a big hug, and maybe add a kiss. Definitely a kiss. Instead, I scooted off the bench and held out my hand. "Let's go get ice cream."

"Ice cream?" His head flinched back briefly, brows pulled tight, but he clasped my hand. He didn't gingerly hold it in awe and trace all the lines on my palm, but my entire body warmed from his touch anyway.

"My dad and I always got ice cream to celebrate a good day or a milestone. From my perspective, what you said is something to celebrate."

A painfully beautiful smile spread across his face, which pretty much stole my heart for good. It was too soon to say that to any sane person, so it stayed in the vault, but that right there—that smile would make it into the memory jar before the night ended.

Eli gestured toward the door. "Then ice cream it is."

"Let me tell Lexi. She'll hang with Tony when he's done, so it's no biggie." Lexi had never been needy or possessive, and Tony's set would be over soon anyway. It was hard to let go of Eli's hand, knowing I might not get another chance to hold it for some time.

Less than ten minutes later, Eli and I had ordered ice cream at Dream Cream and found a seat on the bench outside the shop. He'd gotten coffee chocolate chip in a cone, and I'd ordered a sundae with extra whipped cream.

"I'm glad I ran into you tonight." I licked whipped cream from my chin. No one had ever accused me of gracefully devouring a sundae. "Thanks for the excuse to pig out."

"You're welcome." He'd grown quiet since we'd arrived. Whatever his interest in me, he wasn't ready to act on it. For all I knew, he was thinking about his wife now, maybe even feeling guilty about what he'd admitted. If I wanted to know this man, it'd require baby steps. Not my strength. "I keep thinking about what you said at the bar—"

"Erin, I—"

I held up my hand. "Let me finish, please. I only want to say that I could really use a new friend. It seems like you could use a new friend, too. So from now on, I'll drag you out of your house to take walks with Mo, and you think up new excuses to eat more ice cream."

He tipped his head, blinking at me as if he wasn't quite sure what to make of me. Most of the time that was probably a good thing.

"The walks will keep us from gaining weight." He licked his cone.

"They won't hurt, that's for sure."

He tossed the uneaten remains in the trash. "I only see one problem with your plan."

"Please don't tell me you don't like ice cream, 'cause that's a deal breaker. I got a little suspicious when you ordered a coffee flavor." An animated grimace accompanied my odd sense of humor. "No true ice-cream lover picks coffee over all the other choices. Were you thinking that sounded more macho than raspberry ripple or tutti-frutti?"

"I can't say that I've ever been accused of acting macho." He grinned.

"Some people see stuff through rose-colored glasses. Mine are more like mirrors in a fun house. Things get a little weird and distorted, but it's entertaining!" At least I hoped he thought so.

"Duly noted. But let's get back to your plan's flaw."

"Only one? Wow, I'm getting smarter every year. Okay, lay it on me. What's the flaw?" I shoveled a huge amount of my sundae into my mouth to stop the nervous chatter.

"Maybe it's not a flaw but a request."

I swallowed the giant ball of ice cream and fudge so I could speak. "Ask away. You'll find me to be a very easygoing friend—open to lots of things."

He cocked his head, his expression so soft it made my heart mushier than the puddle of fudge and whipped cream in my cup. "Well, then, maybe I have my answer."

"But I don't know the question." I held my breath.

He leaned forward, elbows on his knees, head down. "I wonder if, at some point in the future, this new friendship might develop into something more . . ." He glanced up at me without turning his head.

Breathe. "Like I said, I'm open to lots of things."

Dream Cream's orange neon sign lit the easy smile stretching across his face. "I'm glad your ex was a thief."

"Me too."

CHAPTER FIFTEEN

AMANDA

Any other day, I might've raved about the walnut paneling and Concord dentil crown molding in Kevin's law firm's conference room. The beauty of the oval burled-wood table would've mesmerized me. I might've affectionately stroked the butter-soft leather chairs and even admired the freshly vacuumed emerald-green carpet.

I'd never before been to his office, which was luxurious. Formal. Pristine.

Everything I typically loved.

But words like "divorce," "foreclosure," and "the FBI" echoing off all its surfaces put those things in a new perspective.

My swollen feet stretched my favorite leather pumps to the point where the stitching might pop. If I could've kicked them off without being noticed, I would've. Instead, I swiveled in the chair between Kevin and Stan, my back sticky from sweat, while legalese muddled my brain. The stress-and-pregnancy-hormone cocktail didn't help my concentration.

"What does 'quasi-judicial' mean?" The bank's notice of intent lay there taunting me while Kevin attempted to once more explain

Maryland foreclosure law. And yet again, my mind shot to something more pleasant, like contemplating the room's artwork.

"Never mind," he said when faced with my drifting gaze. He adjusted his tie. "The key thing is that if you don't file a request to mediate within twenty-five days of that notice, the bank can foreclose on your house in forty-five days."

No amount of Visine had helped soothe my dry eyes. The stinging wouldn't subside without sleep, which I hadn't had in days. Squeezing my big-bellied body onto a twin mattress accounted for half my insomnia. Mom's silent treatment made up the other. So far, none of my nightly staring at the ceiling had revealed the secret to sparing us all the public embarrassment of Lyle's fraud. But Erin was being supportive, and I refused to let my mother bully me. Yes, she certainly had a lot on the line, but so did I. After a lifetime of making her proud, it hurt that she wouldn't hold my hand and face this with me instead of making it harder.

I unclenched my jaw, massaging the ache. "Mediation seems pointless. I can't make the late payments. Even if I could, I can't pay the mortgage absent a lottery win."

Foreclosure would be another ding to my family's reputation and leave me homeless. I'd be less worried if I felt I could stay indefinitely at my mother's. But she'd left the refrigerator door open for two hours the other day and burned her hand getting something out of the oven last night. If her anger didn't subside soon, I might have to move out, probably to someplace unpleasant like Erin's former apartment. I would cry about all of it if weeks of chaos and heartbreak hadn't deadened my emotions.

Kev sighed. "I'll lend you money to tide you over until things get sorted out. Once Lyle's arrested, his lawyers will advise him to show remorse to earn leniency, and encourage him to cooperate with you by signing over a power of attorney to sell the house. We could also try to apply pressure with regard to the divorce settlement and custody agreement."

My generous brother kept talking, but my thoughts raced to Willa and whether she would resent me for putting her father in jail. Or if she might grow up mistrusting all men because of her dad. Nothing my brother offered up helped me solve *those* problems.

Kevin cleared his throat, which brought me back to the conversation. "File the mediation request to preserve the chance to pay off the bank and move on with a little equity in your pocket. Otherwise the bank will accept the quickest sale in a foreclosure to cut its losses and you could lose all your equity. Worse, any expenses the bank incurs in those proceedings get charged to you, so you could even owe money after the sale."

I closed my eyes against the unfairness. Then again, I'd blindly trusted my husband to run our finances. Perhaps I was getting exactly what I deserved.

"Thanks, Kevin. I appreciate your generosity." My hand found his and squeezed it hard. "But I can't take your money. Our whole plan depends on the FBI agreeing to the OIA and Lyle getting convicted, but we've got no guarantee those things will happen. I can't stomach owing both Mom and you money for the rest of my life."

"I already spoke with the US attorney for the District of Maryland. Remember when I interned in that office during my first summer in law school?"

I didn't remember, or maybe I'd forgotten. I could hardly keep track of his career path except to note that it generally trended upward.

"If you get Lyle on tape, he'll bring charges. He's already contacted Agent Crowley to let him know, so today's interview is teed up."

"This could still go sideways." I glanced at the box of documents Stan had amassed. My knee hadn't stopped jiggling for the past ten minutes. "I'm sort of panicking. Mom's both angry and out of it, walking around talking to herself. She accidentally dumped bleach in a dark load of laundry, then blamed me."

Kevin sighed. "Any word from the neurologist?"

"No markers for Alzheimer's or dementia, which is a relief. It seems the lapses are grief- and stress-related. Involving the FBI hasn't helped."

I stared at my fingers, having chipped some of the pink polish off my thumbnail in a fit of nervousness. "She's talking about moving."

Kevin gripped my hand again. "Don't blame yourself for how Mom chooses to respond to the situation she helped create." I blinked into his intense gaze, grateful for the way he'd given voice to something I'd felt too guilty to utter. I hadn't *asked* for that money. Mom had offered it. That didn't absolve either of us from our lack of due diligence, but this wasn't entirely my fault. "The FBI is our best chance of getting things settled properly. This case is below the financial threshold normally required for FBI resources, but the AG's interest might sway Agent Crowley."

Something shifted in my belly, as if Willa had overheard our conversation and grown tense. It felt like a cramp, but I brushed it off as nerves.

"Amanda," Stan interrupted, "I know you're outside your comfort zone, but Agent Crowley is fair and reasonable. Let's be optimistic."

"I appreciate all you've done to help, but you two don't need to sugarcoat this. I know where things stand and that we have to keep moving forward despite my doubts."

The two men exchanged a look that I couldn't quite read.

"We should probably hit the road so we aren't late for the appointment." Stan scooted his chair back, hands flattened on the table, ready to shove off as soon as Kevin agreed.

I could hear my ragged breath. If asked, I couldn't have explained exactly why fear now spread through my veins, holding me in place, but it did nonetheless. The anxiety of the unknown, the humiliating buzz that would follow Lyle's arrest, the uncertainty of my mother's and my financial futures. My eyes were closed when my brother rubbed my shoulder.

"We're all in your corner, and we'll be here to help pick up any pieces. In a year or two, you'll look back on this and be proud of how you handled it." He kissed my temple.

"Let's hope so." Projecting ahead a year or two to a bleak future that in no way matched the life I'd tried to build made me ill. I cradled my stomach, eager to become a mother my daughter could be proud of.

"Let's go." Kevin offered his hand to help me out of my chair. Willa might only be as big as an eggplant at this point, but my distended body made me unsteady, not to mention the pressure she put on my bladder.

Kevin and Stan conversed in the front seat while my heart beat louder with each mile. Through the window, I could see other drivers whizzing past. How many wrestled troubles like mine—marriages gone bad, money crises, self-recriminations?

Twenty minutes later, we'd pulled into the parking lot of the Baltimore FBI office building.

I pressed my hands to my chest in a wasted effort to slow my racing heart. Having never been questioned by any officer for anything—not even a traffic ticket—I let my imagination run wild. What if he didn't believe me? What if I'd upset my mother for nothing?

"You okay? You're sweating," Kevin said over his shoulder.

I fanned myself. "Nervous."

"I won't leave your side." My brother helped me out of the car, and we followed Stan into the building, where we passed through a security check before heading to the elevator bank.

When the elevator doors closed, hot and cold flashes racked my body. My ears rang and I trembled with nausea, pulling away as if we could run back to the car and forget it all. I'd never hated my husband more than I did while riding up to Agent Crowley's office.

"Kevin, I'm afraid." I gripped his arm.

"You've done nothing wrong." He slung an arm over my shoulders.

He wanted me to feel safe, but that required a level of trust I'd probably never again achieve. Before I could reply, the elevator doors opened.

A tall man in a navy blazer and coal-black hair shook Stan's hand. "Stan, good to see you again." He turned his sober gaze on Kevin and me. "Mrs. Foster, I'm Agent Crowley. Please, come to my office."

Four hours and one hellacious drive on I-695 later, I dragged myself into my mother's kitchen. "Hello?"

No answer.

Good. My head throbbed and I thought I might wilt from exhaustion. I couldn't remember the barrage of questions, but the humiliation of having to look at Agent Crowley and share the truth—worse, to convince him of my claims—would stay with me forever. Some time alone and rest to recover my strength before going another round with my mother would be a blessing.

I cranked open the window to let in the breeze. It tickled the hairs on my neck but didn't last long enough to be refreshing. After grabbing at the paper towels and soaking them in cold water, I patted down my face and neck, but it'd take an ice bath to reduce my swelling.

My favorite maternity dress now sported sweat stains that might never come out. I plugged my phone into the charger before collapsing onto a kitchen chair and kicking off my shoes. Bending over to rub my feet proved too much of a challenge, so I leaned back, stretched them out, and wiggled my chubby toes.

Even without my pregnancy-acquired sensitivity to smells, I knew I needed a fresh change of clothes. Heaving myself out of the chair, I then waddled into the living room, at which point I stopped dead. My mother didn't bother to glance up from the book she was reading in Dad's Barcalounger.

Her silent tantrum shouldn't have shocked me. She'd pulled it on Dad when he'd supported Erin's decision not to go to college. She'd used it on Kevin when she caught him and his ninth-grade girlfriend going to third base in our basement. She'd done it to Erin too many times to count. But this one—my first—had lasted for days, and I was sick of it.

Clumsily, I settled my weight on the sofa arm, dropping my shoes to the floor. My stomach cramped again, as it had, on and off, all afternoon.

"Oh, you *are* home." I stared at her until she spared me a glance.

"Where the hell else could I go now? I'll be entombed here in perpetuity once Lyle's arrest hits the local paper."

Whenever Mom whipped out her more colorful vocabulary, a lecture would follow. "I can't keep apologizing, Mom. You're angry with me. I get that. Sorry, *not* sorry, for trying to get your money back in a way that didn't land us both behind bars. In case you're interested, the FBI agreed to deputize me for the OIA once they finish verifying what we told them. It looks like we'll coordinate with the Puerto Rican field office, given Lyle's present course."

"How *exciting* for you." She kept her eyes on her book. The icy sarcasm made me shiver even though I was still sweating.

"You do know you're not the only one affected by all of this, right? Whatever you and I suffer, at least *we* are partly to blame for our mistakes. What about my innocent baby? She's likely to suffer her entire life because of her father's crimes. So maybe think about that while you sit there trying to make me feel worse than I already do. Involving the authorities was the smart choice. Why can't you admit that if we'd done it your way, we probably would've failed?"

She set her book on her thighs. "We don't know that."

"Our chances are much better with coaching and backup." Another cramp grabbed hold. I winced and blew a few short breaths.

"What's the matter?" Her sharp gaze softened as it dropped to my stomach.

After the cramp passed, I slid from the arm to the cushion. "It's been a rough day. Lots of cramping."

Her anger gave way to concern, but her pinched expression made me uneasy. "Are you sure those aren't contractions?"

"I don't know." I shrugged. "I've never done this before—I thought contractions were painful. These feel more like a ball of pressure collecting and releasing. It's probably from stress."

"But it could be more serious, especially if it's been happening all day. You're barely seven months pregnant. If you're having preterm labor contractions, we need to go to the doctor." She set her book aside and came over to lay her hand on my stomach. "Have you eaten today?"

Nothing since the banana and cup of yogurt this morning. "Not much." Everything I ate came back up on me when I was nervous, and I'd puked enough during my first trimester to last a lifetime.

"Amanda! Have you been keeping hydrated?"

To be honest, the past few days had been a blur of terse conversations here, phone calls with Kevin and Stan, and donning a brave face in public despite telling a few people about the divorce. The last thing on my mind had been making sure to drink enough water or juice.

I flinched when another cramp tightened my abdomen.

"That's it. We're going to the doctor. I'll drive." My mother stood and then helped me off the sofa.

She had me alarmed now. Though, admittedly, having her back on my side helped me cooperate.

"Where's Erin?" A month ago I wouldn't have wanted her with me during a crisis. Amazingly, Lyle and the end of our marriage had brought about something I'd craved my whole life.

"She left a while ago." Mom found her purse by the television. "I think she went over to visit that man Nancy helped."

I doubted Eli thought Nancy had helped him. "Oh, she didn't mention those plans to me."

The other morning we'd lain in our beds while she repeated, word for word, her conversation with him at the Lamplight and Dream Cream, but she hadn't said anything about a date.

"Who says there were 'plans'? You know her and her last-minute decisions. Now come on, I'll drive." My mother took my elbow as if I couldn't walk for myself, but I allowed her to feel useful and needed. As a retired widow with grown children, she probably didn't feel that way often. "We can't let this FBI business affect little Willa's health, or yours."

Despite weeks of Mom's befuddled behavior, her laser focus returned. I'd meant to change out of my sweaty clothes, but my doctor had surely seen and smelled worse. Mom hustled me into the car so quickly I forgot my phone, so I borrowed hers.

On the way to my OB's office, conveniently located in a profes-sional wing of the hospital, I called my doctor but got the answering service, who told me to go directly to the emergency room. I also tried Erin, but she didn't answer, so I left a message before slipping Mom's phone back into her purse as she parked in the shadow of the hospital.

It didn't matter how new the furniture, how big the fish tank, or how sunny the large windows were in any emergency room; they still made me nervous. The elderly man and his oxygen tank. The mom with a coughing child at her side and another on her lap. The clunking electric locks of the doors whenever health care workers strolled in and out of the patient waiting room. The sirens of the ambulance and then the hustle of nurses racing someone on a gurney back into the bowels of the hospital.

It took some time to fill out the paperwork and have my vitals taken. Finally, they put me in a small room, hooked me up to an IV saline drip, and strapped some equipment across my belly to measure my contractions and monitor Willa's heart rate.

My mother paced the tight space while we waited for my doctor.

"Mom, please sit. You're making me more nervous." I nibbled at my cuticles.

She sat in a plastic prefab chair. "Sorry."

"Did Erin call back?"

"Not yet." She dug through her purse and pulled out a pack of gum. "I swear, lately everything is hanging by a thread. We're good people. Why are these bad things happening?"

Having already exhausted my own supply of self-pity, I didn't answer right away. The two of us had spent most of our lives deter-mined to avoid walking in the kinds of shoes now shoved on our feet. For a long time, I'd believed my way of navigating life had made me smarter than others, and that that would protect me from this kind of fate. Now I knew better.

I wasn't smarter than anyone, and no one gets through life unscathed.

I glanced at my mother, who still clung to childlike notions of fairness. "Most people are good people, yet bad things happen every day. You and I? We aren't unique victims. Erin's right—we need to learn to roll with life's punches. We didn't deserve what's happened, but if we'd been less prideful, we might've seen it coming. Being gossiped about won't be fun, but worse things could happen, like Willa coming two months too soon."

"Don't even say that, Amanda." My mom shot both hands out. "Please lie there and relax while you hydrate. From now on, you have to pay more attention to your health."

If I'd hoped my perspective affected her, I'd be disappointed. My mother was who she was—a flawed woman who'd nonetheless been devoted to doing her best as a wife, mother, and librarian. I couldn't recall her ever trying to view herself or her behavior in a different light. Maybe at a certain age you don't want to make changes, or maybe becoming a widow had been all the change she could handle. I didn't know, but it didn't matter. I could control only my own way of handling life, which meant I had to let go of my need for perceived perfection.

The monitor tracking Willa's heartbeat—strong and steady— suggested that she'd be a fighter, like Erin. "I thought reading all the parenting books would make me a good mother. But look at me. Floundering on my own and not even managing to get the pregnancy right. I know parents make mistakes, but what if I screw *everything* up?"

My mother got out of her chair and stroked my hair. "You won't screw it up. And you're not alone. Erin and I will help you in every way we can."

A firm hug signaled a détente, and I almost wept from relief. This situation had brought out the worst in my mother, but throughout most of my life, she'd given me a secure home and solid family, a sense of right and wrong, and much praise. On the whole, she'd been a loving mother, and I loved her despite her shortcomings, exactly as I hoped my daughter would see past mine.

Then Dr. Wyler walked into the room with my chart. "Amanda, how are you feeling now?"

My mother stayed at my bedside, holding my hand.

"I don't know. Am I in preterm labor?" I asked.

Dr. Wyler read the monitor. "I'm pretty sure you're experiencing Braxton-Hicks—or false labor—contractions, but let's do a quick pelvic exam to confirm. How long have they been happening?" She disappeared from view while doing the exam.

"On and off all day." I stared at the ceiling.

My mom patted my hand reassuringly.

"Have they gotten stronger or come closer together since they started?" Dr. Wyler asked.

"They've been sporadic, but I had a busy day, so I wasn't paying close attention."

Dr. Wyler pushed back and removed her gloves, smiling. "You aren't dilating, and the data collected since you arrived confirms your account."

"Thank God." The wave of relief slackened my muscles. "So what's happening, exactly, and how do I make it stop?"

"Braxton-Hicks are commonly brought on by too much activity or by dehydration, so make sure that you're drinking enough water and getting lots of rest."

I *had* been screwing it up. Better hydration would be easy, but rest might be tricky given my plans to help the FBI. "When you say rest, do you mean bed rest? I have travel plans this month."

"Where to?"

"The Caribbean . . . Puerto Rico."

Dr. Wyler frowned. "You're not on bed rest, but we discourage international travel around this point in the pregnancy, especially to countries with a high risk of Zika. Puerto Rico's slow recovery from Hurricane Maria means you could face additional risks with its water and such. I strongly advise you to reschedule those plans for next year."

Zika!

"I hadn't thought of that!" I wouldn't put Willa at risk, but now my mom's chance of a full recovery of her money dropped to nil. We couldn't catch a break.

"The good news is you should be fine if you keep hydrated and take it easy. Don't push yourself too hard." Dr. Wyler smiled at my mother and me. "I'll see you at your next appointment. When the IV is empty, the nurses will have you sign some paperwork before you can go home."

"Thank you," I said. After the doctor left the room, my mother's pleasant expression vanished. Uh-oh. "What are you thinking?"

"Nothing." She smoothed her skirt, averting her eyes.

"Mom." I stared at her to force a conversation, refusing to simply appease her.

She sighed, still looking at some distant spot. "I knew counting on the sting operation would be a mistake, and now we have nothing."

"I'm sorry." It figured that the one time I'd ever defied my mother had come back to bite us both. "I promise I won't rest until you're paid back everything Lyle took."

She waved me off. "Let's both focus on the baby."

I laid my head back and closed my eyes as my enmity toward my husband spread through me like the saline solution pumping into my veins.

A future in which I hated Willa's father as much as I loved *her* sounded grim and impossible. I'd never have peace of mind unless we got the title to that yacht before Lyle was apprehended.

CHAPTER SIXTEEN

ERIN

"Hey there, buddy." Eli crouched to pet Mo, who'd jumped up to excitedly hump his leg. Couldn't blame Mo for *that* urge. Eli glanced up at me, smiling, before he stood. "Good to see you again."

Sadly, he didn't scratch behind my ears or offer any other physical affection. Our slow friendship-to-maybe-more track would test my newfound maturity. His "casual cookout" invitation had been a huge first step, but my expectations remained in check.

He stepped back to let Mo and me into his house. Once again, its fresh scent gave me all the homey feels. There were a million things to investigate—the photographs, the knickknacks strewn about, and what appeared to be a collection of awards—but snooping so soon would be rude.

I handed him a box of cupcakes from Hannah's. "Full disclosure—the only things I cook come in a can or other container, so I bought these for after dinner."

"Sugar Momma's?" His inquisitive tone suggested he hadn't heard of it.

"Don't tell me you've never been?"

He shook his head. Using his thumbnail to cut through the yellow-and-turquoise sticker that sealed the carton, he then lifted the lid to take a gander at the double-chocolate cupcakes with sprinkles.

"Obviously you don't get out enough. Lucky for you, I can add Potomac Point tour guide to my list of odd jobs. Sugar Momma's is on the west side of town, across the street from Give Me Strength—the fitness center where I also teach. Hannah makes this bay's best chai and some awesome pastries, too." I smiled, then remembered another facet he'd enjoy. "Actually, she plays great tunes in there, too. Eclectic stuff."

"Guess I'd better book a tour. Maybe you can pencil me in one day next week." He set the cupcakes on the dining room table, then crooked his finger so I'd follow him to the kitchen, where he opened the refrigerator. "Can I get you a drink—tea, beer, wine?"

The Coronitas and limes on the top shelf called to me. "I'll take a beer."

I set my cinch sack on the peninsula and scanned the kitchen while he opened my bottle and sliced a lime. Soapstone counters, walnut cabinetry, oil-rubbed bronze fixtures, all of which looked relatively new. The cozy, warm space suited him and the house. After he handed me the bottle, I said, "If I'd ever had a kitchen this nice, I might've learned to cook. Did you design the renovations?"

If he wrote, sang, *and* designed, my ovaries would explode on the spot.

"Nah." He sipped from his own bottle. "The previous owners had just finished renovating the house when the guy got transferred to the West Coast."

"Great timing for you."

"Very."

Maybe one day I'd get a full tour. The audible tip-tap of Mo's nails could be heard from the other room, where he was likely sniffing out all of Eli's secrets. Lucky dog. "Do you mind Mo's nosy nature?"

"No, but let me make sure my guitars are set up where he can't get at them." He hustled back to the front of the house to check on his instruments. Only one, which Mo had not yet discovered, lay abandoned on the sofa.

"Were you playing before I arrived?"

He lifted it off the cushions. "Fiddling around."

"Writing a song?" Fraught territory, but hope bubbled inside like uncorked champagne. If I could get him to write again, it might help him move forward with his life.

"Not quite . . ."

Something—an inkling—made me give Eli a little push. "Can I ask something? Because I'm curious about the process. If *I* wanted to write a song, how should I begin?"

"Do you play an instrument?" His eyes lit up.

Well, shoot. "One, if you count the tambourine."

His chuckle encouraged me to keep up the schtick.

"I can also hum off-key and do a really appalling beatbox." I proceeded to show off my musical nontalent with a few "boom-pah-chew, boom-boom-pah-chews."

I suspected Eli hadn't laughed aloud much these past two years, so his guffaw was better than a gold medal around my neck.

He rubbed his chin. "Not to be a dream killer, but maybe songwriting isn't in your future."

Eli didn't know me well enough to predict my response to that challenge. "Oh? So you're a lame teacher?"

"Hell no."

Settling my hands on my hips, I said, "Then come on . . . I want to write a love song for my favorite male—Mo."

"A love song for your dog?" Another little smile cropped up. "That won't sell."

"Well, then clearly you're no Cat Stevens." I affected a heavy sigh. "How disappointing."

The last time I'd heard that old "I Love My Dog" song had to have been 1998 or thereabouts. My dad had delighted in introducing me to obscure music that would make me giggle.

"Those are fightin' words." A glint of heat flickered in his eyes, changing the nature of his grin.

He seemed to enjoy this game, so I feigned nonchalance, teasing, "Well, I don't want to tax you or anything. It's okay if you can't write a love song about a dog. I'm still impressed with your past accomplishments."

Eli set his bottle on a coaster, went to the hutch to get a legal pad, then picked up his guitar again. "Have a seat and tell me what, *exactly*, you love about Mo."

I nearly bounced on my toes because—even though we were joking around—I was on the verge of getting him to write something for the first time in years. This could be a turning point for him. My whole body warmed like it did when I helped my students make that mind-body connection. Guess this wasn't all that different, except that I didn't usually have the urge to jump over the coffee table and kiss my yoga students.

"Wait, don't we start with a melody?" I asked.

"I don't, but if you want to, hum what you hear in your head when you think about Mo." He sat on the arm of the sofa—one foot on the coffee table—with his guitar across his thigh.

I closed my eyes, curious about what might come to me when thinking about the most awesome little dog. Unsurprisingly, a happy tune spun through my thoughts. "Something with a snappy beat, and maybe like 'Ba da baah, la-la-*la*-lee da, doodley doo-di-ley, ba da ba daah.'"

"Sing it again." He played a quick scale, and by the time I got to the la-la-*la* section, he chimed in with a chord or two.

"Ohmygosh!" I clapped. "I'm writing a song. My dad would be psyched."

That elicited a pleased grin. Then he fingered the fret board and strummed, approximating the melody I'd laid out. Figuring a slight buzz could only enhance my creative process, I sank onto the sofa and drank more beer. Eli continued to play his guitar, teasing more out of my simple melody than I could've imagined. Out of nowhere, *Sesame Street*–inspired lyrics came to me. "Moey-Mo, whatever goes wrong, you're always there to help me along."

Eli looked up, smiling. "Just *terrible*! Keep going . . ."

He strummed again.

I set down my bottle and rose, lifting Mo to my hip and twirling with my pup in the living room while tossing out another lyric. "When the world shoots me down, you help straighten my crown."

"And there I was, thinking it couldn't *get* any worse." Eli laughed.

I stopped dancing to nuzzle Mo, then set him on the ground, grinning. "Two failures in a row is my limit. Your turn to throw down something better."

I plopped back onto the sofa close to where he'd perched, worried I might've pushed him too far.

His expression softened. He strummed while staring blankly, as if searching for the words in thin air. I waited, enjoying the gentle riff and petting Mo.

"Mmm, mmm . . ." He paused, eyes closed. "The world crashes in, and I lose my way, yet one kiss from you chases trouble away . . ."

He opened his eyes and stared at me, all joking evaporated. My mind blanked except for the wish that he'd been thinking about me when he strung those words together.

"Okay, you win. That's way better than anything I said. You clearly don't have to worry about competition from me." And then, because kidding around made things more comfortable for Eli, I added, "Although I can't speak for Cat Stevens."

"Well, thanks." He set down his guitar but remained seated on the arm of the sofa, head cocked, gaze unfocused yet somehow still aware of me.

I guessed he was wrestling with something, so I switched gears to keep things light. "What's for dinner?"

His brows rose. "Oh yeah. I almost forgot why you're here."

"Not to be rude"—I crossed my legs and wrapped my hands around my knees—"but while your company is pleasant and I appreciated my first songwriting lesson, a girl's gotta eat."

One side of his mouth quirked upward as he stood and gestured toward the kitchen. "Hope you like red meat. I probably should've checked first."

"Eli, I eat everything." I stood, gripping my wrists behind my back. "I'm particularly fond of all the foods that are 'bad' for us, like red meat, sugar, and carbs. Hence the four cupcakes I brought for two people. In other words, I'm not one of those salad bitches."

"Good to know." Eli waited for me to start toward the kitchen.

Instead of preceding him, I looped my arm through his in the least intimate way I could think of.

"Look at us . . . this friendship thing is going along swimmingly." I grimaced. "I have no idea why I said that or what that old saying actually means—only that my mom always says it when things are going well. Wonder why the person who coined it chose those words?"

A "beats me" expression crossed his face. "Maybe because swimming strokes are smooth—you glide through the water nice and easy?"

"Ah. See, this is why you're a writer and I make soap." I released him when we got to the kitchen.

He snorted affectionately. "The way your mind jumps around fascinates me."

"Wish I could claim high-level connections taking place up here." I tapped my skull. "The truth is that I pretty much blab every thought that crosses my mind at the exact moment it does so."

He chuckled. "Let's start dinner."

"Hold up, mister. When you extended this invitation, you didn't tell me I had to *work* for my meal." I theatrically grabbed my chest, teasing him some more. "Now you're making waves in our little friendship pool."

"Can you manage a salad?"

"I'm not sure. It's taken me almost thirty years to get my sister to let me try . . ." Then I stopped, momentarily distracted. Amanda had probably finished up her appointment with Kevin and the FBI by now. I was eager to learn about that, but when she'd left, she'd thought she wouldn't return until after dinner, so right now I'd give the sweet man who was about to cook for me my attention. "But you be the judge."

He seasoned the steaks with garlic salt, pepper, and a dash of Worcestershire sauce, while I chopped a carrot. Thank God he didn't hover or get fussy about salad construction like my family did. After handing me another beer, Eli asked me to follow him to his tiny but magical backyard.

Six-foot-tall arborvitae formed a wall that hemmed in its flagstone patio, and beds of Virginia bluebell carpeted half the remaining green space. An ivy-covered pergola surrounded a teakwood table set for two. Only one thing was missing. "Got any good music we can listen to out here?"

"I recently bought some great old albums, but then lost them . . ." With a smile he tossed the steaks on the grill. "Of course I have music, Erin. The bookcases in the living room are loaded with LPs. Go pick what you want."

The idea of fondling his albums felt a lot like foreplay. That might be crazy talk, but my body still flushed as if he'd cupped my boobs. "Any preference?"

"Nope."

Mo stayed outside with Eli while I went to investigate the collection. He hadn't been kidding. A few hundred records, organized by genre (with a decided preference for country), gave me plenty of options. My bluesy mood required the likes of Stevie Ray Vaughan's *Texas Flood*.

Before returning to the backyard, I stopped to check my phone to see if there was any word from Amanda. Instead I saw a rare voice mail notice from my mother. I almost put the phone down, but something made me listen.

"Erin, it's Amanda. I'm on my way to the hospital with Mom because I'm having contractions. I don't know yet if it's serious, but when you get this message, please call."

Crap!

I tried Amanda's phone first, but when it went to voice mail, I called my mother.

"Hello." Mom sounded anxious.

"Mom, it's me. Are Amanda and Willa okay?"

Eli walked into the kitchen and smiled at the album on the counter, then froze when he noticed my worried face.

"It's Braxton-Hicks—from dehydration—but it'll be okay as long as Amanda rests and drinks more water." Mom paused. "We're waiting for the IV bag to empty but should be home in about an hour."

"Can I talk to her?"

"Sure."

"Hey." Amanda sounded tired.

"I just got your message. I'm sorry I'm not there."

"Mom said you're with Eli."

Eli could probably hear my sister, so I cut short any embarrassing questions she might ask. "Mm-hmm. Are you okay?"

"I'll be fine."

"I'll be there in ten minutes."

"No, don't come now. We'll be leaving soon. But if you wouldn't mind coming home early, I'd like to discuss the FBI problem."

Nobody wants to hear "FBI" and "problem" in the same sentence, and it had to be bad if *that* was a bigger concern than why she was in a hospital bed.

"I can come now."

"No, really. Enjoy your dinner first. I don't want to ruin your whole night."

I wouldn't be able to enjoy dinner now, but I didn't want to stress her out. Eli crossed his arms, patiently waiting.

"Okay. I'll be home in forty-five minutes." I shot Eli an apologetic grimace.

"Thank you. Please give Eli my apologies."

"Don't worry about that. Relax and keep drinking water." I rubbed the new knot in the back of my neck. "See you soon."

After we hung up, I looked at Eli. "I'm so sorry to eat and run. My sister's in the hospital with Braxton-Hicks contractions . . . I don't even know what that means."

"False labor." His voice tightened, and some color drained from his face.

A boneheaded move—bringing up a pregnancy-related crisis to a man who'd lost his wife and child in one. Clearly my path to circum-spection would be long and winding.

"She's kind of shaken up and asked me to come home early." I almost mentioned the FBI, too, but something made me hesitate.

"I understand. You can take your steak to go."

"She won't be home for at least forty-five minutes, so let's make the most of the time we've still got." I smiled, but whatever fun we'd been having had ended for the night. My thoughts split in two, and Eli looked like his had, too.

"Okay, then." He picked up the album. "Good choice. Let me get this set up."

I went outside and pulled Mo onto my lap. His nose twitched as he sniffed out the steaks sizzling on the grill. Normally that aroma made my tail wag, too, but I couldn't stop thinking about my sister.

The Lyle turmoil had stressed her out so much that she'd been neglecting her health. She'd stirred so often she couldn't have slept more than two hours each night. Even I'd found it difficult to get much sleep with the nonstop squeaking of her old box springs. The only silver lining would be that Mom probably felt pretty shitty about her cold-shoulder routine.

But that didn't ease my guilty conscience.

All this time, I'd been telling myself I hadn't done anything wrong by keeping what I'd seen last Valentine's Day to myself. That Amanda wouldn't have believed me. That there was nothing to be gained by confessing now. But lately more troubling questions had arisen. The one I hated most? Why *hadn't* I kept tabs on Lyle after that February run-in? I could blame my own grief, work schedule, problems with Max, and so on . . . but deep down there was another sense I didn't want to examine too closely.

If anything happened to Willa as a result of all this chaos, I'd never forgive myself.

The jamming opening notes of "Love Struck Baby" came through the speakers before Eli reappeared. I dabbed at my eyes, but not before he caught me.

"You're upset." He pulled a chair close to me and sat down, elbows on his knees. "Not to make light of the scare, but Braxton-Hicks aren't typically a serious problem."

"It's not that . . . not really." I might not have said anything, but Eli wasn't exactly the town crier. And now that Amanda had involved the FBI, people were bound to find out eventually.

"Do you want to talk about it?"

"Want to? Not exactly." I looked at him, filling with need and hope. "But I could use a sympathetic ear."

"I'm a good listener."

Everyone says that, but I believed Eli. Once he opened my faucet, everything from Lyle and Ebba to the feds came out in a gush. By the time I'd finished, my tears gushed, too, marking the first time I'd cried about any of it.

Eli swiped them with his thumbs and then held my hands. "You can't blame yourself for someone else's bad behavior. None of this is on you."

"I don't blame myself for Lyle's behavior, but I should've told Amanda what I saw instead of letting her live in her fantasy world, leaving her and my mom as easy prey for that bastard."

"It's not like you maliciously withheld your suspicions." He was being kind, but I could no longer ignore that maybe the tiny part of me that always resented the way Amanda dismissed my opinions might've thought she deserved to eat a little crow. God, that made me hate myself. "You had good reasons not to make waves while everyone was still grieving and she was still early in her pregnancy."

"What if I *was* a little spiteful?" My stomach turned rock hard. "She and I haven't always been close. Maybe subconsciously I figured her not-so-perfect marriage was her problem, not mine. I mean, that makes me a monster like Lyle. And now that she and I have gotten closer, I feel like a fraud."

"First, don't beat yourself up for being human. Everyone has let envy and resentment skew their thinking at some point." He was kind not to react with disgust, but my self-loathing raged on. "If sharing this information now could actually improve the outcome, I'd encourage you to tell her. But a blowup between you two now would be worse than the one you wanted to avoid this winter, because she really needs your help with what's coming. From the sound of it, you need her, too. Leave well enough alone and stick by her from this point on . . . That's really all you can do." Eli rested his chin on his knuckles.

"I wish I could fix it or make it up to her." I'd give anything to make it right.

He squeezed my hands. "Then convince her not to go to Puerto Rico. It's too risky. The stress isn't good for the baby, and no one knows what her ex is capable of at this point. She should let the FBI handle this on its own."

"Then my mom will end up with next to nothing."

He lifted a shoulder. "Sometimes when we make big mistakes in judgment, we pay big consequences."

"But I'm not kidding when I say it wouldn't take much to tip my mom into poverty."

He straightened in his seat. "She'll be alive, and more important, so will her daughter and granddaughter."

The deadened look in his eyes—a reminder of the consequences he'd paid by going camping late in his wife's risky pregnancy—made me shut up.

A flame ominously popped out of the back of the grill.

"Oh shit. I forgot about the steaks." Eli exploded off his chair and flipped them, scowling at himself as he spun around to face me again. "Hope you like them charred."

My whining had ruined his dinner.

"Char is my favorite flavor." I stood and placed my hand on his chest. "Thanks for listening without judging."

He covered my hand with his. "You can talk to me anytime, about anything."

I could've stayed like that—or wrapped my arms around him and held tight—all night. But I needed to lighten the mood before leaving so that the good things that had happened earlier weren't forgotten. "All this talking has made me hungry, so lemme get the salad."

He squeezed my hand before letting go. "It might be the only edible thing at this point."

Mo circled our feet.

"Mo has a fondness for shoe-leather steak, so it won't go to waste. Besides, I didn't really come here for the food, Eli." I didn't wink or smile or do anything that might be construed as teasing, so that he fully understood my meaning.

He picked up the plates. "I suppose we'll have to try this again as soon as your family crises are resolved."

That might *never* happen. "Or sooner. And next time I'll bring ice cream."

He grinned. "Then I'll think up something to celebrate."

CHAPTER SEVENTEEN

AMANDA

Mom was tucking a blanket around my legs in the master bedroom when Erin and Mo barged in. My sister sat at the foot of the bed. "Why are you in *here*?"

Mo scampered around their feet, exploring the one room that had otherwise been off-limits.

"Your sister needs more rest, so we're trading beds for a while." Mom stopped tucking and folded her arms across her chest. "She needs the extra space and pillows to get comfortable."

"Wait." Erin's panic-stricken expression reminded me of Beaker from the Muppets. "So now you and I are sharing a room?"

"I'm as excited as you are, my dear." Mom took an empty laundry basket and began stacking it with a few items of clothing, her brush, and other personal items. "Since I'm not as patient as your sister, you'll have to clean up your own stuff and make your bed every day."

My apologetic grimace didn't register with Erin, who remained somewhat dazed by her new situation.

"Do you need anything else, honey?" Mom asked me.

"No, thanks. I'm fine. The contractions have subsided. Please, let's all relax."

Mom nodded and left the room, presumably to go "unpack" in Erin's room.

"I'm sorry." I reached for my sister's hand. "You must rue the day you agreed to come live here."

"It hasn't been all bad." Erin smiled with concern, squeezing my calf. "Tell me everything the doctor said."

"I haven't been a very good mother to Willa." I patted my stomach.

"She said that?" A fierce scowl appeared.

"She didn't have to." I shook my head. "I was so proud of myself for filing charges and meeting with the FBI, but the stress took a toll. That plus my anxiety about confronting Lyle and Ebba distracted me from watching my diet and my body's signals. But Willa's fine now, and I won't let that happen again."

"I'm sorry this whole situation is ruining your pregnancy. I never wanted this for you, Amanda. I'm sorry I wasn't a better sister . . ."

Where had that come from? "We agreed not to rehash the past, remember? Eyes forward?"

Erin cast a glance into the hallway, nodding. "It looks like this little scare melted the ice between you and Mom."

"For now, anyway."

She let loose a sigh. "Tell me about your meeting with the FBI. Can they prep you to keep your cool when confronting Lyle? He knows you hate conflict, so he'll try to use your emotions against you or, worse, not believe your threat."

"That's moot now." That blow smacked me again.

Her eyes went wide. "The FBI said no?"

I pushed the hair off my face. "Agent Crowley went for it, but my doctor says I can't go to the Caribbean because of Zika and other pregnancy risks."

"I never even thought about *that*, but nothing's worth putting Willa at risk." Erin kicked off her shoes and pulled her legs into that yoga crisscross position, then set her chin on her fists.

"I feel sick about it. I was counting on this plan getting all Mom's money back. Without the OIA, there's no upside. When this all hits the papers, Mom might really lose it."

"Maybe not. I bet once the shit hits the fan, the fallout won't be the boogeyman she's making it out to be. Plus she'll have Willa to focus on."

"I hope so."

"You did the right thing." Erin rubbed my leg. "Mom can't stay mad forever."

I cocked a brow because our mom could hold a world-record grudge. "I'll never stop kicking myself for being so gullible. You saw Lyle clearly. I'd been too busy soaking up his flattery to see the signs. I've been reading up on narcissism. It would seem I'm the attractive, affable type who nurses a narcissist's sense of self-importance. At least until Lyle traded up for Ebba—whose sex appeal and bankbook and ambition would've better fed his own sense of grandiosity." I sighed. "All this time, I thought him a charming, loving man who could be over-sensitive and pouty at times. Not at all someone capable of devastating me, my child, and Mom. You've been dragged into this, too, and poor Kevin's working on my divorce for free. This isn't who I want to be—a burden on my family."

"This is not all on you, and you're not a burden." She grabbed my hand and squeezed, her expression oddly pained. "No wife should have to keep her guard up with her husband. That's on Lyle, not you." She released my hand and swallowed hard. "It's been a rough year because of Dad's death. Even six months ago, we were more like acquaintances than sisters. But now look at us—united. Willa gives us something to look forward to, and something to fight for, too. Things look bleak right now, but we've got each other and our health. Together we'll make it through, so keep the faith."

Erin's confidence—the source of much of my envy—today inspired hope.

Mom peeked back into the room. "I'm too tired to cook, so I'll run to the diner to grab soup and salads."

"I can do that, Mom." Erin moved to stand.

"Keep your sister company. I'll be back soon." She disappeared.

"Any excuse to run away from me." I sighed, discouraged by the distance between my mom and me. "My head hurts from this topic. Let's talk about something fun. Tell me about your date."

"Not a 'date.'" Despite those words, Erin's face brightened. A wisp of a smile—like she knew a juicy secret—tugged at her mouth. "We're getting to know each other as friends. I'm trying not to push like I usually do. He's sweet and wonderful and maybe too good to be true."

She'd used those "too good to be true" words about Lyle years ago, though in a derogatory manner.

"It's unlike you to be moony."

She nodded. "Please don't take this wrong, but I understand you better now. It wouldn't be hard for Eli to take advantage of me while I'm in thrall. The fact that he still loves his wife so much should make me wary, but I can't control my feelings. I love and hate this goofy grin in my heart."

"It's nice to see you swept away, but now my experience makes *me* wary for you." Cynicism—yet another change Lyle had forced on me. "Learn from my mistakes and maybe pump the brakes."

"Eli's got his foot on those, so this engine can't run off the tracks." The dreamy look returned to her face, belying the truth. "I did make him laugh, which he really needed. And I got him to start writing a song today—granted, it was a silly one about Mo, but maybe it'll help him break through whatever's been holding him back. There was a moment there . . ." Her gaze turned hazy, as if she were picturing the scene again.

"If anyone can pull him out of a funk, it's you. You've got a gift for making people smile." People always laughed with Erin, another trait I'd envied for most of our lives.

"Maybe, but you make people happy in a different way."

I'd never looked at it that way, but my sister had a point. Both ways mattered, and neither one was better than the other. They could coexist without competing, like my sister and me. "Maybe you should write Max a thank-you note for the accidental introduction."

"Right? It's crazy how well that theft turned out." She laughed, but I frowned at the reminder of thievery. "I'm sorry, Amanda. I didn't mean—"

"Don't apologize for being happy. I want that for you."

"I want that for you, too." She then laid a hand on my belly. "And for Willa."

"Maybe my silver lining is *this* . . . the way that you and I finally have the relationship we avoided for so long." For a change, my intimate remark didn't make either of us shy away.

"Definitely." Erin smiled. "Let's get your nose pierced to seal the bond."

"Ha!" I laughed just as my phone rang. "Saved by the bell! Ooh, it's Kevin."

"Answer it." Her expression turned serious.

Once again, an otherwise relaxed moment got cut short, but Kevin needed to know I couldn't travel. "Hi, Kev."

"Hey, I wanted to give you the heads-up. Agent Crowley already sent the Puerto Rican office copies of the evidence Stan collected so they can coordinate quickly. They'll need to verify it, but I'm optimistic things will come together. You need to be ready to fly out on short notice."

"I'm sorry, but now I can't go. I ended up in the ER with a mild pregnancy scare this afternoon. Everything's fine, but my doctor warned me not to travel, especially to the Caribbean, where there are higher rates of Zika, among other concerns." I pictured his frustrated expression and felt sick all over again.

"Oh my God. Are you and the baby really okay?" His concern alleviated some of my guilt.

"Yes, thank you. I got home an hour ago."

"I'll let you rest and call Stan, but there's got to be a solution. Maybe I could go in your stead . . ."

"Lyle won't talk to you. He hates lawyers and would be suspicious from the start. The only reason he would've talked to me was to further manipulate me." I twisted a handful of the sheets in one hand until my fingers turned white.

"I'm sorry. I know your worst fear was getting caught up in all the red tape . . ."

"Things look pretty grim for Mom and me now, but I have to put Willa's safety first." Today's scare had put everything in perspective. Even if Mom and I end up broke and estranged, Willa was my priority.

"Absolutely, sis. I'll talk to Stan and see if we can brainstorm any Hail Marys. You rest up."

"Thanks." I hit "End," tossed the phone on the bed, and shrugged when I met Erin's gaze, worn out from the long day of scares and disappointments.

"This effing blows." Her brows were pulled so tight, and the way the light caught that nose ring, it looked like a tiny bolt of lightning struck. She jumped off the mattress, hands on her hips. "What if I go?"

"What?"

Erin paced in the space between the bed and dresser while she formulated her plan. "You know he'd love a chance to throw everything in my face and prove his superiority."

"Erin, this isn't about your ego and his."

"I know. I only mean that, unlike with Kevin, he'd never suspect me of anything other than wanting to fight with him, like usual." She grinned, a gleam in her eye. "He'll never see it coming."

"Maybe, but it's too much to ask." I loved her for offering. Erin had the balls for the job, but did she have the patience? I wasn't sure she'd come *that* far yet. "Plus you couldn't go in half-cocked. You'd need to get screened and prepped by the FBI, follow protocol, and keep your temper in check. Do you even own an updated passport?"

"Yes. You know I like to be ready for anything." Her hands waved about. "Look, I know you and Mom think I'm immature, but I can do this. You can trust me. I'll get Lyle to confess."

The way she'd always baited him used to make me nervous, but now the talent could come in handy. Still, I'd already disrupted her life too much to ask this, too. "What about Give Me Strength? Will they let you call off?"

"Let me worry about all that. This may be the most important thing I can ever do for our family. I know I haven't given you many reasons to be proud of me, but give me this one chance. I can make this right . . . I *need* to do this."

"You're serious?"

"Yes. I love you and Mom, and Kev. We've only got each other now. And this will let me make up for everything . . ." She trailed off.

I was too preoccupied with my own thoughts—the misplaced pop of disappointment that my confident sister would be the one on the front line while I remained on the sidelines—to question what she'd meant by that. "Erin, you don't have to make up for anything. *I* do for making you feel like I'm ashamed of you. That's never been true. I've only ever worried because the way you live without a plan makes me *nervous*."

She sank back onto the mattress and rubbed my thigh. "Don't be nervous. I'm good. Better than good, and ready to do this. Call Kev and Stan. Tell them I'll go." She nodded toward my phone. "Come on. Do it."

"Okay." My heart raced. Our shot at Lyle was back on. My thirst for revenge didn't feel good—it felt *great*. I picked the phone up and hit "Redial." "Kev, Erin is willing to go in my place. Unlike with you, Lyle would welcome sparring with her. Will the FBI accept her as a substitute?"

"I'll check. Agent Crowley may want to meet with her before he decides."

I covered the phone. "Can you meet with Agent Crowley?"

"Absolutely."

"Okay, go for it. Now we have to pray we catch a break with Lyle's travel plans." My heart pumped faster, so I took a breath. As exciting as this was, I had to keep calm for Willa.

"I'll circle back with you once I speak with Crowley and Stan," Kev promised.

After we hung up, I reached out to bear-hug my sister. "This is above and beyond anything I would've asked or expected, Erin."

"It's not a big deal." She patted my back and pulled away. "Hey, are you crying?"

I dashed a stray tear away. "My hormones have been on a wild ride today. Thank you for being here for me. For letting me lean on you. I've never felt closer."

Erin's guilt-ridden expression upset me.

I grabbed her hand. "I'm not blaming you for our past. I played an equal role in our dysfunction. So did Mom. I shouldn't have looked the other way when she took hurtful potshots at you over the years."

She waved me off, pausing to chew on her lip before echoing my earlier statement. "Eyes forward, remember?"

"Deal, as long as I'm not required to get a tattoo or nose ring."

Erin pointed a finger at me, teasing, "Look at you, making jokes. This *is* a turning point."

Mom poked her head in the door. "Food's on the table." She twitched her head side to side like a bird, observing us closely. "What did I miss?"

"Erin's going to Puerto Rico in my place, so everything might actually turn out okay."

"Is that a good idea?" Mom's skeptical expression threatened to undo the nascent connection between my sister and me. "Erin hates rules, but you can't go rogue with the FBI."

"Most 'rules' are BS, but I can follow ones that matter." Erin crossed her arms.

"Mom, please stop treating her like she's eight and jumping off roofs."

"Hey, I could still do that," Erin joked.

I stroked her back and speared Mom with a serious look. "I trust her. Truthfully, Lyle is more likely to believe she'll make good on the threat of prosecution than he would've with me."

"That's true," Mom agreed, making a face that didn't much flatter me.

Unable to argue against my own logic, I vowed to Willa that I'd never, ever roll over again. Not for anyone.

"Now that that's settled, let's eat." I pushed my huge body out of the bed. "I'm starving."

"Finally," Mom said before heading to the dining room.

Erin and I exchanged a glance.

"Do you think she might change if we wore mirrors on our foreheads so she could see her expressions when she spoke to us?" Erin tittered.

"She means well." I walked with my sister, rubbing my stomach, certain that my mother did, in fact, love us both. "For the first time in weeks, I feel hopeful. Willa and I have you and Mom, Kevin and his family, and now Richard Foster, too."

"Which do you think will spark more fireworks, my confrontation with Lyle or Mom meeting Richard?" Erin smirked.

I grabbed her shoulder. "Oh jeez. Don't put that in my head."

"Forewarned is forearmed."

The day when my life would no longer be summed up by battle metaphors could not come soon enough.

CHAPTER EIGHTEEN

Erin

"I'm psyched that we sold out of the products so quickly." I set another jar of lemon-thyme sugar scrub on the counter at Castille's, thinking about the special line for expectant mothers that my sister had suggested because certain oils weren't safe during pregnancy. It had merit. Between that and Mom enjoying the production side of things, Shakti Suds had become a sort of family affair lately. That made it pretty easy to ask Kevin to draw up some papers to formalize a partnership. I couldn't wait to hand Amanda that surprise after I nabbed Lyle.

"Your soaps have been a hit." Nalini, the shop's gorgeous—if a tad uptight—owner, flashed a tight smile. "Your being a local artisan helps me hand-sell them. And it's nice that you can restock quickly."

"Local artisan" sounded swanky.

"Absolutely, but I'm heading out of town for a few days. Let's hope there aren't any soap emergencies while I'm gone."

No matter what I said or did, I could not crack this woman's professional armor, which came wrapped in some Chanel-inspired designer duds, if I had to guess. Pity. Life must be boring for those without any sense of humor.

"I'll manage until you return. Have a safe trip." She tossed her silky, dark hair over her shoulder and went to the stockroom without another word.

I'd take those well-wishes for a safe journey, considering mine was not a pleasure trip. I expected to hit some road bumps—literally and figuratively—in my quest to trap Lyle.

A tropical depression forming a few hundred miles southeast of the island should keep them docked there for a few extra days. Stan was certain Lyle and Ebba wouldn't risk rough seas, especially when they weren't expecting me to show up.

Then again, Stan hadn't had years to watch Lyle operate, as I had. That guy's ego would not be easily intimidated by a little thing like God. But this window of opportunity was our best shot, so we were taking it.

After breaking down the old cardboard box and tossing it in the trash, I jogged down the street to Sugar Momma's to meet up with Eli. My local-tour-guide idea had been pure genius. There was an endless list of places to show him.

The bells jingled above my head as I entered Hannah's store and heard Rhys Lewis's "No Right to Love You" playing.

I waved, calling out, "Hannah Banana, two masala chais with an extra dash of cinnamon, please."

"Two?" She chuckled. "You've got an addiction."

"I'm expecting a friend. He's never been here before, which is a *crime*."

"Yes, it is." She waved me to the tables, a few of which were empty. "Grab a seat and I'll get those set for you."

"Thanks!" I sauntered to the small yellow table in the corner for a little privacy. Hannah brought me two steaming mugs seconds before Eli wandered inside. I waved him over. "Perfect timing."

He'd cocked an ear to listen to the music, even as his gaze scanned the unfamiliar, colorful surroundings. My heart stopped when he planted a quick peck on my temple before taking a seat. "This place looks great."

"You'll learn to trust my recommendations. Potomac Point might be a gentrifying village, but there are little pockets of hipness hidden in the 'new and improved' side of town."

He sipped his tea, brows rising with an approving nod. "This is good."

I raised my hands in an "I rest my case" manner.

"You look upbeat." He stretched his legs out. "Does this mean your sister is doing better?"

"Yes, no contractions these past few days. She's been resting, and my mom makes sure there's always a glass of water nearby."

"I'm glad to hear it." Only the barest shadow of sadness passed over his face, vanishing quickly yet reminding me of his broken heart.

Today was not a day for second-guessing, so I changed the subject. "I also took your advice, sort of. My sister isn't going to Puerto Rico to confront her ex."

"Great news. He sounds too unpredictable—exactly the kind of guy who could be dangerous if backed into a corner. I'm glad she's not taking unnecessary chances." He raised his mug and blew on the surface before taking another sip.

"*I* volunteered to take her place in the sting operation." I still felt the flutter of pride for being trusted to do it.

Eli choked down his tea. "What?"

"I leave tonight, and you can bet I won't leave Puerto Rico without getting Lyle's confession on tape. He's easy to bait because his giant ego cracks in a flash. In one swoop, I'll save my family and make up for keeping quiet back in February."

Eli shook his head. "From what you've described, no one would've listened to you in February, so you shouldn't feel guilty about that. Certainly not enough to justify taking this kind of risk. You've got a history of animosity with this guy, who's now committed a couple of felonies. He's got to anticipate that, sooner or later, people will be after him, so he's probably prepared to defend himself. What if he pulls a gun or worse?"

I closed my eyes to picture Lyle pointing a gun at me. Nope. Couldn't see it. "Lyle's an obnoxious ass, but he's not a killer. And not for nothing, but I can take him in a fight. He's fit, but he's not much bigger than me, and I'm wily." I winked to loosen Eli up.

No dice. His chilly expression gave me goose bumps. "This isn't funny, Erin. You're putting your safety in jeopardy for what . . . money? Money won't mean much if you're dead or seriously injured."

I leaned across the table, patting his hand. "Thanks for caring, but you're overreacting. The FBI will be nearby if anything goes awry."

"It only takes a second for a bullet or a knife to do permanent damage." He straightened his posture as if his muscles were tightening bit by bit.

"I've taken some self-defense classes in the past five years. Trust me, I know my limits."

"That sounds uncomfortably familiar, and to be blunt, I know *mine*."

"What's that mean?" All my happy vibes from earlier fizzled.

He tugged his earlobe as his lips pressed together. "The last time I got involved with a stubborn, passionate woman with all the answers, it didn't work out so well. Not sure I want to sign up for that ride again."

I blinked, suddenly feverish. "Are you saying that I've got to do things your way—play everything safe all the time—in order for us to be friends or whatever?"

He stared at me for what seemed like forever. "This trip's not some little thing. I'm not setting a curfew or micromanaging your life. But you've got no training in undercover operations. You don't know what this woman he's hooked up with is capable of doing, either, so at least be honest with yourself if not with me. You're so determined to get what you want that you can't be objective."

I gulped my chai, which now tasted sour thanks to my bitter disappointment. "If this were that dangerous, the FBI wouldn't go along with it."

"I hope you're right." He opened his wallet and tossed five bucks on the table before he stood. "I wish you well. Truly. I know there's a lot at stake for your family. But I'm sorry, Erin. I can't do this with you. I left Nashville to live a quiet, comfortable life. One without worry."

"You're being unfair." I slapped my hand on the table, then winced when his brows rose. Still, he was in the wrong. "From the moment we met, when I barged my way in with Rodri to get my albums back, you knew what kind of person I was—one who hardly thinks things through, let alone overthinks them. I'm working on that a little, but now you suddenly want me to be someone else entirely."

He shook his head. "No. I don't. I like you exactly as you are. But this right here reminds me that what I like about you is exactly what scares me about caring for someone like you. I don't expect you to understand. You haven't been through what I have. You don't know how hard it was for me . . . still is. How I've struggled with my own guilt for agreeing to the pregnancy, agreeing to the camping trip . . . The tears I've cried. The booze. The anger. I can't do it again. I just can't. I'm sorry."

I stood and reached for his hand. "Wait a sec . . ."

He raised mine to his lips and kissed my knuckles. "Please be safe and take care of yourself."

That sad little smile of his appeared before he turned, shoved his hands in his pockets, and walked away.

I sank back onto the chair with a thud, as if I'd gained two hundred pounds in ten minutes. Aching from losing something we never fully explored.

Dad had always told me to be true to myself, but when it came to relationships, was there a line between self-respect and selfishness? Since my breakthrough with my sister, I've thought about that. About how my attitude—the delight I'd taken in defying my mom and Amanda under the auspices of following my father's advice—helped shape their attitudes toward me. Had I also repeated that pattern with Eli, or were we actually incompatible?

One I could fix. The other, not so much.

Either way, I had a plane—and a liar—to catch.

———

I wished I could roll down the window to get a better view of the island along the one-hour drive to the Puerto del Rey Marina, situated in the northeast coast of Puerto Rico. It'd been too dark to see much of San Juan last night, and my morning had been consumed with interviews and a mountain of paperwork. Now I was trapped in the back of this squad car.

The wireless recording device on my wrist resembled a Fitbit. Much less likely to be detected than the tapes, wires, and recording devices I'd grown up seeing on TV. Still, wearing it made what I'd signed up for suddenly very real, and Eli's dire predictions more fathomable.

Agents Reyes and Jones sat in the front seat, dressed in plain clothes, but neither spoke to me.

My knee bounced restlessly. I needed this win to prove to Eli that I hadn't been foolish. To show my family that I was a capable, fierce muthaducker.

But what if Lyle wouldn't sign the title, or Ebba turned out to be a hothead? She was a real wild card. We still didn't know if she was in on the fraud or if Lyle had duped her, too. She could go batshit crazy as easily as break down in tears.

"We're almost there," Agent Reyes said over his shoulder.

"Great," I lied, fearful that expressing doubts or nerves might cause them to cancel.

"You remember how to turn on that device, right?" Agent Jones said as the car turned into the marina and pulled up to La Cueva del Mar, a canopied restaurant-bar at the water's edge.

"I do." I shook out my hands, a nervous reflex I'd need to keep in check for the next thirty minutes.

"Wait here. I'll go talk to the dockmaster to confirm which slip the target is in. Hopefully, he didn't duck out to sightsee." Agent Reyes exited the car, leaving me alone with Agent Jones.

"Normally, we don't waste resources on a case this small absent corruption of public trust, but I'll be glad to haul this ass off in handcuffs for how he's treated his pregnant wife." He cracked his knuckles.

"Not as glad as I'll be to watch." I looped my arm through my backpack. "I'll be staying on the boat tonight rather than ride back to San Juan in this car with Lyle and Ebba."

"Suit yourself."

Being alone in this marina might not be my safest option, but talking to people around here would help me figure out how to get the boat back to the US to sell.

Agent Reyes returned. "*The Office* is still in its wet slip. You go down the main dock to the fourth row and then go left on that narrow offshoot to the sixth slip on the right. Got it?"

"Yes." I held his gaze, pretending I was talking to Rodri even though Agent Reyes's dark-brown eyes weren't nearly as friendly.

"Repeat it back."

Crap. I hated tests. "Go down the main dock to row four, hang a left, and then it's the sixth boat on the right."

"Sixth slip, not boat. There could be an empty slip."

His level of particularity reminded me of my sister. "Yes, that's what I meant."

"Agent Jones and I will linger around the restaurant and dock. We'll be listening in, so if you want to pull the rip cord, say the code word."

"Okay. Code word is 'bravo.'" Against my will, my heart picked up its pace. My mom and sister were probably sitting together awaiting my call. That pressure wrapped around my chest, but I had no time for a yoga breath now.

"Yes." Agent Reyes put on his sunglasses while Agent Jones pulled on a baseball cap. "Ready?"

I imagined my dad smiling at me. *"Whatd'ya mean you're afraid? My little toughie can do anything!"* No turning back.

"All set." In thirty minutes, it'd be over, one way or the other. I could keep it together that long.

I opened the car door and, as instructed, didn't look back. I scented salt water and fish. Gulls squawked, motors churned, and tourists chattered around me. Smiling as if on vacation, I took in the sun and sights. When I reached the dock, I counted ahead to mark my turn. The closer it got, the more sweat rolled down my back. Fortunately, that perspiration wouldn't screw with the wristband.

I slowed when *The Office* came into view. Stan had called it a trawler, but it was an elegant triple-decker boat. White with navy trim and handsome wood accents made it look exceedingly romantic.

A rush of rage turned my body thermostat way up. I drew two yoga breaths and blew the last one out long and slow before making a move to board the boat. Two steps later, the buxom blonde I'd met in February emerged onto the aft deck.

Seeing her in her swimsuit, relaxed and happy, made the ache for my sister and niece burn. The slutty bitch yawned like she'd just awakened from a nap. If no one had been watching, I might've rushed the boat and pushed her into the sea. That daydream got interrupted when Lyle appeared and said something to her.

Now or never. I grasped a stair railing as I boarded the swim platform and called out, "Hey there, Lyle. Fancy seeing you here."

His head snapped up at his name, and then he went still.

First round went to me.

"Who are you?" Ebba asked, her voice carrying a faint accent.

"You don't remember?" I pointed at myself with a phony, bright smile, surprised she didn't recognize me. Then again, I had shaved my hair after our February introduction. Plus I'd been wearing a winter cap then. "I'm Lyle's sister-in-law, you silly ho."

"What did you call me?" She set her hands on her hips, lips parted.

"'Ho'? Sorry. Is there a better term for a woman who sleeps with someone else's husband? Oh, never mind. I've a better one for you both. 'Felons.'"

"You're a crazy bitch," Ebba said as I joined them without invitation. "Hey! Get off our boat."

Lyle remained silent, intently assessing my every move, sizing up which of us would be the predator and which the prey.

"Lyle, don't let her talk to me that way." Ebba slapped his arm, then swiveled toward me again. "I said get off our boat."

"*Our* boat? Interesting. And here I thought lover boy anted up all the cash." I had to keep my eye on her. She was jumpy, which wasn't helping me keep my cool.

"What do you want, Erin?" He crossed his arms without sparing Ebba a glance.

"If you don't get off this boat, I'm calling the cops." Ebba stomped.

Be smart. Use her. "I doubt that'll turn out like you think. Let's back up, though. You keep saying this is your boat."

She narrowed her eyes. "It's our boat. Our company boat."

Woo-hoo, the bimbo might be headed to jail, too! "Ah yes. Would that be Somniator Partners?"

"Yes—"

"Ebba," Lyle snapped.

I wanted to kiss her for confirming another piece of the puzzle. "Well, I'm sorry to inform you both"—I faced Lyle—"but these are your final minutes of boat ownership, so take a nice last look at your love nest."

"What?" Ebba whined.

"Why so blue?" I asked. "I've always been told that the happiest days of boat ownership are the first and the last. Let's break out the champagne. I feel like celebrating."

"All right. Enough of you and your games." When Lyle moved toward me, I held up my hand and hoped he didn't see it tremble. He shooed me. "Scoot along so no one gets hurt."

"Gosh, I hope that's a threat. That'd make it mail fraud, wire fraud, and assault . . . Tell me what I can do to make you hit me so we can add battery to that list." I glared at him, every muscle in my body taut with frenetic energy.

"What the hell is she talking about?" Ebba finally turned her attention from me and tugged at Lyle's shirt. He remained cool under pressure. "You said you *told* your ex you were leaving her for me. Why is her sister here now making wild accusations?"

I hated Lyle but had to admire his unflappable nature.

Ebba did not share his temperament, which made her the weak link I could break—or who might turn dangerous. "To be fair, Ebba, Lyle did tell Amanda about you after you both fled. What did he say, exactly . . ." I tapped my cheek and pretended to think, trying to decide how far to push. "Something about needing time because he was 'undecided.' Yes, I think that's the word. It seems, however, that he didn't tell *you* about how he stole my mother's money to buy this boat."

"Liar!" she yelled.

So she didn't know. Would that help or hurt my mission?

"I know, I know . . . you don't want to believe me. You believe him." I gestured to Lyle, then set the back of my hand by my mouth as if sharing a secret with her. "My sister did the same thing for years. Turns out he lied to her. Lied to his first wife, too. Now he's lied to you. Sucks, huh? But he gets points for consistency." I chuckled to annoy them both.

"First wife?" Ebba's eyes got wide. "What's she saying, Lyle?"

Before he answered, I interrupted. "The PI we hired collected a whole file of documents to prove every word. Granted, if Amanda hadn't reached out to Lyle's dad, we might not have learned about Deanna so quickly."

Ah, there it was. A flicker of heat flared in his eyes from a second blow he hadn't expected. His father.

Lyle's coloring now looked like he'd been on the boat all week without sunscreen. He glanced past me, up and down the docks. "I don't see any cops, so you must want something specific."

"Oh, I do."

"I've heard enough," Ebba said. "I'm sure losing Lyle was a blow to your sister, but she's obviously unhinged and making crazy claims. Instead of badgering us, you should convince her to not fight the divorce. Lyle and I are getting married whether she likes it or not."

"Bet you have family money," I said.

"So?"

"Better get a prenup."

She scoffed. "I'm done with you and your sister. What a wimp to send you instead of coming herself."

I jabbed my finger at her face. "You shut up unless you want those hair extensions on the ground and your ass tossed in the sea." I could do it without worrying overmuch. Ebba wouldn't drown with those fake tatas to keep her afloat. "The only reason Amanda's not here is because it would be too risky for the baby."

"Whatever," Ebba said, showing no remorse for breaking up a family-to-be. I really should shove her overboard.

But this was it. Time to bluff my ass off. I was good, but so was Lyle.

My heart pounded so hard I thought he might see my chest thumping, so I faced Ebba.

"Go ahead, dismiss me, but I'm here to offer you both one chance to get out of this without serving time." I turned back to Lyle. "I've got a false deed, the letter about the affair in which you claimed to be working on the real estate deal in Florida, the public records for all of your shell corporations, interviews with people you two have dealt with recently, wire transfers from your accounts, and obviously the information needed to track you down here at this marina. Sign over the title to this boat right now and I won't go to the cops."

He laughed, cocky as ever. "Amanda and your mother will never risk the scandal. Nor would my wife put her child's father in jail."

It took every bit of restraint not to rush him and shove *him* off the boat. Only a monster could use my sister's love against her . . . and harm his own child. I'd give him points for knowing my family pretty well, but he should've considered the way painful events change and harden us.

"Don't count on my sister's sympathies, Lyle. Your *wife* has started divorce proceedings and, given the way you're treating your daughter, hardly thinks of you as her child's father. From the bottom of *my* heart, thank you for proving yourself to be the dick I always said you were *before* your child is born. But make no mistake, Amanda won't protect you. Don't believe me? Roll the dice."

He hesitated, his cold blue eyes heating with menace. In contrast, Ebba had fallen silent and turned white as the fresh paint on this old boat. Lyle took another step toward me. I gulped and stepped back, bumping into the side of the ship. Trapped. Shoot. Had Eli been right to worry?

My gaze darted between him and Ebba, but I refused to say "bravo" before I got that title.

Lyle spoke through gritted teeth. "Whatever 'evidence' you think you have is a long way from a conviction. I'm sure Kevin explained how hard it is to prove fraud absent a confession. Is that why you're here? Are you wearing a wire?"

We'd anticipated this possibility, so I pulled up my T-shirt to reveal a red bikini top, then spun around to show them the "absence" of any wires and recording devices. Meanwhile, the bracelet kept track of every word, but Lyle wouldn't think twice about a yoga instructor wearing a Fitbit.

Sticking as close to the truth as possible, I said, "It's just the three of us on this boat. Maybe bimbo here doesn't know all you did, but you and I know the truth, so let's cut the crap and make the deal. You don't want to go to jail, and I don't want the government to seize this boat and auction it off for peanuts, leaving my mom holding the bag. Gimme the title and we all walk away."

"Lyle!" The desperation in Ebba's eyes suggested she'd finally started to believe me. "You said you got a loan."

"I did." He smiled.

"Yes, he did. A loan from my mom that he repeatedly said—verbally and in writing—was for a real estate deal in Florida." I made a show of gesturing around *The Office* with a quizzical expression. "This doesn't look like a South Florida condo complex to me. Oh, and by the way, the first interest payment date came and went, so my mom is calling the entire balance due. Absent a four-hundred-thousand-dollar money order, I need the title to settle up."

Lyle sneered. "I'll give you credit for being the only Turner with the balls to threaten me, but you'll be going home empty-handed. The cops will need time to investigate before they get a warrant, so I'll be long gone. You can't touch me where we're headed."

"Wait a second." Ebba's crestfallen expression gave me a little thrill. If she hadn't ruined my sister's life, I'd almost feel bad for her, because it couldn't be easy to see the ogre in someone you loved. "Is she telling the truth? Did you steal the money?"

"I *borrowed* it." Lyle took another step toward me, but I ducked out of the way. Adrenaline had me on high alert. If I had to, I could jump into the water.

He stopped his advance, choosing another tack. "Ebba, change in plans. We'll be taking off sooner than expected. Go inside while I escort our guest off the boat."

I was running out of time, and if Ebba went inside, I'd lose my weak link. "I never liked you, Lyle, but I never thought you were this stupid. But, hey, if you want to risk your life by sailing stormy seas rather than hand this boat over, no one will miss you." Then I spoke directly to Ebba. "In the meantime, now that you know the score, everything you do to help him escape makes you an accomplice after the fact at best, or a coconspirator at worst, so I sure hope he's worth it."

"Lyle!" Ebba cried. "I don't want to go to jail. Tell me the truth."

"Seriously, lady?" I laughed in her face. "You got involved with a married man—one with a pregnant wife—and you still want to trust him over me?"

"Shut up!" she shouted, then spun and pounded on his chest. He grabbed her wrists, but she screamed, "Just give her the damn title, Lyle. I'm not going to jail for you."

"Ebba, calm the fuck down. Don't let her get in your head. Focus on the life we want. The one we'll have as soon as we sail away. We'll be safe in Venezuela."

"Oh my God, you're guilty." Ebba grabbed her head, visibly shaking. "I thought we'd planned an incredible life, investing in international properties, not one looking over our shoulder. How could you be so stupid?"

"'Stupid'?" His stricken face revealed a crack in that fragile, narcissistic ego. "I did this for us. For the adventure we wanted."

"I thought we had a *legitimate* plan . . ." She started tugging at her hair, turning in small circles, talking to herself.

"Relax," he said.

"No! I'm not sailing into a storm, and I'm not going to jail. This is over. Give up the boat, Lyle, so you don't end up in jail, too."

"You're serious?" The color rose in his cheeks.

My bearing witness to the implosion of his plans had to kill him, so I stood there grinning like a kid with a bag of popcorn.

"Hell yes, I'm serious. I'm not a criminal!" she shrieked.

"Lower your goddamned voice, Ebba, before everyone knows our business." His expression tightened as he punched the wood paneling of the door. "Fuck."

I remained silent and still while he thought. He'd be going to jail. The only question now was whether I'd get that title before the agents came aboard.

He narrowed his gaze at me. "How do I know you won't turn me in after you get what you want?"

I deflected by pulling a thumb drive out of my pocket. "Will it make you feel better if I give you the evidence?"

He snatched it from me. "Ebba, get the laptop to see if she's bluffing."

"I don't care if she has a little or a lot of evidence. I didn't sign up for this. If you want to sail on, you're on your own. I'm going to pack my shit." She turned on her heel and stormed into the main cabin.

With her gone, the air around me energized like a gathering storm. Lyle shot me a death stare. "Back off, Erin, or I'll make your sister's life a living hell."

"You already did, asshole." I focused so my voice wouldn't quaver with rage.

"Walk away or I'll assert my parental rights."

That stopped me. The only thing that mattered more than vengeance and getting my mom's money back was my niece.

His smile broadened. My poker face must've slipped.

Ebba reappeared, saving me from the lack of a ready comeback. She handed me a paper. "Here. Take the title."

"Ebba!" Lyle reached for it, but she pushed at his chest.

"I'm saving you from yourself, Lyle. Let the boat go. We don't need it. We're amazing brokers, and there's rebuilding happening everywhere in the Caribbean. We can work that to our advantage and then get a boat next year. We'll live in the islands without being fugitives. Sign it or I'm gone."

The wee bit of conscience hidden under all that hair surprised me. On second thought, it wasn't a conscience. More like a CYA move. I mean, how many scruples did I honestly expect a mistress to have?

Lyle's strangled expression made me smile. I scanned the title quickly, verifying the Somniator Partners name, then interrupted the stare-down between him and Ebba. "I need a signature to make this official. Let's go to the marina offices and get a notary or whatever while your girlfriend packs your bags. I can recommend a decent hotel in San Juan." I winked because it felt damn good to be this close to getting everything I needed.

Lyle turned on Ebba. "What the hell have you done?"

She raised her chin. "You lied to me about everything, so be thankful I'm willing to let you earn back my trust."

"We were free—no ex-wife or kid, no strings. Going where we wanted, when we wanted."

"I'm no saint, but I'm no thief, either. Fix this and maybe we still can move forward together."

The moment begged for a mocking slow clap, but I wouldn't antagonize him when Ebba was doing the heavy lifting for me.

He turned his back on both of us, scrubbing his hands over his face so hard I thought he might actually hurt himself. "'Maybe'? Well, *maybe* I'll take my chances on my own, then, 'cause it doesn't sound like I've got much to lose at this point."

"Are you saying your freedom and I aren't worth anything?" Her affected pout suggested she would forgive him but would also use this incident to reset the power balance between them for a while. He let out a frustrated growl.

"I'll pack our things." She patted his chest, then turned to me. "Be sure to tell your sister that Lyle is willing to do the right thing for *me*."

He grunted. If she weren't the bitch who stole my sister's husband, I might warn her about the many ways she'd pay for forcing his hand. I could already see the wheels turning and suspected Ebba and her family would end up his next victims if he weren't about to be arrested.

"Move it," he said to me.

We disembarked and headed toward the shore. Agent Reyes watched us from the restaurant. I hoped he and Jones had heard everything and would stand down until I got the document signed.

Ten minutes and some fees and taxes later, I was holding a freshly signed boat title made out to my mother in exchange for her forgiveness of the loan.

"Thank you." I shook the dockmaster's hand. "Can't wait to go explore my new boat."

Lyle closed his eyes, jaw clenched, color feverish. We exited the office and started back for the boat.

"Where are you going?" he asked.

"You don't think I'm dumb enough to leave you on that boat, do you? I'm seeing this through to the bitter end."

"Suit yourself." Lyle stalked off, staying a few steps ahead of me. I glanced over my shoulder to make sure the agents were following us now, which they were, from a distance. When Lyle and I reached the yacht, we climbed aboard to find three large suitcases and two cardboard boxes of personal items already on the deck.

Lyle called, "Ebba?"

"Coming." She appeared with a fourth large suitcase in tow. "This is everything that matters."

Clearly, one benefit of boat dwelling is that you don't need many clothes or other things.

"Lovely doing business with you both." The agents were only one boat away now. "Good luck to you. You're gonna need it."

Lyle noticed the men rushing the boat. By the time his confused gaze snapped to mine, I'd pulled out my phone to snap his picture. "Oh, that's a keeper. Might have to blow it up for when I need a good laugh."

Agent Reyes asked, "Lyle Foster?"

"Who wants to know?" Lyle scowled.

"I'm Agent Reyes of the FBI, and you're under arrest."

Ebba's eyes widened as she sank onto an empty chair.

Lyle growled at me, "We made a deal, Erin."

I could've burst into a little dance right there but didn't want to annoy the officers. Instead, I shrugged. "Oops. Guess you're not the only one who can lie. Sucks to trust the wrong person, doesn't it? I'll let these gentlemen handle it from here. Think I'll check out my accommodations for the night." I handed Reyes the recording device, gave a little wave to Lyle and Ebba, and brushed past everyone while the officers read them both their rights.

I did it! The adrenaline rush made my hands shake while I grasped the title. My dad would be proud. Smiling through relieved tears, I texted Amanda the picture of Lyle with a note that read Woot! Print this with a note, and drop it in the memory jar for me.

Hot damn, this would be an absolutely perfect afternoon—if only it hadn't cost me a chance with Eli.

CHAPTER NINETEEN

AMANDA

"Are you sure you don't want me to come for moral support?" Erin helped me wrestle my way into a maternity maxidress with short sleeves that complied with the strict dress code requirements of the Chesapeake Detention Facility in Baltimore. No exposed shoulders, knees, backs, or bellies. I hadn't paid this much attention to my appearance since my wedding day—a day I couldn't think about without bitterness. "He's going to be pissed as hell and probably try to strike back at you. I think you need backup."

Lyle would be enraged after he got over his shell shock that I'd willingly faced public humiliation in order to bring him down. It hadn't been easy. News of his arrest had hit our local paper when he landed in Baltimore in handcuffs five days ago. Suddenly all the lookie-loos who typically ignored me were "checking in" to see if I needed anything.

When I'd wished to be on friendlier terms with women like Barb and Sandy, I hadn't wanted to field comments like "Oh, you poor thing. It must be awful—aw-ful—to have to deal with this when you're about to give birth." Worse was imagining the things they said behind my back. But Erin had been right. The satisfaction of having done right kept me from shriveling into a ball.

Mom couldn't stand her "well-intentioned" neighbors, so she'd fled town for a while—to Aunt Dodo's, of all places. I supposed, when the chips were down, your best refuge was family. A sister. Mine had been by my side nonstop since returning from Puerto Rico.

"No, thanks. I need to do this by myself, *for* myself." I toyed with my hair. Lyle hadn't seen my new hairstyle. I wanted to look fantastic to make him eat his heart out, so I fluffed its layers. I knew it to be silly and vain—hardly something that would undo how much of a fool he'd made of me—but it was better than nothing.

Then again, his new home—the former supermax prison that now functioned as a pretrial detainment center for federal criminals—probably preoccupied him with bigger concerns than my appearance. Frankly, I was surprised he'd approved my visitation application.

"Are you nervous?" Erin flicked her wrists.

"What do you think? Willa's future depends on me convincing him to give up custodial rights." I'd hardly slept from practicing my speech over and over. Even now, my pulse kicked an extra beat while thinking about it.

"I'm sure his lawyer told him that being cooperative will help with his plea bargain."

Kevin had also offered to meet me, but today wasn't only about legalities. I needed personal closure.

"That doesn't mean Lyle will do the right thing or be mature about this." I closed my eyes momentarily. "We loved each other—or I loved him—for a long time. I need to make peace so I can move on."

Erin's expression told me that peace was the last thing she wanted. Emotional catharsis and resolution didn't mean much to her. But trading insults with Lyle wouldn't bring me to a place where I could be a happy mother, and that was now my number-one goal.

"If I were you, I'd be dancing the jig at what's happening to him."

"I'm not made that way." I wouldn't waste my breath with too much explanation. "I'm proud of how we worked together to get justice, but take no joy in his suffering." Ebba's? Yeah, maybe a little.

Erin thrust her arms upward, head shaking. "He hurt you so much—how can you *not* rejoice in seeing him get what he deserves?"

I stared at her, uncertain I would ever be capable of putting my feelings into words. "I stood before God and swore to love him, for better or worse. Many nights I lay in his arms, feeling the happiest and most loved I've ever felt." I rubbed my stomach. "Together we created this amazing little life that I'll cherish until my last breath. So while I hope this experience keeps him from hurting others down the road, it'll be hard to see him in a jumpsuit, surrounded by guards and razor wire and inmates. To know that, at some point, when he gets out, he'll be a harder, changed version of the man who had, for a few years, been my world . . ."

"If he doesn't have custody, who cares?"

"Willa will. She might want to know him someday, and while I'll protect her for as long as I can, I can't protect her forever. On paper it seems black-and-white, but I keep telling you reality is complicated and unpredictable. What if Lyle spends his prison time constructing some elaborate revenge plot?" I let loose a long breath. "There's a lot running through my mind, and in order to feel good—to feel like the future won't become an ongoing battle—I need to make peace. I need to forgive him so I can be free."

Erin shrugged as if pacified, although I doubted I'd persuaded her. "What if I wait in the car? I don't think you should be alone after you see him."

"I love that you want to be there, but I'll be okay. This is the first real test of the promise I made Willa to become the strongest woman I can."

"Well, she's in luck because we both know you ace every test you set your mind to." Erin hugged me, prompting a round of happy tears for a change.

"Thank you." I grinned, swiping my eyes. "It's nice to know you've got my back."

Erin's expression slipped for a second. Feelings had never been her forte. "I talked to Mom this morning."

I stiffened. "How is she?"

"Okay, I guess. She's been leaning in to the part about the 'loan documents' so Dodo doesn't think she was too gullible." Erin rolled her eyes. "I reminded her about the family brunch on Saturday for the anniversary of Dad's death. The reading of the memory jar will be done with or without her."

"Is she coming home?"

"She won't blow that off."

I wasn't as sure as my sister. "I don't blame her, you know. It's not easy to have people look at you differently and to know you're the butt of their jokes."

"Ignore them. All that matters is that we have each other and soon Willa, too."

"What about Eli? You've been dodging my questions about him since getting back from Puerto Rico."

Erin turned away, fiddling with the brush I'd set on the dresser. "Because that's not important right now."

"It is to me." I stared until she glanced at me.

"Fine." She grimaced. "He dumped me. I mean, if you can dump a friend . . . that's what he did."

"What?" I'd been so self-absorbed I'd let days pass without realizing the truth. "Why?"

"The 'danger' factor of my mission brought up his fears about losing someone. Apparently his late wife and I share a headstrong personality type he can't handle now." Whatever Erin's true feelings about that, she hid them behind an "oh well" expression.

I pressed my hand to my chest. "Helping me cost you Eli?"

"No, Amanda." She shook her head firmly. "*Eli* cost me Eli. I can't turn into a different person—a cautious one—just because he's afraid. I'm sad, but mostly for him, because he's making his life so small."

New tears threatened. My sister had made a huge sacrifice for me—such a testament to the change in our relationship, yet I felt awful. It was one thing for my husband to shatter my heart, but he'd also cost my sister a piece of hers. "Go convince Eli he's wrong."

"I thought about it, but he needs to come to that conclusion on his own. Same goes for Mom and you and everyone else." She handed me my purse. "If we carelessly disregard other people, we should change. But if we're merely being true to ourselves, we shouldn't. How others respond to pain or fear is *their* choice. If Mom moves out of town and Eli lives a lonely life, that's on them, not us."

"It's still hard not to feel responsible." I bit my lip, aware that, in her own way, Erin had matured a lot these past few weeks. "I want to talk about this more, but I have to go. The traffic up to Baltimore might be heavy, and I don't want to miss my visiting-hour window."

My sister smiled at me and offered a final hug. "Good luck!"

I'd need it.

———

Razor-wire fencing, metal detectors, and the mild body search intimidated me, and I wasn't even an inmate. The sound of heavy locks and buzzers and the bright lights and sterile, stark surroundings added to the bleakness, making me tremble.

I couldn't picture my fastidious husband amid other prisoners, eating sloppy food from a tray and living in a six-by-eight-foot cell. He'd taken his chances, but I'd put him here. He had to be terrified. Enough to possibly have some regrets about how he had treated me.

Despite everything he'd done, my stomach burned at the thought of the danger he faced in prison. It would be easier on me if we wouldn't always be connected through Willa. But he could choose to waltz in and out of her life, so I'd be stuck with him forever.

Today we'd be separated by thick glass. The barrier made me sad for all the visitors denied physical contact with an inmate they still loved.

I no longer loved Lyle. Sometimes my hatred for so much about him strangled me. He'd hurt my pride, weakened my belief in love, and in some ways cost me my mother's affection. But I'd also tapped undiscovered strength, gained a sister I could lean on, and found enlightenment about my own insecurities.

While waiting to see him, I wrestled with hyperventilation. He might lash out—as he'd done whenever I'd inadvertently crossed him. He might rage at me for involving his father. He might even twist everything to blame me for his fate.

I was prepared for all that, but what if he dropped to his knees and begged for forgiveness? What if he cried? What if I saw any glimpse of the man who'd made me fall in love with him?

That I even fantasized about such an unlikely scenario scared me almost as much as the prison guards and their guns. I didn't want my husband back, but shamefully, I wanted him to want me back. Was that normal, or was I just in desperate need of therapy?

My thoughts circled until suddenly it was my turn. I stared at the glass, struggling to swallow because my mouth had gone dry. When he appeared, I hardly recognized him with his unkempt hair and chapped lips. His hollowed cheeks and the dark circles beneath his eyes confirmed my suspicions about how poorly he'd fare here.

I couldn't quite swallow.

My nostrils flared as I blinked back heartsick tears, feeling almost bodiless after weeks of not seeing him. I picked up the receiver, as did he. "Lyle."

His name came out more like an exhale than a fully formed word. I couldn't think because my mind kept circling back to one question: How did this become my life?

"Amanda." His blue eyes no longer shone with confidence and affection. He narrowed his gaze and grimaced. "Did you think a new haircut would make me fall in love again?"

That jab lanced—more sting than fatal blow. Seeing him left me too benumbed to feel the pain, so I had that going for me.

Erin's words drifted back to me, reminding me he would take every opportunity to hurt me today. I cleared my throat, undeterred by his childish behavior. "Are you okay?"

"Do you actually care?" He slouched into his seat as if already bored.

"I shouldn't, but you know I never wanted this ending for either of us. For so long, I thought we were happy . . ." A tide of sorrow rose in my chest, cracking my voice. Then I got angry for feeling any pity after what he'd done.

Lyle stared at me from his chair, as still as a photograph in a box frame. I couldn't read any emotion through the glass wall between us. "I'm not sure why you're here. Your sister got the trawler. Ebba's left me. I'll probably spend the next several years in jail. Did you come to dance on my grave?"

"You don't know me at all if you think that." I dropped my chin, the reality of it all too heavy to bear. I reminded myself that Lyle had never been whom I'd believed. He'd never actually loved me, although he'd done a bang-up job of pretending. "I wish I *could* take some joy in this, but I won't give you the power to fundamentally change me. I won't let you harden me or make me vengeful. The truth is that I mostly pray for your safety now."

"You and me both." He stared blankly, so I had no idea if my words affected him. I was counting on his self-preservation instincts to give me what I had come for.

I twisted my skirt in my hand. "Kevin says there are things you can do to reduce the penalties you'll face, so I came to discuss how you could convince my family to go easy in their victim impact statements."

"Ah, now we get to the heart of it." He leaned forward. "You came to get something, not because you cared."

"What I want is for our daughter's benefit, not my own."

He didn't reply.

"Give me full custody. It's not a big ask, since you seemed willing to walk away from her anyway. Under the present circumstances, having the right to make decisions without consulting you would be helpful for me and stabilizing for her."

"You expect favors after the way you and your sister tricked me?"

The air whooshed from my lungs. I'd prepared for this, but it still felt like a punch to the head. You can read about narcissism. Learn that a deep sense of shame and inadequacy lies beneath the bravado. Yet knowing that his real motivations were self-directed didn't make that comment less biting. "It's not a 'favor.' It's an opportunity for you to help yourself. Deep down in your soul, you must know our child is better off under my care. You might not love me, but surely you trust me to do right by her."

"Cutting me out is 'right by her'?"

How dare he! I jumped up from my seat, phone by my hip, and turned away, body tight with fury. Desperation for his consent kept me from hanging up and walking out. Closing my eyes, I focused on Willa and then turned around and took my seat again. My heart was as cold as the metal tabletop in front of me. "You already threw her aside for Ebba. I won't let you hurt her in the future. Absent some *major* changes, you'll never be a healthy influence on her. You're too devious."

"Apparently, so are you."

I shook my head, rejecting that guilt. "I lied to right a wrong. Restitution, pure and simple. Children need stability, love, and discipline. I won't actively make Willa dislike you, but I won't lie about you, either. She'll need to be aware of your silver-tipped lies so you can't spread your poison. I'll read her any letters you send, but I won't bring her to prison to see you."

"Willa." He shook his head. "I never agreed to that ugly name."

Another poke, but I wouldn't rise to his bait. "I'm not here to argue. Please, Lyle. This one time, do the right thing."

He sat back, still collected. "You said this was one of the things you wanted. What's the other?"

"I'd like a power of attorney to sell our house so we don't lose all the equity in a foreclosure. If there's any money left after all the costs and penalties, I'd like you to put your half in a fund for Willa's education. I'm not seeking alimony. With you in jail and then looking for work after a felony conviction, there's no real point. But this is a chance to do something for Willa that you can be proud of."

He stared at me for a moment. "You know, if you'd have shown this much nerve when we were together, maybe Ebba wouldn't have turned my head."

His little digs might've hurt more if they weren't a grown-up version of a temper tantrum. "We can be civil and do the right thing for our child's future, or I can leave and let the chips fall. I'd prefer us not to be bitter enemies the rest of our lives, but I can handle whatever you throw my way. If you don't want my compassion and a chance to reduce your sentence, that's up to you."

"Don't act like you're doing me a favor when it's the other way around."

It was like talking to a wall. All this time, I hadn't *really* understood how Lyle's father could've let Lyle walk out of his life, but now I did. Worse, this conversation was sapping my sanity. It hit me—to my horror—that in addition to settling the legalities, I'd also secretly desired an apology. "You're not sorry at all, are you?"

"Oh, I'm plenty sorry. Sorry I underestimated you. I'll have lots of time to regret that one. I'm also sorry I never counted on Erin riding to your rescue so late in the game. She must've felt guilty for not saying anything when she caught Ebba and me together in February."

Erin "caught" him and Ebba in February? No—that couldn't be. She would've shouted that from the roofs because she disliked him so. But then why couldn't I breathe?

I told myself this was a last-ditch attempt to drive a wedge between my sister and me, but my expression must've betrayed my dismay.

"Ohhh . . . she never told you about our run-in at the Kentwood Inn?" A sickening grin crept across his face. "Thinking about her kicking herself for that will be one of the few things that will make me smile."

He wasn't lying.

Erin actually hid my husband's affair from me for months.

I had to leave before he hurt me again. Mustering my last bit of backbone, I said, "My brother sent your lawyer all the documents related to my requests. You might want to hear his advice before refusing to cooperate." I almost hung up, but this would be my final chance to speak my truth. "I gave you every corner of my heart, and even after you smashed it apart, I've appealed to the man you could become, hoping we'd both get some closure. I thought if you apologized . . . I don't know. It's clear that, whatever I thought, it was stupid. You duped me for years, but my blinders are off. Your ugly jabs make leaving you here easier on me, so thank you for that much. Good luck to you, Lyle." I hung up the phone, pushed myself out of my chair, and turned my back on my husband and my old life.

The weight I'd been carrying around all month lifted. I might've floated to my car if not for the fact that my new relationship with my sister was as much of a lie as my marriage.

CHAPTER TWENTY

ERIN

"I can't believe you kept this from me all month. Man, it would've been something to see you play cop for a day." Rodri sucked down his espresso and tossed a few bucks at me. "I'm glad Amanda involved the authorities. Nothing's worse than when people get themselves in a jam trying to exact revenge."

"Amanda was never motivated by revenge. More like a desire to avoid scandal."

"Also common."

A wry smile seized my face. "What's it say about me that I sort of enjoy being the center of a scandal?"

"What's it say about me that *I* enjoy when you are?" Rodri reached over to tousle my hair. "Hate to duck out, but I've got to run. Don't pull what little hair you've got left out while waiting for your sister to get back from Baltimore."

"Ha ha." I kicked lightly at his leg.

"Give Amanda my best and keep me updated. I'll catch up with you later this week." He waved before taking his cup and saucer to Hannah and exiting the shop.

I remained seated at the same table where Eli had dumped me a week ago, reflecting on how my life had changed recently. From the little things like where I laid my head each night, to the big things like finally having a relationship with my mom and sister that didn't irritate me.

How different life could've been if the trust we'd built lately had existed years or even months ago. I wished it had, not only for our sakes but so that my dad might've been part of it, too. He would've loved my getting along better with Mom and Amanda.

The brunch on Saturday would be hard, especially if Mom didn't come back. I still missed Dad—thought of him by my first cup of coffee every morning. Knowing he would never experience this version of our family made my heart pinch with regret. Lesson learned too late, but I'd never hold anything back going forward. If my dad *were* living, that vow would earn at least one trip to Dream Cream, maybe more.

That thought prompted another gentle ache—Eli. My knee-jerk reaction to his concerns told me I still had a ways to go on my path to maturity—at least when it came to communication. I couldn't decide if letting go had been respectful of his feelings, or if I'd simply given up. Nothing bugged me more than indecision, which made me grouchy now.

Hannah cleaned the spills and sugar dust that the couple who'd been sitting at a nearby table had left behind. "Erin, you're on a streak. Last week you had one hottie here, this week another. Funny, though, I don't picture you with a cop."

"Rodri is an old friend, nothing more." I flashed a half-hearted smile.

"And the other one?"

"Also a friend, although there was a spark of something there . . ."

"Past tense?"

I screwed up my face while picking at the almond slivers on my pastry. "It's complicated."

The dishrag dangled from the hand Hannah planted on her hip. "You and I both know 'it's complicated' is a lie people tell themselves when what they mean is that they're not ready to face their own fears." She swiped her index finger my way. "Not for nothing, but it's easy to be bold about your hair and your job and all that, but none of that means a thing if you can't be bold with your heart. So you go on and uncomplicate that situation if that's what you really want."

It sounded so much like something my dad might say that tears wet my eyes. "This is why I love it here, Hannah. Where else could I find a pastry-making shrink?"

Hannah chuckled and went back to the register.

For years, I had thought myself bold and my sister fearful. In truth, Amanda had put herself out there—in love, in her career, in all ways that I never had. Even today, she was facing down Lyle in prison while I sat on my butt, drinking chai. Seems I'd had it backward all along.

Maybe it was time to take my own advice. I drew a breath and called Eli.

"Hello, Erin." Hearing his voice made my heart hum.

"Hey, Eli. I'm sitting at our table at Sugar Momma's and thought I'd let you know I'm home safe, and I succeeded." I bit down on my lip, not knowing what else to say.

"I read the news. Congrats. I'm glad for your family, and that you're safe." After a brief pause, he said, "Actually, I was planning on calling you. Do you have time to stop by?"

My knee bounced wildly, and I bit my lip so hard as I smiled it hurt. I checked the time because I wanted to be home when Amanda arrived. "Only a little."

"I'll take what I can get. See you soon."

My hopes soared because he wouldn't ask to see me if he hadn't changed his mind, would he?

On my way out of the shop, I waved to Hannah. "Wish me luck!"

"You make your own luck."

I nodded at that truth, then hopped on my bike and pedaled across town.

———

My stomach was doing Olympic-level somersaults as I climbed his porch stairs. Last time I'd been here, we'd laughed and he'd held me while I'd cried. That evening had been a really good beginning before everything went to hell. Still, I couldn't temper my expectations.

Eli opened the door wearing his shy smile, but we didn't embrace. "Thanks for coming."

"Friends always come when you call."

"Good friends do." He nodded, gesturing to the sofa. "Take a seat. I have a surprise for you." He rolled his shoulders and rocked on his toes.

"Oh?" My skin prickled with anticipation as I sank onto the cushions. "What kind of surprise?"

Eli rubbed his hands together before he picked a guitar off the wall. "A musical kind. I'm working on a song . . ."

"The one about Mo?" My heart thumped at the memory.

"No." Eli chuckled like he had that evening. Then he inhaled deeply and sighed, his expression contrite. "When I left you at that coffee shop, I couldn't shake a new kind of blues. Then I read the news and felt shitty for walking away when you and your family could've used a friend. I spent the past week thinking about my life. About who I am and what kind of man I want to be. I thought a lot about how you burst into my life so unexpectedly, like a rainbow after a storm. Next thing I knew, words were flowing . . . and I wrote this."

I was still reeling from the bliss of being compared with a rainbow when he began to strum a pretty melody and sing:

Oh, the cold, it hurts my skin
When I feel the whispers of the wind

316

And the colors come and go
But I wonder if they'll ever know

That the grace you showed me
Brought me back to the world you see
And with your guiding light
I know where I want to go tonight

Can't hold me back
'Cause I'm gone, I'm gone
And finding my
way out of the storm
I'm healing now before your eyes
Watch me grow, watch me grow
As I follow where you go

See the world around me change
I'm no longer stuck inside my cage
fighting shadows that are mine
Now I'm ready to take flight

And with your guiding light
I know where I want to go tonight

Can't hold me back
'Cause I'm gone, I'm gone
And finding my
way out of the storm
I'm healing now before your eyes
Watch me grow, watch me grow
As I follow where you go

I'm no longer
a tear falling down
Now that I've got reasons
to pick myself off the ground
I'm hearing voices
telling me to move on
You give me reasons
to pick myself off the ground

By the time he'd finished, each hair on my body stood on end. I wanted him to sing it again so I could focus on the lyrics, most of which I'd missed because my mind had blanked from a gush of excitement. I'd inspired him. Me—Erin Turner. I'd become a muse. My dad would love it! *I* loved it, and I really hoped this song was his way of saying he didn't want to walk away, even if my impulsiveness scared him a little.

He set the guitar down, eyes aglow, licking his lips, watching me. My body seemed disconnected and adrift somehow, yet anchored in the incredible moment.

"Eli, it's amazing! You broke through your writer's block. That's everything. I don't even know what else to say . . ." *"Thank you"* came to mind, but sounded too self-important.

"I'm glad you like it. It felt good to put pen to paper again." He slid off the arm to sit beside me on the sofa. Everything moved in slow motion. I studied the satisfied upturn of his mouth, the two-day stubble he scratched along his jaw, and the smile lines deepening around his eyes. His expression turned serious as he leaned closer and grabbed my hand. "I'm sorry I threw down an ultimatum. You were right. You've never pretended to be anything other than who you are, and that's exactly what draws me to you. I wouldn't want to change it, or make you think there's anything wrong with your way of life."

Boom! I wasn't often speechless, but those words meant so much I soaked them up like a cactus in the rain.

I stared at the faintly whiter skin on his ring finger where—once upon a time—his wedding band had been. "Thanks, but you weren't completely wrong, either. Until recently, I've always thought that no one should have a say in what I do, because I'm willing to live with the fallout. Now I get how those consequences don't affect only me. They affect everyone who cares about me, which means I ought to at least consider others before plunging headlong into something that could have negative consequences."

We stared at each other in silence.

"I've decided maybe Karen came through that woman at that exact moment because she thought you could help me find my way back to the world." He turned my palm over in his hand and traced the lines, like I'd fantasized about a couple of weeks ago. I'd never understood how Amanda and Mom got mushy at those Hallmark movies, but now I was about to cry over the connection building right here. "Do you think we could pick up where we left off last week?"

That did it. The tears spilled onto my cheeks, and I was even willing to thank Nancy Thompson if I ever saw her again.

"On one condition." My voice trembled like the rest of my body.

"What's that?"

I sniffled while swiping my cheek and smiling. "We seal the deal with ice cream."

He stared at me, heat in his eyes, which shot me off on another roller-coaster ride. "I'd rather seal it with a kiss."

"Oh!" I nearly fell off the couch. "Not many things rank higher than ice cream, but I'm thinking that might."

"You set a high bar."

"I try!" Nervous laughter didn't keep my mouth from going dry. It seemed impossible that any kiss could live up to my expectations.

Then Eli gently brushed his fingers through my hair before trailing his thumb along my jaw and cupping my face.

I set my hand on his thigh, closing my eyes because I could barely breathe beneath the intensity of the look in his. When his lips brushed mine, my body got so hot my bones seemed to melt. He swept his tongue to seductively dance with mine, slowly at first, then building with confidence and desire. My heart surged with yearning so strong I almost pushed him back against the cushions.

He eased away, smiling at me, scanning my entire face, perhaps seeking reassurance that it had been as good as we'd both hoped it would be.

I wrapped my hands around his neck, feeling simultaneously eager yet shy. "I may never need Dream Cream again."

He laughed, and we were about to resume the kissing when my phone rang. Amanda's ringtone. Oh God! This zenith of happiness had made me forget all about my plan to be home to greet her.

"That's my sister. She went to see her husband in jail today, so I should take it."

"Absolutely." He sat back while I dug my phone out of my pocket.

"Hey, how'd it go?" My body now tingled for less pleasant reasons.

"Not exactly as expected. When will you be home?" Her cool voice quavered.

My stomach dropped. "I can be there in ten minutes."

"Good. I'll be waiting." The clipped tone and the fact that she hung up without her usual pleasantries put me on high alert. What the hell had Lyle done now? I dug my hand into my hair, staring into space.

"I'm sorry, Eli. I need to go. Something must've happened . . ." I looked at him. "Really, though, you have no idea how sorry I am to leave."

"I have some idea." He smiled. "Go be there for your sister. I'm not going anywhere."

After a hug and another quick kiss, I said, "I'll call you later."

"Good luck." He walked me to the door and waited until I pedaled off before closing it.

For the mile-or-so ride home, my heart ping-ponged from ecstasy to concern. I parked my bike in the garage and went in through the kitchen. "Hello?"

"In here," Amanda called.

I found her at the dining table, hands clasped on the tabletop, posture and expression stiff as our mom's starched shirts.

"Oh God, you look white. Is Lyle fighting you about Willa, or refusing to sell the house?" I collapsed onto a chair in disbelief.

"I don't know. I've given up predicting what he will do, or expecting him—or anyone—to be honest with me or care about my feelings." The pointed words seemed directed at me.

Her hard edge made me uneasy. "Try to relax. He put up a brave front to knock you down a peg or two, but Lyle can't handle jail well. If his lawyer tells him it should help reduce his sentence, he'll capitulate. Willa will be safe. We'll protect her."

"Will you?" Amanda's cold eyes burned through me. "Like you protected me?"

Sarcasm? My stomach started sinking to my toes. Her anger confused me after the way I'd helped her.

She glowered at me with open disdain, much the way Lyle had always glared at me when no one else was looking. What did he say to turn her against me . . .

Oh! Oh no.

My heart pounded in my ears as the past came roaring back.

Praying I was wrong, I joked, "Let's hope sting operations don't become a new family tradition."

Amanda shook her head. "Stop, Erin. I know that you've been lying to me for months. Lyle told me about the Kentwood Inn."

"Oh." Damn it! My pores sweated like the plumbing pipes at my old apartment. All week I'd been so focused on how Lyle would attack Amanda I'd never considered that he would also pay *me* back. He'd done it, all right. In the worst way possible.

Although frantic to shore up our fragile bond, I froze, unable to think of how to explain myself.

"That's all you have to say?" My sister's heartsick expression made my insides blister. "You knew for months that Lyle was running around behind my back yet never warned me. Exactly how often did you snicker about that with Lexi?"

"It wasn't like that . . ." My chest ached at the possibility of us returning to the way things used to be—polite at best, snarky at worst.

"No? You didn't get any thrill from making a fool out of me? Didn't secretly love the fact that my life wasn't at all what I thought it was? Didn't go to bed heady with this knowledge, like a spectator, eagerly waiting for the bottom to drop out of my life?" Her eyes narrowed, framing a look of disgust. Those ugly accusations slayed, especially because I couldn't claim none were even the *faintest* bit true. "And then to rush in like some great savior at the end, when in fact none of it would've happened if you had even once told me what you saw."

I dropped my chin, on the verge of crying. "I'm sorry. But I knew you wouldn't have believed me."

"So it's my fault?" she asked, her blue eyes full of betrayal.

"No, that's not what I mean. But think about it, Amanda." I gripped the edge of the dining table. "How many times did you dismiss anything I said about Lyle's behavior? Every single time." I slapped the tabletop for emphasis on each of those three words. "It's not like I caught them in bed or even kissing. They were coming out of the inn in the early afternoon, claiming to have finished a business lunch, which was plausible. Despite my suspicions, I had no proof. And you two had recently bought your house and announced your pregnancy, so I wondered if my dislike for Lyle had made me paranoid. Plus we were still mourning Dad's death. You know none of us were back on track yet. I worried that an unsubstantiated accusation would make you so angry you'd totally cut me out."

No one could blame her for her doubt, but seeing it made me shrink inside. I was shaky and desperate at once.

"I might believe you if you'd at least mentioned it once the truth came out. All these weeks—all my tears—yet you never said a word." Her lip trembled, but she fought back her own tears. She smoothed her palms across the tabletop, regaining her composure. "It was bad enough to be humiliated by my husband, but to learn that you've been holding on to this, leaving me unarmed so Lyle could use it against me . . . I feel doubly foolish for believing we'd finally gotten close."

"I swear to God I would never consciously withhold anything out of spite or jealousy. When you told me about Lyle, I almost said something but figured Mom would blame *me* for everything instead of Lyle. It seemed pointless to upset everyone more at a time when we needed to rely on each other." My logic didn't seem to budge my sister even an inch. Remorse bloomed like algae, choking me. "Wasn't it kinder to keep quiet once the truth came out? That was my only intent. I love you . . . I'd never intentionally hurt you."

Amanda stared over my shoulder, through the window. She avoided eye contact even as she rose from the table, spine straight but shoulders soft. Defeated and remote. "All I know is that I can't count on *anyone* to be unconditionally honest and on my side. I've never felt more alone in my life, despite everyone in town gawking and checking in on 'poor Amanda Foster.' Maybe Mom's got the right idea. There's nothing keeping me in Potomac Point now. It'd be easier to live and work in a school district outside the reach of the stain of Lyle's name and Mom's suffocating anger. I could move nearer to Kevin and get Marcy's help with Willa."

Six months ago, those words wouldn't have taken a shovel to my chest and carved out half of me. "Amanda, wait. Where are you going?"

"For a walk. I need to think." She waddled across the living room and through the front door, closing it quietly behind her with a finality that stole my breath.

My screwup had pushed my mother, sister, and me as far apart as we'd ever been, and I had no idea how to—or if I could—fix it. I would've dissolved into a puddle, but there wasn't time.

I sat at the table with my eyes closed, begging my dad for some sign. A direction. Advice. Nothing happened. No ray of light, no whispers, no sign that he was there unless he remained silent to force me to move on without him.

No matter what came next, we could not let Amanda believe she was on her own. With my dad unavailable to me, I'd have to rely on my mother. I pulled Mo onto my lap to cuddle while I called her.

"Hello?"

"Mom, it's me. I know you're still ticked off at us for involving the authorities, but you need to come home today."

"Is something wrong with the baby?" Her distress rang out.

"No!" Knock on wood. That was about the only thing that hadn't gone wrong in the past hour. "But Amanda's talking about moving out of town after Willa's born."

"Has something *else* happened?" Her tone hardened.

"She saw Lyle today . . ." Closing my eyes to brace for her meltdown, I explained how he'd used what had happened in February to hurt Amanda. Afterward, I held the phone away from my ear, expecting a major tongue-lashing the likes of which used to send me to sulk on our roof. The ensuing silence was worse. "Mom?"

"I'm here." Instead of fury, I heard resignation and fatigue.

Unaccustomed to skirting the blame, I remained poised in self-defense mode. "I'm sorry. I know you prefer to steer clear of all this, but I'm really worried about Amanda."

"Did she pack a bag?"

"Not yet."

"Good. And how are you holding up?"

"Me?" What had Aunt Dodo done with my mother?

"Yes. Obviously you've been holding this in for weeks, probably kicking yourself. That's a lot to handle."

When I released a pent-up sigh, Mo licked me. "You're not mad at me?"

"Mad?" She huffed. "You think your little role in all this makes you special? Lyle took us all for a ride, and we all fell for it. I can't take enough showers to come clean, but it's no more your fault than any of ours."

I wished I owned stock in Kleenex for the amount of tissues I'd used up today. "I appreciate that, Mom . . . so what are we going to do about Amanda?"

She blew out a breath. "I know how she feels—the need to escape—but running here didn't solve anything for me." She went quiet. Then, in a surprise turn of events, she said, "I'll be home tonight."

"Really?"

"Naturally, Erin. When my children need me, I'll always be there. And we have your father's memorial brunch."

"Thank you." It occurred to me that I didn't say those words often enough. "I'm glad we'll all be together for that."

"Yes. All but William." Then she inhaled sharply. "I just had a brilliant idea. I'm going to beg Nancy for an emergency session. William might finally show up if we're gathered together in his honor."

———

It'd been a year, but sitting in our living room surrounded by somber faces and silence made it feel like Dad's funeral all over again. That remained the worst day of my life.

I remembered how Max wouldn't stop shadowing me, as if he'd expected me to shatter into a thousand pieces if left alone. Inside, I'd already broken, so there was nothing he could've done to stop it. I'd stood in the corner, wishing I didn't have to listen to our neighbors sharing personal stories about my dad. It hurt to hear them laugh about this time or that, while it was all I could do not to drop to the floor and wail. The absence of music had thrown me, too. My dad had always had a record playing, but I couldn't bear to hear music that day, so we'd left the turntable untouched.

Kevin had leaned against the wall, keeping little Billy on his hip, as if acutely aware of the fleeting gift fatherhood could be. I couldn't believe my mom slinked away from the company and put herself to bed. If I'd tried that, she'd never let me hear the end of it.

My stomach had twisted while I watched Lyle speak to our company as if he'd been part of the family for decades. But even that hadn't infuriated me as much as watching Amanda break into hostess mode—refreshing pitchers of iced tea and replenishing platters of food. I couldn't understand why she gave a shit about what the community thought of the wake when we'd just watched our father go into the ground.

It'd taken me all year to realize that busywork helped my sister process her feelings. Like now, she was fluffing the pillows and neatening the magazines on the coffee table.

She hadn't said ten words to me since our argument. In fact, she'd rarely made eye contact. Kevin had come alone today because Billy had a fever and an ear infection, so he kept glancing at his watch. Even Mo hid, curled up by the potted philodendron in the corner.

Mom had drawn the curtains "to keep the neighbors out of our business." The effect? Thin slants of sunlight mixed with dim lamplight gave the room a gloomy aura. Perhaps it was the perfect setting for the occasion and Nancy's hocus-pocus.

"Should I get the memory jar? We might have time to read some before Nancy arrives." I'd barely finished my sentence when Amanda answered.

"I'm not in the mood for that today." She looked at Kevin instead of me.

"But that was the plan—" I started.

"No, that was your wish, not 'the' plan. I'm not interested in reading the notes I put in there this winter when, unlike you, I was ignorant of the truth. Sorry to rob you of whatever jollies you'd get in reliving how foolish I was."

"Amanda, you know that's not . . ." But before I finished my thought, she turned away.

Mom tapped my shoulder. "Let's put off the jar. By December we might all be in a better place to keep the tradition going."

"Agreed," Kevin said, offering Amanda a shoulder squeeze while shooting me a conciliatory smile. Our whole lives, he'd been the Switzerland in any battle between Amanda and me. He then said to her, "I thought you'd be in a better mood after learning that Lyle signed all the papers."

It bummed me out that *we* couldn't celebrate that together. "That's a win to put in the jar."

My mother shook her head at me. It took me a second to grasp that even though Lyle's cooperation had definitely been the best possible outcome, the situation still sucked for my sister. "Sorry," I mumbled.

I shoved two Ritz crackers in my mouth, followed by a cheddar cheese cube.

"There she is!" Mom, who'd been peeking through the drapes, exclaimed.

I'd been going back and forth about Nancy since the thing with Eli and Karen. On one hand, Eli'd encouraged me to keep an open mind, convinced that Karen had been in the room with us that day. But it would take more for me to believe my dad could pass messages through Nancy as if she were a supernatural mailbox. With our family's personal business being publicized recently, the woman had easy access to a trove of details she could spin into so-called messages from beyond.

I'd yet to master Kev's ability to hide his skepticism, but in my desperation to bring the family together for Amanda's sake, I would go through this charade one last time.

Mom clapped her hands together and raced to the door, opening it before Nancy rang the bell. "Welcome back. All the kids are here today, so surely William won't ignore us."

Nancy smiled. "Don't think of it as being ignored. We don't know how or why some spirits can come through and others can't. He may be trying."

Nice dodge, Nancy, I thought, then winced because that had hardly been open-minded.

"Well, he'd better try harder. We need him more than ever." Mom nodded sharply. "I made a pot of coffee."

"None for me, thanks." Nancy hung her purse on the coatrack in the corner and introduced herself to Kevin and Amanda.

Nancy and I greeted each other with the polite nod of civil foes. "For those who haven't been through this, all I ask is that you keep an open mind and heart. Try not to say anything unless I ask, and then only yes/no answers, please."

"Okay. Let's get started." Kevin pulled out a seat for Amanda and then sat beside her.

Nancy sat next to him and Mom flanked Amanda's other side, forcing me to sit beside Nancy.

Amanda glanced at everyone, but when she caught my eye, she looked away.

"As your mother knows, I encourage everyone to say a silent prayer for your intention today and, if it helps, to close your eyes so your other senses awaken." Nancy placed her hands on the table. "Think about a specific memory or let your feelings about your father flow through you. As I get messages, I'll relay them. Many may have nothing to do with him. I can't control who comes to me, but I hope we hear from William."

Kevin shot me a look that mirrored the incredulity I felt, to which I responded with a subtle shrug.

Surrendering to the inevitable, I relaxed my shoulders and closed my eyes. I don't know how many minutes passed before Nancy spoke.

"I'm getting something about red shoes. Do red shoes mean anything to anyone?" Nancy's eyes remained closed.

"I have red shoes," my mother said. "And Erin has those beat-up red sneakers she always wears."

Most women probably owned one pair of red shoes, so once again Nancy's "gift" underwhelmed. What also didn't shock me was my mom's inability to stick to yes and no answers.

"I hardly think Dad gives two you-know-whats about red shoes," I grumbled.

Mom gave a sharp grunt of disapproval. To Nancy's credit she took a deep breath and kept her eyes closed.

For my own sanity, I mentally checked out and thought about how to convince my sister to forgive me so we could prepare for Willa's arrival and I could tell her about kissing Eli. After all we'd been through, I refused to concede the ground we'd gained to Lyle's viper tongue.

For most of my life, I'd thought our differences too big for us to be close. Now, I knew we could bridge those if we learned to respect them rather than judge them. But there'd never before been a time when we didn't speak to each other, so I first had to win back her trust.

"Dorothy . . . I'm hearing a man say the name Dorothy . . . ," Nancy said.

"My sister's name is Dorothy!" Mom's hands went up with another hopeful smile.

"Why would Dad bring up Aunt Dodo? She made him crazy," I said. More to the point, finding the name of my mother's siblings would take almost no skill at all. So far, Nancy was batting a big fat zero. I'd give her credit for not quitting, though.

Kevin's mask started to slip. He stole another glance at his watch and shot me a "spare me" look. Nancy closed her eyes again, so I made a silly face. From the corner of my eye, I saw Amanda scowl at me.

"Buttonwood . . . ," Nancy said, eyes opening. "The base of the sycamore tree."

My heart stopped as my mouth fell open.

"What?" Amanda asked, yanking me from the memory. "You look spooked."

"Dad and I planted that sycamore in the backyard."

My mother clapped her hands together. "He's here."

"Why would he show up to talk about a tree?" Kevin asked, all lawyerly.

"I'm not sure." And then I thought about red shoes and Dorothy and I leaped from my chair. "I know! I know!"

I ran to the garage for a shovel and then raced out the kitchen door to the tree trunk.

Within a minute or two, my family had gathered around me as I paced, trying to figure out where to dig. "It's so big now . . . I don't think I can get to the doll."

"What doll?" Kevin probed.

"From *The Wizard of Oz*. Remember the little action figures? I buried Dorothy when we planted this tree." I continued walking around the tree trunk, trying to remember where it might be.

My mother waved her hands and gazed at the clouds as if spirits circled overhead. "William, what kind of nonsense is this? I need answers, not toys."

"Erin," Kevin called, stopping me in my tracks. He reached for the shovel. "You'll never get to that doll now. This trunk is massive. How about you try to think about whether there's actually any significance to this memory? Why did you two bury the doll with the tree?"

I squeezed my eyes closed, trying to recall every detail, reenacting the scene aloud.

"Why can't we plant an apple tree so we have fresh apples for Mom's pies?" I'd said to my dad, hands on my hips. "Or a cherry tree—I love cherries."

"So do I, but this sycamore will grow to be huge and provide lots of shade for us." He dug up the first shovelful of dirt.

"Whoop-de-do!" I sank onto the bag of fertilized soil I'd dragged back there and crossed my legs.

He patted my knee. "Come on now. This buttonwood will be here for generations, like a piece of Turner family history. You and me—we're putting something in the ground that will outlive us."

I opened my eyes, staring up at the massive canopy of leaves now shading us all. "He went on and on about how deep its roots grew. I'd said, 'Who cares? You can't see the roots, unlike the apples or pink flowers of the other trees.'"

Amanda stared at me, wide-eyed and accepting, as if she'd known that if Dad did show himself, it would be to me. That wouldn't help us mend fences.

I turned to Mom. "Dad said that roots were more important than the pretty flowers. At first I thought he'd said that because he knew it hurt my feelings that everyone always complimented Amanda's looks but no one ever called me pretty." I avoided my sister's gaze and glanced instead at Kevin. "But then he talked about how roots kept the tree safe, and that it was like that with a family, too. That all the people in a family could stretch in different directions like branches, but the roots would always bind them together and keep them strong. And then I said that must be why people called it a family tree. And then he said something about how there is never anyplace as important as home . . . and that's when I ran inside to get Dorothy and bury her with our tree, 'cause, you know, that's what she said."

Kevin laughed at me, head shaking. "Sounds exactly like something you and Dad would do. Good metaphor, too."

"Except sometimes branches get diseased and need to be pruned," Amanda quipped and turned to go back inside.

I bit my tongue and followed her, as did the others.

"None of this helps us with the gossip or selling the boat," Mom groused as we filed in through the kitchen door.

We returned to the dining room but didn't take our seats. "Maybe the point is that none of that matters as much as this right here." I circled our little group with my index finger. "Instead of focusing our energy on everything out there, we should be grateful for and help each other."

"Works for me." Kev scratched his head. "I was dreading coming today, and had no idea what to expect, but I actually feel better. It's been an interesting way to mark our loss."

"I'd think you'd be happier, Mom," I said when faced with her befuddled expression.

"Is that all?" She looked at Nancy with an air of desperation. "Is he saying anything else? A special message just for me?"

My heart squeezed. I'd grown up believing I was his favorite person, and maybe I was—who knows for sure? But he'd been my mother's favorite, and her raw longing made my eyes sting. For the first time, I *wanted* Nancy to make up some loving message to make my mother feel better.

Nancy closed her eyes but then shrugged. "I'm sorry. I'm not hearing anything now."

"Don't be sad, Mom." I hugged my mother and kissed her temple, teasing, "Be happy that you get to prove my naysaying wrong. That's gotta be satisfying."

Mom snorted.

"Mom, Dad showed you every day how much he loved you and relied on you to keep us all in line," Kev gently added. "Maybe this tree business is his way of reminding you he's still right here standing guard over you."

She nodded but didn't speak.

"I think I'll leave you all to digest the message." Nancy took her purse and smiled at us. "I wish I would have met William. He sounds lovely. If you need anything more, you know how to reach me."

Once she was gone, Kevin said, "Marcy won't believe this. I'm still stunned. But I can totally picture Erin and Dad out there having that conversation."

"I miss his way of seeing things." I gave my sister a pointed stare. "It's pretty clear he wants us to stick together, no matter what."

"It's not so easy when you can't trust each other," Amanda said, showing no signs of softening, despite the miracle we'd experienced.

"I don't want to butt in where I don't belong, but you're being harsh, Amanda." Kevin rubbed her shoulder. "I get it—you've been through the wringer—but Erin didn't set out to hurt you. And how can you say you can't trust her when she's gone and made plans to make you a partner in her business?"

I'd forgotten that I'd asked him to start the paperwork before I went to Puerto Rico. This wasn't exactly how I had expected to surprise her with a possible new chapter in our lives.

"What?" Amanda asked, while Mom splayed a hand across her chest.

"When we met with Agent Crowley, Erin asked me to draw up a partnership agreement for Shakti Suds." Kevin's brows knit as his gaze bounced back and forth between my sister and me.

Now that I had Amanda's attention, I said, "You've been offering to help me with the admin stuff, so I thought together we might actually make decent money, which we could both use. Then everything else happened this week, and I forgot to mention it."

"You want me to be your partner?" Amanda's eyes turned misty.

"I did—I do if you can get past your anger." I turned to Mom. "I didn't think you wanted the responsibility, so don't get offended. I still like mixing products with you."

"Oh, for Pete's sake, I'm not offended. I'm a librarian, not a soap maven. I only help you because you're here and it's something to do." She waved her hands.

"Well, you can still help us—or me, if Amanda isn't interested." I turned back to my sister. "You're pretty quiet."

Amanda looked at Mom and Kevin. "I'm floored."

"So you're not interested?"

"I didn't say that . . . I'm still reeling from the whole thing with Dad. And, honestly, I'm still hurt by your secretiveness."

I held my hands out from my sides. "I've explained and apologized. I can't go back and fix it, but I wouldn't make the same choice today. You have to know that."

"I suppose I do." She nodded. "Maybe I overreacted—things would be so much worse for us if you hadn't gone to Puerto Rico. And I know that cost you a shot with Eli. I'm sorry about that. And I'm sorry I didn't accept your apology sooner."

I wrapped her in a hug. "It's okay. It's been a terrible time, and you've got extra hormones swimming around."

She held me tight. "Thank you."

When we broke apart, I said, "By the way, Eli and I patched things up. I didn't tell you because, well . . ."

"Because I haven't been speaking to you." She wiped her eyes. "I'm happy for you. When will we meet him?"

Before I could answer, Kevin said, "Looks like my work here is done. I'll follow up on the house sale and boat stuff this week, and email those partnership papers."

He kissed us all goodbye before leaving.

Despite my sister's and my reconciliation and a message from Dad even I had a hard time ignoring, my mother's sour expression remained fixed.

"Are you still upset that Dad didn't say more?" I asked.

"No. It's just that all of you get to move on—with your business, with a new boyfriend, a baby—but what's better for me? I'm still a widow—a notorious one who lent a criminal so much money." She covered her face.

I grabbed her hands and gently pulled them away. "Mom, it's been a stressful and painful year. But look at this—we're all under the same roof again, learning to trust each other and work together. Accepting the things that are different about each other. Isn't that worth more than a few lost dollars and a little embarrassment? At the end of the day, the worst thing anyone can say about you is that you love your children and are extremely generous. Is that so awful?"

"And you know I'll need help with Willa." Amanda stroked her arm. "Dr. Blount's given you a clean bill of mental health, so once Kevin sorts out all the legal stuff, I'm hoping you'll want to babysit a few days a week."

She nodded blankly without directly answering either of us. "I need to go for a little drive."

Maybe she thought she'd get more answers from Dad at his grave.

As she backed out of the driveway, I said, "I'll follow her to make sure she's okay."

Amanda nodded, so I ran to the garage, jumped on my bike, and took the chance she had gone down Elm Street. Her red Prius came into view two cars ahead, so I hung back. My mother drove the speed limit, and a plethora of stop signs made it easy to track her, especially when she headed north on Balsa Road. Not much out that way but Saint Bernard's cemetery, as I'd expected.

I didn't go there often. For me, seeing Dad's headstone—thinking about him lying beneath that cold field, surrounded by other skeletons and headstones—disturbed me and made his absence sharper.

My mother got out of her car and trod to the third row of graves, where she sank to her knees. I laid my bike on the ground and quietly came up behind her, heartsick to find her crying.

"Mom," I said, startling her.

"Oh, Erin. Why'd you follow me?" She scowled, wiping her eyes.

"To make sure you were okay."

"Well, I'm not. I haven't been okay since your father died, and I'll never be okay again. He was the heart of this family . . . he was my heart. Now that's gone."

I sat in the grass beside her and rubbed her back. "It's not gone. He's part of all of us. You know I didn't want to believe in Nancy's hooey, but I can admit when I'm wrong. Dad is with us, even if we can't see him. He's here, Mom, and if we lean on each other, he'll always be with us and we'll be fine. Even if you don't believe that yet, you have to try. Willa will be here soon, and we have to give her everything Dad would've wanted for her, right?"

My mother glanced at his grave, nodding.

"I know you feel lost without him, but of all the women he could've picked, he picked you because he knew you were strong and principled and the exact right person to help him build a family. Don't give up on yourself or the rest of us now."

Her mouth twitched. "I don't know if I can get used to this wiser version of you."

I smiled. "Don't worry. I've got plenty of crazy ideas floating around my head that'll keep you on your toes for years to come."

My mother elbowed my side, chuckling. "Your dad loved you best."

"He didn't *love* me best. He showered me with affection because I fit in the least and he wanted me to feel okay about that."

She squeezed my hand. "I'm sorry I didn't do that for you."

My throat tightened. I half expected a flock of doves or a double rainbow to accompany that unexpected apology. What a day!

"It's okay. We still have time." For once, hugging my mother felt authentic.

I still missed my dad something fierce, but peace finally came from knowing that, like that tree, our family would continue to grow strong in our love and commitment, thanks to him.

CHAPTER TWENTY-ONE

AMANDA

Six weeks later

The old sycamore provided much-needed shade today. The "Over the Hill" and silver "30"-shaped mylar balloons Mom and Aunt Dodo had tied all around the deck for Erin's birthday stood erect and unmoving in the humid, stagnant summer air.

I took a seat between my mom and Lyle's father, Richard, jostling Willa, who fussed in my arms after waking from her nap.

"I'm so glad she's thriving," Richard said, gathering her little fingers around his index finger. "I was worried when you called to tell me she came early."

Three weeks early, but my little Muffin's lungs were formed, and she'd shown no signs of trouble so far. "She's a perfect little pip-squeak, isn't she?"

I smiled, as I'd been doing since her birth. My heart could scarcely contain all the love and happiness that seemed to grow exponentially with each new day.

Eli picked up his guitar again and played a soft melody. Willa's eyes widened, and unblinking, she stopped fussing.

"You're a baby whisperer," I said. "Can I record you now to play whenever she gets fussy?"

Eli shot me a gentle smile while Erin gazed at him with such open warmth it brought on another wave of joy. She'd been spending more nights at his house lately—possibly to avoid being awakened by late-night feedings. Even so, she still visited most afternoons at Mom's.

After a day of purging and reorganizing, Kevin's old room turned office now did double duty as a nursery. I hoped to get a full-time teaching job by Christmas, but in the meantime planned to sub when I could and continue at the nursery school a few days per week this fall. Mom had agreed to sit with Willa during those hours. It wasn't the perfect plan I'd once needed, but it was doable.

Little Billy lay passed out on Kevin's shoulder after the comedown from his sugar rush. "We've got to get going so we can drop Richard at the airport on our way home."

"Happy birthday, Erin." Marcy gave her a little hug from behind.

Erin patted her hands. "Thanks for coming."

"Good to see you, honey." Mom stood to give Billy a peck on the cheek and say goodbye to Kevin and Marcy. "And don't forget, honey: I can come up and watch him next week if Marcy wants to go with you to that conference in New York."

"I'll help," Dodo added.

My mother smiled at her sister, but I suspected she'd rather not have Dodo micromanaging her time with her grandson the way she'd micromanaged this little picnic. Their relationship made me smile, though, because like with so many sisters, despite the friction, they had each other's backs.

"Thanks. We'll let you know." Kevin nodded at Richard. "You ready?"

Richard sighed. "I hate to go, but yes. I left my bag by the front door, so I'll meet you by the car."

Kevin and his family disappeared into the kitchen as Richard turned to my mother. "Thank you for welcoming me to visit Willa during Erin's birthday weekend. It's been a real pleasure to meet you all, especially my beautiful little granddaughter."

Mom self-consciously toyed with her hair, not quite meeting Richard's intense gaze. "Certainly. You're part of the family now."

Aunt Dodo's brows rose high on her large forehead as she stared into her cup of coffee.

Richard smiled, while Erin shot me "a look" that wasn't all that different from Dodo's. But Richard Foster had been unobtrusive and kind, affirming my decision to include him in Willa's life, so I was grateful that Mom hadn't made him feel unwelcome.

He turned to Erin. "Happy birthday, young lady. I'll see you all again in the fall."

I thought to invite him to Thanksgiving but would wait to see how things played out in the coming weeks. One could push Madeline Turner only so far so fast, and I didn't want to give Aunt Dodo a heart attack in this heat.

Richard squeezed my shoulder. "Thanks for my little soap package. Good luck to you girls with your men's line."

"You're welcome!" Erin said, rubbing her hands together victoriously.

In the past weeks she'd developed a line of men's products, and I'd worked to build a customer database and regular newsletter, and set up a reward program for repeat customers. But more important than the ultimate financial success of the venture was its meaning for my relationship with my sister.

After Richard left, Erin asked, "Did anyone talk to Kevin about the boat?"

Mom cleared her throat. "He thinks I should involve a boat broker. It'll cost me something in commission, but the boat will probably sell faster."

The Office currently called a slip in the bay home, but I'd never set foot on it. Erin had taken pictures, but seeing them made the images of Lyle and Ebba's love cruise too pointed, killing my interest in a private tour.

"Listen to Kevin," Aunt Dodo instructed.

My mother started to clear the table without answering. Their relationship reminded me of what Erin and I used to be, and made me grateful for the change. When she went inside, Dodo turned to me. "So custody is secured? And your house is already under contract?"

"Yes, Aunt Dodo. My neighbor's good friend wanted my house, so I sold it without a broker, which offset the late fees I owed."

"You kept it so beautifully—no wonder someone wanted it. I'm glad for you. And what of Lyle?" Aunt Dodo had an abrasive way of asking questions like a grand inquisitor, but I'd long ago learned the best way to handle her was to answer quickly and move on.

"He's accepted a plea bargain for some fines and a four-year sentence but could get out sooner on good behavior."

"Does he get visitation?"

"Not while he's in prison. As for the future, I'm reserving judgment to see how things go. He is Willa's father, and if he's reformed or she wants to meet him, I'll deal with it then."

Erin cleared her throat in an obvious attempt to change the subject.

"Quit hogging the baby." My sister unapologetically stretched across the table and took Willa out of my arms before turning to Eli, who'd set down his guitar. "I think she looks like me, don't you?"

"So much so I thought she *was* yours," he teased, his arm slung loosely around Erin's waist.

Willa did have my sister's chin. She also had my fair complexion and blonde hair, and Lyle's eyes—bright-blue buttons beneath high, arched brows.

No one mentioned that, but everyone had to see it. I couldn't guess how long it would take for me not to see him every time I looked at her, but his looming presence didn't diminish my love for her. If anything, it might slowly erode my hatred for him. No matter what else he'd done wrong, without Lyle, I wouldn't have my daughter, and she was worth any suffering I'd endured.

I'd lost a husband but gained a daughter and my sister. Since husbands can be replaced, I figured I made out okay in the end.

AN EXCERPT FROM

TRUTH OF THE MATTER

A POTOMAC POINT NOVEL

EDITOR'S NOTE: THIS IS AN EARLY
EXCERPT AND MAY NOT REFLECT THE
FINISHED BOOK

CHAPTER ONE

Anne Sullivan Chase

Ten more minutes—fifteen, tops. I can stick this closing out for that long without falling apart. A revenge plan of some kind might've cushioned the blow, but payback won't put my family back together. I've survived losses before. The only new ground this time will be helping my daughter, Katy, cope with the fallout. I have a plan for that, but at present I'm best served by relaxing my shoulders, sipping my water, and maintaining my carefully blank expression.

That last part would be easier if I hadn't left our home for the last time less than an hour ago. Without drapes and carpets, the McMansion had felt cooler than the inside of its Sub-Zero refrigerator. A fitting end.

Recollections of those final moments spent in the foyer bombard me. On the wall, unfaded squares where my original paintings had hung. The faint echoes of the shrill bell on the pink bike Katy used to pedal across the floor, and of the futile marital arguments about missed soccer games and inconsiderate in-laws that replaced laughter and "I love yous." The aroma of cocoa on rainy mornings spent seated in the family room's window bench, where I'd stared past the pool to the wooded perimeter, wondering how I could be a mother and wife yet so lonesome.

Like shadows, my memories record the history of a family that will no longer live under one roof. Of the atrophied dreams and broken promises flayed by the sharp blade of divorce. But the worst part of my morning was the look on Katy's tear-streaked face before she jumped into the yellow Jeep that Richard bought her on her sixteenth birthday, and sped away from me like a canary freed of its cage.

Now, while the brokers leave the conference room to confirm the wire transfer and the buyers exchange a celebratory kiss at the other end of the table, Richard turns to me. "Jim will be in touch to finalize the transfer of stocks and other things before the end of the week."

It's not surprising that my husband of seventeen years treats the end of our marriage as nothing more than another negotiation. His emotional IQ had dipped in direct inverse relation to his legal career's spike. He's probably quite self-satisfied for being so "generous" with our divorce settlement, but, honestly, I'd prefer less money in exchange for seeing even an ounce of regret in his eyes.

I say nothing about the stocks because "Thank you" seems unwarranted for something I earned in exchange for years of waiting patiently—raising our daughter largely on my own while supporting him as he built his practice—on the promise of the life we would one day share. Surprise! Instead of planning empty-nest vacation weekends in Bermuda, he dumped me to bestow those perks on Lauren, the interloper.

I hate Lauren. A blow-up-pictures-of-her-face-and-toss-darts, stopping-barely-short-of-wishing-harm-on-her kind of hate. And I've never hated anyone in my life, so I haven't mastered control over the crippling surges of vengeance. It's frightening, to be honest, so I redirect my thoughts and ask Richard about his plans with our daughter.

"Where are you taking Katy for lunch?" At the first hint of his confused expression, I grip my purse to keep from pounding my fists on the table. "Don't tell me you forgot."

Sorry *not* sorry about my irked tone.

"I did." He proceeds to scrub his face with both hands in one deliberate motion. God, that annoys me. Each gesture, word, and outfit are chosen with care. "I promised Lauren—"

"You cannot blow off Katy for your girlfriend today of all days." Technically Lauren's his new fiancée, but I won't give her that respect. Three and a half months ago, Richard confessed his affair and asked for this divorce. Nine weeks ago, he moved out. His eagerness to move on is driving his acquiescence on financial and custody matters. Still, Richard's already put a ring on Lauren's finger although technically our divorce isn't finalized. "Lauren sees you plenty. Katy needs your reassurance today. She's having a rough time with the changes. Please be there for her, Richard."

Ah, finally. The tiniest trace of guilt disrupts the cool surface of those Pacific-blue eyes. "I'll have lunch with Katy."

Again, "Thank you" seems unfitting. I settle on "Good."

"But don't act like I'm abandoning her. *You're* taking her out of town." He drums his fingers on the table, glowering.

He probably doesn't expect me to smile in response, but I can't help it. Purchasing my gram's old Cape Cod–style home in the sleepy bayside town of Potomac Point has been my only silver lining in this situation.

Yes, part of me is fleeing Arlington to avoid both the pitying whispers of "friends" and bumping into Richard and Lauren. But my childhood summers on the water had been a salve after I lost my mother, and living there should help Katy deal with *this* loss. Plus, I want to spend more time with my gram before her dementia erases every shared memory.

Katy and I deserve something good in our lives, so I won't apologize for it.

Still, Richard knows me well enough to suspect I wrestle doubts, mostly because of Katy's intensifying anxiety about leaving her friends and changing schools. Yet every parenting book promises she'll gain new confidence from learning to adapt. Real confidence, not the false kind she gets from tap-dancing to her father's tune for praise. Once we get through these rocky first weeks, the change of pace will be good for us both.

"Please let me live with Dad," Katy had pleaded before driving off. Each of those words had whistled through the air to pierce my heart like poison-tipped darts, and not only because I've devoted myself to parenting her. Richard hasn't and won't.

From the moment we accidentally conceived her in college, he's loved the "idea" of his mini-me—our gorgeous, intelligent daughter— yet, over time, his priorities undermined her bit by bit, pecking away at her like a crow.

Despite this act he's putting on now, he doesn't want Katy disturbing his next family, but of course he won't tell her that. Once again he's left the black hat on the table for me to wear while I flounder for some way not to devastate her—exactly like he did when he dropped the divorce bomb on me in May and then took off for New York for a few weeks to work some big deal.

Frankly, I expected him to do or say something to reset the balance of power today. For once, control is something *I* can deny *him* for a change. He leans forward, hands stretched out on the table, wedding band already removed. I cover my wedding rings before pulling both hands onto my lap.

"Anne, you'll be better off once you admit that you weren't any happier in our marriage than I've been lately. Trust me, there's someone out there who's more capable of meeting your needs than I ever was. You deserve that, too."

Blandishments? My temperature is steadily climbing. At this rate, I could blow like Vesuvius before the brokers return. All these years I've set aside my own ambitions and managed our home and daughter while he focused on his career, and this is how he repays me? In any case, the last thing I want now is another man in my life after having spent my entire adulthood with this one.

"Gee, thanks." I refuse to look away although something uncomfortable slithers through me—perhaps an acknowledgment of my willingness over time to settle for a B-minus marriage instead of striving for an A-plus one.

Our passion had begun to ebb once he'd graduated from law school and gone to work. Truth be told, Richard practically lived at his office while building his practice, which then left me little opportunity to be either an outstanding or a poor wife.

Then Katy started showing signs of extreme sensitivities around four—a hyperawareness of others' opinions, banging her head against a wall when she made a mistake, crying too easily over every little thing. Richard called them tantrums, but I worried she might have deeper issues. Managing her behavior and schedule required more and more of my attention, exhausting me.

Between Richard's long hours, my volunteerism, and Katy's needs, it seemed as if sex became scheduled like every other obligation, and our conversations veered toward efficiency rather than intimacy. But we'd had Katy to connect us, and I thought we'd rediscover each other and spontaneity once she went to college.

The actual result? Richard now enjoys a thriving practice and new family while I'm living in a chronic state of confusion with a teen who constantly misconstrues me.

He's still handsome, though: thick dark hair with hints of silver, cheekbones I envy, and a gorgeous mouth. Vital, too, thanks to vigorous exercise and boundless energy. Everything comes easily to him, as with Katy. Maybe that's why neither of them is patient with how hard the rest of us work for the things that matter.

"Seems I can't do anything right today." He sits back. It saddens me that this exchange has probably reaffirmed his relief to be ditching me. I bury every bit of grief beneath the thick seams of resentment and righteous indignation his adultery has handed me.

To look at him now, I wouldn't recognize the man who'd pursued me during our junior year at the University of Richmond. He'd been relentless, coming around the studio where I'd painted, or bringing his books along to the James River Park's green spaces where I'd sketched. Like my gram, he'd encouraged my wildest artistic dreams. That praise, the belly kisses and hushed whispers as we lay naked and spent, the love notes stuck in my backpack, the flowers he'd bring for no reason—all his ardor tricked me into believing that, despite being twenty, naive, and pregnant, we could build a happy life together—a family like the one I'd lost when my mother died.

Since then, I've come to call that zeal his "acquisition mode," as he's wooed new clients with the same intensity. His surname suits him, because he much prefers the chase to maintenance.

Lauren will be in my shoes soon enough. The day some major new client or other woman crosses his radar, I'll have the last laugh. Of course, I'll feel bad for her two young children, who'll be casualties of his whims. Like Katy.

If Richard and I were alone now, I might literally reach across the table to slap that self-pitying look off his face. Look at him sitting there as if everything is about *him*. He doesn't get it and never will. My mood—the *root* of my concern—is about Katy.

Yes, I'm a woman in my prime. A woman of some means. A woman with talent, some might even say. But first and foremost I am a mother.

"What'd you do with the furniture? It can't all fit in Marie's old house." Richard's question temporarily throws me.

"Severed Ties took what we didn't need." The high-end consignment store pays the original owner 50 percent of its profit on sales. "Whatever I make will be put toward Katy's college fund."

"Keep it." His full lips bend into a conciliatory smile. "I can pay her tuition."

Here he goes again, sounding generous when really he's trying to buy me off so he can boast to others about how fair he's been. He's never understood this about me: I don't care about hoarding money or things. Never did and never will. "And I can afford to contribute."

Some might consider me lucky because, along with my suitcases, I take a comfortable nest egg and alimony—enough that I'm not panicked about establishing a career after all these years at home. But he's still gotten off pretty cheaply for betraying me and our old dreams. Naturally, I don't share my feelings or let him see my pain.

"Fine, Anne." He rolls his eyes and checks his watch. "Jesus, I'm trying to be a decent guy."

Too little, too late.

A laundry list of insults cycles through my mind like ticker tape, but I literally bite my tongue when another image of Katy's splotchy face from this morning flickers through my mind. All the time spent filling her life with love and opportunity means very little in light of one inescapable reality: by letting our family fall apart, Richard and I have fundamentally failed our daughter.

Condemning my husband is pointless. However we got here, the result is the same.

The brokers return, confirm the payments, congratulate us all, and quickly show us out. Even though I never loved that house, the finality of what's happening hits me like a board to the face. My married life and home are truly lost to me. There will be no going back. No fixing what broke. I'm starting over at thirty-seven. That prospect festers like an ulcer. All I know is how to be a wife and mother.

My hands tremble for a split second as I grapple with my purse strap. Please, God, don't let Richard see my strength falter. His affair humiliated me. He can never know how badly he's hurt me, too.

The buyers walk ahead of us, holding hands. The woman is decked out in a Trina Turk "Vanah" dress, diamonds and sapphires in her ears and around her neck and wrists, and cute platform espadrilles. Her husband is attractive in a Tom Hardy way and carries his success like Richard does—chin up, shoulders proud.

I can picture him—much like my soon-to-be ex—proudly moving into that home that has three times more space than any family needs. What he doesn't yet know is that four stories and a dozen rooms make it too easy to slink away from each other for entire evenings. Bit by bit that disconnect—the physical space between each person—becomes the sort of emotional distance that loosens family bonds. Not that you see it happening in the moment.

I've often wondered whether Richard and I might've stayed together if we'd remained in the two-thousand-square-foot home we'd previously owned. Questions like that keep me up nights.

A decade ago, we were excited. Happy. A young family on our way up. The problem with rising so high so fast? When you fall—and that fall will come, usually when you least expect it—you smack the ground so hard a part of you dies.

Once reanimated, you feel more like a roamer on *The Walking Dead* than a person.

Richard leans in as if he might kiss my cheek, but stops short when I flinch. "Good luck, Anne. Hope you don't die of boredom in that small town."

His condescension pricks the ugly bitterness that has blistered beneath my skin since his May confessional.

"Well, I survived life with you, so how bad can Potomac Point be?" I pat his shoulder twice. "Don't worry about me. Save your energy for staying sane while Lauren has you stuck at home raising her young kids. I'll be sure to send postcards from Paris and Prague to give you goals to look forward to in another twelve or fourteen years."

I turn away and walk to my car without looking back so he can't see my brave face slip. The truth is I'd wanted more kids but, after the agony of a late-term miscarriage, chose to focus all my love on Katy and her anxieties. Once she'd turned six, Richard no longer wanted to bring an infant into our lives. Another decision to regret, I suppose, because both Katy and I might be better off if we had another person in our shrinking family.

By the time my car door closes, fresh tears blur my vision. Contrary to my goal, I did not escape that closing with my dignity intact—behaving no better than my teen daughter.

It takes a bunch of tugging and a good lick to wrench my wedding rings from my finger. In the sunlight their dazzling sparkle is full of false promise, so I drop them into my purse. I stretch the fingers of my bare left hand, which now looks as unfamiliar as everything else about my undone life.

Richard wasn't the husband I'd hoped he'd be, and ours hadn't been the perfect marriage. But I've given so much of myself to that life that I can't stand the way it's ending. He's skipping forward as if our years together meant nothing, leaving me behind on an uncertain path. Seeing him quickly—and happily—replace our family stings like an ice-cold shower.

I've been telling myself I'm not running. Telling myself that this move will be for the best.

Please, God, let me be right.

ACKNOWLEDGMENTS

As always, I have many people to thank for helping me bring this book to all of you—not the least of whom are my family and friends for their continued love, encouragement, and support.

Thanks, also, to my agent, Jill Marsal, as well as to my patient editors, Chris Werner and Tiffany Yates Martin, whose keen eyes made this book so much stronger. And none of you would know about my work without the entire Montlake family working so hard on my behalf.

A number of people helped me with different elements of this book. It started with my friend's husband, Brian Ong, a forensic accountant, and some of his coworkers (Lindi Jarvis, Toni Mele, and Lisa Dane), who helped me understand how husbands like Lyle plot and try to get away with these crimes, and how wives like Amanda often seek ways to recover money without involving the police. They provided a lot of details I ended up not including in my story, but I appreciated their time and advice. When I came up with the idea for the yacht (instead of a plane, as apparently is more common), my mother's BFF and her husband, Ria and Bobby Baiz (who recently sold their house to sail into retirement), helped me better understand how Lyle might go about planning his escape, and how he might get caught. My daughter's friend Meghan Kloud, an EMT, stellar student, and athlete, told me how Madeline's fainting spell might be handled on-site. Jo Schaller, a Connecticut detective, and two former federal agents, who asked to remain anonymous, helped me flesh out what Amanda could and couldn't do in her quest to track Lyle down. Despite all the research, I may have made some mistakes (or taken some liberties for the sake of fiction), so I own those and beg your forgiveness! The wet-bathing-suit memory comes from a friend with two sisters, Linda Kolodny Jens, so thanks for that one! I also need to thank my mother-in-law, Carol Day, a medium, who helped me create Nancy Thompson's character and the scenes in which she's delivering messages from beyond. I'm also so proud of my beloved daughter, Kayla, a budding songwriter, who wrote Eli's song for me to use in this book.

I also want to thank my beta readers, Jane Haertel and Katherine Ong, for their feedback on the early draft.

I couldn't produce any of my work without the MTBs, who help me plot and keep my spirits up when doubt grabs hold. And my Fiction From the Heart sisters also inspire me on a daily basis.

And I can't leave out the wonderful members of my CTRWA chapter. Year after year, all the CTRWA members provide endless hours of support, feedback, and guidance. I love and thank them for that.

Finally, and most importantly, thank you, readers, for making my work worthwhile. Considering all your options, I'm honored by your choice to spend your time with me.

ABOUT THE AUTHOR

Photo © 2016 Lorah Haskins

Wall Street Journal and *USA Today* bestselling author Jamie Beck's realistic and heartwarming stories have sold more than two million copies. She is a two-time Booksellers' Best Award finalist and a National Readers' Choice Award winner, and critics at *Kirkus*, *Publishers Weekly*, and *Booklist* have respectively called her work "smart," "uplifting," and "entertaining." In addition to writing novels, she enjoys hitting the slopes in Vermont and Utah and dancing around the kitchen while cooking. Above all, she is a grateful wife and mother to a very patient, supportive family. Fans can get exclusive excerpts and inside scoops, and be eligible for birthday gift drawings by subscribing to her newsletter at http://eepurl.com/b7k7G5. She also loves interacting with everyone on Facebook at www.facebook.com/JamieBeckBooks.